MASSACHUSETTS
Brides

*Three Old-Fashioned Romances Bloom
in the Heart of New England*

LISA HARRIS

BARBOUR
PUBLISHING

Published by Barbour Publishing, Inc., P.O. Box 719, Uhrichsville, Ohio 44683, www.barbourbooks.com

Our mission is to publish and distribute inspirational products offering exceptional value and biblical encouragement to the masses.

 Member of the
Evangelical Christian
Publishers Association

Printed in the United States of America.

Dear Reader,

From the windswept Boston seacoast to the lush Connecticut Valley, Massachusetts, in the late 1800s is a place of unparalleled beauty and rich history. Writing these stories about Michaela, Rebecca, and Adam was like taking a step back into history for me and one I thoroughly enjoyed. It also was a journey of self-discovery for my own life. As my characters struggled to face life's challenges of loss, forgiveness, and finding God's will, I found myself learning spiritual lessons alongside them. What a wonderful reminder that in the midst of life's conflicts, faith can be renewed and love worth keeping found.

My prayer for each of you is that you might discover the freedom of following God with all your heart and that you might lean on Him no matter what circumstances you are facing right now. He is faithful.

Stop by my Web site at www.lisaharriswrites.com. I'd love to hear from you.

Blessings,
Lisa Harris

The steps of a good man are ordered by the LORD:
and he delighteth in his way.
Though he fall, he shall not be utterly cast down:
for the LORD upholdeth him with this hand.
Psalm 37:23–24

Michaela's Choice

Dedication

To my son, Gabriel.
I thank God for you daily and for the blessing you are to our family.
May you always find refuge in Him.

Prologue

Michaela Macintosh woke to her own screams. The terror of that night had returned, bathing her in a pool of sweat. It was the same dream she'd had since the night of the fire. The house appeared, and she found herself standing in Leah's bedroom with flames licking at her flesh. In slow motion, Michaela tried desperately to reach out through the horror surrounding her to find her husband and daughter. The muddled screams had grown louder until she finally awoke, realizing the frantic cries were her own.

The door to her room opened, and by the pale light of the moon, she watched as Aunt Clara slipped in and sat on the bed beside her shivering form.

"It's all right." Aunt Clara put her arms around Michaela and held her tight. "It was only another nightmare."

Michaela tried unsuccessfully to control the sobs that came and finally gave in, crying until there weren't any tears left. There had been fewer nightmares in the last six months, but when the dream did come, it brought with it the stark reality of that night. Longing to push the lingering images away from her, she forced herself to take slow, deep breaths. But unanswered questions continued to haunt her.

After several minutes, the intense feelings of panic left, only to be replaced with a deep void. "Why did Ethen and Leah have to die? I miss them so much."

Aunt Clara stroked her hair, gently pushing the damp strands away from Michaela's face. "I wish I could take your pain away. All I know is that God has promised to go through the valleys with us, and He will carry us through times of trouble. 'The LORD redeemeth the soul of his servants: and none of them that trust in him shall be desolate.'"

Listening to the words her aunt recited from Psalm 34, Michaela knew that God had compassion for her. Yet at the moment, He seemed so far away.

"Do you want me to stay until you fall asleep?" Aunt Clara asked.

Michaela nodded and closed her eyes, emotionally exhausted from the ordeal. *When will You take away the pain, Lord?*

Aunt Clara's strong alto voice broke through the quiet of the night. "'What a friend we have in Jesus, all our sins and grief to bear. What a privilege to carry, everything to God in prayer.'"

The words from the hymn worked as a salve on Michaela's spirit, and before long, she drifted off into a dreamless slumber.

Chapter 1

Michaela looked out her second-story bedroom window toward the ocean. A ship followed the breeze into the harbor, its majestic white sails billowing in the wind. What would it be like to sail on a vessel that could take her to another place? Another time? Another life?

That's what she wanted now—to get away. Far away where she could forget. But she knew she would never be able to. How could she erase the moment her life changed forever? How could she get over losing a spouse and a child? It had taken only an instant for the fire to snatch their lives away—an instant to tear her entire life apart. All she could do now was try in vain to push back the memories that constantly invaded her thoughts.

Michaela opened the door of the mahogany wardrobe that sat in the corner of her room. Ethen's skilled hands had created the masterpiece with its ornate front panels and twisted barley crown. When he and his brother, Philip, had taken over their father's cabinetmaking business ten years ago, they'd found success in what they did.

Ethen had been the dreamer and early on had shown an incredible talent to see beyond a raw piece of wood to the finished product. Philip also was gifted in woodwork, but he excelled on the business side and had the ability to take Ethen's artistic flair and turn it into a thriving business. Now Philip was the only one left to keep the family business going.

Michaela pulled a dress from the inside of the armoire inlaid with cedar and breathed in the fragrant scent of the wood. Of all the dresses she owned, this had been Ethen's favorite. How many times had he told her that the tiny green-flowered print brought out the red in her hair and accented her fair skin?

Today she wore it because the collar, trimmed with antique lace, was high enough to hide the scars that still covered her neck and left shoulder. Pausing to look at her reflection in the beveled mirror beside the wardrobe, she ran her fingers across the scars to where they stopped at the base of her neck. The doctor told her that with time the disfigurement would fade, but the raised welts were still noticeable.

Why was it that everything seemed to point back to that night a year and a half ago, reminding her of what she had lost? Turning away from the mirror, she dressed quickly, then pinned the small watch that had been her mother's onto the dress's bodice. She had thirty minutes until her first student arrived. Aunt Clara had been right. Teaching piano lessons gave her a way to occupy her time and stay busy.

Normally she enjoyed the time interacting with her students, but at the moment, music was the last thing on her mind. Today the committee would decide Anna's future and whether or not they would allow Michaela to raise her. Five-year-old Anna, with her bright smile and angelic face, had lost her parents in the same fire that had taken Ethen and Leah. She'd become the one constant source of joy in Michaela's life.

Hurrying down the narrow staircase that led to the parlor below, she prayed fervently that God would answer her prayer that the board would grant her custody of Anna.

The curtains of the small parlor were open, letting the morning sun spill across the rose-colored walls. She loved this old house. It was the home she'd come to after her parents were killed in a buggy accident when she was only fourteen years old. And the home she'd come back to after Ethen and Leah died.

She ran her hand across a brightly flowered slipcover her best friend, Caroline, had made last winter for Aunt Clara's sofa. As a child, Michaela had called this the happy room because it reminded her of family and love. Countless Christmases had been spent here in front of the stone fireplace, singing carols and drinking hot chocolate, or celebrating a birthday with presents. She had never lacked for anything—especially love.

Pushing memories of the past aside, Michaela stepped into the kitchen. The sunny yellow room featured a nice-sized window overlooking her aunt's garden, exquisite no matter what time of the year with its array of flowers and assorted shades of greenery.

Aunt Clara stood in front of the cast-iron stove, wearing the familiar white apron over her dress while frying a pan of eggs and potatoes. Her brother-in-law sat at the table.

"What brings you by so early, Philip?" Michaela greeted her aunt with a kiss on her cheek, then turned to her late husband's younger brother.

"Your aunt's dresser's almost ready." Philip raked his fingertips through his dark, curly hair and leaned back in his chair. "I had a question to ask her about the mirror we're getting ready to mount."

"Truth is, he just wanted a homemade meal." Aunt Clara put her hands on her hips. "How can a man expect to work as hard as you do with no one to fix you a proper meal every day?" She took a step toward him and offered a smile. "Marietta told me that Molly Granger's back in town. She's a beautiful girl—"

"I manage just fine, Aunt Clara." Philip laughed, then took a bite of his eggs. "I haven't gone hungry yet."

In spite of her somber mood, Michaela smiled at her aunt's matchmaking attempts. Finding a wife for Philip had become one of Aunt Clara's ambitions. Barely a Sunday went by that she didn't invite at least one single woman over for dinner if Philip was able to join them. After last week's disastrous meal with Julia Hurst, Michaela was certain it would be weeks before Philip returned for another Sunday meal. The woman had talked nonstop for two hours, sharing anecdotes about the pet Pekingese her father had given her for her birthday. Even Michaela had longed to slip out of the room during the tedious monologue.

"One of these days you'll meet the woman you've been waiting for, and you'll thank me." Aunt Clara clicked her tongue and began dishing up another plate. "This is for you, Michaela. You need to eat, too."

Michaela raised her hand in protest. "I don't think I want anything this morning. Maybe just a glass of orange juice."

"Nonsense. You have to eat." Aunt Clara finished piling the food on the plate and set it on the table.

Michaela poured a glass of juice from the pitcher, trying to ignore the growing ache in her temple.

"You need to go down to the shop and see the dresser, Michaela," Aunt Clara said. "The detail in the woodwork is exquisite. I don't know how you do it, Philip."

"I'm glad you like it. Truthfully, though, the dresser's not the only reason I came by this morning." Philip's cheerful expression turned serious. "The committee's making their decision about Anna today, aren't they?"

"Yes." Michaela sat down, and the pounding in her forehead intensified. "I'm spending the afternoon at the orphanage. Caroline's in charge of today's fund-raiser, and I told her I'd help out. I should have their decision by the time it's over."

"How are you feeling?" Worry lines creased Aunt Clara's forehead.

"Scared. . .anxious. . .worried." Michaela spread a spoonful of homemade cranberry and apple jam on a biscuit and took a tasteless bite. "I'm trying not to think about it, but I don't ever remember being as nervous as I am right now."

"I saw Agnes in town yesterday." Aunt Clara pulled out one of the wooden chairs from the table and sat beside her. "She sounded optimistic that things would work out for you and Anna."

Michaela fiddled with the white linen napkin in her lap and shook her head.

"If it were up to Agnes, Anna would be mine, but unfortunately, the decision's not hers to make."

"The people in this town respect you," Philip said as he added a spoonful of sugar to his coffee and slowly stirred it. "They know what a wonderful Christian woman you are and that all you want is what's best for Anna."

"But am I doing what's best for her?" Michaela clenched her hands into fists in her lap. "I've prayed so hard, but sometimes I'm just not sure. Part of me understands their hesitation in letting a child be adopted into a home where there isn't a father, but Anna's like a daughter to me. She was Leah's best friend ever since they could toddle around together, and she practically lived at our house."

How many times had she sat in the parlor with Anna and Leah in their dress-up clothes, surrounded by dolls and teacups? They'd spent countless hours baking gingerbread cookies in the kitchen and swinging from the big oak tree in their backyard. The realization that she'd never have another sunny afternoon with Leah hurt so badly at times, she could hardly take another breath.

"Does the pain ever go away?" She rested her forehead against her fingertips for a moment, trying to hold back a flood of tears that threatened to overflow.

"No, not entirely." Aunt Clara shook her head slowly. "It's been almost ten years since I lost my Henry, and I still miss him. The pain eases, slowly at times, but it will ease."

Michaela took a deep breath, then let it out slowly. "I feel so lost. I don't know what direction my life is headed. It used to be enough to be a mother and a wife, but now that's gone. It's almost as though in losing my family, I lost my identity, and now I don't even know if they'll let me be a mother again."

Aunt Clara caught Michaela's solemn gaze. "Keep praying and looking to the Lord for direction. He'll show you the way. You're young and have many options open before you."

Philip reached out and squeezed Michaela's hand. "I need to get back to the store, but promise me you'll stop by on the way home if you find out anything."

Michaela nodded and stood up. "I'll walk you outside."

"Thank you for breakfast." Philip kissed Aunt Clara on the cheek and followed Michaela out the front door.

Resting her hand in the crook of Philip's arm, Michaela accompanied him slowly down the brick walk toward the street. The sun filtered through the trees, warming her face but failing to reach the depths of her heart.

"Do you have any lessons this morning?" he asked.

"Four, including Sammy."

Philip let out a deep chuckle. "Sammy Hauk?"

"The one and only."

"Sammy's name invokes visions of last summer's disastrous church picnic when he let a snake loose in the middle of Mrs. Lindberg's prized cakes."

Michaela felt the corners of her mouth curl into a smile at the memory. "He's a character."

"You're working too hard, Michaela." Philip stopped at the front gate and turned to face her. "I worry about you."

"Staying busy is good for me."

"Not if you run yourself ragged. You need more rest. Time to do something just for yourself."

"You're beginning to sound like Aunt Clara." Michaela squeezed his hand. "I enjoy what I do."

"And you're very good at it. But I do worry about you."

"Don't. I'm fine. And after today, if the committee will let me adopt Anna. . ." She let her voice trail off, afraid to envision the two of them together as a family. Afraid of the pain that would come if the board said no.

Leaning against the fence, Michaela tried to push aside the discouraging thoughts. "Caroline talked me into bringing two cakes to the bake sale today. We should raise enough money to be able to buy each of the children the coats, sweaters, and shoes they will need this winter, as well as supplies for school. And did you hear the news that Samuel Perkins is donating ten new beds for the children? Anna told me—"

He tilted her chin with his index finger and smiled. "You're rambling."

She chewed on the inside of her lip. "I ramble when I'm nervous."

Grasping both her hands, he held them tight. "I know this is hard, but I'll always be here for you. I never told you this, but when you and Ethen first got married, he made me promise that if anything ever happened to him, I'd take care of you."

Michaela reached up and wiped away a stray tear from her cheek. "He loved you so much. You were more than just a brother. You were his best friend, and he trusted you completely."

"I take my promises very seriously. If there's anything you need, anything at all. . ."

He gathered her into his arms, and for a brief moment, everything in her world felt right again.

☙

Her last lesson over, Michaela glanced at her watch, pleased to find that she still had plenty of time to eat lunch with her aunt before leaving for the orphanage. Not finding Aunt Clara in the kitchen, she wasn't surprised to see her working in one of the flower beds behind the house.

"I don't know how you do it." Michaela walked past a grouping of plants her aunt had arranged on a small, rustic table and stepped onto the velvety grass. "You truly are an artist."

A slightly terraced lawn surrounded the fishpond Michaela's uncle had put in shortly before he died. Solid oak trees stood valiantly around the yard, shading the ground from the harsh summer sun. But the most treasured place was where Aunt Clara had planted her prize garden of roses, columbine, rhododendron, and cardinal flowers.

"There are many different kinds of artists," her aunt said with a smile. "You're an artist with your music."

Michaela stopped where Aunt Clara worked and sat down on the grass beside her. "You can smell the saltwater in the air today." She breathed in deeply, attempting to allow the familiar scent to soothe her spirit.

Clara eased herself up to a standing position. "I plan to go by the store this afternoon. Do you need anything?"

"I don't think so." Michaela plucked a blade of grass and twirled it between her fingers. What she needed couldn't be bought at a store or found at any seller's stand. Anna was an intricate part of her life. One she couldn't bear to lose.

Clara's concern showed in her eyes as she spoke. "Still thinking about the committee's decision?"

Michaela stood and followed her aunt into the house. "I'll know soon enough, so there's no use fretting about it."

Clara turned around to face her niece. "Somehow, I have the feeling the board's going to grant your request."

"I hope you're right," Michaela whispered. "I hope you're right."

Chapter 2

Michaela walked the short distance to the Mills Street Orphanage, praying the entire way. From her vantage point, it was going to take a miracle for the committee to allow her to keep Anna, so she was praying for a miracle. Tightening her grip on the box that held the two cakes she'd baked the day before, she slowly made her way up the walk toward the Romanesque-style home where Anna lived.

"Looks like you've been busy." Caroline Hodges greeted Michaela at the front door of the orphanage with a broad smile and peeked inside the box. "Yum. You made my favorite. Chocolate."

Michaela grinned at her friend's predictable response. "I knew if no one else bought them, you would."

Caroline reached up and brushed back a wisp of her short, curly bangs with her fingertips and laughed. "You know me far too well."

Together they entered the familiar parlor of the large house where Michaela had spent numerous afternoons visiting with Anna. The furniture, a collection of hand-me-down items, from a circular sofa to several Chippendale chairs, had been rearranged to make room for the assortment of desserts that would be sold during the fund-raiser.

"This is going to be quite an afternoon." Caroline smoothed down the front of her blue taffeta skirt, then busied herself in arranging the table. "We've just opened for business and already sold three cakes and two pies."

Michaela eyed the heavy pine table already laden with a variety of home-made pies, cakes, and colorfully wrapped boxes of peanut brittle, taffy, and other candies.

Noting a box filled with pralines, Michaela resisted a second look. "I can tell you right now, I'm going to have to stay out of this room. If they taste as good as they smell. . ."

Caroline moved a few of the confections and set Michaela's cakes in a prominent position on the white tablecloth. "You know yours will go for the highest price."

"Caroline." Michaela shook her head at the biased compliment and grinned. "Spoken by a devoted best friend."

"It's true. I had to promise myself I wouldn't take a single bite." Caroline giggled, fairly drooling over the rich assortment of goodies. Her love for sweets had helped contribute to her pleasant but plump figure. "If I gain another pound, I'll have to buy a whole new wardrobe."

The sound of children's laughter floated into the parlor, and Michaela glanced past Caroline into the adjoining room. "Have you seen Anna today?"

"She's wearing the sweetest pink calico dress with a matching apron. She'll be so excited to see you." Caroline turned from the table and looked at Michaela. "I almost forgot. The committee's making their decision today, aren't they?"

"Yes." Michaela's voice quivered. "Agnes is supposed to let me know their answer this afternoon."

"I know that many people are praying for you." Caroline reached out and rested her hand against Michaela's arm. "Agnes had to run out for a bit, but she'll be back soon."

Michaela turned as someone called her name. She sighed, spotting Vivian Lockhart entering the room from the other side of the house, and wished there was a way to avoid the nosy woman.

"I know she's a difficult person to get along with," Caroline whispered to Michaela, "but her mother donated fifty dollars to the orphanage this morning. I'll be forever in your debt if you talk to her." Before Michaela could respond, Caroline hurried away to help an older woman who had just brought two home-made pies to sell.

Vivian looked dramatic, as usual, in a pink organdy day dress with matching pink ribbon trim. Knowing there was nowhere to hide, Michaela smiled and waited as Vivian approached.

"It seems like I haven't seen you for ages, Michaela. You look wonderful, and that dress is gorgeous."

Michaela knew her outfit could never be called stylish but thanked her for the compliment anyway, barely getting out the words before Vivian began again.

"Tell me, what have you been up to?" True to her nature, Vivian didn't wait for Michaela's answer. "I hear you're trying to adopt one of the poor orphans. I told my mother what a perfect solution for both you and the child. So sad for her to have lost both parents in that terrible fire. Of course, my mother wasn't convinced it's a good idea with your being a widow, but you know how Mother is."

Exactly like her daughter, always talking without thinking first. Michaela gritted her teeth but stifled a reply when she felt someone tug on her skirt. Looking down into the eyes of a dark-haired five-year-old, all traces of frustration toward Vivian left.

"Anna!" Michaela gave the small child a big hug, her heart softening at the sight of the young girl.

"I knew you'd come today." Anna's brown eyes brightened and lit up her entire face.

"Tell me, sweetheart, what have you been up to?" Michaela knelt down and pushed back a strand of hair from Anna's heart-shaped face, tucking it behind her ear.

"Right now we're eating lunch, and this afternoon we're going to play all kinds of games. There's even going to be prizes."

Michaela could hear the children's happy chatter as they finished lunch in the dining room. "I'm going to be here the whole afternoon."

Anna clapped her hands together and gave Michaela another hug.

Vivian had already gone to talk to a group of women who'd just entered the room, and Caroline, who was busy arranging the food table, seemed to have everything under control.

"Would you like to go for a walk before the games start?" Michaela asked.

Anna nodded, and after checking with one of the staff members, Michaela and Anna headed to their favorite spot. Several hundred feet behind the house stood a huge oak tree. It was the perfect thinking spot, Anna had told her one afternoon, and then and there, they had proclaimed it their special place. When they got to the tree, Michaela sat down next to Anna and leaned back against the thick bark.

"It's a beautiful day, isn't it, Anna?" A clear blue sky fanned out above them, dotted only by a few puffy white clouds.

"I suppose."

Michaela looked down and caught Anna's sullen expression. "What is it?"

Anna crossed her legs and fiddled with the hem of her dress. "I had another dream last night. I was looking for my mommy and daddy, but I couldn't find them."

Michaela pulled Anna into her lap and held her close. A tear trickled down the little girl's face. "I tried to save them, really I did."

"I know, sweetheart. It wasn't your fault." Michaela knew the words were true, yet she often struggled with the same feelings of guilt for not having been able to save Ethen and Leah. "Sometimes I have bad dreams, too."

"You do?" Anna's eyes narrowed at the thought.

"Sometimes I dream I'm trying to save Ethen."

"And Leah?"

"Yes. And Leah."

"Leah was my best friend."

Why did so many people have to die, Lord? My husband and my daughter? Anna's parents? How can I even begin to take away Anna's pain?

Michaela took a deep breath and searched for the right words. "Do you remember what to do when you're sad or afraid, Anna?"

"Yes." Anna snuggled closer into Michaela's arms. "I try to remember how much God loves me. And I remember that they're in heaven with Jesus, and someday I'll see them again."

"That's exactly what you need to think about."

Anna leaned her head back and looked into Michaela's eyes. "I wish you were my mother."

Michaela desperately wished the same thing. She pulled Anna tight against her and breathed in the faint scent of lavender from her hair, struggling with how much to tell Anna about her attempts to adopt her. Surely it was best for her not to know in case the committee turned her down. For now, her frequent visits would have to do.

"Why don't you tell me about your friends." She rocked Anna slowly back and forth, treasuring this time they had together. "What did you do yesterday?"

They talked until the bell rang, announcing the beginning of the activities. Michaela stood, took Anna's small hand, and led her back to the house. For the moment, unpleasant memories from the past were forgotten.

By the time the afternoon's festivities had ended, the children's faces were lit with smiles, and laughter filled the yard. When the dinner bell sounded, Michaela told Anna she needed to take care of something and went to find Agnes. The decision should have been made by now. It was time to face her future.

Let it be with Anna, Lord. Please, let it be with her.

♋

Michaela sat down in an old but comfortable chair across from a heavy pine desk. Like the entire home, Agnes's office was decorated simply. Bookshelves covered two walls, while a third showcased a large picture window that overlooked the front courtyard. Michaela studied the green lawn that was bordered with a colorful assortment of flowers as Agnes took a seat behind the desk.

"The time you spend here means so much to the children." Agnes pushed a pair of wire spectacles up the bridge of her nose and smiled. "They're always asking when you'll be back."

"They do a lot for me as well." It hadn't taken long for the weekly visits to the orphanage to become one of the highlights of Michaela's life. "At first I thought being around the children would be too painful, but instead it's helped me tremendously."

"I admire your courage." Agnes's smile faded. "I wish I could do something, but these decisions are not left up to me. I know you'd be a wonderful mother for Anna, but the committee has made their decision. I'm so sorry, Michaela. They want Anna to be adopted by a couple."

Michaela stared out the window, her stomach tightening as the reality of the decision hit her. Tears stung her eyes, and she blinked rapidly to stop the flow.

"If you were to marry again, I know the board would reconsider—"

"I can't marry for those reasons." Michaela's knuckles whitened as she gripped the sides of her chair and battled for control over her emotions. "That would be wrong."

Agnes tugged on her ruffled blouse. "You're right. I'm sorry to have even suggested it."

It wasn't fair. How could they have decided against her? Anna needed a home with someone who loved her. Why couldn't that be her? Michaela folded her hands, then pulled them apart nervously. "I'm sorry, Agnes. I know this isn't your fault; it's just that I felt so sure this was God's will for Anna and me. I love her so much, and after losing Leah, well, I thought God was giving me another daughter."

"If there's anything I can do. . ." Agnes picked up a pencil and tapped it against the desk, obviously dismayed by the outcome of the board's answer. But Agnes didn't have to live with the consequences of their decision.

"Please tell Anna and the others good-bye for me." Michaela shook her head numbly and stood. "I need to go home."

"Before you leave, there is one more thing." Agnes dropped her gaze and tapped rapidly again against the wood with the pencil. "There's a couple interested in adopting Anna."

Michaela's eyes grew wide with disbelief, and a feeling of panic swept over her. *No, Lord, please don't take her away from me so soon.*

"They've been by several times and are interested in the idea of adopting an older child, possibly even two. They want to take their time and get to know her, but they plan to make a decision soon."

Michaela bit her lip, determined to hold back the tears until she was home in the sanctuary of her room. *Don't do this to me, God. It's too much.*

"I know this coming at the same time as the committee's decision is not easy, but I felt like I needed to let you know. They're a wonderful Christian couple who have never had children and feel called by God to adopt."

"I wish more couples felt that way." Michaela's words came automatically as she battled to calm the turmoil raging inside.

"Michaela, what you do here with the children means more to them than you will ever imagine." She dropped the pencil onto the table and leaned forward in her chair. "I believe that someday God is going to bless you with more children."

Michaela looked at Agnes, a raw ache radiating through her body. "You don't know what God's going to do. God took away my husband. He took away my baby. And now He's taken away Anna. Don't try to tell me what God's going to do!"

⚘

How dare they come between Anna and me.

Michaela walked along the crowded street the few blocks toward Philip's shop, her feet pounding the ground beneath her. How could the members of the committee make a decision like that? Couldn't they understand the relationship she had with Anna was as strong a bond as a mother had with her biological child? How could they just rip Anna out of her life in order to follow what seemed appropriate to society?

She'd prayed about this situation for a long time and felt this was what God wanted her to do. They might not be a traditional family, but she and Anna understood each other. They loved each other. Why couldn't they see that?

The front room of the cabinetry shop was quiet when Michaela entered the building, slamming the door behind her.

"Philip?" Michaela ran her hand across an unfinished table. A splinter lodged in her index finger, and a pool of blood rushed to the surface. She pulled out the piece of wood, easing the sting of the injury. If only the pain in her heart could fade as quickly.

"Michaela." Philip entered the room from the back, his clothes layered with a thin covering of sawdust. He ran his hand through his dark hair as if trying to smooth it out. "Did you find out anything?"

"They won't let me adopt Anna." Saying the words aloud only resulted in making them seem real.

"I'm so sorry." He bridged the gap between them and gathered her into his arms. "I know how much you love her."

"I'm so angry, all I want to do is scream." She took a step back, her voice rising with each word. Even Philip couldn't take away the hurt this time. "They met me briefly during one interview, and with that, they think they have all the information they need to decide our fate.

"What about the fact that I was at her mother's side when Anna was born? I took care of her when her parents were sick and helped to plan her birthday parties. I was the one who held Anna while she sobbed over the death of her parents."

She crossed the room, her mind numb with grief. Turning sharply to face Philip, she slammed her palms against the top of a wooden dresser. "I don't understand, Philip. What does God want from me? Wasn't I a good enough mother for Leah? Is this His way of punishing me? I lost one child and now I'm losing Anna."

"No, Michaela, of course not!" Philip came and stood beside her. She could see the disappointment reflected in his eyes. "You were a wonderful mother to Leah. I can't tell you why this happened, but I do know that God isn't punishing you."

She wanted to believe him, but the hurt wouldn't let her.

"Is there any way to reverse their decision?" He reached out and pushed back a strand of hair that had fallen into her eyes.

She shook her head. "The decision is final, unless, of course, I get married. Then they might reconsider their decision."

"You don't have a suitor hidden anywhere, do you?"

Michaela raised her head and allowed a slight grin. Only Philip could make her smile at a time like this. "Not the last time I checked."

"Then we'll have to think of something else." He glanced at the clock that hung on the back wall. "It's almost dinnertime. Would you like to go eat? Maybe it would help get your mind off everything for a little while."

"I do believe you're always thinking about food." Michaela had been right to come. Philip was the one person who could help her get through this.

"I work up a big appetite. Just ask your aunt," he said with a lopsided grin.

Michaela looked at Philip, still in his work clothes. His hands were calloused, and his arms showed the strength of someone who was no stranger to physical labor. Looking into his familiar blue eyes, she saw her friend and confidant, and for the moment, some of the anger seemed to dissipate. "Thank you."

"For what?"

"For always being there for me. For knowing how to make me smile."

⚜

Philip looked at Michaela and felt an unexplained stir.

"What is it?" Michaela asked.

"Nothing," Philip stammered, his heart beating faster at the idea that had suddenly taken form in his mind. *Could this be the answer, God? If I marry Michaela, we could be a family. We could adopt Anna.*

Sunlight came in from the window behind Michaela, casting a golden glow around her. Her red hair shimmered in the light, and the downward tilt of her mouth almost made him want to kiss her. The thought came totally unexpectedly. *Why have I never noticed how beautiful she is, God?* He knew her heart and what a caring and compassionate person she was, but could he have feelings for her? Buried feelings he never knew existed?

They'd become close after Ethen's and Leah's deaths. Michaela had turned to him for the comfort and support she needed, and he had never felt as at ease around a woman as he did with Michaela. He'd always seen Michaela as a sister and a good friend, but now he found himself looking at her as more than his brother's widow. Was there a chance their relationship could develop into something deeper?

"I heard the new restaurant in town has wonderful fish chowder."

At Michaela's suggestion, he pushed his thoughts aside for the moment—until he could deal with them in the silence of his room above the shop. "We could invite your aunt."

"I'd like that." Michaela wiped the back of her hand across her tear-stained face and smiled.

"Let me go get out of my work clothes, then I'll bring the buggy around and meet you out front. I was planning to close up in a few minutes, anyway."

Philip hurried to change out of his work clothes, praying for wisdom the entire way. Something told him, as he went out the back and locked the door behind him, that his entire life was about to change.

❦

"Have a good time tonight," Aunt Clara said as Philip and Michaela walked toward the front of the house.

"Are you sure you don't want to go?" Michaela lingered in the open doorway.

"Positive." Aunt Clara smiled and ran her hand down Michaela's cheek, then turned to Philip. "Thank you for getting her out of the house and helping get her mind off of today. If I hadn't worn myself out in the garden, I might have come, but I'd planned a leisurely evening with a good book I borrowed from Amy Parker, and that's exactly what I'm going to do."

"If you're sure. . ."

"Go on," she exclaimed, hurrying them out the door.

Philip helped Michaela into the buggy, then climbed in beside her. Her satin dress, the color of emeralds, shimmered in the fading sunlight. Her beauty, though familiar, amazed him. It was as if he were seeing her for the first time.

"You're quiet tonight," Michaela said a few minutes after they left the house.

"Just concerned about you." Philip kept his eyes on the road, afraid of his growing feelings toward the woman who sat beside him. "I know you've spent a lot of time in prayer over Anna's adoption, and I've also been praying they'd say yes."

"I want what's best for her, but I can't help believing that what's best for her is me."

For the past hour, Philip hadn't been able to dismiss the idea of asking her to marry him. The thought of them together seemed so right. Philip loved Anna, and the three of them had spent countless afternoons together in the past year. They could be a family.

As he allowed himself to steal a glance at Michaela, everything seemed clear. He would ask Michaela to marry him, and they would adopt Anna. Maybe it wasn't love yet, but one thing was for sure: Michaela held a piece of his heart, and he wasn't about to take it back.

Chapter 3

Michaela felt a ribbon of peace encircle her as she walked beside Philip along one of the streets that overlooked the incoming swells of the ocean. She'd enjoyed the well-prepared dinner of corned beef and potatoes, but more than anything else, she'd enjoyed spending the evening with Philip.

There were very few people who understood her the way he did. She had vented and poured out her frustrations, and the entire time he'd listened, never once trying to fix everything or judge her heated reaction toward the board's decision. Instead, he grieved with her, cried with her, and prayed with her.

"Are you all right?" Philip placed her hand in the crook of his arm.

"I think so." The pain lingered, but some of the sting had lessened. "Today was heartbreaking, but I realize that staying angry won't change the situation."

Michaela glanced at Philip. He always knew how to make her laugh and exactly what to say to lift her spirits. As the shadows of twilight moved across the waters, she studied the silhouette of his tall figure. Every movement he made with his broad shoulders and long legs demonstrated strength.

She stopped to hold on to a railing so she could gaze out across the constant flow of the tide. "It's beautiful out tonight, isn't it?"

The last of the fading sunlight glistened off the dark waves, and she didn't think there could be another place as peaceful as this.

"It's getting late." She caught the longing in Philip's voice as he spoke and wondered if he wanted to prolong the evening as much as she did. "I guess I'd better take you home now."

જી

Philip remained silent, lost in thought, as he walked Michaela to the door of Aunt Clara's house. He wondered what it would be like to kiss her.

"Michaela," he began as they reached the door.

"Yes?"

In the silver light of the moon, he could see her face and hear her breathing. He had to slow down. He had to wait until he could sort out the myriad of emotions he felt.

"I'll see you in a few days," he said. "I have to go out of town tomorrow to deliver an order."

"You don't normally make deliveries, do you?" Her eyes widened, but he couldn't read her expression. Did she care that he would be gone for a while?

"A couple of workers are out this week, and it has to be done. I'll be back on Friday." A torrent of emotions erupted as she touched his arm with the tips of her fingers.

"Be careful, and thank you for this evening. In spite of all that happened today, I needed this."

"Me, too." He resisted his desire to run his thumb down her cheek, wishing he had the words to take away the pain he knew she felt.

"I almost forgot; Aunt Clara wanted me to invite you over for dinner Friday evening. Will you be back in time?"

He nodded and felt a rush of anticipation. "I won't be back too late."

"Wonderful. We'll eat at seven."

"Perfect." If only he didn't have to wait until Friday to see her again.

✖

He was in love with his brother's wife.

An hour later, Philip stood in the middle of his workroom, rubbing oil into the Queen Anne desk he'd finished earlier that afternoon. Did the fact that Ethen was dead really make a difference? What would Ethen think if he knew that the feelings he felt for Michaela had crossed beyond innocent friendship to wanting to ask her to spend the rest of her life with him?

Ethen is dead!

Philip poured more oil on the cloth, then pressed it harder against the rich copper-colored grain. He felt at home with a piece of wood in his hands. The process of taking the raw material and forming it into something useful was a progression of change and development. Just like his relationship with Michaela.

For years, Michaela had been Ethen's wife. As a man, Philip had appreciated her beauty and sweet temperament, but his feelings had never gone beyond what was appropriate. She was a friend and close family member. Nothing more. Even after Ethen's death, he'd never imagined feeling the way he did tonight. But now that line had been crossed.

Never again could he watch her smile without his heart pounding in his chest or feel her soft hand against his arm without longing to engulf it in his own. No. Things could never be the same again.

He'd listened to her tonight as she'd poured out her frustrations over losing Anna, and his heart broke with hers. His feelings of loss over Anna's adoption couldn't compare to hers, but he still experienced grief and heartache because she felt those things.

Wait on the Lord: be of good courage, and he shall strengthen thine heart: wait, I say, on the Lord. The verse from Psalm 27 came to mind as Philip moved to the other side of the desk and continued to vigorously polish the wood. For years he had waited for the one whom God would choose for him to share his life with. The one he would someday call his wife. Was Michaela the reason he had never given his heart to anyone else?

Other questions haunted him. Could he share his feelings with Michaela? And if he did, would she understand? Was it even a possibility that she might come to feel the way he did? He threw the rag against the wood and let out a deep sigh. Resting his hands against the decorative panel, he shook his head. He couldn't get over the feeling he was betraying his brother's trust. But Ethen was dead. Ethen would want Michaela to find happiness with someone else. Why not with him?

✂

As soon as Michaela finished her last piano lesson the next day, she made her way to the garden behind the house. In spite of the late summer heat, her aunt had managed to keep the flowers and plants thriving.

"Looks like we'll have plenty of fresh vegetables this fall." Michaela greeted Aunt Clara with a smile. Night had brought with it an array of uncertainties and fears, but in the light of day, she'd managed to keep her emotions under control.

"I might have gone a bit overboard." Aunt Clara glanced up from a healthy tomato plant. "I don't know why, but I went ahead and planted twice what I normally do."

"We both enjoy it, and no one complains when you give the extra away." Michaela sat down in the warm grass and stretched her legs out in front of her.

"I guess you're right." Aunt Clara went back to tending to her plants like a mother doting on her young. "There's a letter from Daniel for you on the porch rail."

"I must have missed it when I came out." Michaela stood and walked back toward the porch, eager to read the news from her brother. "Did I tell you Philip will be coming over for dinner tomorrow night?"

"Good. I thought I'd make some of my mother's Irish stew."

Michaela picked up the envelope and tapped the edge against her palm. "Philip certainly won't complain."

"That boy could use some home cooking, though what he really needs is a good woman."

"You know I've tried to introduce him to some of the women at church, but he always says they're too old, or too young, or they talk too much." Michaela slipped the thin paper from the envelope. "I've decided to stay out of it from now on. Seems to just get me into trouble."

Michaela took the letter over to a small wrought iron bench on the other side of her aunt and sat down. "I still can't believe it's been six years since Daniel and Emma left Boston."

Michaela looked down at the wrinkled paper and began to read aloud.

Dear Aunt Clara and Michaela,

It's well into summer here, and every year I seem to enjoy living in this area more. I wish you could see this beautiful part of Massachusetts someday. Cranton is only a short distance from the Connecticut River, and we are surrounded by forests of pines that blend into the farms and orchards around us. This is a place that grows on you, and I can't imagine living anywhere else.

We have some good news to tell you. Emma is expecting again. I guess the news comes with mixed emotions and concerns since we have already lost two children.

The doctor is worried, but he told us if she can carry the baby past the next two months, she has a good chance of delivering a healthy baby in late December. Please remember to lift us up to the Father in your prayers. Emma is strong, but the last two years have been very difficult. Losing two babies has been hard on her, both physically and emotionally, yet she amazes me with her strength and faith in God.

Things on the farm are going well. The crops have been very good this year. We also have several prize pigs we will butcher this fall. Our apple trees are thriving, and we have a growing number of cattle and horses. I thank God every day for the land and what it gives us. I have come a long way from a newly married youngster who many said had a foolish dream of becoming a farmer.

Our closest neighbor, Eric Johnson, has a farm about twice the size of ours. I think I've mentioned him to you in previous letters. He's a widower with six children whose wife died soon after we arrived. Yet he's helped us so much since our arrival in Cranton.

Yesterday one of his boys came over with a big pot of stew when they heard Emma was feeling poorly. Eric's going with me to Springfield when I sell two of my horses to help ensure I get a good price for them. I guess he has lived out here close to eighteen years now. His kids truly are a blessing, as they work hard alongside him to keep the farm going.

We're planning a fall celebration for the church and the community next month. Something we really look forward to each year. We may not have all the conveniences and luxuries found in Boston, but we will have the best supper you could imagine, with smoked beef, chicken, steak, and all the trimmings.

    Michaela, we want you to know we're keeping you in our daily prayers. May God continue to heal your heart.

All our love,
Daniel and Emma

"I wish I could go see them and help Emma." Michaela set the letter down beside her and lifted up a silent prayer for Emma's pregnancy. It had been a bitter loss for the entire family when Emma miscarried during her first pregnancy, then again a year later.

"Why don't you go?" Aunt Clara looked up from the plant she was trimming.

"I couldn't leave you here alone." Michaela got up from the bench and began weeding around a bed of pink roses.

"Why not? It would be good for you to go away for a while and get some rest. The timing's perfect." She rested her hands on her hips. "I don't know why I didn't think of it earlier. Might help you get your mind off Anna, and besides, you've been working too hard lately."

"I wouldn't exactly have nothing to do if I went. I would have to help run a farm or at least do the cooking and cleaning. What do I know about farm work?"

"Michaela." Aunt Clara's glance held a measure of determination. "Maybe going to see your brother is just what you need. It would give you a chance to step back from things and figure out what direction you need to take with your life."

Michaela pulled out another weed. *Is this Your will for me, Lord?* From somewhere deep inside her, she knew her aunt was right. She had buried so many feelings and emotions deep within her, and just as this garden needed to be weeded and taken care of, the day would come when she would have to finish dealing with the pain from her past. If she didn't, she would never be able to go on with her life. She also knew herself well enough to know that if she took the time to think about going, she would never leave.

"I'll send a telegram tomorrow." Michaela stood and headed back into the house. A small measure of peace began to grow, giving her the confirmation she needed.

"If you like, I can send it for you," Aunt Clara said. "I need to go out this afternoon."

Michaela turned to her aunt and smiled. "I think someone's afraid I might back out."

"Not at all."

"Well then, it looks like I'm going to Cranton."

❧

On Friday, Michaela went to the orphanage with mixed emotions. She would be leaving on the train for her brother's farm in a week, and while she felt the excitement of her upcoming trip, part of her wanted to stay close to the familiar. Her aunt was right. Time away was exactly what she needed. It would give her the chance to think and see things more clearly.

Still, her stomach tightened as she thought of how Anna might react to her going away for a while. Michaela waited until after music class when the kids were playing outside and she could talk to Anna alone.

"Miss Agnes said I might have a new mommy and daddy," Anna said after sipping some tea from a small cup and saucer Michaela had given her the previous Christmas. They sat in the front parlor at a small table with four chairs: one for Michaela, one for Anna, and the other two for Anna's stuffed bears, Oliver and Sam, who had joined them for the tea party.

"Have you met them?" Michaela asked, pouring another cup of tea for Anna. She attempted to ignore the sharp sting of pain at the thought of someone else raising the little girl.

"She has long dark hair, and he has a funny mustache." Anna's face turned somber, and the corners of her mouth curved into a frown. "I don't want them for my mommy and daddy. I want you."

Michaela took a deep breath and reached over to grasp Anna's hand. "Wouldn't it be nice to have a mommy and a daddy?"

"I'm not sure." Anna scrunched up her nose. "They're going to visit me again. I heard them tell Miss Agnes they would like a girl and a boy. Maybe Johnny Philips. Does that mean he would be my brother?"

"I suppose it would. Would you like a brother?"

Anna just shrugged. "I told Miss Agnes I wanted you to be my mommy. She said you wanted to be my mommy, but you couldn't right now. Why?"

Michaela took a deep breath, trying to explain the situation as simply as she could. "You know I would like to be your mother, but some people who care about you decided it would be better for you to have both a mommy and a daddy."

"Oh." Anna did not sound convinced. "Will I still get to see you?"

"I'm sure we can work it out. No matter what happens, you'll always be very special to me."

Michaela knew she needed to talk to Anna about her upcoming trip but ached with the knowledge they would be apart. "I need to tell you about something. My brother and his wife, Emma, are going to have a baby, but she's sick. I told them I wanted to stay with them for a while to help Emma with the cooking and cleaning."

Anna sat still for a moment. "So you have to go away?"

"Yes, they live in Cranton, near the Connecticut River. Do you know where that is?"

Anna shook her head.

"I have to take a train to get there." Michaela tried to make it sound like an adventure.

"I took a train to New York once."

"I remember." Michaela smiled, trying to ignore the ache in her heart.

"When will you be back?"

"Sometime after Christmas."

Anna cocked her head. "Will you come and see me when you get back?"

"Of course I will." Michaela ruffled the little girl's hair, then tilted up her chin with her finger. "I wouldn't miss that for the world."

"Maybe I'll be living with my new mommy and daddy by then." Anna picked up Oliver and wrapped her short arms around him.

Michaela motioned for Anna and Oliver to come sit in her lap. Pulling them close, she stroked the young girl's hair and prayed for a miracle.

Chapter 4

Philip made his fifth inspection in the mirror of the apartment above the store. His thick black hair lay in neat curls, and the dark blue suit that had been recently cleaned and pressed matched the color of his eyes. He straightened his collar and tried to relax.

Funny, though twenty-nine years old, he suddenly felt like a teenager again, asking Mary Lou to the social at church. But that had been fifteen years ago, and he wasn't interested in Mary Lou with her freckles and pigtails anymore. Today he only had eyes for Michaela.

He hadn't slept for two nights, praying and wrestling with thoughts he hadn't known existed until a few days ago. He knew he couldn't wait any longer. In spite of the apprehension he felt over his newfound feelings toward Michaela, God had granted him peace. Tonight he would tell her how he felt.

His hands shook as he picked up his hat and slowly walked out the front door and down the busy sidewalk that would take him the short distance to Michaela's home. He had no idea how Michaela felt, but realizing he cared for her, he also knew he wanted to spend the rest of his life with her. He hadn't known how long these feelings had lain dormant in his heart, but he could never keep them from her, no matter what her response would be.

What had changed? Philip still wasn't sure, but it seemed natural for them to be together. He wanted to spend the rest of his life making her happy, not because he felt sorry for her, but because he loved her.

The sun beat down on the dusty street, and Philip wasn't sure if he was perspiring because of the heat or because of his nerves. He'd never thought twice about eating dinner with Aunt Clara and Michaela. In fact, it was something he did at least once a week, usually on Sundays. Aunt Clara was constantly reminding him that he needed more home-cooked meals instead of the fare he typically bought from one of the street vendors. After tonight, though, he knew things would never be the same.

Ten minutes later, he stopped and stood at the gate of Aunt Clara's two-story home, fiddling with the paper wrapped around the small bouquet of flowers he'd brought for Michaela. The Victorian home stood on a street among other similar houses with their corbeled brick exteriors, round-arched windows, and decorative features. He had saved enough money in the past few years to build a house for the two of them near the sea, if that was what Michaela wanted.

"Philip?" Michaela poked her head out the front door.

"Michaela. . .hello. . . How are you?" He fumbled through the gate toward the porch where she stood. She looked beautiful in her plum-colored dress with its high collar.

He offered her the flowers. "You look lovely tonight."

"You're always so thoughtful." She brought the flowers close to her face and took in a deep breath. "Roses are my very favorite."

Nervously, he followed her into the house. She turned and smiled at him, leaving his heart racing in anticipation.

"Did you have a good trip, Philip?"

"It was fine. Very uneventful."

"Sit down if you'd like." Michaela pointed to the rosewood armchair in the corner of the room.

It was the one he always sat on, but the familiarity of the situation did little to alleviate his anxiety.

"Dinner's almost ready. Aunt Clara went out to the garden to get some lettuce."

"Something smells delicious." Philip wiped his hands against his pant legs and took a deep breath before sitting in the cushioned chair.

"Aunt Clara made Irish stew for dinner." Michaela rested her hands on her hips and turned to him before leaving the room. "Would you like something to drink? I made lemonade this afternoon."

"That would be nice. Thank you."

He watched her flutter out of the room like a springtime butterfly. *Let her feel the same way I do, Lord.*

A minute later, Michaela came back into the room with two glasses of lemonade. "I have something I need to talk to you about," she said, handing him one of the tumblers. "But I want to wait until after dinner. We can sit out on the swing later if you'd like. It's such a beautiful evening."

"Sounds perfect." He took a long sip of the sugary drink and attempted to relax. "I'd like to talk to you about something then as well."

"Of course." Michaela raised her eyebrows in question. "Are you sure you're all right? You seem. . .I don't know, nervous."

"I'm fine." For the first time in their relationship, he had nothing to say to her. He could talk about the large furniture order he received today from a wealthy couple living outside of Boston or the fact that the wife of one of his employees had just given birth to her eighth child, but he wasn't in the mood for small talk.

Aunt Clara entered the room, and Philip jumped out of his chair to greet her, thankful for the reprieve. "You look lovely this evening," he exclaimed. "Michaela told me you made some of your famous stew."

"My mother's recipe." Clara smoothed her white apron and beamed at the compliment. "Straight from Ireland."

"Shall I finish making the salad, Aunt Clara?" Michaela asked.

Clara nodded. "And as soon as that's done, we can eat."

❧

"The weather's perfect tonight." Michaela looked up at the stars that seemed to hover above them like thousands of tiny white diamonds. After a feast of stew and homemade bread, the wooden swing in the backyard was a perfect place to relax and enjoy the soft breeze that filtered in from the ocean.

"What did you need to talk to me about?" Michaela shifted in her seat so she could see his face better.

The light of the gas lamp revealed a guarded expression on Philip's face. Something was different tonight. He'd acted strangely all evening, and she couldn't imagine what he had to tell her.

Unless. . .he'd met someone.

She smiled at the idea. That must be it. She watched with interest as Philip looked down at the ground, rubbed his hands together, and shifted his weight in the swing, causing it to rock sideways.

"What is it?" Michaela pressured him with a laugh. "If I didn't know better, I'd say you look like a lovesick puppy."

Philip squirmed again, and the swing banged gently against the wooden post, but he still didn't speak.

"That's it!" Michaela's eyes widened in excitement. She was right. He'd found someone.

"Who is it? Do you want me to guess?" Michaela started making a mental list, wondering if it was someone she knew. Vivian was far too outspoken for Philip, but she had seen him talking to Elizabeth at church several times. Or maybe it was Hannah. She was a widow with two small girls, but Philip had always said how much he loved children. Then there was always her best friend, Caroline—

"You're right, I think I've found someone." Philip raised his gaze to meet hers, and a solemn shadow crossed his face. "The problem is, she doesn't know. I'm close to this person, but I don't know how to tell her what I'm feeling."

Michaela reached out and rested her hand on his arm. "Philip, you have nothing to worry about. You're extremely handsome and a faithful Christian. You're talented and own a successful business, you're kind and generous—I could go on.

What else could a woman want?"

He pulled his arm away but held her gaze. "So you think I should tell her how I feel?"

"Definitely." Excited about the possibility that Philip had found someone, her matchmaking skills began to work. "Wait a minute, what about the church social that's coming up? You could invite her, then slip away for a short walk after lunch and tell her how you feel. That would be perfect." She stood and continued mulling over the possibilities. "You need to wear the suit you're wearing tonight—"

"It's you, Michaela."

"And don't forget to bring her flowers. Women love flowers. . . ."

"Michaela, I said it's you."

Michaela sat back down on the swing and looked him straight in the eye. "What did you say?"

"I—I just didn't know how to tell you," Philip stammered. "I'm in love with you, Michaela."

"I don't know what to say." She was shocked at his declaration of love. Michaela had certainly not expected him to name her.

Philip gazed into the distance and wrung his hands together. "Are you disappointed?"

"Disappointed?" Michaela stood, shaking her head in disbelief. She turned to face him. "You're like a best friend to me—a brother."

He let out a short sigh and frowned. "I don't want to be a brother to you. I want much more than that. I want to ask you to marry me."

Philip wanted to marry her? Philip, who had been an anchor in her life since the fire, no longer looked at her as her husband's wife?

Ethen.

Michaela stopped suddenly as a wave of panic swept through her. How could she even think about loving someone else and betraying her husband's memory? "What about Ethen?"

Philip grasped the wooden post beside him and shook his head slowly. "Ethen's gone. He would want you to be happy again."

"I know, but. . ."

A slight grin played on Philip's lips. "At least you would know he approved of the man."

"You were his best friend." Her mind spun with the implications of what he was saying. Philip loved her and wanted a relationship with her. But was that something she could give him?

Philip held up his hand as if to stop her. "You don't have to say anything now; just think about it. You and me. We're so right for each other. It makes sense."

"Philip, if I ever fall in love again, I don't want to do it because it makes sense. I. . ." Michaela sat beside him and took his hands, squeezing them gently. "I'm sorry. You took me totally by surprise. You know I'm crazy about you, Philip, but I never thought about you—about us—being romantically involved."

"Never?" He frowned, and she could hear the disappointment in his voice.

"I'm sorry, but no. I don't know what to say. It's not you. I've just never thought about there being anyone else." Michaela struggled with her words. The last thing she wanted to do was to hurt him, but she also knew she had to be honest. "I think I want to get married again someday. I just don't know if I'm ready for that now. I'm not over Ethen yet. I still miss him so much."

"I know. Just promise me you'll think about the possibility of us together." He shrugged his shoulders and gave her a hopeful look. "Give me a chance. We could start over. I want to court you, Michaela. I want to take you out to dinner, buy you flowers, and escort you to church."

"Oh, Philip." Michaela stood and tilted her head. "You know, the funny thing is, you do all those things already. When did you realize you were in love with me?"

"The other day when you were upset about the board's decision and we went out to dinner. You were smiling and laughing. You hadn't done that for so long, and I liked being the one to make you smile again. I want to be that person in your life."

Michaela walked over to one of the trees next to the swing and leaned against the rough bark. Philip meant so much to her. He had been there through the most difficult time of her life, and he continued to be there today. He was the one who'd told her Ethen and Leah were gone. He had stood by her at the funeral as the tiny casket was lowered into the ground beside her husband's. He had cried with her over the emptiness she felt. She knew he understood, because he had always been a part of her life and had felt his own loss of a brother and niece.

She also knew someday she wanted to find the right man, fall in love again, and get married, but she didn't know if that time had come yet.

They were both quiet for a few moments, until she finally broke the silence. "Philip, something happened while you were gone." She went back to the swing and sat beside him. "Maybe this isn't the best time to tell you, but you need to know, especially now. Emma is expecting another baby, and she's having a hard time. I decided to go help them out until the baby's born. I've already sent a telegram to my brother, and I'll be leaving next week."

"Don't go." He leaned closer, and she felt the desperation in his voice. "Don't you see? If we marry, we could adopt Anna. It would be perfect. Michaela, I know you care for me. You could come to love me."

He was right. If they married, they could adopt Anna and become a family. Wasn't that what she wanted? A family? Her breathing quickened at the torrent of emotions she faced. It seemed like such a logical solution. But what about love?

Finally, she shook her head, her eyes pleading with him to understand. "Philip, I can't marry you for those reasons. It just wouldn't be right. Please understand. I need some time to think."

"I'm sorry." He sat back again and raked his hand through his hair, undisguised pain evident in his eyes. "I don't want to pressure you. Things just seemed so clear to me all of a sudden."

"No, I'm glad you told me."

"Promise me one thing. When you come back, will you let me court you?"

Michaela thought for a moment, trying to interpret what her heart felt. "I can't make you any promises except that while I'm gone, I'll do a lot of praying. I realize I still need to let Ethen go so I can get on with my life. I don't know right now, but maybe it will be with you."

"Remember one thing, Michaela. I'll always be here for you. You know that, don't you? No matter what happens between us."

Michaela looked into his deep blue eyes and smiled. "That's one thing I will always know."

⚘

"I'm not surprised one bit," Aunt Clara said to Michaela as they washed the dinner dishes. "I've wondered for some time if Philip didn't care about you—in a way other than friendship, I mean."

"Why didn't you say something?" Michaela demanded as she set the last of the dishes in the cupboard.

Aunt Clara wrung the wet rag and washed the counter. "I wasn't sure he realized it himself, and besides, I may always play the part of the matchmaker, but something held me back when it came to the two of you."

Sitting at the small table, Michaela rested her chin in her hands. "How could you tell?"

"There was something in his eyes when he looked at you, the way he held your hand a little too long, and the way he smiled whenever you entered a room."

"You noticed all of that?" How could she have missed something that had been clear to Aunt Clara? "Why didn't I notice?"

"You're still in love with Ethen."

Michaela fell silent. Her aunt was right. How many other things had she failed to notice because she was still wrapped up in the past?

Aunt Clara shook out the dishrag and laid it across the sink before sitting beside Michaela at the table. "What you've been going through is normal, but at some point, you have to look forward instead of behind."

Michaela shook her head. The revelation of Philip's affections seemed more like a dream than reality. "I care about him, but I don't know if I could fall in love with him."

Aunt Clara reached over and put her arms around her niece. "When the time is right, and it's the right person, you'll know. Give it time."

⁂

Philip wandered down the quiet street toward his home, wondering if he'd done the right thing in confessing his feelings toward Michaela. The pale moon shone above him, casting eerie shadows against the storefronts. He'd never felt uncertain about his future before. Spending the rest of his life with Michaela had seemed like the perfect solution. But was that all it had been? Had he mistaken a possible marriage of convenience for love?

At his cabinetmaking shop, he took the steps two at a time and entered the empty room above the store. He'd lived here for seven years and never felt lonely—until now. He'd never met a woman he wanted to share his life with, raise a family with, and grow old with together. Now that he'd revealed his feelings to Michaela, she was leaving and would be gone for months. He felt at a loss—how was he to win her heart now?

He looked around the room. Discarded clothes lay across the back of a wooden chair. A pile of books had been scattered across the small table beside a mug of forgotten coffee. As a bachelor, he'd never needed much more than the basics. A few simple furnishings had been adequate, but an unfamiliar sense of longing overcame him.

He didn't know what reaction he'd expected from Michaela, though he would have welcomed a shared confession of love. Clearing the table, he laid the stack of books on the shelf and dumped the leftover coffee. Love from Michaela wasn't realistic at this point. His one fear was that his feelings for her, even if never returned, would affect the friendship that had developed between them. He loved her too much to let his feelings change what they had.

Marrying Michaela still seemed like the perfect solution—not just for the two of them, but for Anna as well. They could give her what she needed most—a family to call her own. And there could be more children as the years passed. His business did well enough for him to support a large family if that was what Michaela wanted.

He sat on the edge of the bed and ran his fingers through his hair. What did Michaela want? That was the question that really mattered. He shouldn't have been surprised at the fact that she'd never thought of the two of them as something other than simply friends, but he'd dared to hope that once he declared his love, it would awaken unexplored feelings in Michaela's heart. The same thing he'd experienced when he looked at her that day in the wood shop with the sun streaming through her hair.

But there wasn't only their relationship he had to consider. In less than a week, Michaela was leaving. And where that left him, he had no idea.

෯

Michaela tossed and turned, trying to sleep after Philip's confession. She cared about him, but was it enough to build a marriage on? It had only been recently that she could admit to herself she might want to marry again—someday. Still, she didn't know how she could ever love someone as much as she loved Ethen.

Part of her wondered if God hadn't placed a second chance at love right before her eyes. Somewhere deep inside, she knew this wasn't the way. She could never marry Philip unless she knew she loved him with all her heart. If she married him now, she'd only be giving him second best.

Chapter 5

A cool breeze blew outside, perfect for a summer day on the beach. Michaela studied her reflection in the bedroom mirror, wondering if the dress she chose was right for the outing. She had already tried on four others and still couldn't make up her mind. The yellow fabric hugged her waist and draped gracefully past her hips. Its fashionable leg-of-mutton sleeves and lacy collar made it a favorite of hers.

When Philip had asked her to spend the afternoon with him, she hadn't even hesitated in telling him she would love to. Their relationship had changed because of what he had told her, and it could never be the same again, but she still wanted to spend time with him before she left.

On Sunday at church, she had noticed some of the things her aunt had mentioned. The way he held her gaze longer than necessary and grasped her hand after helping her out of the carriage.

No, things could never be the way they had been before.

Michaela had expected to feel uncomfortable around him, but she didn't. It had been a long time since a man had looked at her and told her that he loved her. It felt good to be wanted again—to be cherished and desired.

"Michaela?" Aunt Clara knocked on the door and peeked in. "Philip's here."

"What about this dress?" Michaela smoothed her hands against the silky fabric, wondering again about the attire she had chosen.

"It's always been one of my favorites." Aunt Clara folded her arms across her chest and studied her.

"Mine, too, but—"

"Am I sensing a bit of nervousness on your part?" A grin broke out across Aunt Clara's face. "I hadn't expected this."

Michaela fell back against the bed and groaned. "I don't know how I feel. This whole thing with Philip took me by surprise. It's been a long time since I worried about how I looked, but for some crazy reason, I want to look just right today."

Aunt Clara sat beside her on the bed. "You look beautiful, and I know without a doubt Philip will agree with me."

"Do you remember when I first fell in love with Ethen?" Michaela sat up and straightened the collar of her dress.

"It seemed as if the two of you had been in love forever." A dreamy look crossed Aunt Clara's face, and Michaela wondered if her aunt was remembering when she first fell in love with Uncle Henry. "I remember when you realized how you felt."

"I was eighteen years old, and suddenly I took twice as long to get dressed whenever I knew I was going to see Ethen." Michaela faced the mirror and pulled her curls back into a large chignon, then ran her fingers through her short bangs. "He took me to a church picnic one Sunday afternoon. We had always been friends, good friends, but I hadn't really thought beyond that. I looked at him as we sat beside the lake and knew at that moment that I loved him and wanted to spend the rest of my life with him."

Aunt Clara shook her head slowly. "You seemed so young."

"But I'm not anymore. I'm thirty-two years old." Michaela stood and faced her aunt, her hands resting against her hips. "Oh, Aunt Clara, do you think someday I might be able to love Philip the way I loved Ethen?"

"I can't answer that, sweetheart." Aunt Clara wrapped her arms around Michaela and held her tight.

"I could have Anna." Michaela's heart churned inwardly. "If I marry Philip, we could be a family."

Aunt Clara cupped her hand on the side of Michaela's face. "I know how alone you've felt at times. Sometimes I wish I'd found someone else—someone to fill the lonely spot in my life. Someone to grow old with me and laugh at my jokes."

Michaela nodded, wishing it didn't have to seem so complicated—or was it? "Philip is comfortable and familiar. He knows me, and we'd be happy together."

"It's a choice you're going to have to make."

Michaela took a step backward and looked toward the door, needing a change in the direction of the conversation. "What about Ben White from church? I've seen the way he looks at you."

"Michaela!" Color rushed to Aunt Clara's cheeks, and she quickly changed the subject. "I think Philip's waited long enough."

Michaela tried not to laugh at her aunt's reaction and followed her down the narrow staircase and into the parlor where Philip waited for her. He stood when they entered the room.

"You look lovely." His gaze lingered on Michaela's face.

Aunt Clara cleared her throat. "I made a picnic lunch. Fried chicken, baked beans, cake, and lemonade."

"Sounds wonderful. Thank you." Philip picked up the food box Aunt Clara had prepared for them and turned to Michaela. "I have the buggy out front if you're ready."

Michaela kissed her aunt on the cheek. "We'll be back before dark."

"Enjoy yourselves," her aunt replied.

Michaela sat next to Philip in the buggy. Suddenly, she felt shy around him. His short, curly hair lay in dark waves across his head, and she couldn't help noticing how handsome he looked in his white shirt and dark blue pants. She let out a soft laugh, realizing how much time the two of them must have spent getting ready.

"All right." He turned and looked at her, his dark brows raised in uncertainty. "What is it? My hair, my clothes? You look as though you're about to burst."

"It's not you; it's us." She rested her fingers across her mouth, trying to stop the erupting giggles.

"What do you mean, it's us?"

"We've been friends for so many years, and we know just about everything there is to know about each other."

His brow creased. "And that's funny?"

"No. What's funny is I spent two hours getting ready this morning, and I know you did the same thing."

A ripple of laughter broke from his lips as he nodded in agreement. "Does that mean there's a chance for me?" A solemn grin quickly replaced his laughter. "For the two of us?"

"Let's give it some time." She felt a tug of emotion pull on her. "You've helped me find contentment and never let me forget that someone cares about me."

"I've always cared for you, Michaela."

"I know, but loving someone is different." She let her gaze wander down the street that bustled with the noise from other buggies and pedestrians. Love was a complicated issue. She turned her attention back to him, not wanting to hurt him but knowing she needed to be honest about how she felt. "I can't say that I'm in love with you, but I do know you've made me very, very happy."

"And I intend to keep on making you happy."

They were silent, and she knew they both realized the possibility of a relationship had come at a difficult time. Determined to put thoughts of leaving aside, Michaela smiled as Philip shyly reached for her hand and placed it safely in his own.

❧

"I love the sea." Michaela leaned back against a rock, pulling her knees against her chest. She took a deep breath and let the salty air fill her lungs. "It's so beautiful. Constant and yet ever changing at the same time."

Philip stood beside her, throwing pebbles into the tide as it rolled in a continuous motion. It was getting late. They would have to go back soon, but she didn't want the day to end. This would be the last day she'd spend with him for months.

"It's been a good day, hasn't it?" Philip took a seat beside her on the sand and stretched out his legs in front of him.

"It's been perfect. I can't remember the last time I spent a whole day doing nothing but relaxing."

"It's about time. Of course, it's been quite awhile since I took a day off as well. I guess we both need to learn to enjoy the beauty God's placed around us."

"What's your excuse?" Michaela dug the toes of her boots into the sand and watched the white spray of water as the incoming tide splashed against a small outcropping of rocks along the shoreline. "I'm running away from the past. What are you running from?"

Philip looked out across the ocean as if contemplating her question. "I don't know. My room's lonely at night, so I'd rather work than go home. It's something I've only been able to admit recently."

"Why haven't you ever married? I know I've tried more than once to set you up with someone."

Philip arched his arm backward, then threw another rock into the oncoming tide. "How could I forget? You and Ethen were always trying to get me hitched. Remember Sassy Winter?"

Michaela laughed at the forgotten memory. "I'll admit I was a bit out of line with her."

"A bit?" He nudged her gently with his shoulder. "She never quit talking during the entire dinner, and none of us could get a word in edgewise. Half of the time I didn't even know what she was talking about. What was it she was interested in?"

"Her father left her a rather large inheritance, and she spends it studying rare plants. From what I understand, she's really quite knowledgeable on the subject."

Philip shook his head. "Well, it was beyond me. In fact, it seems that most of the women I've met talk incessantly. Except for you, of course. You seem to understand that the amount of conversation is not equal to the level of intelligence."

She smiled at the compliment, and for a moment they both sat still, listening to the rhythmic sounds of the ocean and the occasional cry of a shorebird.

"Shall we walk for a bit?" He helped her up from her sitting position but didn't let go of her hand as they walked along the sand. "It isn't that I was in love with you when Ethen was alive. You were Michaela, the girl next door who married my brother. But now I realize what it really means to love someone. I never felt this way toward anyone before. I knew God's timing was always right and that one day I would meet someone, but little did I know that person had always been right here with me."

Michaela looked out across the gray-blue waters, not knowing what to say. "I'm sorry. I promised I wouldn't pressure you, and the way I'm going on—"

She squeezed his hand. "You're not. I just have a lot to think about. You've always been there for me, and I don't want to lose you first of all as a friend. Part of me wishes I wasn't leaving for Cranton tomorrow."

"Don't." He stopped and rested his index finger against her lips to quiet her. "Don't talk about that now. Let's just enjoy the rest of today."

She closed her eyes and felt the gentle touch of his lips brush hers.

"Michaela. . ." He reached forward and kissed her again. This time his hands encircled her waist. As he drew her close, she felt herself melt into his embrace. This was what she wanted. She wanted him to hold her and tell her how much she meant to him. Part of her was certain this must be a dream, but as she looked into his eyes, feeling his warm touch and the smell of fresh cedar that lingered from his work at the shop, she knew it was real.

If only she could put the past behind her and let go of Ethen, she might be ready to love again.

❧

That night Michaela picked up the Bible she kept on the small table next to her bed and set it in her lap. In the morning she would board the train for the other side of Massachusetts. It might as well be the other side of the world.

The image of Philip seemed so real, his kiss so poignant, that she felt torn between going to help her brother and sister-in-law and staying here with Anna and Philip. Emotions swirled within her, leaving her confused. Maybe it was best that she was going away for a while. It would give her time to sort out her feelings without any distractions. She couldn't say she loved Philip, at least not the way she had loved Ethen, but tonight when he kissed her, he'd stirred something within her that hadn't been awakened for a long time.

Sitting up in her bed with the thick, cream-colored quilt her mother had made over twenty years ago wrapped around her, she opened her Bible to the fourth chapter of Philippians. Pastor Simon, who had performed her wedding twelve years ago as well as the funeral for her husband and daughter, had shared with her this chapter. She'd almost worn out the page in the Bible, reading it whenever she needed encouragement. When she finished the first half of the chapter, she read the seventh verse again.

" 'And the peace of God, which passeth all understanding, shall keep your hearts and minds through Christ Jesus.'"

"God. . ." She struggled with the words to begin her prayer. "I hardly know what to say. I read of Your promises for peace and strength in Your Word, but sometimes You just seem so far away. How do I find this peace that passes understanding? The peace You promise?"

She closed her Bible and pulled the book tightly against her chest. "Sometimes I think I'm healing and getting my life back together; then I see the face of my little girl, and I don't understand why she had to die. I want to let go of the past, but I don't know how.

"And Ethen. . .I miss him so much, God. I feel lonely without him, so lost. We had plans for the future, and now they're all gone. Philip loves me, but I don't know if I can open up my heart to him. I don't know if I can let anyone inside. I know to love Philip isn't betraying Ethen, but I still find my heart holding back. And now losing Anna. . . O God, give me the strength and the courage to live again. Help me to remember You are near so I might once again find peace in my life. The peace that transcends all understanding."

Michaela laid down her Bible next to her on the bed and closed her eyes. Had she been letting God heal her, or had she instead been holding in her pain and refusing to let go of it? She knew she could never truly love Philip or anyone else until her heart healed.

≈

"Are you sure you'll be all right?" Michaela stood at the foot of her bed and voiced her fears to Aunt Clara, concerned she'd made the wrong decision in leaving. Her trunk was already packed and sitting beside the dresser, along with the two other small bags she planned to take.

"It's not like you'll be gone forever. Just until the baby is born and Emma gets back on her feet." Aunt Clara shook her head and smiled. "Besides, there are plenty of people at church who have promised to look in on me now and then."

"I know; it's just hard not to worry."

Her aunt cupped Michaela's face in her hands and looked deeply into her eyes. "You may not always feel this way, but the past few months have given you a strength that often comes through adversity. You're not going alone. God will go with you and sustain you. He has 'engraved each of us on the palms of His hands.'"

Michaela smiled and let her aunt's paraphrase of Isaiah 49:16 comfort her spirit. "You always know what to say."

"I know you're nervous, but I'll be fine and so will you. Is everything packed now?" Her aunt took a step back and glanced around the room. "Philip should be here shortly to take you to the station. I made him promise not to be a minute late."

"I just need to change my clothes and make sure I haven't forgotten anything."

Michaela studied her aunt, memorizing each feature. She loved her so much, from her wrinkled face that had always shown Michaela so much kindness to the white hair she wore in a neat bun at the base of her neck. She had been Michaela's mentor, her adviser, and most of all, her friend.

"I'm going to miss you so much, Aunt Clara." Michaela gave the older woman an affectionate hug as she tried unsuccessfully to stop the tears. "I wish you were coming with me."

"So do I. I'll miss you, but I'm too old and set in my ways, even for a trip across the state. You'll be back before you know it."

Michaela looked into Aunt Clara's eyes, praying that she would one day possess the same measure of godliness and wisdom.

"I believe this time away will be very important for you. Philip loves you very much, and nothing will change his feelings for you between now and when you come back. I'll go downstairs to watch for him while you finish getting ready."

Michaela sat on the bed and looked around the room that had been hers as a teenager and again when she moved back after the fire. It seemed silly to say good-bye to a room, but for some reason she needed to. It was a simple room filled only with a bed, armoire, dresser, and chair, along with a few things that helped give the room a homier look. If she decided to marry Philip when she came back, this room would once again be empty.

"Philip's here," her aunt called from downstairs.

Gently, Michaela closed the lid to the trunk. It was time to go.

✃

"You promised you'd write me," Philip reminded Michaela as he helped her out of the buggy once they reached the busy train station. The smell of burning coal hung in the air as passengers hurried across the platform or waited on long wooden benches for the next arrival.

"I haven't forgotten."

She was glad Philip had insisted on taking her to the station. She found herself holding on to the familiar, afraid it might change while she was away.

"I assured your aunt I would check in on her, so don't worry about a thing. She'll probably outlive us all." Philip smiled, causing her heart to skip a beat.

She laughed. "You're right."

"Six months is a long time." Philip set the trunk on the platform and handed her the tickets.

"The baby is due around Christmas, so if everything goes well, I'll be back the first of next year." She flinched at the words. It sounded like a lifetime away.

"That's forever." Philip reached out and brushed her cheek gently with his hand. "I love you with all my heart, but I'll wait for you as long as you need me to."

Michaela gazed into his eyes and knew that here was a man who loved her unconditionally—a man who wanted to spend the rest of his life with her. She prayed that someday she would be able to say the same of him.

The conductor called out, "All aboard!" and Philip reached down gently and cupped her face in his hands. As their lips met, Michaela found herself responding to his kiss. She lifted her arms around his neck and felt his hands tighten around her waist. She longed for him to hold her forever, never letting go. Finally, she backed slowly away from him, and without another word, she boarded the train.

Chapter 6

Michaela woke to the sun peeking into Daniel and Emma's second-story guest room. Soft rays of light streaked across the pale green walls that matched to perfection the handmade quilt on the bed. Crawling out from under the covers, she went and stood beside the window that overlooked the front yard. Several old trees stood tall, their twisted limbs swaying in the morning breeze. Beyond them lay pastures of grazing cattle, hillside orchards, and, eventually, the Connecticut River.

Her first week in Cranton had passed quickly. More than happy to jump in and take over the cooking and housework, she'd found little time to dwell on her loss of Anna or even the possibility of a future with Philip. Turning away from the window, she swept her hand across the smooth top of the pine dresser. Perhaps the truth was she simply hadn't allowed herself to imagine what her return to Boston might bring.

Her gaze moved across the room and rested on a rocking chair and empty bassinet. She wasn't the only one whose arms ached for the soft touch of a child. Daniel and Emma had never even been able to hold their babies. All they had left were two tiny grave markers. She prayed that someday this room would echo with the laughter of her brother's children.

Shaking off her melancholy mood, Michaela mentally went over her plans for the day. The church social was to take place today, and she was looking forward to meeting some of the people who lived in the area. She'd spent the previous day baking and planned to take two chocolate cakes and several loaves of fresh bread to the celebration.

After putting on a lavender dress with dark purple trim, Michaela hurried downstairs. The strong aroma of coffee filled the cozy room where Emma sat at the kitchen table reading her Bible. Her dark hair hung neatly in one long braid down her back with loose curls framing her face. Her dress, a deep chocolate brown, pulled tight across her stomach, showing the first signs of pregnancy.

"Good morning, Emma." Michaela smiled at her sister-in-law, glad to see that the color was back in her cheeks this morning. "You must be feeling better."

"I am." Emma glanced up from her Bible and returned the smile. "I thought the least I could do was get up early and make some coffee."

"It smells wonderful." Michaela poured herself a cup of the hot drink and took a long swallow. Despite the fact that Michaela had been unable to spend much time with Emma since she and Daniel had moved to Cranton, Michaela still considered Emma a close friend.

Emma shut the heavy book and walked toward the cupboard. "I know the doctor wants me to rest as much as I can, but I get so tired of staying in bed."

Michaela squeezed Emma's hand, knowing how much this child meant to her. "In a few months, when you're holding your baby in your arms, you'll forget all about the struggles you're going through right now."

"I know." Tears misted in Emma's eyes as she ran her hand across her abdomen in a slow, circular motion. "Sometimes I get so scared that I'll lose this one, too."

The ache in Michaela's heart intensified as she struggled with what to say. "I know how bad it hurts to have lost a child. Aunt Clara always reminds me how God has promised to go through the valleys with us and that He will carry us through times of trouble."

Emma wiped away a stray tear and let out a soft chuckle. "I don't know why I get so emotional. Daniel's always teasing me about how I'm laughing one minute, then crying the next."

"It's all right." Michaela handed her a clean rag from the counter.

Emma dabbed at her eyes with the cloth and let out a deep sigh. "I know you understand. That's one of the reasons I'm glad you're here." She waved her hands in front of her. "Enough of this. We have a celebration ahead of us."

"Do you feel well enough to come?" Michaela set a black iron skillet on top of the stove and pulled some potatoes from a wooden bin to start breakfast.

"I'm sure going to try. The Johnson farm isn't far away, so if I start to feel bad, Daniel can always bring me home."

Michaela set to work chopping enough potatoes to fry for the three of them. "I'm glad you're coming. It will do you good to get out of the house for a while."

"You're spoiling me, you know." Emma set three plates on the round table, then added the silverware.

"That's why I came."

"I didn't realize how much it would help me. Just knowing I don't have to worry about Daniel fending for himself is a great relief."

Michaela cracked an egg into a bowl, the corners of her mouth tilting into an affectionate smile. "It certainly doesn't look as if he's been starving."

"I heard that." The front door banged shut, and Daniel's deep laughter floated in from the front room. He stomped into the kitchen, leaving traces of mud across the recently mopped floor.

"How do you put up with this man?" Michaela set her hands on her hips as Daniel gave his wife a kiss on the cheek.

A rosy blush crept up Emma's face. "I thought somebody had to, so it might as well be me."

Michaela laughed. "You'd better go get washed up for breakfast."

Twenty minutes later, Daniel slid into his seat, and Michaela placed a steaming hot plate of eggs and potatoes in front of him. "You know, I've missed you, little sister."

"It has been way too long." She smiled at the familiar teasing that had always been a part of their relationship. "Emma, are you hungry?"

Emma waved her hand toward the stove and frowned. "I was going to try to eat, but I think I'll just have a dry piece of toast. That's about all I can handle this morning."

Daniel reached over and squeezed his wife's shoulder. "Ladies, we need to hurry if we're going to make it to the Johnson place before the celebration gets into full swing."

❦

"What a beautiful home." Michaela leaned forward in the wagon as Daniel pulled on the reins and stopped in front of the Johnsons' charming gray-shingled farmhouse, with its large porch and symmetrical front windows.

"The man in the black shirt is Eric Johnson," Daniel told Michaela as he helped her down from the wagon. "He and his wife had six children before she passed away a few years ago."

Eric Johnson leaned against the porch rail, his tall, lean figure towering over most of the guests. Several children, whom she assumed to be his, played quietly nearby. Michaela wondered how a single man could raise such a large brood of kids, though each one of them looked properly cared for and well dressed.

She followed Emma to the house, then stopped for a moment, captivated by the man who stood before her. Taking a closer look at the farmer, she studied him. His broad shoulders were supported by his equally muscular frame, and he was tanned from hours of work in the sun. His hair, dark as coal, lay perfectly against his forehead.

"Michaela." His firm hand met hers as Daniel introduced them. "It's good to finally meet you. Emma and Daniel have told me so much about you."

"It's nice to meet you as well, Eric." Michaela noticed the dimple in his right cheek when he smiled. "Daniel's mentioned what a big help you've been to them."

"Just being neighborly." Eric rested his hand on the shoulder of the child closest to him. "Let me introduce you to my children, Mrs. Macintosh."

The smallest of the group ran up and grasped Michaela's hand. "My name's Ruby. I'm six, and I think your dress is beautiful."

Michaela bent down to give Ruby her full attention and was drawn to the little girl's dark brown eyes, long lashes, and radiant smile. "Thank you, Ruby. I'm very glad to meet you, too."

Eric let out a soft chuckle and proceeded to introduce the rest of the children. "This is Rebecca, my oldest."

Michaela stood to look at the rest of the children, still holding Ruby's hand. Rebecca wore her long hair in a simple twist, allowing two soft tendrils to escape, one on either side of her face.

"Hard to believe it," Eric continued, "but she just turned seventeen. She's a wonderful cook."

"It's good to meet you," Michaela said warmly to the young woman who had inherited her father's dark hair and striking good looks.

"I'm glad you could join us, Mrs. Macintosh."

"And this," Eric said, pointing to the next in line, "is Samuel. He's fourteen."

"Do you like frogs?" He pulled one out of his pocket and held it up to Michaela's face. She took a step back, then stifled a laugh at the slimy pet.

"Samuel!" Eric gave him a sharp look and pointed his son in the direction of the barnyard. "That belongs outside and not in your pocket. What do you say?"

The young boy hung his head and stared at the ground. "I'm sorry, ma'am. Sarah's a girl, and she likes frogs just like me. I thought you might like them, too."

Samuel marched off the porch to let his frog go, avoiding the stern look from his father. Despite the reprimand, Michaela was certain she saw a sparkle in Eric's eyes.

Eric cleared his throat and turned to the next child. "Matt, my youngest son, is twelve."

"Do you have something to show me as well?" Michaela asked, noticing his hands hidden behind his back.

"No, ma'am." Matt brought his hands out from behind his back and held them up.

Eric looked at his youngest boy and ruffled his hair. "Next," he continued, "is Adam. He's my right-hand man, I guess you could say. When I'm gone, he's in charge."

"How do you do, Adam?" It wouldn't be long until he was as tall as his father.

Adam pulled at the collar of his shirt. "Just fine, thank you, ma'am."

"Adam is sixteen, and last but not least is Sarah. She's my only blue-eyed beauty," finished Eric. "She takes after her mother's side of the family."

Sarah, with hair the color of corn silk to match her blue eyes and fair skin, looked as if she were about to burst.

"Isn't this the most exciting day?" Sarah took a step closer to Michaela and clasped her hands in front of her. "Except for Christmas when you get presents, of course. Personally, I think this is the best day of the year. There's so much good food and games and. . ."

Michaela was sure Sarah would have continued indefinitely if her father hadn't glanced in her direction. Sarah quickly closed her mouth.

"I'm looking forward to this day, too, Sarah." Michaela stifled a laugh. "How old are you?"

"Nine." Sarah gave her father a crooked grin, then looked away.

"Make yourself at home," Eric told Michaela. "I know there are quite a few people looking forward to meeting you."

Michaela followed Emma inside the house, her attention immediately drawn to the piano in the corner of the large room. The dark wood shone like it had just been polished, and Michaela longed for a chance to play, already missing the calming effect the music brought.

She crossed the hardwood floor past a grouping of chairs and colorful rugs. Two large windows with bright red gingham curtains gave the room a warm and welcoming atmosphere. A stone fireplace took up most of the far wall and stood as the focal point of the room.

The women were finishing lunch preparations in the kitchen. Emma quickly made the introductions, and several commented on the cakes Michaela had baked for the festivities.

"I think I'll forget lunch and just have a thick slice of your cake, Michaela," said Mary, a young woman with a pleasant smile, as she shifted the infant on her hip.

"I think I'll join you," another woman who'd introduced herself as Mae chimed in.

"Tell us about Boston." Several of the women gathered around and listened for the response to Mary's request. "It's been forever since any of us have been to the city."

Michaela felt instantly welcome and at home with these women as she talked about her hometown and answered a variety of questions ranging from fashion to transportation to church. Before long, lunch was ready, and Michaela helped carry the dishes out to the backyard, where several tables had been set up.

Lunch was wonderful—chicken, beef, ham, and all of the trimmings. Michaela's cakes received rave reviews, and she promised to make another one for the next gathering. She ate until she could hardly hold another bite, and before she knew it, it was time to clean up again.

In the kitchen, Michaela was happy to be partnered with Rebecca, Eric's oldest daughter, in drying the dishes.

"Do you enjoy school?" Michaela asked.

"Very much." Rebecca's smile confirmed her answer as she handed a dry dish to Sarah. "My favorite subject is math. I'm thinking about becoming a teacher, though I also love to sew."

"My mother was a teacher."

"Where does she live?"

Michaela felt the slight aching of her heart as she fingered the towel between her fingers. "She died when I was eleven."

"I'm sorry." Rebecca handed Michaela another dish to dry. "My mother died a few years ago. I still miss her."

"I miss my mother, too."

They were both silent for a moment, until Michaela decided to ask another question. "How much more schooling do you have left?"

"This is my last year. Then I can work on my teacher's certificate." Rebecca reached for another dish from the soapstone sink and began to wash it. "Father's been very supportive. He even found someone to help out with the house so I could have time to go to school."

Michaela wondered about this man, Eric Johnson, who'd spent the last few years not only running a farm, but raising six children alone. She'd noted his relaxed manner during lunch as he mingled among his guests, making sure that everyone felt at home. Somehow, despite the tragedy of losing his wife and being forced to be sole provider and parent for his family, he seemed to have found a sense of peace.

Sarah nudged between Michaela and Rebecca and grinned like a conspirator. "Did Rebecca tell you she has a beau? His name's Jake, and he's here today."

"Sarah!" Rebecca gave her sister a firm look, and Sarah quickly closed her mouth. "Never mind about that. What do you do in Boston?"

"I teach piano lessons. I noticed you have a piano in the front room."

"Unfortunately, none of us knows how to play," Rebecca admitted.

Michaela laid down her towel and rested her hands against the counter, surprised at the revelation. "You can't be serious."

"My grandmother sent it out here on the railroad," Rebecca said with a laugh. "She thought it would help us become cultured. She thinks Pa should have moved us all to the city after Mama died. She's sure we're going to grow up unrefined and unsophisticated without the benefits of living in a large city like Boston."

"Rebecca." Michaela toyed with an idea that was forming in her mind. "I could teach you how to play the piano. I could teach all of you." Michaela handed the last dish to Sarah, whose eyes were almost as wide as the plate she now held.

"You'll teach us how to play the piano?" Sarah asked.

"I could come out every Saturday and teach you one at a time." The more she thought about it, the more she liked the idea.

Rebecca shook her head. "That seems like a whole lot of work, Mrs. Macintosh—"

"I love teaching, and what good is your piano sitting in there without someone to play it? Plus, I already miss my piano, and it would give me a place to practice."

"I'll have to ask Father, but it sounds wonderful." A wide grin covered Rebecca's face.

"I'm going to go ask him right now." Sarah's enthusiasm got the best of her, and she ran out of the kitchen in search of her father.

※

"Come on, Mrs. Macintosh, it's baseball. You have to play," Sarah insisted a little while later.

Never being one to miss out on the fun, Michaela had followed Sarah and the others out into the open field behind the Johnsons' barn, despite the fact she had doubts about the whole thing—including how ladylike the game was.

"How can you live in the city and not know anything about baseball?" Eric leaned against the wooden bat and shot her a grin.

"Yes, come on, Mrs. Macintosh, it's fun." Sarah, who had followed Michaela around all afternoon, now pulled on her arm.

"I don't know anything about baseball," Michaela protested for the third time.

"It's easy!" Adam tossed the white ball into the air and caught it with one simple swipe of his hand.

"Daniel?" Michaela looked to her brother, hoping he would back her up.

"Come on. You can be on my team." He winked at her, obviously not planning to intervene.

Michaela groaned.

"It's simple." Adam stepped forward and attempted to give her a swift course on the game. "All you have to do is hit the ball and run around the bases, or if you're playing in the field, you try to catch the ball."

The first person up to bat was Eric. Michaela held her glove ready like Adam had shown her. He hit the ball and it bounced right toward her, rolling to a stop between her legs. She reached down to grab the ball, keeping Eric in her line of sight the entire time. He ran toward second base. She threw the ball as hard as she could. Adam ran for her off-centered throw, then tried to beat Eric to the base. She let out a soft groan. He was safe.

Ten minutes later, her team was called up to bat.

"You're up, Michaela," Daniel said when it was her turn.

They were winning, three to two, and Michaela had picked up a few things about baseball along the way, but she still felt ridiculous standing at home plate with the bat grasped between her hands. She tried to remember everything she'd been told. *Bend legs, lean over slightly, watch the ball.* Eric, who was pitching for the opposing team, threw the ball toward her, and she swung.

"Strike."

She looked over at Daniel and the Johnson kids, who were cheering her on. Eric threw the ball again. This time Michaela thought she detected a slight smirk on his face.

"Strike."

Michaela took in a deep breath and stared straight at him. Inky black hair curled slightly over his ears, and dark stubble shadowed his square jaw. Their gazes met, and an odd sensation swept through her. Feeling off balance for a moment, she tried to shake the feeling. Determined to concentrate on the game, she sucked in her breath and raised the bat.

Eric threw the ball. She swung. A crack sounded from the bat, and a cheer went up from behind her as she stood there watching the ball fly toward second base.

"Run! Run!" someone screamed behind her.

Michaela threw down the bat, picked up the hem of her dress, and ran for her life.

❧

An hour later, Michaela leaned against the rail of the Johnsons' front porch, enjoying the end of the sunset. The murmur of voices filtered into the night, joining the low croak of a lone frog. Fireflies danced in the distance, their soft glow shimmering in the murky twilight.

"It's a beautiful night, isn't it?"

Michaela jumped at the deep male voice and turned around. "Eric?"

He came and stood beside her, keeping an arm's length between them. "I'm sorry if I startled you."

"No, it's fine. I was just enjoying the sunset." She brushed a hair out of the corner of her mouth and looked up at him. Despite her height, he still towered over her.

Eric rested his palms against the rail and leaned forward. "My mother always said that sunsets were gifts from God that should be shared."

She smiled at the expression. "I like that."

"Then you don't mind if I join you for a few minutes?"

"Of course not." Michaela watched the breeze tug at his hair and brush the top of his collar, then shifted her gaze to the orange and yellow of the sunset. "This has always been my favorite time of the day. Just before evening fades into night and there's still a splash of color across the sky."

"I have to agree. It's beautiful." He cleared his throat and glanced at her. "Sarah tells me you offered to give the children piano lessons."

Shadows masked his expression, and she suddenly wondered if she'd made a mistake in agreeing to teach the children without talking to him first. "I hope I wasn't out of line."

"No, I didn't mean that." He angled his body toward her, one elbow still resting against the wooden rail. "What I meant was that six kids is a lot of lessons."

"It's something I really enjoy. Plus, it's a pity to have such a beautiful instrument that no one plays."

He let out a soft chuckle. "I have to agree with you on that one. If you're sure you wouldn't mind, I would be happy to pay you—"

"I'm not looking for a source of income." Michaela wondered if she'd left the wrong impression. "It really is something I enjoy. Just let me play it every once in a while and I will be more than happy. Are Saturdays all right with you?"

"Saturdays would be perfect."

❧

Eric watched as Michaela pulled her embroidered shawl around her shoulders and tried to interpret the torrent of unfamiliar feelings that rushed through him. All afternoon he'd been aware of her. Then when she'd caught his gaze on the baseball field, something had awakened within him.

Six years ago, he'd lost Susanna. She'd been the love of his life and there hadn't been a woman since who'd captured him the way she did.

Then today, Michaela Macintosh had stepped out of the wagon, and somehow her laughter and bright smile had found a way into the recesses of his heart. He'd watched her interact with his children and the other guests—like this was the place she belonged. He shook his head at the image. For six years he and his children had worked the land, harvested the crops, and built up a farm to be proud of. Nothing needed to change.

Or did it?

"When we first moved out here, the town was no bigger than a whistle-stop on the railroad line." Eric spoke and tried to get his mind off her silky red hair and soft, fair skin. "Since then, it's grown to become a viable place of trading and business."

The sun had sunk into the horizon, and the light of the moon captured her face. He caught her grin, and she laughed. "You forget I'm from Boston."

He shook his head and smiled. "In my mind, Boston can't compare to quiet nights like this. Here we have the best of both worlds."

"You do have a point. I have to admit I do find this part of the country very beautiful."

Daniel stepped out onto the porch behind them. "Michaela? I'm sorry to interrupt you. Emma needs to go home. She's exhausted."

"Of course. I just need to gather my things." Michaela pulled her embroidered shawl tighter around her shoulders and turned to Eric. "It's been a wonderful day. Thank you."

"I'm glad you could come." Eric followed them into the front room, disappointed she had to leave so soon. "The next time there's a baseball game, I'm going to insist on being on your team."

"My double play was simply beginner's luck." She laughed, then caught his gaze. For the second time that day, something passed between them. The color of her eyes had darkened from a pale icy blue to a deep indigo. For a brief moment, he found himself lost in them—but this was a place he wasn't sure he could afford to stay.

He tried to push away the emotion. He didn't have time for someone like Michaela in his life. In fact, he didn't need someone else. While certainly not perfect, his children were well adjusted, and his life was complete. He blew out a long sigh and watched as she rode away in Daniel's buggy. If that were true, then why did his heart suddenly feel a deep twinge of emptiness?

⁂

At the farmhouse, Michaela got ready for bed, attempting to shove aside Eric's lingering image. When he'd looked at her, his dark brown eyes had seemed to pierce through to the deep alcoves of her heart—to a place she wasn't ready to let anyone enter.

Heaving a sigh, Michaela yanked a sheet of paper out of the desk drawer, then slammed it shut. She'd write Philip a long letter. Maybe there she could lose herself in what was comfortable and familiar. Quickly filling the page, she told him about her first week in Cranton and asked if he'd delivered Aunt Clara's dresser or had a chance to check on Anna.

Writing had the calming effect she desired. Just as Philip's presence always had. She had no doubt if she decided to marry him she would be happy. But what about love? That was the question she had to answer.

Chapter 7

Leaving the small church building where she and Daniel had attended the Sunday morning service, Michaela settled back in the buggy for the ride home. Fall had arrived and, with it, a spectacular visage of color as the trees exploded into vivid shades of autumn. A measure of peace enveloped her as she enjoyed the beauty of the endless acres of farmland, towering green pines, apple orchards, and maple sugar houses scattered across the valley.

She'd enjoyed seeing the Johnson children again and, as at previous times, was amazed at their well-mannered behavior. There had been a few whispers between the siblings during the service, but a sharp glance from their father had stopped the misbehavior before it got out of hand. Even little Ruby, who was dressed in a darling lavender pinafore, had managed to sit through the minister's long lesson without much difficulty.

Two weeks ago, Michaela had begun teaching piano lessons at the Johnson home, and she was pleased with the children's interest. Adam and Sarah, in particular, possessed some musical talent, though her biggest challenge was to get Sarah to sit still long enough to take her lesson.

Daniel cleared his throat and guided the one-horse buggy onto the road that led to his farm. "I couldn't help noticing that a few of the single men were being extra friendly toward the new girl in town."

"Daniel!" Michaela's eyes widened in disbelief at her brother's comment.

"You have to admit, it was kind of obvious." Daniel let out a deep chuckle and shook his head. "I thought Joel Lambert was going to get a crick in his neck from turning around so many times. And Hiram Williams; that man had stars in his eyes when he looked at you."

Michaela folded her arms across her chest, unwilling to accept his assessment of the morning worship service. "I don't believe a word of what you're saying, but if anyone does ask, you'll have to spread the news that I didn't come here to find a husband."

"Then they're going to be some unhappy fellows."

Michaela ignored her brother's last comment, half wishing Emma had felt up to coming to church so she could help set Daniel straight. Michaela's brother had always been a tease, but this was a subject she'd rather not discuss.

She should have mentioned what had happened between her and Philip before she left Boston, but each time she thought about telling them, something held her back. If she didn't understand her own feelings toward him, how could she begin to explain their relationship to someone else?

"What about Eric Johnson?" Daniel raised his brows. "Not only is he a successful businessman, but he's a strong Christian as well."

Michaela heard the blatant implications of Daniel's question as he tried to take on the role of matchmaker. It wasn't the first time Daniel had presented Eric in a good light.

Despite the fact she'd determined to forget the perceived attraction she'd felt the first day they'd met, Daniel's comments did ring true. Eric appeared to be an outstanding member of the community. She also hadn't missed the interested looks given by several of the single women after services as he strode by their circle.

A tiny black bug landed on her forearm, and she flicked it away. "I've enjoyed spending time with his children. While I'm sure they all have difficulties at times, they really are quite well behaved. Rebecca, for example—"

"I wasn't asking about his children." Daniel turned his head toward her and sent her a knowing glance before he turned his attention back to the road in front of them. "I wanted to know what you thought about their father. He's rather good-looking, don't you think?"

Michaela felt the heat rise in her cheeks, and she turned her head away from Daniel. They passed a large house that was set back from the road and surrounded by towering pines and the huge white blossoms of hydrangea bushes. She studied the rough stone columns of the house and the long porch that would be a welcome shelter in the summer months, then considered his question.

Yes, she'd noted Eric's striking dark features. His eyes were the color of coffee, and when he smiled, his entire face lit up. Each step he took was marked with the confidence of a man who knew who he was and where he was going. She also wondered about his past sorrows. He'd lost his wife at a young age and had been left to raise their children alone. A situation like that could destroy a family, yet on the outside he appeared stronger because of it.

"I suppose one could say he's handsome, now that you mention it." She kept her voice even toned. "But I'm not interested."

Daniel turned and looked at her. "If you're not interested in getting to know anyone here, what about back home? Any suitors lurking in the wings?"

Michaela hesitated. "Maybe."

"I'm sorry." Daniel reached over and squeezed her hand. "I promised Emma

I'd stay out of any form of matchmaking. It's just that I hate to think you might be lonely."

"I stay too busy to be lonely."

The shrill cry of a bird called out above them, breaking through the relative quiet of the afternoon. Why hadn't she mentioned Philip to her brother? He was a wonderful man who would make a fine husband for someone—for her—if she chose to say yes to his marriage proposal. Maybe it was time to tell Daniel the truth.

"There is someone. . . ."

He shot her a surprised glance. "You don't sound very sure."

"You remember Philip, Ethen's brother?"

"Of course."

Michaela brushed a piece of lint off her skirt, wondering why Philip's proposal still seemed surreal to her. "He asked me to marry him before I left to come here."

"Did you give him an answer?" Daniel's brows rose in question.

"I haven't yet. It all came about rather suddenly. I've always felt close to Philip, but I've seen him more as a brother. And since Ethen died. . .I've just never thought about anyone else."

"And now?" Daniel asked.

"Before I left, I began to seriously consider his proposal."

Daniel shrugged, shaking his head. "Then why did you come out here?"

Why did the situation seem so complex? "I needed to come. He's sure of his feelings toward me, but I needed some time to think about things. Some time to get away and put the past behind me."

Daniel's warm hand embraced hers. "Then I hope you find what you're looking for while you're here."

❧

"Mail call!"

Three days later, Daniel arrived from town with not only the sugar and other items Michaela had requested, but a letter from Philip as well. She took the bacon she was frying off the stove and sat down at the table before tearing open the envelope.

"I'll leave you alone." Daniel sampled a piece of the meat, then left to check on Emma.

My dearest Michaela,

It's only been a short time since you left Boston, but it feels like it's been much longer. I pray that you are adjusting well to life in Cranton and are enjoying the time you have with Daniel and Emma.

I also pray that I wasn't too forward in telling you the truth about my feelings. I never imagined that our relationship could ever be anything more than that of a close friendship. But I will also never regret the change that has taken place in my heart. Please know that I only want what's best for you, and whatever your decision concerning our relationship, I will accept it without question.

I spoke briefly with Aunt Clara after church last Sunday. . . .

Michaela could hear Philip's voice as he continued to describe how Ben White had finally found the courage to ask her aunt out to dinner, and how Vivian had announced her engagement to Charles Randolph, a fact that didn't surprise Michaela at all. Charles Randolph was the son of one of the city's bankers and very well-to-do. Many people from church sent their regards, especially Caroline, who never failed to ask about her.

I visited Anna yesterday, and she's doing well. She asked about you and wanted me to tell you she misses you. I wish I didn't have to tell you this, but I spoke to Agnes as well. There's a family who's decided they want to adopt Anna. . . .

Michaela reached the last paragraph and drew in a sharp breath, her heart breaking at the news.

"What is it, Michaela?"

She glanced up from the letter. Emma stood in the doorway of the kitchen.

"It's Anna." Michaela pinched the bridge of her nose with the tips of her fingers, trying to hold back the tears. "I knew this was coming, but I didn't realize it would happen so soon."

She stood and walked over to the large window that framed a view of the cornfields. "Philip spoke to Agnes. A family has decided to adopt Anna."

Emma came and rested her arm across Michaela's shoulders. "I'm so sorry. I know how much she means to you."

The well of sadness seemed to deepen with each second that passed. Anna had found a home, and it wasn't with her.

※

An hour later, Michaela picked up two half-full buckets of milk and carried them out of the stall. She'd wanted to be alone with her thoughts, and the best place she could think of was the barn. Besides, Betsy and Maude needed milking.

She'd spent the past hour in prayer, and still the pain rippled through her, as fresh as when she first read the news about Anna.

I should be happy for her, Lord. Happy Anna will have a mother and a father. . . Happy because once again she'll have a place she can call home.

But she wasn't. How could she be happy when she knew she'd just lost Anna forever? Michaela shut the gate behind her and walked toward the house.

In a split second, Michaela found herself facedown in a mixture of mud and warm milk. She sat up and glanced around, thankful no one had seen her fall. Standing up, she stepped gently on the wet ground to make certain she hadn't sprained anything.

All right, Lord. Are You trying to test my sense of humor? If You are, it's not likely to please You today!

Michaela picked up the two empty buckets and carried them toward the house, setting them on the porch. Not wanting to track mud into the house, she quickly decided she'd need to take off her boots and dress.

Emma was asleep, and Daniel had left to work in one of the fields and wouldn't be back for several hours, so no one would see her. She sat on the steps and began to remove her boots, then heard someone call her name.

Michaela jerked her head up, dismayed to see Eric Johnson pulling up in the wagon.

"Of all days," she mumbled, knowing she must be a sight in her mud-streaked outfit. There was no escaping an encounter with their neighbor.

"Eric." Michaela forced a smile to cover her growing sense of frustration. *What else do You have in store for me today, Lord?*

Eric stifled a laugh, which only fueled Michaela's anger. She shoved a stray wisp of muddy hair out of her eye.

"I guess there's no need to ask what happened," he said finally, "though I'm not sure if it was the pigs or—"

"It was not the pigs." She gritted her teeth and prayed he wouldn't make a joke out of it.

"I'm sorry."

Michaela took a deep breath to calm her nerves. She was not only mad about making such a fool out of herself but upset with Eric for showing up at the worst moment possible. She clenched her jaw, determined not to say what was on her mind.

"I shouldn't have laughed—"

"I really don't see the humor in all of this," she spouted, wanting to run inside the house. Her temper thundered within her, in sharp contrast to the tranquil, cloudless sky above her.

Michaela glared at him, then looked down at her mud-streaked form. Wiping her hands across the bodice of her dress, she let out an unladylike chortle. "I guess I do look a bit ridiculous, don't I?"

"I really am sorry," Eric said, still unable to hide his grin.

Michaela took another look at her grimy dress. Uncontrolled laughter bubbled out of her mouth. The tension broken, Eric looked at her wide-eyed for a moment. Soon they both were laughing until tears streamed down their faces.

Drawing the back of her hand across her cheek, she cleared her throat and attempted to compose herself. "You never said why you stopped by."

Still smiling, Eric shifted in the wagon seat. "I'm on my way into town to pick up some supplies, and I wondered if you needed anything. Besides soap."

Michaela snickered and shook her head. "Daniel went early this morning, so I can't think of anything."

He took off his hat and nodded his head. "You'll be all right then?"

She laughed again and nodded. "I'm fine."

"Then I'd better get going."

"Michaela?" Emma's voice sounded from inside.

"I'll be right in, Emma." Michaela wiped at a muddy spot on the sleeve of her dress, then turned back to Eric. "I need to go get cleaned up."

"Of course. I'll see you later."

Moments later, Michaela climbed up the stairs, abandoning her boots and ignoring the empty buckets on the porch.

"What happened?" Emma asked as she stepped out onto the porch.

"I slipped in the mud right before Eric showed up." Michaela ignored her sister-in-law's knowing glance. "He was simply on his way to town and stopped by to see if we needed anything."

Michaela followed Emma into the house, forgetting the mud dripping on the freshly cleaned floors and remembering only Eric Johnson's penetrating gaze.

❧

Eric left Daniel's farm with a smile on his face. It had been a long time since he'd met a woman like Michaela Macintosh. She was beautiful, funny, and intelligent. He'd seen the interested looks of several of the women at church directed at him, but not one of them had captured his attention like Michaela. And the fact that she had caught his attention surprised him.

He'd been lonely since Susanna's death, but the children and the farm kept him busy. There simply hadn't been a lot of time to grieve and long for what could have been. Slowly, the heartache had lessened as the pain from her passing began to ease.

A flock of nighthawks flew above him, their wings beating through the sky with apparent ease. As they passed overhead, he thought about the journey before them as they headed toward the coast, then on to an endless summer farther south. Life was about change. Nothing stayed the same. The Bible talked about change and a time for everything. A time to be born and a time to die. . .a time to weep and a time to laugh. . .a time for love. . .

Eric flicked the reins, urging his horses to pick up their pace. He'd never seriously considered courting again, but he'd also never met a woman he thought he might enjoy getting to know. There was something about Michaela that made him curious to find out what she thought about life. She was obviously generous and kindhearted. She'd shown that by her generosity in teaching his children. Life hadn't been easy for her, and yet from all outward appearances, she'd not let it turn her bitter.

Maybe he didn't need a woman in his life to ensure his family survived, but didn't he long for the companionship of a partner and spouse? The image of Michaela's slender form streaked with mud brought a smile to his face. He'd seen the red hue that brushed across her cheeks at his presence. Even caught in an embarrassing situation, she'd managed to appear poised. For the first time in years, Eric wondered if he should let his heart take a risk—and maybe Michaela was the woman he'd take that risk with.

Chapter 8

The following Saturday, after the breakfast dishes were washed and put away, Michaela saddled up Honey and headed over to the Johnson farm. The wind blew through the trees, lending a pleasant coolness to the early fall morning. Emma had been feeling particularly well these past few days and had shooed Michaela out the door, promising her that Daniel would be close by all day and able to help her if she needed anything.

During the past few days, Michaela had spent every waking moment cleaning and cooking—anything to keep her mind off Anna's adoption. Times of prayer had come interspersed with tears of frustration. She knew God had a plan for her life, but she longed for His confirmation of what that was.

"Mrs. Macintosh!" Sarah jumped off the porch steps and ran toward Michaela with Ruby in tow. "Rebecca said if it was all right with you, we could give you a tour of our house today before lessons."

As soon as Michaela had secured her horse, Sarah grabbed her hand and hurried toward the front porch. "You've never seen our room."

Michaela laughed quietly, certain Sarah's suggestion was simply a way to delay her lesson. The previous week, it had been obvious that Sarah had not practiced her scales during the week, and more than likely the same would hold true for this week.

"Make it quick," Rebecca said to the girls after greeting Michaela with a broad smile. "We can't keep Mrs. Macintosh here all day."

Sarah and Ruby each took one of Michaela's hands and led her into the house.

"Did we ever tell you that Father built the house?" Sarah's voice bubbled with her usual excitement. "Each year he added on until it was big enough for all of us."

Michaela followed the girls up the narrow staircase to the second floor, the one section of the house she'd never seen.

"There are four bedrooms upstairs," Sarah informed Michaela. "Ruby and I share a room." Sarah wrinkled her nose and stuck out her bottom lip, apparently not thrilled that she had to share a room with her little sister.

The girls led her to a room where there were two small beds with pink and white matching quilts and a simple pine dresser. White lace curtains hung gracefully on the window that overlooked the front yard, and several hooked rugs lay scattered about the floor.

"This is our room." Ruby threw herself atop her bed and grinned.

"It's beautiful." For a moment, all Michaela could see was Leah's room. Ethen had painted the walls pink, and she'd hand-stitched the quilt from scraps Aunt Clara had given her. She'd planned to make a quilt for Anna's room, but now someone else would fill that place in Anna's life.

Rebecca called up the stairs, drawing Michaela out of the past as she followed the two sisters back downstairs. Rebecca stood in the kitchen drying dishes. Determined to shove aside the ache in her heart, Michaela complimented her on the house.

"Rebecca did most of the decorating," Sarah said. "Father says she has a knack for it."

Rebecca tousled her younger sister's hair, then wiped her hands on a white apron embroidered with tiny yellow flowers along the bottom. "Our mother did most of it. I've just added a few things." Rebecca pointed to a fresh loaf lying on the counter. "She's the one who taught me how to cook. I thought you might like a piece later."

"I'd love one." Michaela smiled, savoring the pleasant aroma of ginger that filled the air.

She studied Rebecca for a moment, impressed at how she was able to help manage the household at such a young age. She had her father's brows and the same expressive eyes that seemed to smile when she was happy. Her long black hair had been parted in the center, then pulled back smoothly and arranged into a simple chignon, leaving a frame of bangs to soften the look.

At first Michaela had been afraid that in offering to give them piano lessons, Rebecca might feel defensive, but instead Rebecca seemed to yearn for the chance to develop a friendship with her.

Rebecca drew her arms around Sarah and held her tight. "You're first this morning." Rebecca glanced up at Michaela to explain. "We drew numbers last night to decide the order."

By the end of the morning, Michaela had given each of the children thirty minutes of lessons and had eaten several pieces of homemade bread with ice-cold lemonade. Ruby, her last student for the day, slipped outside as soon as her lesson was over, leaving Michaela to gather up her music.

"How are they doing?"

Michaela glanced up from the piano bench. Eric stood casually in the doorway, causing her to wonder how long he'd been standing there. The heat in her cheeks rose as she remembered the last time he'd seen her, covered in mud.

"Your children show talent." She stood slowly, stretching the muscles in her back that had tightened after sitting for so long. "And if not talented, they certainly have energy and enthusiasm."

"My children will never be accused of being dull or boring." Eric stepped into the room and leaned against the back of a cushioned chair, folding his arms across his chest. "I wanted to thank you for what you're doing. It's always seemed like such a waste to have a piano no one could play."

"Hopefully that will change, but I have to warn you. They have to practice, which means months of scales and mistakes."

"I think we can deal with that."

The intensity of his expression made her heart race unexpectedly. Michaela turned back toward the piano, inwardly fighting her reaction to his presence. Letting out a deep sigh, she quickly gathered the music into her arms. What was it about him? Had it simply been too long since she'd spent time in the company of a man other than Philip or Daniel? Still, the effect he had on her was disturbing.

"Mrs. Macintosh, would you like to stay for lunch?" Rebecca asked as she stepped into the front room, her hands clasped behind her back.

Michaela gave her a smile of regret. "I appreciate the offer, but I really do need to head home." She pulled the music against her chest and took a step toward the door. "Maybe another time."

Rebecca thanked her again for the lesson, then went back into the kitchen, leaving her and Eric alone again for the moment. He followed her outside, his towering profile a strong presence.

"How's Emma doing?" Eric's long stride took the porch steps two at a time. "How's she feeling?"

Michaela slowed her pace. "The doctor says she's doing well, but I know they both would appreciate your continued prayers."

"I certainly will." Eric untied the lead rope on her horse and brought the animal to her. "I know they're both grateful you're here right now. Daniel wanted to plant some extra crops this fall, and it will be easier with you helping to care for Emma."

She shoved her music into her leather bag. "I'm actually a city girl, but I have to admit, this valley is growing on me."

"City life never was for me." Eric scuffed the toe of his boot in the dirt and smiled. "I spent one summer in Boston, and that was enough to convince me never to return. I wouldn't be surprised if after Emma's baby comes you decide to stay."

She shook her head and ran her fingers down the horse's mane. "I have a life waiting for me back in Boston."

Eric held out his hands, and after hesitating briefly, Michaela allowed him to help her into the saddle. A tingle of anticipation raced through her. For the first time since she'd arrived, Boston and Philip seemed a world away.

❧

A knock on the kitchen door drew Michaela away from the bread she was kneading. Rebecca stood on the back porch, shivering in her long-sleeved dress.

"Rebecca, come in." Michaela ushered the young woman to a chair beside the warm stove. "Where's your coat?"

Even in early October, the temperature had begun to drop in the late afternoon, and though the sun had yet to set, the wind brought a brisk coolness with it.

"I wasn't thinking." Rebecca leaned closer toward the stove, warming her hands for a moment.

"Is something wrong?" Michaela left the bread and sat down beside her, trying to read her troubled expression.

"It's Father." Rebecca met Michaela's puzzled gaze. "He's furious with me."

Michaela wondered how Eric would feel if she got involved in something between the two of them. It certainly wasn't her place, yet if Rebecca trusted her enough to come to her, she couldn't send the young woman away. "Do you want to tell me what happened?"

"It's Jake Markham." Rebecca chewed on her thumbnail. "He's sweet on me, and, well, I guess you could say I feel the same about him."

Michaela smiled at the picture of young love, remembering the time when she first fell for Ethen. Her aunt and uncle had been extremely cautious at first, and Rebecca was even younger than she had been.

"He thinks you're too young?"

Rebecca nodded. "The problem is, if I were thirty, I'd still be too young."

Michaela chuckled at the unrealistic image of Eric locking his daughters away for the rest of their lives. "I suspect that if you give him some time to get used to the idea, he'll be extremely supportive."

Rebecca leaned her elbows against the table and rested her chin in the palms of her hands. "Maybe, but it's just so hard to talk to him about boys and womanly matters. He doesn't understand."

"It's hard for fathers to let their little girls grow up." Michaela's heart ached for the young woman, knowing full well how difficult it was to grow up without the love and comfort of a mother.

Rebecca blew out a sharp breath. "Jake came by this morning to ask Father if he could court me."

"What did your father say?"

"He said absolutely not." Rebecca slapped the palms of her hands against the table and leaned forward. "He said we can discuss the subject after I finish school. You have no idea how humiliating it was."

Michaela stood and went back to kneading the bread, giving herself time to think. She remembered the intense feelings she felt toward Ethen, as well as Aunt Clara's questioning her readiness to marry. "You've made bread before."

"Of course." Rebecca's brow rose in question.

Michaela continued to knead, pushing down the dough with the palm of her hand against the wooden board. The pungent smell of yeast permeated the room. "When you first mix the ingredients together, it takes a bit of time for the flour, milk, and sugar to mix together and become soft and pliable."

"I suppose."

Michaela formed the dough into a ball, then set it into a bowl. "Give your father some time to get used to the idea that you're growing up. He'll let you, but he loves you very much and simply wants what is best for you."

"What if I don't agree with what's best for me?" Rebecca let out a soft chuckle. "What if he wants to make me into a loaf of white bread and I'd rather be a pan of sweet cinnamon rolls?"

Michaela brushed the loose flour off her hands, smiling at the image. "Raising children is not easy, but you're blessed to have a father who loves and cares for you."

"I know." Rebecca fiddled with a loose thread on her sleeve and frowned. "It's just that sometimes I think if I had a mother, it would be much easier to talk to her about. . .certain things."

Michaela sat beside Rebecca and squeezed her hand. It seemed natural to talk to her like a daughter—except she must never forget that role was not hers. "I'm always here whenever you want to talk, but give your father a chance to be there for you. He loves you."

❧

Michaela stepped out of Daniel and Emma's warm farmhouse and into the brisk November weather. Shivering, she quickly saddled Honey and headed into town. With Christmas only a few weeks away, she needed to shop for gifts.

Despite the chilling wind that blew across the valley, she enjoyed the short trip into Cranton. Lazy brooks weaved between a patchwork of farms and the jagged confines of stone fences, reminding her she was miles away from the bustling sounds and smells of Boston.

Soon the clattering of hooves and voices drifted toward her as the town came into view. After securing Honey's lead rope to a post outside the general store, Michaela hurried inside, thankful for the warmth from the woodstove in the corner. She wouldn't find the selection she was accustomed to in Boston, but Mr. Cooper made sure the shelves were stocked for the Christmas holiday.

After greeting Mr. Cooper's daughter-in-law, Meredith, who stood idly behind the counter engrossed in a dime novel, Michaela began her search for appropriate gifts. Changing her mind several times, she finally made her selection—a lovely brooch for her aunt, two pairs of gloves for Daniel and Philip, and a hand-embroidered shawl for Emma.

Michaela couldn't resist buying a small coat and hat for Emma's baby. She wished she were a better seamstress and could have made things for everyone, but this would have to do.

Next she picked out a small doll for Anna and some candy wrapped in bright paper and ribbons for each of the Johnson children. She made her way toward the front of the store and laid her gifts on the counter.

"How's Emma?" Meredith pulled a pencil from the dark bun on the top of her head and tallied the purchases.

"She's doing well. The baby's very active, which the doctor says is a good sign."

The two women chatted for another minute until Michaela paid her bill and placed her purchases in the leather pouch she'd brought with her. Putting her gloves on, she hurried out to Honey.

At the sound of footsteps behind her, Michaela looked up to see Eric. He took off his Stetson, revealing his dark, tousled hair. She studied his black shirt and well-fitting trousers, trying to ignore the unwelcome stirring of her heart at his nearness.

"Michaela, how are you?"

He smiled, and she refocused her gaze to his face, but even there, the dark brown recesses of his eyes seemed to reach into places in her soul she didn't want him to find. "Fine, thank you. Just finished my Christmas shopping."

"Isn't it a bit early for that?"

She shivered as a cold gust of wind blew across her face. "I need to send some gifts to Boston, and I want to make sure they get there in time."

"Then I guess it's not too early." He rotated the brim of his hat between his hands. "I was just about to get a hot cup of coffee at the hotel. Would you care to join me?"

Michaela hesitated, then nodded. It would be nice to warm up before heading home.

The waitress seated them at a small table in the corner of the restaurant and told them she would bring their coffee right away. A dozen tables with blue-checkered tablecloths surrounded a large stone fireplace that kept the room comfortable in spite of the cold outside.

"I have to tell you how much I've been enjoying teaching your children," Michaela said when the waitress left.

Eric rubbed his hands together and blew on them. "We have our share of conflicts, but they're wonderful children."

Michaela took off her gloves and laid them on the table. "Do I detect a bit of pride in your voice?"

"A whole lot, actually." Eric smiled, and the dimple she'd noticed the day they met reappeared.

The waitress set two steamy cups of coffee in front of them. Michaela warmed her hands on the hot mug, surprised at how her feelings of nervousness had dissolved. "Daniel has told me how much things have changed in Cranton since you arrived."

"We certainly didn't have anything as nice as this." He shook his head slowly. "Hard to believe it's been almost eighteen years. When Susanna and I came out here, we had little more than the clothes on our backs and a dream of a better life to keep us going."

"She must have been beautiful. Your children certainly are." Michaela took a sip of the coffee, enjoying the warmth that flowed through her body.

"Susanna Elizabeth Stevens. That was her maiden name. She told me it wasn't until she was five that she could pronounce her whole name." He chuckled at the memory. "And you're right, she was beautiful."

For a moment, his gaze drifted toward the fireplace, seemingly lost within the crackling flames. "Sometimes, for just a moment, I forget she's gone; then it all comes back to me."

"I'm sorry. You don't have to talk about it if you don't want to—"

"That's all right." His smile returned, replacing the momentary look of sadness. "We had a good life, full of happy memories. I like talking about her."

Sensing his desire to share, she encouraged him. "Please go on."

He leaned back in his chair and folded his arms across his chest. "Our parents knew each other before we were born, so we grew up together on Nantucket Island. Her father was a retired captain of a whaling vessel. Mine was a minister. We married at eighteen. Too young in many ways, but we were committed until death do us part. I just never expected it to happen so soon."

Michaela shivered in agreement despite the warm room. His words rang far too true. How many times had she felt the same way about Ethen? She had always imagined them growing old together, surrounded by their children and grandchildren. But that would never happen.

Eric ran his thumbs around the edge of his mug. "We moved out here wanting something we could call our own. Lots of people went out west to California to look for gold, but we decided to stay a bit closer to home.

"Rebecca came right away, and every few years there was a little one arriving. Susanna loved babies. She said she always wanted to have a baby in the house because they added so much joy. The sad thing is that what brought her joy is also what brought me and the children so much pain." He sobered. "She died giving birth to Ruby."

Michaela took another sip of her coffee, feeling the depth of his pain from her own experience. "I know you miss her tremendously."

"I do. I'm reminded of what we made together every day, and yet, over the years, the pain has lessened, to a degree anyway."

Michaela leaned back in her chair and studied the man sitting across from her. Here was someone who understood the pain of losing a spouse. On the outside he seemed to have found a measure of peace over the event. The familiar question returned. How long would it take for her pain of losing Ethen and Leah to lessen?

"I remember when Daniel and Emma went back East to be with you." His gaze softened. "Our church prayed for you."

"Thank you so much." She turned and watched the orange and yellow flames of the fire, reminding her of the flames that had taken the lives of her family and Anna's parents. "I'm sorry, it's just that. . ."

"You don't have to explain. I understand." He seemed to sense her need for them to change the subject. "Tell me about Boston. I understand you taught piano there."

An hour later, Michaela glanced at her watch, surprised they'd talked so long.

She pushed aside the partial cup of coffee that had long since grown cold. "I really need to go. I told Daniel and Emma I wouldn't be long."

Eric placed a few coins on the table, then pushed back his chair. "I'm sorry to have kept you so long."

"Not at all. I've thoroughly enjoyed myself."

He helped her put on her coat before they walked toward the front door. "Rebecca's excited you're helping her plan Thanksgiving dinner."

"I'm looking forward to it. Hopefully Emma will feel up to coming."

A cold wind greeted them as they stepped outside the hotel restaurant. Michaela pulled her long coat closer.

"She had to grow up so fast when her mother died, and I've always felt guilty about that," he confessed. "The truth is, now she really has grown up."

Michaela untied Honey from the post and turned to Eric. "She came to talk to me the other day. I hope you don't mind."

Eric's brow lowered, and Michaela wondered if she'd made a mistake in talking to Rebecca.

"I'm sorry if I overstepped my bounds—"

"No, please don't feel that way. It's just that. . ." He shoved his hands in his coat pockets and shook his head. "It's hard raising a family alone. Rebecca was so angry with me, but I have to do what I think is best."

"And she knows that, trust me. You're a lucky man to have such a wonderful family."

He grasped her hand and helped her into the saddle. Slowly, she pulled away, still feeling the warmth from his touch. She felt the wind whip around her and shivered, wondering if she would ever find the courage to open up her heart and love again.

Chapter 9

The sun shone Thanksgiving Day, and though a thin layer of snow still covered the ground outside, the Johnson house stayed warm from the fire in the living room. The day before, after preparing the turkey, Michaela had helped Rebecca make three pumpkin pies and what Michaela had been told was Eric's favorite, Marlborough pudding, a traditional dish made from stewed apples, sugar, and nutmeg that was baked in a piecrust. Today they worked to finish the rest of the special meal before the guests arrived.

"I can't believe you talked my father into letting me invite Jake's family over for Thanksgiving dinner, Mrs. Macintosh." Rebecca looked up from the onion she was chopping and smiled. "Thank you."

"You're welcome." Michaela finished peeling the last potato that she'd later mash and serve with cream and butter. "Didn't I tell you that you just needed to let your father get used to the idea?"

Starting on another onion, Rebecca nodded. "He still hasn't agreed to let Jake call on me, but at least maybe this way he'll get to know him better."

"Exactly."

Rebecca set her knife down on the counter and leaned forward. "Have you ever thought about letting someone court you again, Mrs. Macintosh? You'd be good for my father."

Michaela's eyes widened in surprise as she poured the potatoes into the boiling water. Surely Rebecca wasn't trying to play matchmaker. "Not really. I—"

Her answer was interrupted as Eric walked into the kitchen. All she could do was pray he hadn't caught the last of their conversation. Yes, she had thought about courting again, but with Philip, not Eric Johnson.

"How long until supper, ladies?" Eric leaned over and kissed his daughter on the top of her head. "I understand that a certain young man is joining us."

A soft blush crossed Rebecca's face as she began vigorously chopping one of the onions. "Everyone should arrive about four o'clock."

"Good." Eric walked near to where Michaela was working on the potatoes and picked up a spoon. "That will give me plenty of time to talk to Jake."

Rebecca's knife clattered against the counter. "Father, promise me you'll be extra nice to him."

Eric didn't answer but instead began peeking under several of the covered dishes. "Did you make any Marlborough pudding?"

Rebecca nodded. "It's already finished."

Spoon in hand, Eric stopped when he found the dessert.

"All right, Eric Johnson." Michaela set her hands firmly against her hips. "You're about to be in trouble with both of us."

His mouth curved into a smile. "Someone's got to sample the food."

Michaela shook her head like a stern schoolteacher. "No sampling until dinner, and promise your daughter you won't do anything to embarrass her."

"Of course I won't." Eric winked at his daughter, then left the room.

Rebecca turned to Michaela. "You don't really think he'd do anything to embarrass me, do you?"

"He's your father, Rebecca. He loves you. He's probably just as anxious as you are." Michaela added some salt to the boiling potatoes. "This is new territory for both of you, and you're going to have the normal ups and downs in your relationship with your father, but he would never hurt you on purpose."

Rebecca nodded. "I know you're right. I'm just so nervous about today. Don't you think Jake's handsome?"

Michaela laughed as Rebecca proceeded to tell her how his eyes were the clearest blue she'd ever seen and how, being interested in politics, he knew absolutely everything about Governor Long. Michaela listened intently to the young girl's stories about Jake and remembered similar conversations shared with Aunt Clara about Ethen. It was good to feel needed. For the first time in a long time, Michaela felt truly happy.

❧

Two hours later, the three families finished the meal. The entire day had been a success. Even Emma had felt up to coming to the celebration.

Michaela helped Rebecca serve the pumpkin pies and Marlborough pudding.

"This looks fantastic." Eric smiled at his daughter and took the plate Rebecca offered him that held a thick slice of each dessert.

Michaela served Jake and smiled. True to his word, Eric had helped put the young man at ease and seemed to take today as an opportunity to get to know him better. It was obvious by the smile that hadn't left Rebecca's face that she was pleased with the way the afternoon was turning out.

A fork clattered against the china plate. Perplexed, Michaela watched Adam gulp down his glass of water.

She eyed her piece of pumpkin pie, wondering if something could be wrong with the dessert, but it looked perfect. She sampled a bit of the pie and froze.

Instead of the sweet pumpkin flavor she'd expected, it tasted as if she'd just taken a spoonful of salt.

"What's wrong?" Rebecca noticed the startled looks on everyone's faces.

"It's the pumpkin pie." Michaela felt a wave of nausea wash over her. This dinner meant so much to Rebecca.

Rebecca took a bite, then promptly spat it out. "What happened?" She sat motionless in her chair beside the one person she'd tried to impress all day.

"I think you switched the sugar for salt, sweetheart." Eric's sympathetic smile didn't faze Rebecca.

"I couldn't have. I. . ."

A quiet giggle came from the other side of the table. Sarah sat hunched down in her chair, her hands across her mouth. "I'm sorry, it's just—"

"This is not funny, Sarah," Eric warned her.

Michaela stood from the table and began gathering up the plates of uneaten pie. Jake sent Rebecca a sympathetic glance but seemed to be at odds at how to remedy the situation. Sarah's giggles continued despite the sharp look from her father.

Eric crossed his arms and leaned toward his middle daughter, who sat across from him. "Sarah Phoebe Johnson, if you know anything about the extra salt in your sister's pie, you'd better tell me right now."

Sarah's giggles stopped.

"Sarah. . ."

She bit her lip and looked at her father out of the corner of her eye. Michaela set the stack of dishes at the edge of the table, wondering what she should do. Rebecca had spent days planning this meal, and if Sarah had something to do with the ruined pie, she knew it would crush Rebecca.

"I. . ." Sarah stifled another laugh.

"You still think this is funny?" Eric kept his voice low, but it was laced with anger.

"Yes—no." Sarah's gaze dropped to the floor. "I switched the sugar for the salt in the filling when Rebecca wasn't looking yesterday. She was so busy, she didn't even notice what I did. It was supposed to be funny."

Rebecca let out a sob, then fled from the room. Eric stood and threw his napkin on the table. Sarah slid down farther in her chair.

"Eric." Michaela took a few steps toward him until they were only inches apart. She knew she shouldn't interfere, but Rebecca was the one who needed her father right now. "Let me talk to Sarah. Go find Rebecca. She needs you now."

Eric nodded and stepped out the front door to find his daughter.

"I'll get the dishes." Mrs. Markham stood to finish clearing the table, while

Michaela nodded at Sarah to follow her up to the girl's room.

Sitting across from her on the bed, Michaela watched as Sarah chewed on her thumbnail. "I remember one summer when I was eleven years old. It was the worst summer I'd ever had. I'd been sick a lot and wasn't allowed to go outside and play most of the time. Then, in late August, we celebrated my brother's eighteenth birthday. He would be leaving soon to go to school, and my parents wanted the day to be extra special. I was in charge of serving the punch at the party. The more they planned, the more jealous I got. They'd never thrown a party like that for me, so I decided to do something so no one would forget I was around."

Sarah leaned forward. "What did you do?"

"Attempting to make it look like an accident, I dumped the punch off the table and onto my mother's beige carpet."

"Guess your parents didn't think that was funny, either."

"No, they didn't." Michaela prayed for the right words. "Truth was, I loved my brother a lot, and I didn't like the changes that were taking place. I knew he would be leaving, and I didn't want him to go."

Sarah shook her head. "Sometimes it seems like everything's changing."

"What are you really afraid of, Sarah?"

She was still for a moment. "If Rebecca gets married, things will never be the same again."

Michaela smiled and patted Sarah gently on her arm. "You're right. Things won't ever be the same again. But it also means that before you know it, some handsome boy will be calling on you."

Sarah groaned, but it was obvious she wasn't totally displeased with the idea. "I suppose I would hate it if Ruby or one of the boys did something like that to me."

"I think you're exactly right." Michaela smiled. "Besides that, you'd have to come up with a lot better idea to chase Rebecca's beaus away, because I don't think some extra salt in the pie would deter very many of them."

Sarah dropped her gaze. "It was awful, wasn't it?"

Michaela nodded in agreement. "I think you have a few people you need to talk to, starting with your sister."

❧

Eric hurried out of the house and into the barn. Climbing up the sturdy ladder to the loft, he found Rebecca sitting on a bale of hay with tears silently streaming down her face.

"How'd you know I'd be here?" Rebecca looked up at him. The hurt in her eyes broke his heart.

"You told me one time this was your favorite place to think."

Eric rubbed his hands together, more from nerves than the cold wind that blew through the cracks in the walls. Sitting down beside her, he prayed for wisdom. "I'm sorry about what happened."

"Why would Sarah do something like that?" Rebecca wiped her cheeks with the backs of her hands and shook her head. "I know it's silly to care about a bunch of stupid pies, but—"

"Your feelings aren't silly." Eric took his daughter's hands in his. "Today was important for you. I know that."

Rebecca looked up at him; her gaze seemed to plead with him to understand. "I really care about Jake. I know you're not ready for me to grow up, but I'm seventeen. You married Mother when she was barely eighteen."

Eric let out a soft laugh at the truth behind her words. How come his own daughter seemed so much younger than he and Susanna had been when they married? The truth was, his daughter was just as mature and responsible as he had ever been at eighteen. He just didn't want to admit it.

"I never thought I'd have to go through all of this alone, Rebecca." It was times like this when he missed Susanna the most. Missed her support and encouragement. Her wisdom. A man wasn't meant to raise six children alone. For the first time in a long time, he felt the cold reality of being a widower.

Eric turned and placed both of his hands on her shoulders. "Rebecca Margaret Johnson, you are my firstborn, and I love you unconditionally. I know that I could never take the place of your mother in raising you. There are simply too many emotions you feel that, as a man, I can't understand. But what I do know is that you and I are going to get through this together. Just give me some time to get used to the idea of another man caring for you."

Rebecca cocked her head and lowered her brows in question. "Does that mean you'll let Jake court me?"

"I didn't say that." He saw the disappointment in her eyes. It was time, and he knew it. "Though I suppose I should consider it. Especially if it means I'll get more dinners like tonight's."

Rebecca's face lit up. "Do you mean it? Will you talk to him?"

Eric nodded, realizing that in agreeing to Rebecca's request, he was letting go of her. Before he knew it, he'd be walking his daughter down the aisle, and she'd leave his home to live with someone else. He'd known the day would come, but he wasn't ready yet.

"I suppose this means Jake will be coming around a bit more?"

"You like him, don't you?"

He had to admit the truth, even though he doubted he would ever meet someone good enough for his daughter. "He's a fine young man."

"What about you?" Rebecca reached out and straightened the collar of his shirt.

He raised his brow in question. "What about me?"

"Have you thought about courting again?"

Eric leaned back, pushing the palms of his hands against his thighs. Had Rebecca noticed his interest in Michaela? "You think we need a woman in our lives?"

"After tonight?" She flashed him a broad smile. "Yes."

He combed his fingers through his hair. "Courting would mean a lot of changes for us. We're used to doing things on our own. You'd have to stay with the children while I'm out eating at a restaurant or taking her out on a picnic."

Eric liked the idea but had worried about his children's reactions. He had thoroughly enjoyed having coffee with Michaela earlier this week. In fact, since Susanna's death, he hadn't felt as comfortable talking with another woman as he did with Michaela.

Rebecca folded her arms across her chest and smiled again. "Of course, it would have to be the right person."

"Are you thinking about anyone in particular?"

Rebecca nodded, and he caught the gleam in her eye. "There is one person I've thought for quite a while now would be perfect for you. Michaela Macintosh."

❧

Michaela handed Mrs. Markham the last dish to dry, then wiped down the long counter. She'd found the woman's company pleasant but couldn't keep her mind off Eric and the conversation he was having with Rebecca. Silently, she prayed that God would give him the wisdom he would need, not only for tonight, but in the weeks and months to come.

Eric stepped into the kitchen and addressed Michaela. "Can we talk?"

Michaela nodded at Eric's request and followed him outside onto the front porch, where they could have a semblance of privacy. He leaned against the porch rail and looked at her, his brow furrowed into deep creases. Michaela's stomach constricted. This time she had overstepped her boundaries. She never should have suggested talking to Sarah. It wasn't her place. It was Eric's.

"Eric, I need to apologize—"

"Wait, please." He held up his hand in protest. "I need to say this."

Michaela swallowed hard and let her gaze sweep across the terrain, now a maze of shadows in the fading sunlight. Whatever he had to say, she deserved it.

Eric cleared his throat. "When you first offered to teach piano to the children,

I was thrilled to have them gain that experience. I have slowly had to realize that there are many things I simply can't do as their father. I struggle with talking to Rebecca about becoming a woman and to Sarah about how to dress like a lady. A man wasn't meant to be both father and mother to his children. We need someone like you in our lives."

Michaela's hands clenched the rail. Surely he wasn't planning to propose some kind of marriage of convenience. Eric took a step toward her. "I just wanted to thank you for being a friend to my children. I know I haven't always put you in an easy position, but you've been there for them when they needed you, and I appreciate that."

Michaela felt the heat rise to her face, thankful she hadn't made a fool of herself by saying something she'd regret later. If all he was saying was thank you. . .

She coughed softly. "God has blessed you with six marvelous children, and I've enjoyed the short time I've been able to spend with them. However, I by no means want to overstep my bounds—"

"You haven't, trust me. In fact, I was afraid you might feel that way, and I wanted to assure you that you hadn't."

Sarah stepped out of the house and onto the porch, a somber expression on her face. Michaela felt sure it would be awhile before Sarah attempted another stunt like she'd pulled today.

Sarah stood in front of her father, her hands fidgeting at her sides. "I apologized to Rebecca and the others, and I want you to know how truly sorry I am."

Eric gathered his daughter into his arms, and Michaela slipped back into the house to let them be alone.

She found Emma lying on the couch in the parlor. "Are you all right?"

"Just resting. It's been a long day, but I didn't want Daniel to have to leave early. I believe he and Mr. Markham are caught up in a game of chess."

"I think everyone has had a nice day today."

"I noticed you and Eric spending a lot of time together today." Emma propped herself up on her elbow. "Do you simply enjoy his company, or could it be something else?"

"Eric's a good friend and nothing else." Michaela immediately regretted her sharp tone. "I'm sorry, Emma. It has been a long day, and I'm tired."

Michaela rubbed her temples with her fingertips. She needed to take a step back. Her emotions were becoming far too entwined in the lives of this family. She'd be leaving in a few weeks, and then what? Maybe if she went riding for a bit, she could clear her head.

"Since I rode Honey out here, I think I'll go on home. If I'm not there by the time you get back, I'll be there shortly."

Emma pulled her shawl across her shoulders. "I need to get home soon, as well. Don't stay out too long. It will be dark soon."

A crisp, chilly breeze played with the loose wisps of hair peeking out of Michaela's hood as she left the Johnson farm. Squinting against the brightness of the setting sun, she took in a deep breath of the frosty air.

She touched her skirt pocket and felt the crackling of paper under the material. She had received another letter from Philip yesterday. Anna had celebrated her sixth birthday, and he and Caroline had spent part of the day with her, giving her the tea set Michaela sent and a wooden pony Philip had carved.

The most important news had followed. The couple planning to adopt Anna had changed their minds and decided to adopt only a boy.

The answer seemed so clear. Wasn't Philip everything she could want in a man? He was a strong Christian with high moral standards who treated her with respect and one who would cherish and take care of her.

Michaela sighed, remembering how many times Daniel and Emma had each tried their hand at arousing her interest in Eric. He might be a handsome, eligible bachelor, but that didn't mean he was the one for her.

Michaela pulled gently on the reins and brought Honey to a stop. She looked toward the west, where the yellow and red of the sunset spread across the sky like a bucket of spilled paint. Philip had asked her to marry him, and she was going to accept.

Michaela turned Honey and headed toward the farm, ready to tell Daniel and Emma her decision. She'd kept her feelings for Philip quiet for too long. It was time to move forward with her life.

After bedding Honey down for the night, Michaela hurried into the house, where she found Daniel and Emma sitting in the parlor. A smile played across Michaela's lips.

"Eric proposed?" Daniel set down the book he was reading and looked up at Michaela with a sly grin across his face.

Michaela put her hands on her hips and gave her brother an exasperated look. "No, but it does have to do with proposals. I've made a decision. I'm going to marry Philip."

Emma leaned forward on the sofa. "I knew his feelings for you were strong, but if we'd realized you shared his feelings, we never would have teased you about Eric. It's just that you've rarely spoken of Philip."

"I know." Michaela sat on the edge of the mahogany armchair across from them. "I may not have talked about him much, but in these past couple of months,

I've been forced to think about where I want my life to go. Marrying Philip is what I want. He's kind, compassionate, and he loves me unconditionally."

"You don't have to convince us. As long as you're happy, then we're happy for you." Daniel stood and pulled her to her feet, wrapping his arms around her. "Philip's a good man, and I know he'll make you very happy."

"Why don't you send him a telegram and tell him?" Emma suggested, drawing her legs up beneath her. "You know he'll be elated."

"I wish I could tell him myself." Michaela felt the ache of homesickness increase for a moment, but she knew her place was here for now. Philip would wait for her, of that she had no doubt. And Anna would be there as well. A wave of peace washed over her. "I'll go into town tomorrow."

After the baby came, she would go home to Boston, where she belonged.

Chapter 10

Sarah tried the scale for the tenth time.

"Have you been practicing?" Michaela asked.

"Well. . ."

"Sarah, if you don't practice, I can't teach you anything. You have to practice."

"The other kids are always on the piano."

Michaela felt her patience waning. "I happen to know that your father worked out a time schedule so each of you have at least thirty minutes a day."

"Yes, but. . ."

"Sarah, you have to practice."

"Then I'll be able to play as good as you?"

Michaela decided to use a new approach. "Can I tell you a secret?"

Sarah leaned forward, her face lit with a grin.

"God has gifted you with a talent in music that far exceeds my own. Not only do you have a beautiful voice, but you have talent to play the piano as well."

Sarah pulled back, looking doubtful at Michaela's assessment. "Do you really think so?"

Michaela nodded. "I know it's true. But even someone as talented as you are has to practice."

Someone yelled outside, and Michaela and Sarah hurried to the window. Eric and the boys were running in circles around the front yard, chasing the chickens.

"The chickens are loose!" Ruby ran outside, whooping in delight.

Michaela steered Sarah back to the piano. "We'd better get back to our lesson."

Fifteen minutes later, the front door slammed. Eric stomped into the house, followed by the boys.

"Someone left the gate open to the chicken coop." Eric flopped down in a chair and started taking off his boots. "Do you know how difficult it is to catch over thirty chickens?"

"I saw how difficult it is." Michaela stifled a laugh.

Eric didn't smile. "Does anyone know who left the gate to the chicken coop open?"

By now all the children had gathered in the room, but Eric's focus was on Sarah and Ruby. If Michaela remembered correctly, it was their responsibility to gather the eggs each day and feed the chickens.

"I'm sure we shut the gate." Sarah nudged Ruby with her elbow.

"Did you latch it?" Eric leaned forward and rested his elbows against his thighs.

The girls looked at each other and squirmed in their chairs.

"The animals are part of our livelihood." Eric pulled off his other boot and set it beside him. "You may think it's humorous to watch your father run circles around a bunch of squawking chickens, but I don't."

Several of the children let out quiet chuckles. Michaela bit her lip, trying not to laugh. Eric's gaze swept the room, then stopped at Michaela.

"Looks like we're even," she said with a grin.

Eric raised his brows in question.

"Have you forgotten the day I fell in the mud? I seem to recall at least one person who couldn't keep a straight face."

The sides of Eric's mouth slowly curled into a grin as he shrugged in defeat. He turned to Ruby and Sarah. "I guess I owe you an apology. I had a frustrating morning in town, and I shouldn't take it out on you. I'm sorry."

The girls ran to give their father a hug, and Eric kept an arm wrapped around each of them. "But that doesn't excuse the fact that you weren't careful. From now on, please make sure you latch the gate so this doesn't happen again."

Two heads bobbed in unison.

Eric turned to his oldest daughter. "How long until dinner, Rebecca?"

"Ten minutes."

"Good, because I, for one, worked up quite an appetite."

"Can Mrs. Macintosh join us for dinner, Father?" Sarah asked.

"You'll have to ask her."

"Will you stay?" Ruby ran and jumped into Michaela's lap.

Michaela pulled the young girl close and nuzzled her chin against the top of her head, breathing in the familiar scent of lavender. "How could I refuse? Daniel and Emma's dinner's on the stove, and I've been wanting some more of Rebecca's excellent cooking."

Rebecca blushed and headed into the kitchen.

Eric carried his boots toward the front door. "Everyone needs to get washed up."

Michaela went into the kitchen to help Rebecca with dinner. "What can I do to help?"

"The bread still needs to be sliced."

Michaela cut the fresh loaf of bread into thick pieces while the children began to trickle in and take their places at the table.

"Smells delicious." Eric entered the room and kissed his oldest daughter on her forehead. "Nothing like a roast with vegetables."

After Michaela finished helping Rebecca serve the meal, Eric pulled back the empty chair beside him and motioned for her to sit. "As our guest, you're working too hard, Michaela."

Michaela slid into the chair and glanced around the long table at the children who had, in such a short time, become an integral part of her life. Eric led the family in a prayer, which was followed by echoes of "amen" around the table.

"This meal is wonderful, Rebecca." Eric put a large spoonful of vegetables on his plate.

Rebecca smiled, obviously pleased with her father's compliment. "Sarah and Ruby planned to ask you to stay for dinner, Mrs. Macintosh, so I tried to fix something extra special."

"I'm honored to be here." Michaela spread homemade jam over a thick slice of bread. Besides the roast and bread, there were mashed potatoes, green beans, and apple cobbler for dessert.

Michaela took another bite of her roast and listened to the children's laughter as they shared what had happened throughout the school week. The animated conversation centered on school and the upcoming Christmas holiday, and she found herself enjoying the lively banter between Eric and his children.

After a short lull in the conversation, Eric turned to Michaela. "I've never asked you what you think of our house."

She waved her hand in the air. "It's beautiful. The girls gave me a tour a few weeks ago. They told me you built it yourself."

Eric set his fork on his plate and chuckled. "It's become one of those never-ending projects. We started off small, but with each child, we needed a bit more room and thus added on every few years."

"Tell us about Boston." Sarah leaned forward expectantly.

Michaela wiped the corners of her mouth with a napkin, then set the cloth in her lap. "My aunt and I live on the outskirts of the city, not far from the ocean."

Sarah's eyes widened. "I've never seen the ocean! What's it like?"

Michaela smiled at Sarah's innocent wonder. "It's hard to describe, it's so vast. As far as you can see, the blues and greens of the ocean spread out before you—wave after wave making its way toward the shore."

"What about the city?" Samuel spoke for the first time.

"Boston is full of people, businesses, and crowded streets. There are so many stores and restaurants, you can easily get lost if you don't know your way around. There are also museums, art galleries, and a university."

"Sounds wonderful." Samuel squirmed in his chair, excitement mounting in his voice. "Someday I want to go back East for school."

"Samuel wants to be a doctor," Eric said, the pride obvious in his voice.

"I'm sure you'll make a fine doctor."

"What do you do in Boston?" Ruby asked.

Michaela played with the linen napkin in her hands. "Before my husband died, I worked with him. He and his brother owned a cabinetmaking shop."

"Is it a big factory?" Samuel asked.

Michaela nodded. "There are about a dozen men who work there, plus a showroom where they sell the furniture. My job was to keep up the books."

"But you don't do that anymore?" Sarah asked.

Michaela shook her head. "Lately I've been teaching piano lessons. It's something I've always wanted to do."

"And now you teach us." Ruby grinned and turned to whisper something in Sarah's ear.

"Girls," Eric said, "if there is something you need to say, say it so the rest of us can hear you."

They giggled, then looked at Michaela.

"Girls...," their father prompted again.

"We were wondering," Sarah began. "Could we have a sing-along this afternoon?"

"Yes." Ruby's head bobbed up and down. "You could play the piano and the rest of us could sing."

"That would be fun." Rebecca stood and began clearing the dishes.

"Only if Michaela agrees." Eric turned to her, and by his expression, he seemed pleased with the idea. "We haven't done that for quite a long time."

"Sounds like fun." Michaela smiled but inwardly fought a wave of sadness. Sitting at the table with Eric and his children, she suddenly realized how familiar her presence in this house had become—and how at ease she felt. She wouldn't be here to be a part of Rebecca's courtship or Adam's upcoming graduation. She swallowed hard. And then there was Eric.

Eric's voice stopped her thoughts from wandering to a place she was afraid to go. "I need all of you to help Rebecca clean up the kitchen. I need to take care of something outside, then I'll be in."

Michaela joined in the familiar task of drying dishes. Sarah and Matt put them in their right places, and before long the kitchen was in order, ready for the next meal. As soon as they were done, Sarah and Ruby begged to be allowed to show Michaela the new litter of puppies in the barn.

"Pa's not back yet," Sarah pleaded. "Can we, please?"

Rebecca nodded her head. "Just don't be long."

Michaela followed the girls outside to the barn, where she was introduced to Sarah's brood of animals.

"She's adorable." Michaela took the puppy Ruby handed her and was greeted with a face full of wet kisses. The puppy couldn't have been more than a few weeks old.

"And this is Red," Ruby announced, petting an older dog.

Michaela was then introduced to five cats, Pinky the pig, and Beaker, Sarah's favorite chicken. She was campaigning so it wouldn't end up on the dinner table.

After a few minutes, they stepped back outside and into the bright sunshine, with Red still jumping and barking around them.

On the way back to the house, Sarah pointed to their garden, freshly tilled for the winter months.

"The garden is our job." Ruby puckered up her nose.

"We have to make sure there are no weeds," Sarah added.

"Running a farm takes a lot of work," Michaela said to the girls.

"Most of the time it's fun," Sarah jabbered. "There's harvesttime when all the people in the area get together for a big celebration, swimming in the summer, horseback riding, and best of all, Christmas is coming."

"Christmas was always one of my favorite times of the year." Michaela felt a rush of emotion. "I always loved the lights and the trees decorated so beautifully. My mother and I used to make gingerbread men and frosted sugar cookies."

Ruby stopped and looked up into Michaela's eyes. "If you like Christmas, then why does your face look so sad?"

Michaela took a deep breath, wishing her feelings weren't so transparent. She ruffled Ruby's hair. "I had a little girl who would have been about your age. She and her daddy died in a fire on Christmas Eve."

Ruby's eyes narrowed. "Then this Christmas, maybe we can help make you happy again."

Michaela smiled as each of the girls took one of her hands, seemingly trying to comfort her.

"Our mother died when I was born," Ruby said as the three of them slowly walked back to the house together. A gentle wind blew, rustling the leaves in the trees. "Father's always sad on my birthday."

"I know she loved you." Michaela knelt down and faced Ruby. "For nine months, she carried you inside of her and dreamed about what you would look like, what you would become someday."

"Really?"

"Really."

They were silent for a moment until Sarah spoke again. "We'd better go back to the house. I just saw Father go inside. It's time for the sing-along."

༄

Michaela ran her limber fingers across the keys, enjoying a final chorus. Her high soprano voice and Eric's deep bass blended with the children's voices, which rang with energy and enthusiasm. Even the boys, who hadn't seemed excited about the idea, looked as if they were enjoying the singing.

"It's going to be dark before long." Eric slapped his hands against his thighs and pulled Ruby against his side. "This has been wonderful, Michaela. Thank you."

There were groans of protest from the children until they saw their father's stern look, reminding them he meant what he said. "I'll be happy to take you home, Michaela."

"You don't have to do that." Michaela stretched out her fingers, then tilted her head from side to side to loosen some of the muscles in her neck.

"It's no problem at all." Eric grabbed his coat from the hook beside the door. "Honey can follow behind the wagon."

"All right then." Michaela put on her coat and said good-bye to the children before following him outside.

"It's beautiful out tonight." Sitting next to Eric in the wagon, Michaela watched as the last sliver of sun sank into the horizon. "I remember sunrises with my grandfather. We would sit on one of the rocks along the beach until the sun made its appearance over the ocean."

"I miss the ocean." There was a wistful tone to Eric's voice. "It used to be one of my favorite places. Someday I want to take the children to the coast and show them the ocean."

"They'd love that." Michaela's spirits brightened at the idea. "Come to Boston. I'll be there and can show them around."

They rode in silence for a moment as a mass of stars took their places with the full moon in the sky.

After a few minutes, Eric spoke. "How long do you plan to stay in Cranton?"

"I'll go back to Boston after the baby is born and Emma's back on her feet. Probably just a few more weeks now." The slight tug of disappointment returned.

"What do you want to do when you go back?"

"I'll continue teaching piano for a while—"

He shook his head. "That's not what I mean."

She turned and looked at him, her brows raised in question. "What do you mean?"

"I know it's really none of my business, but while you seem so good at taking care of others, I wondered what your dreams are."

It was something she'd never thought about. Two years ago, she'd known exactly what she wanted. She loved being a mother and a wife. But all of that had changed. How could she even begin to understand what she wanted out of life?

When she didn't answer, Eric gently slapped the reins, his gaze seemingly lost in the distant horizon. "After my wife died, I felt so out of control. All my time and energy went into working the farm and caring for the children—until finally I realized if I didn't take care of myself, both emotionally and spiritually, I wouldn't be able to do anything after a while. All I want to say is that it's all right to think about what your own needs are."

The words seemed to pierce straight through her soul. She regularly turned to God, full of requests and needs, but wasn't there supposed to be so much more to her relationship with her heavenly Father? When was the last time she'd studied her Bible? What about times of worship and adoration? She suddenly realized how empty she was spiritually. Could the fact that she'd been neglecting her relationship with God be the reason she felt both spiritually and emotionally drained? It seemed so simple, but somehow she'd missed it.

" 'O come, let us worship and bow down: let us kneel before the Lord our maker.'" Michaela spoke the words from the Bible aloud, barely more than a whisper.

Eric must have heard her quiet voice. "One of David's psalms?"

Michaela nodded and clasped her hands in front of her. "You know, you're right. I've been so busy trying to stay busy, it seems my prayers have become nothing more than one-sided requests when I'm hurting or needing something. I can't remember the last time my heart was full of praise and worship."

Eric slowed the horses as they came to the top of a slight ridge and started down the other side. "That's an essential part of our relationship with Christ and in our healing."

Michaela unfolded her hands and played with the folds of her skirt. A light snow had begun to fall. She watched a flake land on the material, then slowly melt. "It's still so hard. I want to forget the past, and I'm good at staying busy so there isn't time to think. Losing Ethen and Leah was the hardest thing that ever happened to me."

"Psalm 147 says, 'He healeth the broken in heart, and bindeth up their wounds.'"

Daniel and Emma's frame house appeared in the distance. In the past few months, it had become a haven of safety for her, but she had neglected to let Christ be her true refuge. Eric had reminded her of something she'd ignored in her life, and she knew she couldn't just leave it at that.

Eric stopped the horses in front of the house. "I really enjoyed spending the afternoon with you."

"Thank you for such a wonderful afternoon, Eric."

Eric jumped down from the wagon and hurried to the other side, where he helped Michaela down. As her foot hit the ground, she lost her balance and fell against Eric's chest. She looked up into his eyes, and before she knew what was happening, his lips met hers.

For a moment, she felt herself responding.

"No!" She pushed herself away, still feeling the burning sensation on her lips.

"I'm sorry." Eric looked down at her. "I didn't plan to kiss you, Michaela. It just seemed so natural."

"It's not that; it's just. . ."

Questions flashed through her mind as she tried to stop the panic rising in her throat. What about Philip? She started to slowly back away from Eric.

"Wait, Michaela." Eric gently brushed a snowflake off the end of her nose. "Tell me the truth, Michaela. Is it just me, or do you feel something as well?"

Michaela took a deep breath, trying desperately to make sense out of her jumbled emotions. She knew she felt a strong physical attraction to Eric, but was there something more? Something deeper?

No! I'm going home to Philip.

"Is there someone back in Boston?" He glanced down at his boots. Swallowing hard, he looked off to one side, clenching his jaw and waiting for her response.

"No. . .Yes!" Michaela's eyes were wide with confusion as she looked at Eric. "I'm sorry. I wasn't expecting this."

"Neither was I."

"There is. . ." *I have to tell him the truth. I have to tell him about Philip.*

Michaela searched for the right words, but something held her back. Her mind spun out of control. She couldn't think clearly. She had to get inside the house.

"Maybe I'm wrong." Eric drew a deep breath. "I thought there was something between us. I apologize. It just all seemed so real today with you and the kids, and the ride home. Then when I kissed you. . ."

"I'm sorry." Michaela wiped away a tear with the back of her hand, turned around, and ran toward the house.

Daniel and Emma were sitting on the sofa and talking when Michaela burst into the parlor. "Daniel, would you please put Honey into her stall?" Michaela hurried into her room and threw herself on the bed.

What was the matter with her? How could she have reacted this way over a kiss? And more important, why hadn't she told Eric the truth?

If deciding to marry Philip was supposed to simplify her life, why did things suddenly seem so complicated? Marrying Philip was the right decision. But if that were true, why had Eric's kiss turned her heart, and maybe her life, upside down?

⅜

Eric dug the pitchfork into the loose hay, trying to get his mind off Michaela—something he hadn't been able to do for the past two hours. He wiped the sweat from his forehead with his sleeve and sighed.

Michaela Macintosh.

She had captivated him from the moment he first laid eyes on her. These last few weeks, he found himself thinking more and more about this woman who had come into his life. He loved the way she worked with the children and her willingness to teach them piano.

She was beautiful, too. He had found himself watching her and wondered if she noticed. He loved how she constantly pushed back the stray lock of hair that always fell in her eyes and how her eyes crinkled when she laughed. When he accidentally brushed next to her, her skin was soft against his arms, and he couldn't help wondering what it would be like to hold her.

Then tonight, when he kissed her, he realized he loved her. He had known for a long time now that he missed her when she was gone, and when they were together, he couldn't keep his eyes off of her. Yes, he knew now that he loved her, but how could he have been so wrong about her feelings toward him?

Eric scooped up another mound of hay and added it to the pile. He had begun to think she was the one God had brought into his life to make him whole again—a second chance at love. He was lonely and knew he wanted to marry again, but it had to be someone who loved the children and whom the children loved as well. After today, it had all seemed so clear. How could he have been so wrong?

The barn door creaked open, and Rebecca stepped into the light of the lantern.

"Rebecca." Eric leaned against the pitchfork. "Is something wrong?"

She shook her head and walked toward him, pulling her coat closer around her. "No, I saw the light and thought you must be home. What are you doing?"

He followed her gaze to the two piles of hay. He'd worked for an hour and done nothing more than move the pile a few feet to the right. He shook his head and ran his fingers through his hair. "I couldn't sleep."

Rebecca stifled a yawn and sat down on a packed bale of hay. "What happened with Mrs. Macintosh?"

Eric closed his eyes briefly, cringing inwardly at the memory. "I kissed her."

Shadows dancing across Rebecca's face revealed a smile. "That's wonderful."

He shook his head and set the tool against the wall before coming to sit beside her. "It was supposed to be."

"I don't understand."

Eric leaned back against the barn wall and sighed. "I thought you were the one who was supposed to come to me about relationships."

"Talking helps. That's what you've always told me."

Eric closed his eyes again, but all he could see was Michaela standing in front of him. "I don't know, Rebecca. I must have totally misread her."

"I'm sorry. I, well, all of us kids really like her." She reached out and took his hand. "I just want you to be happy, Father."

Eric squeezed his daughter's hand, then stood and picked up the pitchfork again. "Go on to bed. I'll be in later."

He watched as his daughter slipped out of the barn and headed toward the house. He'd allowed her to shoulder far more responsibility than a young woman should have to deal with. All this time he'd thought he'd been handling things fine without a wife, but instead, he'd unknowingly placed a large burden on his daughter.

He needed Michaela. His family needed Michaela. And if he was right, Michaela needed them. If she could just find a way to let go of the past, then maybe, just maybe, she'd be able to take another chance at love—with him.

Chapter 11

Michaela rose early the next morning after a restless night. She would see Eric at church today and dreaded facing him after last night's scene. What a fool she had been. Why hadn't she just told him about Philip?

Needing to talk to someone, Michaela fixed a breakfast tray for Emma, then knocked gently on her door.

"Good morning." Michaela entered the room. Emma sat snuggled under a thick quilt reading a book. "Are you hungry?"

"You're just in time. I'm starving." Emma set the book down and pushed her long braid off her shoulder.

Michaela placed the tray on the small table beside the bed and handed Emma the steaming plate. "I'm sure glad food doesn't turn your stomach anymore."

"Me, too, except now that I can eat, I can't get out of bed." Emma laughed and took a small bite of eggs.

"Is Daniel out working already?" Michaela walked to the window and looked out across the white snow that glistened in the morning sunlight. "His breakfast is on the stove."

"Daniel's been up for hours. I don't know how he always manages to get going so early."

Michaela rubbed her hands together, then turned to face Emma. "Can I talk to you about something?"

"Of course. What is it?"

"I spent half the night thinking and praying. I had such a nice time yesterday afternoon with Eric and the kids. We ate a delicious lunch Rebecca fixed, then had a sing-along." The knot in Michaela's stomach grew, and she paced the short side of the room. "On the way home, he brought up some things that really challenged me spiritually. Things I needed to hear."

"I'm not sure I see what the problem is." Emma took a drink of her milk before setting it back on the tray.

"He kissed me."

"Oh." Emma set her fork down and gave Michaela her full attention.

Michaela took several more broad steps across the room. "Last night I lay in

93

bed and all I wanted to do was take the next train away from here."

"Did you tell him about Philip?"

Moving back to the side of the bed, Michaela sat beside Emma, her gaze fixed on the dark brown sheen of the hardwood floor. "That's the problem. I didn't tell him."

"You didn't tell him!" Emma's voice rose slightly. "Why not?"

Michaela stood again, knowing there could be no excuse for her behavior. She had to tell him the truth, but the very thought of telling him made her stomach turn. She didn't want him to think she'd purposely deceived him. It hadn't been that at all.

She ran her hands down the sides of her dress, wiping away the moisture. "I don't know why I didn't tell him. I keep asking myself that same question over and over. When he kissed me, I couldn't think."

"He deserves the truth, Michaela."

"I know."

Emma set her plate on the tray and pulled the covers over her swollen abdomen. "Could it be you have feelings for Eric and don't want him to know about Philip?"

Michaela inwardly winced at the question, trying to disregard any truth to the notion. "The time I've spent with Eric and his children has been wonderful, but. . ."

"And now?"

"It doesn't matter." She shook her head. "Philip loves me, and I belong in Boston with him. I'm going to marry Philip."

Michaela stood up and walked back to the window. Whatever her feelings toward Eric and his children, nothing could erase the mistake she'd made. Why hadn't she told Eric about Philip? All along there had been plenty of opportunities.

"Come and sit down." Emma patted the top of the quilt beside her, and Michaela complied. "Eric's the kind of man any woman would be blessed to have for a husband, and he cares about you. I know I shouldn't say this, but be careful about closing the door unless you're sure. If you really are in love with Philip, then that's wonderful, but just make sure you're not marrying Philip because it's convenient and safe. Don't do something you'll regret later on."

Michaela fought against the wisdom of her sister-in-law's advice. "It's true that I don't love Philip the same way I loved Ethen, but I don't think I'll ever love anyone as much as Ethen. Philip loves me. We'll have a good life together."

Emma bit her lip, and it was obvious to Michaela she wanted to say more. Needing to be alone with her thoughts, Michaela stood and went to the door.

"I'd better get ready for church. Do you need anything else?"

"No, but come and talk to me anytime you need to."

Michaela turned around, her hand against the doorknob. "Thank you."

❧

Michaela looked for Eric as she sat down on the pew next to her brother. All the Johnson kids were there except Ruby, and there was no sign of Eric.

The service began, and after singing two songs, the minister stood before the congregation.

"'If the Son therefore shall make you free, ye shall be free indeed.'" He began the morning's sermon, quoting from John 8:36.

Michaela forced herself to concentrate on the lesson, but the memory of Eric's hurt expression the night before continued to haunt her.

As soon as services were over, Michaela followed Daniel out to the wagon without getting a chance to talk to the Johnson children. He hated to leave Emma even for a short amount of time and wanted to hurry back to the house. Michaela sat silent for the first five minutes, thinking only of the words from the sermon.

"I think starting next week I'll let you ride to church alone," Daniel said as they passed the town cemetery and rode into the shadows of the covered bridge. "Emma's due date is right around the corner, and I don't want anything to happen while I'm gone."

"We can switch off until the baby's born, if you like." Michaela stared out across the landscape but saw little.

Daniel reached over and patted his sister's hand.

"You've seemed a bit. . .I don't know if depressed is right, but maybe distracted lately. I hope you're not working too hard."

"No, it's not that." Michaela decided to tell him the truth. "It's Eric."

"He's interested in you?"

Michaela grasped her Bible tightly against her chest and nodded. "I didn't realize he had feelings for me. Everyone kept hinting, but I just ignored it. I guess I should have noticed, but I didn't want to."

"I'm not surprised."

"There's more." Michaela felt another wave of guilt consume her. "I didn't tell him about Philip."

Daniel's brows rose in question. "Why not?"

"I'm still trying to understand how I feel. When Ethen and Leah died, I wanted to die, too. Sometimes I feel like my life is spinning out of control. When I decided to accept Philip's proposal, I felt like I had control over my life again." She rolled a piece of the fabric of her skirt between her forefingers.

"Then today I realized the truth. God's the only One who can truly set us free from our past. I have to let Him be totally in control of my life."

" 'If the Son therefore shall make you free, ye shall be free indeed.' "

Michaela knew she was free through Christ because her past sins had been forgiven. But what did it really mean to be set free?

"In Christ we have freedom from sin." Michaela struggled to formulate her thoughts. "What about freedom from other things? The fruits of the Spirit are clear—love, joy, peace, patience, and so forth."

She let her gaze scan the horizon. "What I'm trying to say is, aren't we free from what's contrary to these fruits?" Things began to grow clear for her. "As Christians, we leave the past and our sins behind, and in turn we are to live like the Spirit. That means we give up hate, discord, sorrow, and impatience."

"You're right." Daniel tilted his head and nodded in agreement. "I've never thought about it that way."

Michaela took a deep breath and looked at her brother. "I felt convicted today during the lesson, because I'm still carrying with me the pain, sorrow, and even guilt over Ethen's and Leah's deaths. I know God understands our pain and that the grief we go through is a part of healing, but instead of healing, I've been holding on tightly to it."

Michaela clenched her fists together in her lap. "I haven't walked with the Spirit of God, allowing Him to restore me and fill me with the joy of His presence."

The grief that had been bottled up inside her for so long began to flow down her cheeks, but Michaela's heart lit with joy. "See, God is the only One who can give me back my joy. Not Philip. Not anyone."

For the first time in two years, Michaela felt a true sense of deep peace surround her.

Daniel reached over and took her hand. "So what about Philip? Does he still fit into things?"

Michaela nodded her head and smiled. "I think so, but that's what I have to pray about."

℁

Michaela sat in her room later that afternoon, thinking about what she and Daniel had discussed. She knew she needed to talk to Eric, but even more important, she needed some time with her heavenly Father.

"God, I realize how much I need freedom from the past, and You're right here, waiting for me to give it up to You." Tears began to flow down her face, but she didn't attempt to wipe them away. "I need the peace You've promised. The peace that passes all understanding."

Ethen wouldn't have wanted her to sit and mope, wishing things were different. It certainly wouldn't change anything. She could almost see Ethen sitting in the chair across the room, looking at her with his smile that had been only for her.

"I have to say good-bye, Ethen," Michaela said aloud. "I have to go on with my life. I realize you would want me to be happy, and instead I've mourned for something I can never have again. I miss you so much. And Leah, with her dark hair and bright eyes. My little angel. Please take care of each other for me and know I'll never stop loving you. I just can't stop living."

It was time to move on.

❦

An hour later, a knock on the door jolted Michaela out of a deep slumber. In her dream, she'd been running through a green valley after someone, but in the hazy fog, she couldn't tell who it was. Pushing aside the vague impression of a tall, dark-haired farmer, she stumbled to the door and opened it a crack, still trying to wake up.

Daniel stood at the door, his hands shoved in his pockets. "I'm sorry to wake you. Hiram Williams is here to see you."

"Hiram Williams?" Michaela stifled a deep yawn.

"From church."

She shook her head, not understanding why Hiram would want to see her. "What does he want?"

Daniel grinned. "Let's just say this isn't a business call."

"Oh." Her mouth curved into a frown at the implication. "Tell him I'll be right out."

Michaela glanced in the mirror, making sure she looked presentable. She smoothed out her dress and put a stray strand of hair in place. Taking a deep breath, she went into the parlor.

"Hiram." He stood to greet her, rotating the brim of his hat between his hands. "How nice to see you."

Michaela recognized the tall redhead from church. He had a big smile and a face full of freckles. She had never spoken to him other than to say a polite hello at church services.

"I hope you don't mind me dropping by." He gave her another sheepish grin as she took a seat across from him. "I tried to catch you after church today, but you left in quite a hurry."

Michaela leaned against the back of the Boston rocker. "Daniel and I needed to get home to Emma. The baby is due in less than three weeks now."

"I'm sure they're very grateful you're here to help out with things. Running a farm is a big job. I know from experience, though winter is a bit slower." Hiram continued talking, hardly taking a breath. "I own a farm not ten miles from here. My father farmed it until he died three years ago, then I took it over. I'm an only child, so naturally, the farm is mine now."

"That's nice." Michaela forced a smile, wondering when he would get to the point of his visit.

"I had a really good crop this year." He rested his forearms against his thighs in an apparent attempt to get comfortable. Michaela smiled inwardly at the picture he made. The hefty farmer seemed out of place in a parlor filled with dainty porcelain dishes and Emma's collection of lacy sandwich plates.

"In fact, this has been the best year yet," he continued. "I won't bore you with all the details. I'm sure coming from the city, farming might not be one of your interests?"

He said it like a question, and Michaela wondered what he wanted her to say.

"Actually, I've learned a little about farming since I've been here. I have to admit, though, I'd never milked a cow before I came here."

Hiram let out a deep belly laugh. "And I've been milking cows since the day I could walk."

Michaela gave him a weak smile and wished Daniel would come and rescue her. "Was there something you needed?"

"Well, yes, actually." Hiram cleared his throat. "Each Christmas Eve we have a big celebration. It's a wonderful time with caroling, a bonfire, and, of course, lots of food."

"Sounds like fun."

"Oh, it is. Normally we have it every year at the Hurn farm, but since he's been laid up these last few months, it will be at the Johnsons' farm. They have such a nice-sized house, and it's not as crowded."

Michaela nodded, waiting for the inevitable invitation.

"I was wondering. . .well. . .if you'd like to go with me this year."

Michaela hated to turn him down. He seemed to be a nice man, but nevertheless, she couldn't accept his invitation. "Mr. Williams. . ."

"Please, call me Hiram."

"Of course. Hiram." She started again. "I'm flattered you would want to ask me, and I'm sure I'd have a wonderful time with you. The truth is, there's someone back in Boston. We're engaged."

Hiram squirmed in his seat, then stood abruptly. "I'm sorry. I had no idea."

Michaela stood as well, feeling awkward over the entire situation. "Please understand, it's nothing personal. I'm sure there are several women at church who would love to go with you."

Hiram scratched his head, then put his hat on. "I guess I'd better get going then. I apologize for taking up your time."

"I'll see you next Sunday at church?"

"Of course. I'll be there."

Michaela followed Hiram to the door. Stepping out onto the front porch behind him, Michaela froze. Eric stood at the bottom of the steps.

"Eric?"

"Michaela." Eric turned to face her. "I stopped by to talk to you, but if you're busy. . ."

"Hiram was just leaving."

Hiram mumbled good-bye, then mounted his horse and rode off toward his farm.

"I didn't know you and Hiram were friends." Eric followed Michaela into the house.

"Actually, we're not. I mean, I don't really know him at all. He just stopped by to ask me something."

"I see."

"I noticed you weren't in church this morning." Michaela stalled for time as she sat in the chair, wondering how much Eric had heard of their conversation. Eric sat across from her, looking more nervous than Hiram had, if that were possible. "I didn't get a chance to talk to your children. Daniel wanted to hurry back to Emma."

"Ruby was sick, but she's feeling much better now."

"I'm glad to hear that."

Michaela's stomach lurched, and again she wished Daniel would come into the room, but he was in the barn and Emma was asleep.

"I came to talk to you about last night. I felt I owed you an apology, but now. . ." He stood and paced, his boots echoing across the wood floor. Turning sharply, he faced Michaela. "Why didn't you tell me you were engaged to someone in Boston?"

"I don't know." She shook her head and gazed miserably at his clenched jaw. Why couldn't she have handled the situation better? "I owe you an apology." She bit her lower lip. "I never meant to give you the impression I was interested in you. Romantically, that is. I love being with your family, but that's it."

Michaela's heart pounded in her chest as she forced herself to continue. "When you kissed me, it took me off guard. I should have told you I'm getting married. I'm sorry."

"It certainly would have made things a lot easier if you had told me." Eric sat across from her again, his hands gripping the arms of the chair. "I assumed with all the time you were spending with the children, maybe part of it was because you enjoyed being with me as well."

"You assumed wrong." Michaela's voice rose in frustration. Immediately, she wished she could take back the harsh words, but still, it wasn't entirely her fault. She'd never meant to give him the impression she was interested in him.

"Your children are wonderful, and I've enjoyed teaching them. I've even enjoyed the few times we've talked together. But my personal life is just that—personal."

Eric sat quietly for a moment, and Michaela knew she'd hurt him.

"If you'd rather not come out to the house for any more lessons, I'd understand completely." Eric's tone sent icy shivers down her spine. "I can tell the children you're needed here with Emma."

Michaela shook her head and took a deep breath, trying to calm the pounding of her heart. "I made a commitment to the children, and I'll be there. I'll be leaving in a few weeks, anyway. I want them to get in as much practice as possible before I leave."

"The children will miss you." Eric cleared his throat and stood. "I need to get home and make sure Ruby's all right."

Michaela followed him to the door. Eric took the porch stairs two at a time and in one seamless motion jumped on his horse and rode away. She stood at the door and watched until all she could see was his shapeless form on the horizon.

Chapter 12

Mrs. Macintosh!" Ruby greeted her at the door of the Johnson home the night of the Christmas Eve party. Candles filled the parlor, adding warmth to the frosty night. A handful of people had already arrived and now mingled in small groups around a tree that had been decorated with mauve-colored silk bows and dainty gold balls for the occasion.

Ruby held Michaela's hand tightly, her face bright with the excitement of the holiday. "Your dress is beautiful!"

"Thank you, sweetie." Michaela glanced down at her green taffeta dress. She'd been afraid it might be a bit elaborate with its full bustle skirt and silk ribbon lace, but Emma had assured her it was perfect. Glancing at the other guests, she had to agree Emma had been right. Everyone had taken advantage of the occasion and pulled out their finest outfits.

"Tomorrow's Christmas." Ruby tugged on Michaela's arm and pulled her closer. "Do you have a present for me?"

"A present. Let me see." Michaela put her index finger against her chin and pretended to think. "I guess you'll have to wait until tomorrow to find out, but I'll let you in on a secret." Michaela bent over and whispered in Ruby's ear. "I think you'll find a little something under the tree for you from me."

Ruby in turn cupped her hands around her mouth. "Can I tell you a secret?"

"Of course." Michaela smiled, enjoying the little game with the youngster.

"I have a present for you, too."

"You do?" Michaela pretended to look surprised.

Ruby nodded and reached inside the pocket of her dark blue dress. "You said Christmas makes you sad, so I wanted to give you something to make you happy."

She held out a small gift she had obviously wrapped herself. "You don't have to wait until Christmas. You can open it right now."

"All right." Carefully, Michaela unwrapped the shiny red paper held together precariously with a white ribbon.

Ruby stood with her hands clasped behind her back, her eyes glowing with excitement.

Inside the package was a small gold-encased cameo brooch. Certainly, it had to be a family heirloom. Michaela swallowed hard, not sure what she should do. "It's beautiful, but where did you get it?"

Ruby crinkled the edge of the wrapping paper and smiled, obviously pleased with her gift. "It's mine. Pa says when we give something away that's special to us, we're giving from the heart."

Michaela glanced around the room, looking for Eric. "Your father's right, but this looks very expensive."

"What am I right about?"

Michaela drew out a sigh of relief when Eric appeared beside her. "Ruby gave me a gift for Christmas." Michaela held up the brooch, hoping Eric could read the concern in her expression.

"Where did you get this, Ruby?" Her father ran his hand across Ruby's silky hair, then pulled her gently toward him.

Ruby's chin rose as if she was determined her gift would go unchallenged. "It was Mother's, and now it's mine to give to anyone I want. I gave it to Michaela because I want her to be my new mother. I never knew my mother because God took her away to heaven, and I think it's time I had a mother like everyone else."

Michaela stood up straight, her jaw lowering in surprise.

"Ruby." Eric hesitated. "This brooch is yours to do with what you want. If you want to give it to Michaela, then that's fine. But, as much as you want a mother. . ." Eric glanced at Michaela, a note of sadness in his voice. "Michaela's going back to Boston soon. That's where she lives. She's going to marry a man there."

Ruby's smile faded, and it broke Michaela's heart to see her so disappointed. But Eric was right. She would be going home soon and could never be Ruby's mother.

"Are you sure you don't want to keep this, Ruby?" Michaela bent down, holding the gift in the palm of her hand. "I would understand if you wanted to since it was your mother's."

Ruby looked from Eric to Michaela.

"I'll tell you what, Ruby." Eric leaned over and picked up his youngest daughter. "You and I will make a special trip into town next week, just the two of us, and you can pick out a special gift for Mrs. Macintosh then. How does that sound?"

Ruby squished her lips together, contemplating her father's offer. "All right," she finally agreed. "You won't have your feelings hurt, Mrs. Macintosh?"

Michaela smiled and ran her hand down Ruby's rosy cheek. "Not at all. I'll never forget how special you made my Christmas."

Ruby grinned widely, then reached out to give Michaela a big hug, bringing her within inches of Eric's face. The back of his hand brushed Michaela's arm, and she took a step back at the brief contact.

Eric cleared his throat. "I think it's time to start the singing. Do you still feel like playing?"

Michaela nodded, thankful for the distraction.

"Wait, before you go. . ." Eric's hand touched the sleeve of her dress. Ruby had walked off and they were alone for a moment. "Can we call a truce? I'd like it if we could remain friends."

"I'd like that, too." Michaela forced a smile. "I still feel so horrible about yesterday—"

Eric held up his hand to stop her from continuing. "I'd just as soon put that behind us."

Michaela nodded and went to sit at the piano. She played song after song, and the front room rang with animated voices full of Christmas cheer. After an hour or so of singing, the festivities moved on to a contest prepared for the children. While the men got the bonfire started out behind the barn, Michaela brought out the maple syrup gingerbread cookies she had made especially for tonight, along with several colors of frosting and goodies to decorate the cookies.

The children crowded around the table in the kitchen and began to work on their cookies. Michaela was pleased at not only how seriously they took the project, but also how creative many of them were.

"This is fun." A dark-haired little boy placed two small candies on a snowman for eyes.

"Look at my star, Mrs. Macintosh." Ruby held up a cookie for her to see.

"It looks wonderful." Michaela smiled, hoping Ruby had forgiven her for not accepting her gift.

The guests mingled, both in the house and outside where they stood near the bonfire, roasting chicken and drinking hot cocoa. It was a perfect evening.

Someone screamed outside.

Michaela hurried out onto the front porch to see what had happened. To the far left, she could see the barn. Orange and yellow flames roared with intensity, shooting up from its roof. A dozen men worked as fast as they could to put out the fire and get the animals to safety. Women huddled outside with children, keeping them away from the fire and watching in disbelief at what only minutes ago had been a time of joy and celebration.

Ruby ran after her father toward the flaming building. None of the men seemed to notice the small girl entering the burning barn. Without considering the consequences, Michaela hurried off the porch.

In a dreamlike state, Michaela ran toward the barn. All she could think of was the little girl in the fire. The flames singed the hairs on her arms, but Michaela felt nothing.

"Leah!" She screamed at the top of her lungs, desperately trying to reach her before it was too late.

"Not again, God," she cried. "Please don't let it happen again!"

Inside the barn, the heat was intense. Michaela heard a cracking sound from the ceiling.

"Leah!" Michaela screamed and ran for the little girl who stood in the path of a falling beam.

Seconds later, there was darkness. And then nothing.

Chapter 13

What's going to happen to Mrs. Macintosh?" Sarah wrapped her arms around her legs, rocking back and forth on a cushioned chair. "I don't want her to die."

Eric sat with his children in the parlor, exhausted yet unable to sleep. The barn was a total loss, though they'd managed to save most of the animals. If not for the falling snow and lack of wind, they might have lost the house as well.

The barn, though, was the least of Eric's worries. No matter what Michaela felt about him, upstairs in Rebecca's room lay the woman he loved. Michaela had saved Ruby's life and taken the brunt of the force when a beam collapsed, striking her on the back of her head.

Adam sat on the floor, resting his elbows on his knees. "Do you think Mrs. Macintosh is going to live?"

"All we can do is pray and wait for the doctor." Eric stood and walked across the room to the window. Outside, the earth was covered by a deep layer of snow.

The sun would be up in a few hours, but Christmas had been all but forgotten. Eric refused to give up hope. She had to be all right. He turned at the creaking of the stairs and the subsequent appearance of the doctor. "How is she?"

The doctor rubbed the sides of his temples with the tips of his fingers. "I honestly don't know at this point. She's asleep right now. It's difficult to know how much damage was done. There were a few burns on her arms, but thankfully they're not too serious. The wound on her head is deep, but I'm more worried about internal damage."

"What about Emma?" Daniel came in from the kitchen with a steaming cup of coffee in his hands. An hour after the fire began, his wife had gone into labor.

"It's a good thing you didn't try to take her home last night." The doctor pulled off his wire-rimmed glasses and rubbed his eyes. "The contractions are strong, but she's doing fine. It won't be long now before the baby's here. Mrs. Santon's staying with her, and I'd say in the next few hours, there'll be a new little boy or girl in the house."

Daniel let out a sigh of relief.

Setting his glasses back on the bridge of his nose, the doctor glanced around the room. "All of you need to go to bed and get some sleep. There's nothing else you can do tonight."

Eric stifled a yawn. "The doctor's right, kids. We've got a lot of work to do in the morning."

He picked up his youngest daughter, who had fallen asleep in Sarah's lap, and carried her upstairs to her room. After getting her settled, he closed the door quietly behind him, his gaze resting on the door to Rebecca's room, where Michaela lay. He cried out to God, begging Him to save her. He still loved her so much. If only she felt the same for him.

⁂

The presents lay unopened under the tree Christmas morning. Slowly the children woke from a restless night and joined Eric in the parlor. Unable to sleep, he'd come downstairs in case the doctor had news for him. The fireplace cast ominous shadows on the walls as rays of morning sun crept through the window.

"Has there been any word?" Rebecca came in from the kitchen with a cup of hot coffee and handed it to her father.

"Thank you." He took a deep sip of the strong brew and shook his head. "Nothing yet."

Daniel lay sprawled across the sofa, his open gaze fixed on the ceiling. Eric doubted he'd slept, either.

There were shouts upstairs, followed by the shrill cry of a newborn.

"The baby!" Sarah jumped up from the chair she was sitting on and clapped her hands together.

Daniel bolted to the bottom of the stairs, anxiously awaiting some word about his wife and child. After a few minutes, Mrs. Santon appeared with a broad smile across her plump face. "You're a father, Daniel! Come see your son."

Daniel ran in front of her up the stairs, two at a time.

Eric drained his mug of coffee and stood, his heart aching for good news about Michaela. "There are chores to do, children. Sitting around won't help anyone. Let's all get to work. Rebecca, I'm sure the doctor and Mrs. Santon could use some breakfast, as could the rest of us."

"Certainly." Rebecca picked up his mug, then scurried into the kitchen.

Eric stretched his arms behind him, trying to relieve some of the tension. He made a mental list of what needed to be done. Not only did the charred remains of the barn need to be cleared away, but he was going to have to make plans to rebuild.

"Eric." The doctor stood at the bottom of the stairs, his clothes crumpled

106

from staying up most of the night. "It's Michaela. She's awake now, and she's calling for you."

Eric paused. Why would she want to see him? In his mind, he was the last person Michaela would be asking for. He took a step forward. "Are you sure?"

The doctor nodded. Slowly, Eric climbed up the stairs.

He entered the room, and his heart skipped a beat when he saw her. Her eyes were open, and he could see the pain reflected in them. Several layers of gauze were wrapped around the top of her head, and one side of her face was swollen and bruised. "Hi."

She offered him a weak smile.

He sat down beside her. "How are you feeling?"

Her eyes closed briefly, then opened again. "I don't know. My head hurts and feels like it's spinning in opposite directions."

Eric pushed back a strand of hair from her face and let it tumble against the pillow. "The doctor said you wanted to see me."

A teardrop fell down her cheek. "Everything's so fuzzy. I'm scared."

He took her hand and held it tight. "Do you remember anything about last night?"

She shook her head. "I thought it was my daughter, Leah. I had to save her. I thought God was giving me another chance to bring her back." Another tear flowed down Michaela's face. "She won't ever come back, though, will she?"

Emotion welled inside Eric's chest, knowing the pain Michaela was experiencing was not only physical. "It was Ruby in the fire, Michaela. You saved her life."

Her free hand touched the side of her temple. "It hurts so bad."

Eric wished he could take away her pain. Wished he could erase the scars from the past that had been ripped open last night. Hoping a distraction would help, he told her about Emma's baby.

Michaela smiled at the news. "What did they finally decide to name him?"

"Nathaniel James."

"I like that." She shifted in the bed but made no effort to pull away from his grasp.

She closed her eyes, and he wondered if she'd drifted off to sleep. Deciding to slip out and let her rest, he pulled his hand free and stood to leave the room.

"Please don't leave me." Her eyes were wide open now, and the glazed look he'd noticed before was gone.

"I'm so sorry this had to happen." He longed to hold her in his arms, but instead he sat down beside her and took her hand again. "I know it reminds you of what happened to your husband and daughter."

She nodded and squeezed his hand.

There was something he had to tell her. "I won't say this again, but when I saw that beam fall on you. . ." He closed his eyes, and for a moment he was there again, seeing the horror in her eyes, the screams that filled the air, the panic within his chest. "I knew without a doubt I loved you and didn't want to lose you."

He raked his free hand through his hair. He shouldn't be telling her this. Not here, not this way. She was in love with someone else. But she had asked for him. . .

"I know there's someone else, but I just need you to know how I feel."

Her voice was quiet, barely above a whisper. "I don't know how I feel anymore. If I love him, then why do I want you with me right now? Please stay with me." She held tight to his hand.

Eric wondered if she knew what she was saying.

The doctor stepped into the room to check on her. "She needs to rest."

Eric turned back to Michaela, who had fallen asleep. A peaceful look covered her face, and he resisted the urge to run his finger across her cheek.

"After a couple of days, she should be all right. The beam must have skimmed her head instead of actually hitting her directly. That's probably what saved her life."

"She saved my little girl's life as well."

❧

Late the following day, the doctor allowed Michaela and Emma to go home. The cleanup for the barn was almost finished, and Eric thanked God the snow had stopped any further damage, especially to the house. Two chickens had died, but the livestock had survived and was now holed up in Daniel's barn until another shelter could be built.

The morning after Michaela went home, Eric saddled up his horse and headed for Daniel's farm, needing to see for himself how she was doing.

"Good morning, Eric," Daniel called out from the front porch.

"Guess you have your hands full." Eric dismounted the horse and pulled his coat closer around him to block the chilly wind that had picked up.

Daniel finished hammering a loose porch rail, then greeted Eric with a firm handshake. "Several of the women at church have already been by with meals and have even helped clean the house for me."

Eric held up the pouch he was carrying. "Rebecca sent over some home-made bread and jam with me."

"No one's going hungry around here!"

"How is the baby?" Eric followed Daniel inside the house, thankful for the warmth from the stone fireplace.

"Besides the fact he keeps us up all night?" Daniel let out a deep chuckle. "Couldn't be better. He's perfect."

"I remember those nighttime feedings." Eric set the gift on a side table. "How's Michaela?"

"I think she's asleep. The doctor says she'll recover fine as long as she gets enough rest."

"The kids have been begging to come see her, but I told them they needed to wait until she's up and around." Eric stood in front of the crackling flames and rubbed his icy hands together.

"Maybe tomorrow. Would you like me to see if she's awake?" Daniel asked as a hungry cry from the baby sounded from the bedroom.

Eric nodded. "If you don't mind."

A minute later, Daniel came out of Michaela's room.

"I'm sorry, Eric." He shut the door behind him. "She's sound asleep. This whole ordeal has been both emotionally and physically draining for her."

"I know." He tried not to worry, but he knew the experience had been traumatic for her. And he wanted to be with her. "Please tell her I came by and if she needs anything, I'm here. Anything at all."

"I'll tell her."

❧

Michaela groaned and pulled out the last dozen stitches of the sweater she was knitting for the new baby. "Remind me not to attempt another project like this."

Emma chuckled as Michaela held up the lopsided sweater. "Nathaniel won't care. I'm just glad you're up and around." Emma picked up a skein of blue yarn and laid it in her lap.

"I feel so much better."

"He's such a good little boy." Emma watched her son sleep in the small crib beside her in the parlor. "I can't believe how small he is."

Daniel walked in from the kitchen with a slice of cake Mrs. Winters had sent over. The grin that crossed his lips hadn't left his face since the baby's arrival. He sat down on the sofa beside his wife. "Eric came by earlier, Michaela, but you were asleep. He asked if he could bring his children by to see you tomorrow if the weather is not too bad. They've been worried about you."

Michaela sighed. She could remember every word of her last conversation with Eric. She'd asked him to stay. For some reason, she'd needed him beside her to take away the fear she felt.

He'd told her he loved her.

She choked back the wave of emotion, confused by her reaction. If she wasn't careful, she'd start crying again.

"I'm sorry." She set the sweater down and walked over to the fireplace. Flames crackled. She could smell the soot and feel the intensity of the blaze. "I haven't felt like myself lately."

"It's all right." Emma's voice was reassuring.

"When I saw Ruby running toward the barn and the fire, I relived it all over again. It was Leah, and God was giving me a second chance to save her." She turned around to face them. "I know it sounds crazy."

Emma shook her head. "It's not crazy at all."

The wind howled and the windows shook with the impact.

"There's another storm coming." Daniel stood up and looked out the window. "I'd better go out to the barn and make sure the animals are secure. It's likely to be a bad one."

"Bundle up," Emma insisted. "The temperature has dropped."

Michaela shivered unconsciously, wishing she could get Eric and the feel of his strong hand around hers out of her mind.

Chapter 14

Philip Macintosh got off the train and stood on the tiny platform, wondering what his next move should be. Snow flurries whipped around him beneath a darkened sky. Maybe he had been foolish for coming to Cranton without telling anyone, but after receiving the telegram from Daniel about Michaela's accident, he'd had no choice.

Philip tightened his long coat against the wind. He couldn't believe how desolate the town looked. The snow had drifted into deep piles along the sides of the buildings, and few people braved the harsh elements. He didn't blame them.

The sun would be setting soon, taking with it any lingering traces of light. His best option would be to find the nearest hotel and get a good night's sleep before traveling to Daniel's farm in the morning.

Philip picked up his bag and started for the center of town. The hotel proved easy to find, and soon he made his way through the front door, thankful for the warmth of the lobby. Rubbing his hands together, he took a seat at a table next to the fireplace and ordered a cup of hot coffee.

A man was talking to the hotel manager at the nearby desk. Philip turned his head when he heard mention of Michaela's brother.

"I hear Daniel's wife had a boy." The manager leaned his elbows on the counter.

The second man nodded. "I saw him yesterday. They seem to be doing great."

"Sorry to hear about the fire that destroyed your barn," the first man continued.

"I'm just thankful no one was killed."

Philip leaned toward the men. What about Michaela?

"So, Daniel's sister, Michaela—is she all right?" The manager slid his glasses up the bridge of his nose.

"Got quite a knot on her head, but she's doing fine. We were worried for a while, but the doctor says with a little rest, there shouldn't be any complications."

"That's good to hear."

"I need to get on home, George. I'm afraid it'll be a rough ride. I wouldn't

111

have come in today if it hadn't been absolutely necessary. Been the first break in the weather all week, and now things are stirring up again. I've got to get home before dark, and at that I'm not likely to make it."

The man headed toward the door with broad, determined steps. Philip decided this was his chance.

"Excuse me, sir." Philip stood and quickly crossed the room and introduced himself. "My name's Philip Macintosh, Michaela Macintosh's brother-in-law. I just got into town, and I wondered if you could tell me how to get to her brother's farm. I guess I'll have to wait until morning, though."

"Do you have a horse?"

"No, sir, I just got off the train."

"I'm on my way home right now, and my farm is right past theirs. I had to pick up a few supplies, so I brought the sled. You can come with me if you'd like." The man shook Philip's hand. "Name's Eric Johnson, by the way. We'd better get going if we're going to make it before nightfall."

"Nice to meet you. I sure appreciate this." Philip left enough money for the coffee and a tip and followed Eric out the door. "Didn't think I could make it out there tonight."

"God must have wanted our paths to cross. I had planned to leave over an hour ago, but I got held up." Eric raised his voice against the howling wind as they hurried to the sled. "Another storm isn't far behind us. I guess you heard about the accident."

"That's why I'm here."

"She's doing fine now. The doctor said the beam that hit her just missed doing some very serious damage."

"I'm just thankful she's alive."

The snow was picking up and the wind whipped against Philip, making further conversation impossible. He climbed into the sled, anxious for the moment he'd see Michaela again.

❧

"Looks like another severe storm's about to hit." Michaela paced the living room floor, wishing the long stretch of winter weather would be over soon. For the past week, as soon as one storm let up, there seemed to be another one hitting even harder. She knew that Eric had planned to go into town today, and she prayed he'd made it home safely.

"You're pacing again," Emma commented as Michaela started across the room once again.

Michaela shrugged and continued her trek. "The storm's getting worse."

Emma stuck her needle into the taut fabric, then pulled it out gently.

"Would you like to help me with the quilt? It would help you get your mind off whatever is bothering you."

"Eric was supposed to go into town. I was hoping he made it home all right. I'd hate for the children to be alone right now."

She looked at the quilt Emma patiently stitched together, piece by piece. The vivid reds, greens, and yellows were already starting to form the intricate pattern. If only life was as simple as following a pattern. Instead, it was full of detours, turns, and at times, heartache.

Someone pounded on the front door. Michaela jumped. "Who could that be?"

Daniel opened the door.

"Eric!" Relief flooded through her as she hurried toward the door. She stopped when she noticed a man standing next to him bundled in a heavy coat. "Philip?"

"Boy, are you a sight for sore eyes." Philip picked her up and swung her around. "I didn't think I'd ever get here."

"How did you. . . ?" Michaela looked to Eric, then back to Philip, confused.

Eric strode across the room to the crackling fire. "Found your brother-in-law in town as I was leaving. Didn't want him to have to spend the night in town."

Philip held her for a moment, then went to stand by the fireplace beside Eric, his gaze never leaving Michaela's face.

"After I got the telegram about the accident, I left Boston on the next train." Philip rubbed his hands together. "Never imagined it would be so cold." He turned to Eric. "I'm sure Michaela's told you. We're planning to get married as soon as she gets back to Boston."

Eric's gaze locked momentarily with Michaela's. She looked away, not able to bear the mark of pain in his eyes. What had she done?

Eric shuffled his feet and cleared his throat. "I need to get home before this storm blows full force." His voice was void of emotion as he quickly made his escape to the front door. "It was nice to meet you, Mr. Macintosh."

A brief gust of wind blew in, and he was gone.

Michaela's gaze lingered on the closed door for a moment before she turned back to Philip. "I can't believe you're here."

He smiled at her and took her hands in his. "I was so worried. I know it's crazy to come all the way out here, but I just had to see for myself that you were all right."

"I'm fine." Michaela squeezed his hands, then showed him where the board had hit her. "Just a very bad bump on the head and a headache that lasted for days."

Emma stood up and motioned Daniel to follow her into the kitchen so the two of them could be alone. "We'll get you some hot tea."

"Michaela." Once they'd left the room, Philip ran his thumb down the side of her cheek, his face lit with relief. "You don't know how much I've missed you."

He reached down and kissed her slowly on the lips. Michaela pushed away any feelings of doubt. Seeing him put everything back into perspective. She was going to marry Philip, and together they'd adopt Anna.

Chapter 15

There you are." Michaela stopped along the side of the Johnsons' new barn, where Philip stood high up on a ladder, nailing shingles onto the roof. The last couple of days had been a whirlwind of activity as the men in the community gathered to rebuild Eric's barn.

Philip finished driving a nail before glancing down at Michaela. He blew out a puff of air and smiled. "Hi."

Michaela took a step back and studied the gabled structure, amazed at how much work had been accomplished. "You men have done a wonderful job on Eric's new barn."

"Good thing there was a break in the weather." Philip looped his hammer on his belt and climbed down before stretching his back. "Is that for me?"

Michaela handed Philip the steaming mug of coffee. He took a deep sip. "I sure needed this. The snow might have stopped, but it's still icy cold."

She shoved her hands into the deep pockets of her wool coat. "Lunch will be ready soon. There's quite a feast prepared, including roast beef, ham, potatoes, bread—"

"Stop, you're making my stomach growl." Philip held up one of his hands and grinned. "I want to finish the section I'm working on, then I'll come in."

He took another sip, keeping his eyes focused on her. She could feel the heat rising in her cheeks at his intense gaze.

She tilted her head, lowering her brows in question. "What is it?"

"The trip out here's been good for you, hasn't it?"

Michaela nodded and breathed in deeply. There was a peace about her she hadn't felt for a long time. "I've been able to sort through things—let go of some things from the past."

Philip took a final gulp of the coffee and handed the empty cup back to Michaela. "There's a glow about you that you didn't have back home. I'm glad to see you happy and relaxed. We've all been worried about you."

"And who is we?" Michaela chuckled and fingered the rim of the mug. It was nice to have someone fuss over her.

The blue of his eyes lightened in the bright sunlight. "Me, for one. Aunt Clara. Caroline."

"You've talked a lot about Caroline this week."

He smiled at her teasing. "She and I tried to visit Anna as often as we could. Anna enjoyed it."

"I'm glad."

He ran his gloved hand down her sleeve. "The board said we could adopt Anna as soon as we're married."

Her heart soared at the possibility that the three of them could be a family. "I can't wait to see her."

Philip pulled the hammer out of his belt and jingled the sack of nails he held. "I'd better get finished. Can't believe we're heading home tomorrow. Seems like I just got off that train, and now I have to get right back on."

℁

Philip paused to watch as Michaela turned around and walked back toward the house. Tomorrow they'd leave for Boston, and in a few weeks she'd become his wife. Eric approached Michaela, halfway between Philip and the house. She pushed a stray piece of hair behind one ear and fiddled with the mug.

"The barn looks wonderful."

Michaela raised her head and smiled at Eric. They were close enough that Philip could hear their conversation.

"I'm grateful for all the help I've got."

"Eric, I . . ."

A loud ring sounded from the porch as someone hit the dinner bell.

Clang.

Clang.

"I wanted to tell you. . ."

Clang.

Clang.

"Come on, let's eat." Someone slapped Eric on the back as three of the men who had been working on the barn surrounded him. "I'm starved as a bear."

Philip watched as Michaela stood still in the snow while the men joked and laughed on their way to get their lunch. Her lips formed a frown, but he couldn't read her expression. What had she wanted to say to Eric?

Philip decided to join the group for lunch and finish the shingles later. He hurried across the hard ground to catch up to where Michaela still stood. "Ready to eat?"

"Yes." He watched as she glanced one last time at Eric before turning back to him. "Yes. I'm ready."

Philip cupped Michaela's elbow with his hand, but his focus remained on the man ahead of them. Was Eric the one who had brought life back to Michaela's heart?

❦

"I can't believe you're leaving." Emma cleared the last cup from the breakfast table, then wiped it down with a wet cloth.

Michaela held the sleeping baby in her arms, enjoying his sweet fragrance. "I'll be back. I have to make sure little Nate knows who his favorite aunt is."

"The wagon's ready." Daniel opened the back door and came into the kitchen.

Michaela handed the baby back to Emma, trying not to cry. She wrapped her arms around her sister-in-law for a moment. "I'm going to miss you so much."

"We're going to miss you, too."

"I want you both to know how much I've appreciated your hospitality these past few days," Philip said as he picked up the last bag and held open the front door for Michaela. "I know it was a bit unexpected."

"Just promise to take good care of her." Emma reached up and kissed him on the cheek.

"You know I will."

Michaela hurried toward the wagon, struggling to hold back the tears.

She had said good-bye to the Johnson children the night before. A few tears had been shed, even by the boys, and Michaela promised she would write as soon as she got to Boston. There had been no time alone with Eric. No time to tell him how sorry she was for everything. She let Philip help her into the wagon, forcing herself to put Eric out of her mind.

The ride to town seemed short, and Michaela wondered if she'd have a chance to come back again. She looked out across the snow-covered ground. A bird flew overhead, singing a lonely tune. Crystals of ice sparkled in the snow below. She studied the scene, trying to memorize each detail so as not to forget.

At the station, Michaela stood silently on the platform as Philip put her bags on the train.

"I'm going to miss you, Michaela." Daniel wrapped his arms around her tightly. "Promise you'll come back."

Michaela smiled through the tears, trying desperately to hold on to her emotions. She would miss them all so much.

"All aboard!"

"It's time, Michaela."

Taking one last look at her brother, Michaela followed Philip onto the train and waved good-bye for the final time.

❦

He'd been a fool.

Eric pushed his stallion as fast as he could across the frozen terrain. Forests of pine trees seemed to fly by, but only one thing seemed clear at the moment. Michaela. He never should have let her leave without talking to her. He'd let his pride get in the way of letting himself become vulnerable.

At the Cranton station, he jumped off the horse and quickly tied the lead rope to a post. His stomach turned as he caught sight of the empty platform. He was too late.

❦

Michaela sat across from Philip and looked out the window of the train, waiting for it to leave the small station. The familiar valley stretched out before her, a sharp contrast from the bustling streets of Boston.

"You'd better hurry if you're going to get off the train."

Michaela turned to Philip, lowering her brow in question. "What did you say?"

He leaned forward and took her hands. "From the moment I arrived, I saw something in your eyes when you looked at him. You've never looked at me that way."

Michaela opened her mouth to respond, but he put a finger to her lips. "I've been awake all night trying to decide what to do. I'm a part of what's familiar to you, what's comfortable. . . . But you don't love me, Michaela. You love Eric. And if I'm not mistaken, he loves you as well."

Michaela closed her eyes, trying to make sense of everything. Philip had been a part of her life for so long. At a time when she'd needed him, he'd always been there. Yes, he was familiar and comfortable. . .but was that all? "I don't know. I. . ."

"Do you love him?"

She closed her eyes and could see Eric—the dimple on his right cheek when he smiled. The sound of his laugh. The tenderness he showed to his children. She loved him. "I didn't want to."

"I know." Philip reached out and wiped away a tear that had fallen down her cheek. "Go on. You'd better hurry."

❦

Michaela stepped off the train moments before it roared away from the station. It was clear to her now. In not wanting to let go of the past, she'd held tight to what was familiar and comfortable. And in turn, she'd confused feelings of safety and protection for love. Her relationship with Philip would always be important, but she knew now she could never love him.

White light reflected off the snow that still covered parts of the ground. She watched the train pull out of the station, slowly picking up speed until she could see only a small puff of smoke lingering on the horizon.

Stepping out of the shadow of the station building, she saw Eric cross the street toward her.

"Eric."

"Michaela?" His surprise to see her was obvious.

"You came to see me off?" She didn't know what to say now that he stood in front of her.

"I wanted to, but I thought you were leaving with Philip. Why are you still here?"

Tears streamed down her cheeks. Eric took a step closer and gently wiped them away with his hand.

"I realized I love you." Michaela's voice was barely above a whisper. "And I couldn't go with Philip. I thought I could love him, but then I met you and everything changed. I've just been too stubborn to admit it, even to myself."

A smile spread across Eric's face. "Did you say you love me?"

Michaela nodded shyly, surprised at her boldness.

Eric let out a shout of joy. "So you'll marry me?"

Laugher exploded from her lips. "You're asking me if I'll marry you?"

"Will you?"

There were no longer any doubts as to who she wanted to spend the rest of her life with. "Yes!"

He picked her up by her waist, swung her around, and gently put her back down. He brought her face toward his and kissed her slowly. Michaela laid her hands against his chest, enjoying the sweet taste of his lips against hers.

After a moment, he pulled back, still cupping her face in his hands. "I suppose this isn't the most appropriate place for displays of affection, but I can't help it. I love you, Michaela Macintosh."

Michaela just looked at him, realizing she'd been given a second chance for love. "What will the kids think?"

"They're going to be six of the happiest kids in the county. I've seen nothing but gloomy faces around my place since you told them you were leaving."

Eric brushed back the tears from her cheeks with the back of his hand. "I was going to buy a train ticket for Boston and come after you. You must be some catch to have men traipsing all over the country for you."

"I finally realized the truth. There's only one man for me."

No more words were needed as Michaela felt his strong arms surround her and his lips met hers.

Epilogue

Six months later

Ladies and gentlemen, may I present to you Mr. and Mrs. Eric Johnson."
Michaela pressed her gloved fingers against her heart, then looked up at Eric, who stood beside her at the front of the church. His broad smile reached the corners of his eyes, and she resisted the urge to reach up and ruffle his inky black hair. Mrs. Eric Johnson. Soaking in the happiness of the moment, her gaze moved to the children who stood beside them as attendants. Rebecca, Adam, Samuel, Matt, Ruby, Sarah. . .and Anna.

Her breath caught in her throat as Anna reached up to grab her hand. It was still hard for her to believe that the little girl who had stolen her heart was now an official part of the family. In the midst of preparing for the wedding, the news had come from Agnes at the Mills Street Orphanage that the committee was going to let her and Eric adopt Anna.

Eric ushered them both toward the back of the church, not seeming to mind that Anna had chosen to be escorted by the bride and groom behind the rest of the children.

Familiar faces smiled back at Michaela as they made their way up the aisle. Emma stood beside Daniel, holding a plump Nathaniel in her arms. Caroline looked radiant next to Philip in her bright yellow dress and fancy straw hat with gold trim. Aunt Clara, whose love and wisdom had been indispensable over the past few years, leaned against Ben White, her husband of two months. Even Jake Markham had come with his parents, though his intentions were no doubt to see Rebecca and not to witness the wedding ceremony.

In the sunlit foyer of the church, Michaela felt a tug on her skirt.

"Momma?" Anna looked up at her with wide eyes.

Michaela bent down to tousle the girl's dark hair. "What is it, sweetie?"

"Are we a family now?"

"Yes we are, Anna." Michaela nodded as a tear of joy slid down her cheek. "We're a family." Michaela wiped her cheek, then stood to face Eric, still holding tight to Anna's fingers. "I can't believe my whole family's here. I don't ever remember feeling so happy, so complete."

"God does have marvelous ways of working things together for the good of His children, doesn't He?" Eric wrapped his strong arms firmly around her waist.

"Aunt Clara is happily married to Ben." Happiness radiated at Michaela's voice. "Philip realized he loved Caroline. But best of all is Anna. I have to thank God every day that couple decided to adopt only a little boy. I never imagined it would end this way."

Eric pulled Michaela closer.

"This isn't the end, Mrs. Johnson," he said and kissed her gently on the lips. "This is only the beginning."

Rebecca's Heart

Dedication

To Mariah Lauren, my precious daughter.
May you always seek Him first in everything you do.
And to my fantastic critique partners.
Thank you for taking this journey with me.

Prologue

R ebecca Ann Johnson, I'm about to make you the happiest girl in the world." Jake Markham pulled an envelope out of his pocket and handed it to her.

"I thought I already was the happiest girl in the world." Rebecca clutched the envelope between her fingers and laughed. "I'm marrying you tomorrow, aren't I?"

Jake leaned across the blue cushioned sofa and stole a kiss. Her heart fluttered at the intimate gesture as she studied his familiar profile. Curly fair hair framed his smooth face. Square jaw, clear blue eyes. A solid, muscular form from helping his father work the Markham farm.

Mrs. Jake Markham.

Tomorrow she'd become his wife and someday, she prayed, the mother of his children. Heat rose to her cheeks, and she turned back to the gift.

"What is it?" Rebecca didn't try to hold back her enthusiasm as she drew two slips of paper out of the offered envelope. "Train tickets?"

"They're your wedding present. I planned to give them to you tomorrow after the ceremony, but I couldn't wait."

"I don't understand." Rebecca's brows scrunched together. She scanned the details on the train tickets, her excitement over the gift quickly waning. "These are one-way tickets to Portland, Oregon."

"Exactly. It's what we've always dreamed about, Rebecca." Jake leaned forward and grasped her hands. "There's plenty of land. We can settle somewhere along the coast if you'd like, or maybe in the Willamette Valley. It's supposed to be beautiful. Snowcapped mountains, forests of thick evergreen trees—"

"Wait a minute." Her mind spun with the implications of the tickets she held. "I know we've talked about the possibility of settling out west someday, but I never thought you were considering leaving now. These tickets are for next month."

"I know." Jake's face erupted with a smile. "My father gave us three hundred dollars for a wedding gift. We don't have to wait any longer."

Rebecca stood and walked to the large front window of her parents' gray-shingled farmhouse and took a steadying breath. Cranton, nestled in the lush Connecticut Valley of western Massachusetts, had been her home for all of her nineteen years. One day she dreamed of seeing more of the world, but right now she wanted to enjoy being married before she had to take on the responsibilities of settling somewhere else.

He didn't even ask me what I thought.

Her fingers touched the windowpane as she stared out across the lush acres of farmland bordered with stone fences. Tall elm trees and stately pines rose from the rich soil. Mayflowers dotted the apple orchards to the south. The white blossoms of the hydrangea bushes were beginning to fade but for now still held their beauty. This was her home.

Jake crossed the room and stood beside her. "What's the matter, Rebecca? I thought you'd be excited."

Tears welled in her eyes. "You actually believed I'd be thrilled, despite the fact you never asked me what I thought before buying the tickets? I don't know if I'm ready to leave my family yet—"

"You're just nervous about tomorrow and not thinking clearly." Jake took another step toward her and ran his hand down the sleeve of her lavender day dress, but Rebecca pulled away. "We've talked about moving west—"

"You talked about it, and while I'm not against the idea, it was always something for us to consider for the future. Not now."

Unexpected anger seared through her like a hot iron. Her resentment didn't come from the fact he wanted to move away. She was hurt because he'd never asked her what she thought about leaving so soon after they were married.

Her hands curled into fists at her sides. "What in the world were you thinking, Jake Markham? Buying these tickets without even discussing the matter with me?"

"I thought you'd be happy."

The confused look that crossed his face didn't quell her anger. "What about my family and your father?" Rebecca paced across the hardwood floor to the other side of the room, pausing at the large stone fireplace. "Did you even stop to consider what they might think about this sudden move?"

"I've discussed it with my father, and he's excited for us. Told me if he were twenty years younger, he'd consider coming along." Jake raked his fingers through his hair. "If my mother were still alive, I know she'd feel the same way. As for your parents, I'm sure they'll be delighted you're getting such an opportunity."

"You've already told your father?" Folding her arms across her chest, Rebecca stomped her foot. "Is this how you see our marriage? You make all the decisions without even asking me what I think? Jake, I don't know if I can—"

He bridged the gap between them, and Rebecca felt his arms wrap around her. His lips pressed firmly against hers. For a moment she forgot why she was so angry as she yielded to his kiss. She loved Jake Markham and planned to spend the rest of her life with him. He was the one she'd dreamed of growing old with.

But he never considered asking me what I thought about the entire matter, Lord!

Rebecca pulled away from him, still feeling the pressure of his lips against hers. She touched her fingers to her mouth, the sweetness of his kiss slowly replaced by a swell of uneasiness in her heart.

"I thought this was what you wanted, Rebecca." His eyes pleaded with her to understand. "I just want to make you happy."

"No, Jake." She looked up at him and shook her head. "This is what you want. You don't know me at all."

And I don't know you either.

An hour later Rebecca smoothed her fingers across the silky white fabric of her wedding dress. She'd promised Jake she'd consider his decision, but today's experience had showed her something she now realized had been a part of their relationship all along.

She wanted a marriage like her parents'. Things hadn't always been easy for her father and stepmother. Both had lost their spouses years ago, and when they married each other, they brought seven children into the union. Still, despite the difficulties they'd faced, with God as the center of their relationship, they'd worked things out together.

That was the kind of marriage Rebecca wanted. Looking back, she realized this wasn't the first time Jake had made a decision concerning them both without consulting her first. Usually they were small incidences, but even when it came to the details of their wedding, Jake had made a number of decisions without her input.

He had been the one to set their wedding date and decide the minister from Springfield should perform the ceremony, not their well-loved preacher from Cranton. At the time it hadn't seemed to matter, but he always told her, never asked. It wasn't that she didn't respect God's roles for a husband and a wife, but could she live the rest of her life with a man who didn't respect her feelings?

Rebecca threw the dress on her bed and sat in front of her mirrored dresser. Undoing the French knot twisted at the back of her head, she began to brush out her long, dark hair. She'd allowed herself to get so caught up in the notion of being in love and taking care of wedding plans that she hadn't even noticed Jake's lack of concern over how she felt about matters. This time, though, he'd gone too far.

Suddenly everything was clear. If she married Jake Markham, she knew she'd be making the biggest mistake of her life. Her stomach clenched at the reality of what her decision meant. Come tomorrow, Jake would expect to see his bride walking down the aisle. Instead, Rebecca planned on being as far away from that altar as the train could take her.

Chapter 1

Eight months later

Rebecca held up the tailored slipcover for a closer inspection. Why couldn't her own life look as neat and orderly as the tiny, meticulous stitches in which she prided herself? She felt more like one of the jumbled spools of thread in her younger sister Sarah's sewing box. Twisted and tangled. Out of control.

She ran her fingers across the downy texture of the linen-and-cotton-blend fabric, fighting the all-too-familiar sense of restlessness. The indigo-on-white pattern of the lily blossom would work perfectly with Scarlet Bridge's padded chairs and sofa. *That* wasn't the source of her frustration. Already the material was beginning to take the shape of a stylish slipcover—one of Boston's fashion rages.

Rebecca finished the last few stitches of the chair cover and whispered a prayer of thankfulness that the front showroom of Macintosh Furniture and Upholstery was finally without customers. Despite their location on the outskirts of Boston, the store brought in a considerable number of wealthy clients from the city.

Letting out a deep sigh, she leaned back in her wooden chair and glanced around the showroom. Fine-quality chests of drawers made from imported wood, mahogany highboys, and dainty tea tables filled the room, along with a large assortment of bedsteads and dining tables. While many of the products the store sold were ready-made furniture, some, like the walnut dresser with its glossy marble top, were custom-made in the workroom in back of the store by Philip Macintosh and his employees.

It wasn't as though she didn't enjoy working for her stepmother's best friend, Caroline Macintosh. Quite the contrary. She'd always found pleasure in taking a plain strip of fabric and turning it into something useful. Before she left home, she'd been the one to sew the red gingham curtains that framed the large living room windows and the colorful slipcover that hid the faded sofa beneath it. Her father had always told her she had a knack for decorating, and she was thrilled she could finally put her talents to good use.

But for some reason, even the enjoyment of working with Caroline to fill

129

the numerous orders for slipcovers wasn't enough to squelch the edginess she felt inside.

Eight months ago she never would have imagined that she'd be sitting in Boston, surrounded by yards of brightly printed cottons and linens. At the time, the invitation from Philip and Caroline had seemed like the perfect solution. Once everyone had recovered from the shock of her calling off the wedding, Jake used his train ticket and left for Portland. Four weeks later she arrived in Boston.

Clipping a loose thread with a pair of scissors, Rebecca shook her head. Shouldn't she at least have a twinge of guilt over breaking Jake's heart? She still felt certain that marrying him would not have been God's will for her life, but she had yet to discover His plan for her. Marriage and children had always been her dream, and she thought she'd found what she was looking for with Jake. That is, until he presented her with those train tickets without one thought as to how she might feel. How could she have been so wrong about someone?

The back door to the workroom opened, pulling Rebecca out of her somber deliberations. Caroline, with her swollen abdomen and ever-pleasant smile, bustled into the room.

"Morning, Rebecca."

Rebecca set down the slipcover and forced a smile. "You're sure in high spirits today."

"I should be happy." Caroline hurried past a row of mahogany side chairs, then stopped to catch her breath at the tailor's bench where Rebecca worked. "I'm married to the most wonderful man in the world, I'm going to be a mother in five weeks, and"—she dropped a copy of the *Boston Herald* on the table—"look at this."

"What is it?"

Caroline sank into a padded chair across from Rebecca. "Our first advertisement."

Rebecca picked up the newspaper, scanning the page until she found the small ad halfway down.

Stylish Slipcovers!
Looking to update your parlor without spending a fortune?
Go to Macintosh Furniture and Upholstery Co.
Here you will find samples of our stylish slipcovers.
Tailor-made from brightly printed cottons,
these covers are a necessity for all households.
Remember—Macintosh Furniture and Upholstery Co.
is the only place you need to go.
C. Macintosh & R. Johnson

"R. Johnson." Rebecca frowned and laid the paper back down on the table. "You added my name?"

"Of course. You're the backbone of this venture." Caroline leaned forward and squeezed Rebecca's hand. "What's wrong? You don't look very happy."

"I don't know."

Biting the edge of her lip, Rebecca walked toward the front of the shop. Miniature replicas of ready-made furniture had been artistically arranged among yards of cream and gold silk fabric in front of the window, advertising their goods to everyone who walked by the brick-faced building. Leaning against the top of one of the hand-carved dressers, she stared past the colorful display to the bustle of traffic on the street outside and watched the busy scene unfold before her.

Everyone seemed to have a purpose and direction. Drivers traversed the cobblestone street toward known destinations. Pedestrians weaved carefully through the traffic to their next appointments. Was she the only one who didn't know where her life was headed?

"Do you ever question God's will for you?" Rebecca turned back to Caroline. She wanted to confide in her, but how could she when she didn't understand her own growing dissatisfaction? "I feel so unsure about everything."

"Do you still miss Jake?"

"No." Rebecca blinked back the tears and tried to work through the jumble of emotions so she could explain clearly how she felt. "I miss what we planned together—a home, children."

"You're twenty years old, Rebecca. You've got your whole life ahead of you and a God far bigger than any earthly problem. Trust Him to show you His plan for your life, in His timing."

Rebecca allowed a slight smile to cross her lips. "So you're telling me to have patience?"

"Patience isn't an easy virtue, is it?" Caroline ran her hand across her stomach and let out a soft chuckle. "There was a time when I was convinced it would take a whole lot more than patience to win Philip's heart."

Rebecca paced the length of the shop again, back to where Caroline sat. "What do you mean?"

"I don't know how much Michaela told you, but Philip was once quite smitten with her."

Rebecca's stepmother had told her parts of the story. In the end, it had been Eric Johnson, Rebecca's father, who had stolen Michaela's heart. And shortly after that, Philip had discovered Caroline was the one he truly loved. "I guess God does work things together for good."

"And the same is true for you. I believe coming here was God's will for you." Caroline picked up one of the slipcovers Rebecca had just finished and ran her hand across the fabric. "It's giving you time to figure out what you want to do with your life. Look at your work. God has given you an incredible gift. This is absolutely flawless."

"I do enjoy it."

Rebecca reclaimed her chair across from Caroline, smoothing out the silky folds of her Napoleon blue taffeta dress. Maybe this was the direction God had planned for her. She could help Caroline build up her business and maybe even open her own shop one day. Still, if living in Boston was God's will, then why did she feel such a stark emptiness inside? Something was missing, and she knew it wasn't Jake.

Caroline fingered one of her blond tresses. "Since you've been here, business has doubled because of referrals for your work. I may have had the inspiration of combining Philip's cabinetmaking business with the fabric slipcovers, but I'm not near the seamstress you are."

Rebecca dropped her gaze at the compliment. "I don't know about that—"

"It's true." Caroline waved her hand in the air. "Besides, after the baby comes, Philip is insisting I stay home more. I don't know what I'd do without you."

Rebecca smiled. It did feel good to be needed.

Caroline eased out of her chair. "Pretty soon I won't be able to stand without help."

Rebecca grabbed Caroline's hand to help her up and grinned. "Pretty soon you'll be holding your precious son or daughter in your arms."

"I can't wait." A warm, satisfied look swept across Caroline's face. "Which reminds me, I promised Philip I'd rest this afternoon. You don't mind watching the store, do you? Philip will be out back in the workroom if you need anything."

"Of course I don't mind. That's fine."

Caroline picked up the newspaper and pulled it to her chest. "Patience Hutton is supposed to drop by and pick up the rosewood table Philip repaired for her."

Rebecca began folding the leftover pieces of the indigo fabric and setting them in a pile. "He showed it to me this morning. It's beautiful."

"He did a good job. You can't even tell it was broken." Caroline paused at the bottom of the staircase that led to the apartment she and Philip shared above the store. "Have you met Mrs. Hutton yet?"

"I don't believe so."

Caroline leaned against the door frame. "Now there's a woman I'd love for us to get as a client."

"Why's that?"

"Her home is supposed to resemble a museum. She has a collection of silver pieces that have been passed down in her family for five generations, as well as all sorts of family heirlooms."

"How wonderful to be able to pass down treasures like that to your children."

Caroline nodded. "Now it's just her and her son. I believe he builds ships for a living, but the family was in the whaling business for several generations."

Rebecca set the last piece of folded fabric on the pile. "Did you know my grandfather was the captain of a whaling vessel?"

"Really? I've always thought that would be such a romantic profession."

Rebecca's eyes narrowed. "What's so romantic about waiting years for your husband to return from an expedition? The whaling and fishing industries are all horribly dangerous lines of work. My father once told me of a storm in which thirteen vessels went down carrying about a hundred and fifty fishermen. Think of all the widows and orphans those sailors left behind."

"All right, you have a point." Caroline's hazel eyes sparkled. "I was thinking more about the lovelorn bride waiting anxiously day after day for her husband to return from sea."

"Sounds like a tragedy to me."

"All of Shakespeare's romances ended in tragedy. *Romeo and Juliet*—"

"Enough." Rebecca laughed as she added the entire pile of scraps to the bin that held other bits and pieces of leftover fabric. "You're talking to a girl who only knows a tragic end to romance, unlike your happily-ever-after story with Philip."

"Your day will come, Rebecca. I have no doubt about it."

"Maybe, but for now I plan to leave tales of romance, tragic or not, to the storytellers."

A warm breeze off the Atlantic seaboard ruffled Luke Hutton's work shirt as he finished greasing the skids beneath the hardwood runners of the schooner he was building. He was eager for the day she would set sail. Boston's shipyards were full of clipper ships, whaling vessels, private yachts, and commercial fishing boats, but this one he was helping to build with his own hands.

Luke gazed out across the harbor and watched the stately crafts bob in the sparkling blue coastal waters. Folding his arms across his chest, he let out a contented sigh. The smell of the ocean permeated the air, and he could taste the salt from the Atlantic on his lips. It was something he couldn't deny. The sea was in his blood.

"She's going to be a fine sailing vessel, young man." Dwight Nevin stepped onto the deck behind Luke, inspecting the work he'd just completed.

"You're right, sir." Luke turned to greet his boss. "She's a beauty."

Working for Dwight Nevin as a ship's carpenter had been a dream come true. In many ways, Mr. Nevin was the father figure Luke had longed for after the death of his own. And he didn't disapprove of Luke saying exactly what was on his mind. Something he was prone to do.

Luke grinned at the redheaded Irishman, who at fifty-five was as fit as any sailor. "I still predict that one day soon the demand for private yachts will overtake commercial boats."

"Never." Mr. Nevin shook his head and frowned, but Luke didn't miss the sparkle in his eyes.

"With all due respect, sir, it's already happening. Summer resorts are bringing in more tourists every year, while the fishing industry is dwindling. We're seeing an increase in land values along the coast as towns are being influenced by the influx of visitors."

The older man waved his hand in front of him. "A few tourists will never make that much of an impact. The entire commercial fishing industry will never die down."

"Like the whaling industry, sir?"

"Okay, you've made your point." Mr. Nevin groaned and started up the narrow wooden plank toward the small building used as an office for the modest shipbuilding company. "Let the tourists have their fun. Fishing's been a way of life for my family for the past four generations. And your family, too. It's in our blood."

"Maybe, but the future isn't in whaling anymore." A seagull cried out above him as Luke hurried to follow his boss up the plank. "We—you—ought to be looking more into the private sector. You could double, triple, your business if you wanted to."

"Business is fine."

"True, but what about tomorrow? Just think about it. Twenty years ago whaling was a highly profitable business, but now kerosene has replaced the need for whale oil and candles."

Mr. Nevin stopped and blew out a labored sigh. "What does your mother think about this?"

"My mother's like you. She refuses to think that things might be changing."

"You're going out again on a whaling expedition, though, aren't you?"

Luke tugged at his shirt collar, sorry for the reminder. It wasn't as if he dreaded the trip. Sailing would always be a part of him, but lately his interest had focused on building the crafts. "I leave in a month. But this will be my last trip."

"Have you told your mother it will be your final voyage?"

"My mother believes it's God's will for me to captain my own vessel some-day. So far nothing I have said or done, including working for you, has helped alter what she believes to be true."

"What you need to do is to find yourself a nice girl and settle down."

Luke frowned at the older man. He'd heard the very same comment a dozen times. "What 'nice girl' is going to wait three years for me to come back?"

"Find the right girl, and she'll wait."

Luke scuffed the wooden plank with his boot and shook his head. "Not likely, sir."

"Well, I'll tell you one thing, Luke Hutton. You've got initiative, that's for sure. If you can survive the next few years battling the sea, and if I can survive my wife's constant nagging, when you get back I'll have a job waiting for you."

Two hours later, Luke stepped into Macintosh Furniture and Upholstery and breathed in the mixture of cedar, pine, and fresh wood shavings. While building boats was his passion, he'd dabbled with carpentry enough to respect the exper-tise it demanded. And from what he'd heard, Philip Macintosh's craftsmanship was some of the finest in the area.

"May I help you?"

Luke's gaze turned from a skillfully carved table and stopped at the dark-haired beauty who stood in the center of the showroom. "Yes. I'm—I'm here to pick up a table for my mother, Patience Hutton."

Luke took a step backward, annoyed at his sudden awkwardness. What was wrong with him? His boss mentioned he should settle down, and suddenly the next pretty girl he sees is marriage material?

The young woman clasped her hands in front of her. "I was expecting her to come by."

"It was on my way home. I hope it's not a problem."

She laughed then shook her head. "It's not a problem who picks it up. I just meant that we were expecting her this afternoon. The table's ready."

"Good—I know she'll be pleased."

"But you haven't seen the table yet."

Luke cleared his throat. Why was everything he tried to say coming out wrong? "Is there a problem with it?"

"No, but I do want to make sure you're satisfied with the work before you take it."

"Of course."

"If you'll come with me, you can look at it." She headed toward the back of the store, letting him follow. "It's a beautiful piece."

"It's one of my mother's favorites." Luke stopped at the table and ran his fingers across the polished top. "Unfortunately, a recent guest of ours managed to knock it over, cracking the narrow leg."

"That's a shame, but if you take a close look, I don't think you'll even be able to tell where the crack was."

Luke examined the curved leg of the table and smiled. "Excellent work. The wood has been matched to perfection, and the seam is even."

"Do you know a lot about carpentry?"

"Not tables and chairs, per se." Luke rubbed his hands together and caught her gaze. Dark brown eyes stared back at him, and he wondered suddenly what was hidden behind them. He'd heard the laughter in her voice but hadn't missed the unmistakable look of sadness. "I've been working for Dwight Nevin as his apprentice. Right now we're building a fifty-foot, two-masted, rigged schooner."

"For fishing or cargo shipments?"

Luke's eyes widened in surprise at her question. "This one is going to be for fishing. Are you interested in the boating industry?"

A dimple appeared in her right cheek when she smiled. "My grandfather was the captain of a whaling vessel. While I never knew him, I've always been fascinated by the sea and the stories it has to tell."

"I come from a long line of whalers, as well." For some reason he didn't want their conversation to end. The table was finished. There was nothing holding him here except one thing. "I'm Luke Hutton, by the way."

"Rebecca Johnson." She shook his hand, then brushed back a wisp of her coal black hair. "I'm related to Philip Macintosh by marriage. Actually, it's a bit complicated. He's the brother-in-law of my stepmother."

"So you have a big family?" He picked up the small table and tried to tell himself her answer didn't interest him. But it did.

Rebecca laughed again. "You could say that. Three brothers and two sisters. Then Anna was adopted into our family, making it seven."

Luke let out a low whistle. "I'm an only child. My father passed away, so now it's just me and my mother." He needed to go, but something about her urged him to stay and prolong their talk. "Have you lived here long? I've been in the shop once or twice before. I don't remember ever seeing you."

"I recently moved here from Cranton."

"Cranton." He searched his memory for information on the small town in western Massachusetts. "That's not far from the Connecticut River, I believe?"

"Yes. It's a beautiful place. Lush farmland, lazy brooks, apple orchards. . . I loved it there."

He caught the look of sadness in her eyes again. Maybe she was simply homesick. He knew from experience that Boston could be an overwhelming city. Hadn't he felt the same way on his last return from sea? The bustling metropolitan area was a stark contrast to the seclusion of life on deck. And Cranton was nothing more than a sleepy little farming community.

"Would it be too bold if I ask why you left?"

She started for the front of the shop. This time he matched her stride and walked beside her. "Caroline, Philip's wife, decided it might be good for business to expand beyond tables and chairs and start offering custom-made slipcovers to their patrons. Business was growing so quickly that she needed the extra help. I thought Boston would be a nice change."

"Slipcovers?"

Rebecca paused at a well-crafted mahogany sideboard and turned to him. "I know they don't take nearly as much skill as fine furniture, but they do seem to be the rage right now—"

"No, it's a great idea." Luke hoisted the table against his hip. "Expanding on the clientele you already have. In fact, my mother mentioned just last week how she thought slipcovers would be perfect in the parlor."

Her hand traced the carved inlay atop the sideboard. Long, slender fingers. Skin the color of cream—

"You could bring your mother by tomorrow if you'd like," Rebecca said, putting a halt to his wandering thoughts. "I could show her samples of what we can do."

He shouldn't. He should turn and walk out of the shop and forget ever meeting Miss Rebecca Johnson. Instead, he caught her gaze and smiled. "That's a wonderful idea."

⁂

Luke placed his mother's table carefully in the back of the buggy, all the time wondering why he'd just told Miss Johnson he'd be back. He knew his return had nothing to do with showing his mother samples of slipcovers and everything to do with seeing her again.

He flicked the reins, urging his palomino to hurry home. His last whaling voyage had taken three and a half years, and considering he was weeks away from departing on his second trip, it made no sense to pursue this unexplained—and unwelcome—attraction to Rebecca Johnson.

It simply wasn't possible. Problem was, he did yearn for a wife and a family. Yet by the time he returned from sea, he'd be close to thirty years old—and no closer to marriage than he was now.

Chapter 2

Rebecca pulled out another piece of brightly printed cotton and held it up for Patience Hutton to examine. It was the fifth sample she'd shown the older woman in the last hour. Up to this point, nothing had been acceptable.

"What do you think about this one?" Rebecca waited as Mrs. Hutton fingered the fabric.

In Rebecca's opinion, the color combination was perfect for the stylish parlor. The shades of light green, delft blue, and sunny yellow would make stunning slipcovers without overpowering the classical style of the room.

Rebecca leaned forward on the elegant Grecian sofa, watching the older woman's reaction. She'd been disappointed when, instead of a visit from Luke Hutton, she'd received a message from his mother requesting her to come to their home. No matter how hard she tried, she hadn't been able to forget those penetrating brown eyes that reminded her of the syrup her brother Adam made each winter from his sugar maple trees. Luke's gaze had caused her heart to tremble, something she hadn't expected—or wanted. Still, the thought of seeing the broad-shouldered, muscular shipbuilder again had kept her dreams flavored with the sweetness of his gaze.

Taking the sample of fabric from Rebecca, Mrs. Hutton walked toward the window, smoothing back a loose strand of silver hair that had fallen from the neat pile atop her head. The bustle of her elegant silk dress rustled as she turned to Rebecca and smiled. "This one is perfect."

Rebecca let out a sigh of relief. After arriving at the Hutton home, she'd learned that not only did Patience Hutton have a stunning place as Caroline had told her, but she was also a woman who was hard to please. No doubt keeping her happy throughout the project would be a challenge.

"And what about the windows?" Mrs. Hutton held the fabric up to the light.

Rebecca nodded at the suggestion. "We could easily hang panels from a cornice using the same fabric."

"Simple but elegant. I like that." Mrs. Hutton sat back down on the sofa, still holding the fabric sample. "Funny, something about the colors reminds me of my childhood home. My mother was Dutch, and our home was filled with delft blue pieces of earthenware from Holland."

"I believe I saw several of them in your curio cabinet?"

"Yes." Mrs. Hutton smiled, obviously pleased Rebecca had noticed.

Those decorations hadn't been the only thing Rebecca noted. In a brief tour of the downstairs, she'd studied the numerous pieces of furniture. Most of them, she judged, had been fabricated prior to the Revolution. A Baltimore clock with its fine inlaid design of vines and leaves, a Sheraton-styled secretary with painted-glass panels, and a number of ornately carved tables. The walls were filled with tapestries, portraits of family members, and a number of detailed needlework pieces.

"Have you always lived in Boston?" Rebecca began gathering the samples she'd brought with her, pleased that having chosen the fabric she could begin making the slipcovers.

"I spent most of my life on Nantucket Island. My late husband and I came to Boston only eighteen months before he died. For some reason I've never wanted to move back. Too many memories, I suppose."

Rebecca's eyes widened with interest. "My mother's parents lived their whole lives on Nantucket Island."

"Really? What were their names?"

"Edmund and Margaret Stevens, but only my grandmother is still alive."

Her face beaming with delight, Mrs. Hutton clapped her hands. "I knew your grandparents well when my husband and I lived on the island. In fact, I still stay in touch with your grandmother."

"Unfortunately, when my mother married my father, it caused a rift in the family." Rebecca placed the last square of fabric, a blend of dark purple and gold, into her large tapestry bag. "I haven't seen my grandmother since I was a little girl."

"I admit, she rarely talked about her family but did mention your mother a few times." Mrs. Hutton let out a soft laugh. "I truly am sorry to hear that you never got to know her, but Margaret always was stubborn. To be honest, it doesn't surprise me one bit."

"My mother used to tell me stories of my grandmother's beautiful flower garden and my grandfather's whaling ship, the *Lady Amaryllis*." Rebecca smiled at the memories. "I'd love to hear more."

"I have an idea. Why don't you stay for lunch?" Mrs. Hutton patted Rebecca's hand. "That will give us time to talk. I believe we're having Irish stew."

Thrilled for the opportunity to learn more about her grandparents, Rebecca nodded. "I'd like that. Thank you."

"First, though, come with me. I want to show you something."

Rebecca stood at the window of Mrs. Hutton's bedroom, admiring the view of the blossoming gardens from the large windows while the older woman rummaged through the bottom drawer of the secretary. Massive oak trees rose up from the green earth, tall and proud, their leaves blowing in the soft wind. Flowers spilled across the edges of the manicured lawn, a stunning mosaic of yellows, oranges, pinks, and reds. Inside, the room was like the rest of the house, full of beautiful furniture, thick carpets, and heavy drapes.

With a large folder in her hands, Mrs. Hutton sat on a padded ottoman and motioned for Rebecca to join her. "I don't even remember the last time I looked at these."

"What are they?" Curious, Rebecca sat down beside her.

"My late husband, Isaac, was quite an artist. He never tired of drawing portraits of friends and family." One by one, she pulled out the illustrations, each full of remarkable detail.

"Here. This is what I wanted to show you. These are your grandparents."

Rebecca's breath caught in her throat as she took the drawing and held it. "When did he do this?"

"I'd say about twenty-five years ago. I remember this picture in particular. We'd just celebrated your grandmother's fortieth birthday. Isaac sketched this portrait of them in the garden."

Tears welled in Rebecca's eyes as she ran her finger across the bottom edge of the paper. In the hands of a true artist, the charcoal pencil had managed to capture every detail of their expressions—including the mischievous twinkle in her grandfather's eye.

"Grandfather looks as if he's up to something."

Mrs. Hutton laughed. "He always did have that Cheshire grin, and yes, he was a prankster, too. You'd think that being the captain of a whaling ship he'd be a bit more serious, but not your grandfather."

"And my grandmother?" Rebecca studied the drawing that had captured the curves of her full face and the soft curls that framed her hair. "What is she like? She's beautiful in this picture."

"And still is. She was always the serious one, though."

Rebecca looked back to Mrs. Hutton. "Do you know why she cut off contact with my mother?"

"Knowing Margaret the way I do, I'd have to say it was her pride." Mrs. Hutton shook her head slowly. "When your father moved your mother away from the island, it broke her heart. She never learned how to love and let go."

"She sent us a piano for Christmas one winter, thinking it would help us become more cultured." For the first time, Rebecca caught a glimpse of what she'd missed all these years, and it filled her with a sense of regret and longing. "I think that was the last time we heard from her. She didn't even come for my mother's funeral."

"If only your grandfather had been alive. He would have talked some sense into her."

"I've thought about going to see her. Nantucket Island's not too far from Boston. I don't know why I've put it off so long."

"She's not on the island right now."

Rebecca raised her brows in question. "Where is she?"

"The last time I saw her, she was preparing to leave for England."

"England?" Rebecca frowned. Had she lost her grandmother just when she'd finally realized what she'd been missing?

"Your grandmother came to America when she was only seventeen. She'd always wanted to return to the village in which she grew up."

"When is she coming back?"

"Late fall at the earliest. She promised to contact me on her return."

Rebecca didn't understand a number of things about her parents' relationship with her grandmother. Nevertheless, as soon as she came back from England, she would make a point of visiting her on the island.

Rebecca thumbed through the rest of the drawings, stopping at a picture of a young boy. "Is this Luke?"

"You can tell?" Mrs. Hutton's wrinkled hand touched the edge of the drawing. "He was only seven years old when his father drew this."

"He has the same eyes and dark full brows." Trying to cover her interest, Rebecca turned to the next page. "Luke was a handsome child."

"*Was* handsome?"

Rebecca turned to the doorway at Luke's voice, letting the portrait flutter onto her lap. He stood there, his lips turned into a half grin. Her stomach lurched. Broad shoulders, square jawline, dark, wavy hair. He shouldn't affect her this way. But he did.

"I. . ." Rebecca struggled to regain her composure. "Your mother was just showing me some of your father's drawings. Your parents knew my grandparents on Nantucket Island."

Luke caught her gaze, sending her stomach reeling. "It's quite a small world, isn't it?"

"Your timing is perfect, Luke." Mrs. Hutton smiled at her son as she gathered the pictures. "You can join us for lunch."

Luke's mouth watered as a generous helping of stew was set in front of him. He'd managed to get away for lunch, and after seeing Rebecca again, he wasn't a bit sorry he'd cut his morning's work short. Her yellow dress, shimmering in the midday sunlight that filtered through the large open window, brought out glints of gold in her dark eyes. She wore her hair the same way as the last time he'd seen her, parted in the center and secured at the nape of her neck, with short, curly bangs framing her heart-shaped face.

"Luke? Haven't you heard a word we've said?"

Luke shot his mother a sheepish grin and set his spoon in his bowl. "Sorry, Mother—my mind must have been wandering."

"You spend far too much time thinking about that boat you're building." Mrs. Hutton pressed her napkin to her lips. "Of course I can't complain too much." She turned her gaze to Rebecca. "It's good to have him around. One of these days he'll find himself a good wife, and I'll be wishing he was back."

Luke stifled a laugh, wondering what his mother would say if she knew what he had been thinking. Finding a wife had never been a priority in his life. Not until lately, anyway. Right now he could hardly keep his eyes off the dark-haired beauty seated across the table. Rebecca smiled at him, and Luke looked away, trying to ignore the strange sensation coursing through his veins.

"I was saying how amazing it is that I knew Rebecca's grandparents so well," his mother said, interrupting his thoughts again.

Luke took a sip of his water. "Of course, with both our families in the whaling business, it certainly makes sense that our paths would cross."

Rebecca's cheeks flushed slightly as she turned to him. "Your mother's promised to tell me about my grandparents."

With the main course cleared away, dessert was served. The lemon cake tasted perfect, but at the moment, all Luke noticed was Rebecca. The clock in the corner of the dining room chimed two o'clock. He needed to get back to work but instead lingered at the table, laughing at his mother's anecdotes from years gone by.

"What brought about the changes in my grandmother?" Rebecca set her fork down, letting it clink softly against the blue china plate. "The picture you paint of my grandparents is nothing like the one I know. Your descriptions make them seem so happy and full of life."

"Honestly, I don't know." Scooting back slightly from the table, Luke's mother folded her hands in her lap. "I'd always felt rather close to Margaret; then gradually we began to drift apart. I noticed subtle changes at first, and I never knew what started it. I'm thankful that in the past few years our friendship has resumed."

Rebecca stared out the open window, a trace of sadness marking her expression. "Maybe I'll have that chance someday, as well."

Setting her napkin on the table, Luke's mother stood. "I hate to cut our lunch short, but I am due shortly at the Mills Street Orphanage to speak to Agnes about an upcoming fund-raiser I'm coordinating."

Rebecca smiled, bringing out the now-familiar dimple in her cheek. "Thank you so much for inviting me to lunch, Mrs. Hutton."

"It was a pleasure meeting you, and we'll be sure to do this again soon. Luke, why don't you walk Rebecca home? I know she would appreciate the company."

Rebecca shook her head. "That's not necessary, really. I'm sure you must get back to work."

Luke paused for a moment, wondering if Rebecca was just being considerate or if she really did want him as her escort. Unable to stop himself, he grinned. He certainly wasn't going to throw away a chance to get to know her better. "It's not a problem at all. I'd be delighted."

Chapter 3

Laughing aloud at one of Rebecca's stories about her siblings, Luke permitted himself to glance at her profile as they strolled down the paved walkway. The Atlantic Ocean, its whitecaps spraying as the tides rolled in, spread beyond them to the east, the bustling city to the west. He breathed in the smell of saltwater that permeated the air, bringing with it the sense of freedom he always felt when he was near the ocean. Today, though, it wasn't simply the allure of the sea reeling him in.

Catching the smile that fluttered across Rebecca's lips, Luke grinned. There was something about Rebecca that had captured his interest from the moment they met at the furniture shop. While her beauty couldn't be argued, he was well aware there was much more to her than a lovely face. In the short time he'd been around her, he'd seen her intelligence coupled with a sense of wit.

"You really didn't have to walk me back to the shop, though I do appreciate it." Rebecca turned to him briefly, allowing him another peek into her mahogany-shaded eyes. He had no doubt this was a place in which he could get lost if he allowed himself the chance.

"I don't mind, really." He shoved his hands into his pockets. "My mother seems pleased with what you have planned for the parlor."

"It took quite awhile for her to choose which fabric she wanted to use." Rebecca chuckled softly, then stopped to gaze across the water, which was sprinkled with dozens of stately vessels. "With that decision made I'll be able to start working."

Motioning toward the northern part of the harbor, Luke pointed out his boss's shipyard. "That's where I'm learning the shipbuilding trade. Dwight Nevin's one of the best."

"What kind of crafts do you build? I believe you mentioned you were currently working on a two-masted, rigged schooner?"

"You have a good memory." Luke grasped the wooden rail beside Rebecca and stared out across the crystal blue water, glad for the opportunity to prolong their walk. "We mainly build commercial cargo and fishing boats, though we have worked on a couple of yachts. I'm trying to convince my boss that the private sector is the way of the future. Not that there won't be a need for the commercial side, of course, but more and more people are pouring money into crafts simply for pleasure."

"Seems a bit extravagant to me."

Luke laughed. "You're exactly right. It's unbelievable what people will spend their money on. Believe it or not, one man had an electrically ventilated dairy built on his yacht where he keeps a cow so he can have fresh milk every morning for breakfast."

Rebecca's eyes widened. "Surely you're joking?"

"Not at all." He smiled, remembering that he'd reacted the same way when first told about the infamous yacht. "Of course, most boats are built to be more practical. Even the private ones."

"I've always thought the ships were so majestic. I think I could stand here for hours, just gazing across the water."

Luke cleared his throat. Before he listened any longer to what his heart was telling him, he needed her to know he was involved in far more than merely building vessels for others to pilot. "Rebecca, there's something I need to tell you—"

"Look at that one. Isn't she beautiful?" Rebecca had turned away from him, missing his last words. The wind tugged at her hair as she pointed at the craft, its white sails blowing in the wind.

"It's a whaling vessel." Luke watched the ship as it headed out to sea, another reminder of his own upcoming voyage. "You'll see fewer and fewer these days than you did twenty or thirty years ago. Soon they'll be nothing more than a reminder of the past."

"That may be true, but there will always be fishermen of one kind or another. Those sailors have such dangerous jobs." Rebecca shuddered despite the warmth of the breeze blowing off the ocean. "I've been thinking a lot about my grandmother. I can't help but wonder if part of the reason she became so cold and distant was because of my grandfather's work. I couldn't imagine living like that. Having to wait, month after month, year after year, for the return of your loved one."

Luke's fingers pressed against the rail. He had planned to tell her the truth, but her words stopped him. No matter how strong the attraction he felt toward her, he was fooling himself to think that anything could come of their newfound friendship. How could he have considered courting her with such little time remaining until his next voyage? And even if she did feel something toward him, he knew now she'd never wait for him. She'd just made that clear.

Turning abruptly on his heels, Luke faced her, forcing a smile. "I'd better get you back to the shop. Mr. Nevin's expecting me at work this afternoon."

Ten minutes later, Rebecca stood at the front door of Macintosh Furniture and Upholstery, watching Luke merge into the busy crowd of pedestrians. His friendly but curt good-bye had made her certain something had happened between his mother's home and the shop, but for the life of her she had no idea what. She'd been confused by the sudden change in his demeanor at the waterfront. In fact, up until that point, she'd even thought she detected a hint of interest on his part. Maybe she was imagining things.

The bell above the door jingled as Rebecca stepped into the shop, thankful it was empty of customers. She laid her bag of fabric samples on the tailor's bench and sank into one of the chairs. It didn't make sense. Maybe she'd been the only one who'd felt the attraction as they talked about common interests such as baseball, politics, and spiritual matters. Of course, she'd been wrong once before when it came to love and marriage. Was God trying to tell her something again?

Rebecca looked up as Caroline entered the showroom from the back.

"How was your afternoon with Mrs. Hutton?" Caroline asked.

"I thought you were supposed to be taking a nap after lunch."

"I'll be on my way upstairs in a minute. Philip asked me to watch the shop momentarily while he stepped out." She rested her hands across the top of her widening stomach. "You didn't answer my question."

Rebecca pulled the pieces of fabric she'd shown to Mrs. Hutton out of her bag and laid them with the rest of the samples. "It was fine. After about an hour, she finally decided on the fabric. It's going to look stunning once it's completed. Then she invited me for lunch."

"Really? That's wonderful. I've heard she's a difficult woman to please. You must have done quite well."

Rubbing the satiny material between her fingers, Rebecca smiled. "Her son ate with us, and the food was wonderful. Irish stew and dumplings—"

"I'm not interested in the menu." Caroline held up her hand and laughed. "What about her son? I have the impression you're leaving out some rather important details to this story."

Rebecca lowered her gaze. The last thing she was interested in at the moment was having a discussion about Luke Hutton. "I'm not leaving anything out."

Caroline sat across from Rebecca and rested her elbows against the table. "And I'm not carrying an extra twenty-five pounds around my waist."

Rebecca laughed but felt the heat rush to her cheeks. "Yes, I met Mrs. Hutton's son, Luke, but it's not an important detail. What is important is that not only does Mrs. Hutton want slipcovers made up for the furniture in her parlor; she wants matching drapes, as well."

Caroline leaned back in her chair. "I'm getting the feeling that Luke is quite good-looking, and you're a tad smitten. Am I right?"

Rebecca let out a low moan. "There's more to men than their looks, Caroline."

"Absolutely, but a handsome face added to the package can't hurt. So is he?"

"Is he what?"

Caroline grinned. "Handsome, of course."

"He's very good-looking." If Rebecca closed her eyes, she knew she would be able to see every detail of his face, from his maple-brown eyes to the slight cleft in his chin. Instead, she stared at the swirls of yellows and blues in the fabric in front of her, willing the image to vanish. "He builds ships, as you told me, and for now lives at home with his mother. Most important, though, he has a strong faith and is very active in his church."

"And you discovered all of this over lunch?"

Rebecca pursed her lips. "He walked me to the shop."

"Now the story's getting interesting."

Rebecca rose from the table and began gathering the supplies she would need in the morning. She had to return to the Hutton home and take the measurements for the slipcovers. Then most of the work would be completed right here in the shop—a place where she wouldn't run into Luke again.

"Rebecca. . ."

"The story ends there." Rebecca shrugged her shoulder. "I don't know what happened, but we were standing at the waterfront, looking at the ships, and all of a sudden his whole demeanor changed. I must have said something wrong."

"Surely you're imagining things."

"I don't know about that. But even if I didn't, what if I make another wrong decision again?"

Caroline leaned forward and covered Rebecca's hand with her own. "Just because Jake turned out to be someone other than the man you thought he was doesn't mean the next beau who comes along will be the same."

Rebecca shook her head. "Maybe, but I do know one thing. I don't think I'm ready to risk another broken heart."

❧

Luke slathered the thick slice of bread with butter then rummaged in the icebox for a slab of leftover ham. Moonlight filtered through the kitchen window, leaving shadows dancing along the walls. The clock chimed one, reminding him of what he already knew. He should be in bed sound asleep. Instead, he hadn't been able to tame his roaming thoughts, leaving him tense and restless.

His sandwich made, Luke slumped into one of the wooden kitchen chairs and took a bite.

"Luke?"

Dropping his sandwich onto the plate, Luke's gaze shifted to the kitchen doorway. "Mother, I'm sorry if I woke you."

"Couldn't sleep?"

He shook his head. "Not a wink."

"Mind if I join you?" His mother pulled the tie of her silk robe tighter around her waist. "The smell of fresh yeast bread aroused my appetite."

"There's plenty left. You know, your cook is spoiling me."

"Just trying to make up for the bland fare you'll be eating at sea." Luke's mother bustled to the counter and made herself a sandwich before joining him back at the table. "Care to let me take a guess at your problem?"

Picking up a crumb with his forefinger, Luke smiled at his mother. "Take a shot. You always were better at figuring me out than I was."

"Let's see. The first clue would be the way you looked at a certain young woman today over lunch. And if that wasn't enough, the sparkle in your eyes as you left to walk her home is more than enough evidence of a man smitten by the aforementioned woman."

"You sound more like a prosecutor than my mother." Luke let out a long groan. "It's that obvious?"

"To your mother? Yes. To her? I'm not so sure. Though I did notice how flustered she became at your arrival."

Pushing his plate away, Luke rested his elbows on the table. "You know I can't think about courting her—or anyone for that matter."

"Why not? Look at your father and me. We married six weeks from the day we met. A bit shocking to many people, I agree, but sometimes you meet someone and know they're the one. A month later your father left on a three-year voyage."

Luke raked his fingers through his hair. "We stood and watched the boats in the harbor on the way to the shop. She mentioned how she couldn't imagine waiting for someone she loved to return from sea."

"So you never told her you're a whaler?"

"I was going to. Then she started talking about how dangerous the profession is. Instead of telling her the truth, I told her I needed to get her back to the shop."

"I like her, Luke. A lot. But that doesn't mean she's the one for you. The sea is in your blood, and you're going to have to find someone who feels the same way. Someone who will allow you to be who you are."

But is that who I am, Lord?

Luke shook his head. "You're right, Mother. It is in my blood, but that doesn't mean I'm going to spend the rest of my life at sea. I want a family someday. And not one I have to leave behind for years at a time."

"The right girl will wait for you. I waited for your father during each of his voyages, never regretting my decision to marry him."

Luke sighed. He'd heard the stories many times of how his mother had kept busy, counting the months that went by at his grandmother's bakery, while his father sailed the world. That wasn't the life he wanted. He was committed to the next voyage and aimed to keep his word to Captain Taft, but after that he was going to retire from sea life. Whether Rebecca would still be around when he returned. . . that was a whole other question.

Chapter 4

*O**nly two weeks left.*

Luke took in a deep breath of humid air and sighed at the somber thought. The ocean, with its green and blue hues, spread out beside him like a well-polished gem. Gulls glided above the sparkling waters in search of their morning prey. Boats bobbed along ripples that moved across the surface of the sea, some of their occupants likely seeking a day's wage in a good catch, others seeking pleasure beneath the warm sun.

Captain Taft would set sail out of this very harbor in a mere fourteen days, yet for Luke the call to stay ashore grew stronger by the hour. And it was all because of the woman who had unexpectedly entered his life—and perhaps a corner of his heart. Rebecca Johnson happened to be everything he'd imagined he could want in a wife. But the timing couldn't be worse.

He'd managed to see her often these past couple of weeks. While she worked on slipcovers and draperies, he'd found excuses to stop by the furniture shop with various messages from his mother regarding the decorating project or found ways to be at home while Rebecca worked. And he'd never been disappointed with a moment of their time together. He felt himself drawn to so many things about her. Not only was she pretty and intelligent; she was hardworking, conscientious. . .and he was leaving.

Something he still hadn't told her.

Unlike his father, he could never rush into a relationship, marry, then leave on another voyage. He would never be able to leave behind a family while he went away for years at a time merely to bring home a ship full of cargo that would add to the country's supply of lamp oil, candles, medicines, and perfumes. The call of the sea might be in his blood, but he saw no reason to be a whaler simply because his father was a whaler. Whatever the realities of the situation he knew to be true in his head, his heart couldn't shake the draw he felt to get to know Rebecca better despite the short time he had left.

The piercing cries of street vendors broke into his thoughts. The rancid smell of fish from a fishmonger's cart filled his nostrils. Carriages, wagons, and traps congested the street beside him. Pedestrians hurried along the storefronts. Escaping this hubbub of activity was one reason he loved the ocean's solitude.

The peace and quiet he found there made up for the backbreaking work and long hours—but even the lure of the sea never completely took away the deeper loneliness he felt. The endless expanse of water could never give him the cherished relationship between a man and a woman.

"Please, mister, 'ere's a beauty."

Luke stopped in front of a street vendor, a little girl selling small bouquets of colorful flowers. She was clothed in filthy rags, her hair oily and matted; it seemed the beautiful, sweet-smelling arrangement had fared better than she. Normally he never noticed the street vendors who spent their days hawking. Selling everything from newspapers to cheese, oysters to peanuts, pies to bottled water, these vendors were simply a part of the city's bustling backdrop with their shrill cries, blowing of tin horns, or tinkling of bells.

For some reason the pinched, haunted look on the girl's face made him take a closer look. He'd spent the noon hour sampling delicious fish chowder with vegetables and sweet bread pudding for dessert, served by his mother's cook. This girl had more than likely eaten nothing but a slice of bread all day, if that.

Luke reached into his pocket and pulled out a few coins. "What's your name?"

The tousled-haired little girl's eyes widened at the question. Instead of answering, she held up one of the bouquets. "Only twenty cents, mister."

He counted out the money, then repeated the question.

The girl's head lowered as she handed him the bouquet. "Mandie."

Luke counted out another twenty cents and handed it to the girl. "Mandie, I want you to find yourself something good to eat tonight."

Before she could object, Luke stuffed the money in her sweaty palm and hurried away. Something should be done about the conditions of children like Mandie, who had to work long hours on the streets for mere pennies. Within five minutes the brick-faced building housing Macintosh Furniture and Upholstery stood before him, and he'd all but forgotten the little street vendor.

※

Humming quietly to herself, Rebecca finished stitching the hem of the drapery panel that would soon grace the window of Patience Hutton's parlor. Slipcovers adorned the two sofas and matching chairs, and the effect was stunning. Tomorrow Rebecca would hang the curtains, and the room's new décor would be complete. Mrs. Hutton had told Rebecca she was pleased with her work. So pleased, in fact, she'd mentioned the possibility of Rebecca's redecorating the sitting room and Mrs. Hutton's bedroom as well.

Placing the scraps of extra fabric in the already full bin, Rebecca ran her hand through the pile of material whose various patterns now enhanced parlors all over Boston and contemplated the idea that had been forming in her mind throughout the morning. She held up one of the fabric scraps she'd used from Mrs. Hutton's green, blue, and yellow slipcovers and smiled, imagining the vivid colors brightening the beds inside the Mills Street Orphanage. Yes. Her idea would work. It might take a bit of coordinating with some of the women at church, but she had no doubt Caroline and maybe even Mrs. Hutton would be eager to get involved with the worthwhile venture.

To finish the project before the cold Boston winter set in, she'd have to work longer hours to complete not only Mrs. Hutton's work but also the work for the half dozen other clients for whom she was currently commissioned to make slipcovers. But her time would be well spent.

Rebecca glanced up as the bell over the front door of the shop rang, announcing a customer. She drew in a quick breath as Luke, wearing a crisp shirt and coffee-colored trousers, made his way through the row of furniture toward the tailor's bench where she sat surrounded by bolts of colorful fabric.

"Good morning, Rebecca."

"Luke. What a pleasant surprise."

Rebecca smiled, noting the sparkle in his eyes, and hoped this unannounced visit truly was a pleasant occasion for him, as well. This wasn't the first time in the past couple of weeks Luke had dropped by the store unexpectedly with a message for her from his mother. His last visit came with an invitation to his mother's sixtieth birthday party, which would be held at the Hutton home the following evening. Still, if she were to guess, she was quite sure most of the reasons behind his visits were purely concocted as excuses to see her. It was a thought that left her smiling inwardly despite the fact that she had no intentions of letting her feelings for Luke go any further than the friendship they now shared. Jake had done more than enough to cause her to think twice about falling in love again.

Luke's tall, muscular figure towered over her, and she noticed the sharp contrast between the white shirt he wore and his skin, perfectly tanned from hours spent in the shipyard. As much as she wanted to fight it, she couldn't help the flutter of butterflies his presence evoked.

She let out a soft sigh and frowned for an instant. Hadn't Jake's presence once set her heart to trembling, as well? She wasn't one of those empty-headed girls who simply fell for every boy who paid attention to her. No, as much as she liked Luke, she had no guarantees he wasn't as capable of breaking her heart as Jake had been. Jake had been so caught up in himself that he'd never noticed what she needed, and she had no intentions of repeating that same mistake. Besides, once she finished working for Mrs. Hutton, more than likely she'd never see Luke again.

He pulled a bouquet of flowers from behind his back, then leaned against a mahogany side table that smelled like the fresh beeswax that had been used on the surface to bring out the shine in the wood. "I met the saddest-looking little street vendor on my way here today, and, well"—Luke tugged on his ear, then handed her the flowers—"I thought you might like these."

"They're beautiful. Thank you." Rebecca took the bouquet and brought it to her face, drawing in the sweet scent of the buds while smiling at his awkward attempts to woo her. Luke Hutton, with all his family wealth and social position, was acting like a flustered schoolboy. Regardless of her hesitations, she had to admit she found his uncertainty endearing.

She stood, then crossed the room to one of the cabinets in the back and fished out an empty vase for the flowers before setting them down on her workbench. "I've always thought it's a pity those poor children have to work such long hours for so little."

"I agree, but what's to be done?"

"I have an idea." She hadn't meant to share her thoughts with anyone until she'd worked out the details, but now that she'd begun, maybe it wasn't such a bad thing to get Luke's insight. "It's not a solution for the young street vendors of the city, but rather the Mills Street Orphanage."

"I'd like to hear your idea." He sat down on the other side of her workbench and rested his elbows against the table.

She fumbled with the flowers, trying to arrange them in the vase, which was slightly too big for the bouquet. With all the other vases being used as displays to complement the furniture, she'd have to make it work.

"Before I tell you my idea, would you like some tea?"

Luke tilted his head slightly. "Don't you think it's a bit too hot for tea?"

"For hot tea, certainly. I meant iced tea." Rebecca let out a soft giggle. "Ever since I arrived in Boston, I've developed quite an affinity for drinking tea, both hot and iced. Caroline's the one who got me into the habit, and now, no matter what the weather, I don't think a day goes by without my having at least one glass of tea using Mrs. Lincoln's recipe."

Luke blinked. "Who's Mrs. Lincoln?"

"The author of a recently published cookbook. It's titled *Mrs. Lincoln's Boston Cook Book: What to Do and What Not to Do in Cooking*. It's said to be an instant success. Her recipe for tea, for example, is exceptional. Have you ever been to the Atlantic & Pacific Tea Company?" She tidied up the bits of thread and scraps of fabric on the table, continuing her monologue. "They sell all those little bins of tea from around the world, and I plan to sample each one eventually. It's far more refreshing than tea cakes or bread pudding, which I'm not terribly fond of anyway, although I do admit that peppermint cakes are my weakness and always tempt me—"

Rebecca stopped. She was beginning to sound more like her younger sister Sarah, who never seemed to know when to stop talking, than a grown woman. What interest, if any, would Luke have in peppermint cakes and the A & P Tea Company? On one level, she'd grown to feel quite at ease around the eye-catching shipbuilder, but the way he was looking at her now, with his handsome visage, made her heart quiver. And she had the bad habit of talking too much when she was nervous.

"I myself love bread pudding." Luke smiled and let out a low chuckle. "Had some for lunch today, in fact. Next time you come visit our home, though, I'll be sure to tell Mother you prefer peppermint cakes over ordinary tea cakes."

Rebecca pushed back a wisp of her bangs and felt her cheeks warm at his teasing. "It's really not necessary, considering the fact that when I'm there I'll be working."

"You won't be working tomorrow night now, will you? You're coming to my mother's birthday party."

"Yes, of course." While she'd truly come to enjoy Mrs. Hutton's company, she wasn't sure how she would feel attending the rather formal celebration. Festivities back home in Cranton had consisted of homemade cakes and pies, along with savory dishes prepared by hardworking farmwives. She was sure this party would be a far cry from roasting meat on a spit or playing baseball in the pasture behind the family barn.

"Good—I'm glad you're coming. And tell me something else, Miss Rebecca Johnson," Luke said, leaning forward, "what else do you like besides the A & P Tea Company's vast selection of teas, Mrs. Lincoln's recipes, and peppermint cakes?"

Rebecca gnawed on her bottom lip and regarded Luke. Surprisingly, she saw no hint of amusement at her expense in his expression. Only genuine interest as he waited for her response. Convinced it would be better to keep the atmosphere light rather than risk the possibility of their conversation becoming too personal, Rebecca laid her finger against her chin, squinted her eyes, and pretended to think hard over the question. While Luke's attraction to her was becoming obvious, she felt certain she wasn't ready for any declarations from him wanting to call on her formally.

"Let's see. I love corned beef, mashed potatoes, my brother Adam's maple syrup—though not together—and baking just about anything. I dislike seafood and eggnog—"

"Being a man of the sea, I can tell you that you don't know what you're missing when it comes to seafood."

She folded her arms across her chest and wrinkled her nose. "I know perfectly well what I'm missing, and besides, you've interrupted me. I wasn't finished with my list."

"Please do continue." Luke's satisfied grin told her he was thoroughly enjoying their exchange.

"I can tolerate corn chowder, which I know I should love along with the seafood, being a favorite Massachusetts fare, and I do love baseball, which doesn't exactly fit into the food category, but I like it all the same."

"That's quite a list."

Rebecca took a deep breath and sat down across from him, hoping she hadn't rambled too much this time and made an utter fool out of herself. "What about you?"

"Well, I suppose I'm rather easy to please when it comes to the subject of food. I have a bit of a sweet tooth, being rather fond of things like the aforementioned bread pudding, and then there's pumpkin pie, apple pie, and cherry pie. Any pie or cake for that matter, I suppose."

"And shipbuilding?"

"Now you're interrupting me." He shot her an amused look. "I also like boats, sailing, and baseball, and I'm rather good at chess."

Rebecca glanced at the front door and, for the first time all day, wished a customer would interrupt them. It was becoming far too difficult to stop the growing attraction she felt toward the young man sitting across from her.

Luke cleared his throat. "Enough about me. You never told me your idea for the Mills Street Orphanage. I'd like to hear it."

Rebecca paused. Jake had rarely shown interest in things she was concerned with. Not that he'd been totally indifferent toward her, but looking back, she realized their conversations had focused primarily on his work and his interests.

"After my father married my stepmother, Michaela, our family adopted my youngest sister, Anna." Rebecca closed her eyes for a moment and smiled at the image of the little girl's face. While the first few months had been somewhat of an adjustment for her, she was now as much a part of the family as any of the Johnsons' other six children. "Anna lost her parents in a terrible fire and ended up living at the orphanage for a couple of years. After hearing her story and realizing the important role the orphanage played in her life, I've wanted to get involved and do something to help make the children's lives better."

Rebecca reached for the large box of scraps and pulled out a handful. "For the past eight months, I've been paid to make slipcovers and drapes of every color imaginable. There are at least four more boxes like this in the back. My clients don't want them, but for some reason I've never gotten rid of them. Now I know why."

"Something regarding your idea to help the Mills Street Orphanage?"

Rebecca nodded. "I propose to get a group of women together and with this fabric make quilts for the orphans for this coming winter."

"That's a great idea."

She smiled at his encouragement but wished his enthusiastic compliment didn't affect her as much as it did. "It's a simple idea, really, and I don't know why I didn't think of it earlier. It's easy to give money or old clothes away, but I wanted to do something with my talents that would help me actually get involved in the lives of the children. I want to help each child pick out the colors for his or her quilt, so it's something special that's theirs."

"That makes your idea even better." Luke leaned back in his chair, his expression serious. "Though I'm afraid I'm guilty on that account."

Rebecca wrinkled her brow. "What do you mean?"

"Take, for instance, the street vendor I bought the flowers from. I gave her an extra twenty cents to buy something to eat, but that's a far cry from getting involved in someone else's life and making a difference. Giving money, while important, is easy. Looking into the faces of the street children and becoming a part of their lives takes things to an entirely different level. And by the way, you need to talk to my mother about your idea. I have a feeling she'll want to get involved."

"Thanks." Rebecca smiled. "I'd planned to."

Luke stood up from the bench, then stretched his arms behind him. "I hadn't intended to stay long. In fact, I don't think I ever told you why I came by."

"No, you didn't." A small part of her wondered if he had come by to ask her if he could call on her in a more formal manner. And a small part of her suddenly longed for him to do so. Could she dare allow herself to daydream about the possibility of a future with him? A home surrounded by a beautiful garden, children. . .

"My mother wanted to make sure you could still come by early in the morning to finish hanging her draperies in time for the party."

Rebecca swallowed her disappointment. "Please tell your mother I've finished the panels and plan to hang them in the morning."

Who was she to think that Luke Hutton, a sophisticated Bostonian from a well-to-do family, would be interested in her, a simple farm girl?

"Good. So if I don't see you before tomorrow night at my mother's party, I'll look forward to seeing you then."

Rebecca watched as Luke stepped out the door into the morning sunlight.

The whole situation was ridiculous. Obviously his visits meant nothing more to him than the fact that he was passing on messages from his mother. It was all business. She glanced at the flowers and ran her fingers across one of the soft petals. And the bouquet, of course, was nothing more than an attempt to help a poor little street vendor. His actions showed he had a heart for the down-and-out, not an interest in her. All the same, she had the distinct feeling that if Luke Hutton ever did ask permission to come calling, she'd say yes without a moment's hesitation.

⅋

He had to tell her. How he could have let things go this far, he wasn't sure. Of course, it wasn't as if he'd officially asked if he could call on her. He'd come close to asking her several times, but what respectable man in his position would dare act on his desires? And he had no idea how she felt about him. Did she share his interest, realizing his frequent visits to the shop stemmed from contrived excuses to see her? Or were her friendly conversation and bright smile simply the way she dealt with all her clients? Either way, she had to know he was leaving. He'd see her tomorrow at his mother's party, and somehow he'd find the courage to tell her the truth.

Chapter 5

Rebecca stood in front of the beveled mirror in the upstairs bedroom of Aunt Clara's home and gazed intently at her reflection. The invitation to Mrs. Hutton's birthday party gave her an opportunity to wear the gown she'd made for herself from one of Caroline's paper patterns. The emerald green satin hung gracefully from her waist with a fashionable tier of frills down the back. Her mother's hair ornament, shaped like a butterfly and glimmering with rhinestones, made the perfect finishing touch.

Letting out a deep sigh, Rebecca chastised herself for taking extra pains over her appearance tonight. Luke obviously wasn't going to ask if he could call on her, despite the number of opportunities that had arisen the past few days. He was simply charming, generous, handsome. . .and loved bread pudding. Period. More than likely she had run him off with her incessant babbling over Mrs. Lincoln's iced tea and how much she loved peppermint cakes. Didn't the basic rules of etiquette state clearly that ladies should avoid talking too much?

She hadn't considered what Luke Hutton thought about her until he looked at her with his dreamy eyes and lopsided smile. Trying to catch hold of her emotions, she worked to straighten the wide satin ribbon at her waist. For a moment, she wished she were back home in Cranton. She missed her family. Missed the gray-shingled farmhouse surrounded by lush acres of farmland, apple orchards, and stately elms.

Not that Boston wasn't a fascinating city. She'd come to enjoy the constant bustle of activity, as well as the contrasting majesty of the Atlantic Ocean. Still, she missed her younger sister Sarah's laughter and her brothers, with Adam's gentle teasing and Samuel's stories stemming from his sense of adventure.

A sharp rap on the door jarred Rebecca from her somber thoughts. Aunt Clara entered the room with a bright smile on her sweet, wrinkled face.

"I'm almost ready," Rebecca said.

Aunt Clara waved her hand. "Ben just arrived home and won't be ready for another few minutes, so you're fine." She glanced in the mirror and pushed back a silver wisp of her hair, which was complemented by her olive-colored dress, then chuckled softly. "He's not a bit pleased that I'm making him wear a dinner jacket to Patience's party tonight."

Rebecca couldn't help but laugh, knowing very well how opposed he was to formal attire. "You know Uncle Ben would do anything for you. He adores you."

After two and a half years of marriage, the older couple still acted like newlyweds. Rebecca frowned at the sudden thought of marriage and newlywed bliss. She still had no regrets over stopping her own nuptials, but the longing for marriage and a family still compelled her—almost as much as it frightened her.

Aunt Clara smoothed down the folds of her dress with the palms of her hands and eyed Rebecca intensely. "Why the sad look all of a sudden?"

Rebecca sat on the cream-colored quilt her grandmother had made years before. "I'm a bit homesick, I suppose."

"Did something happen?"

"Not really." Nothing more than foolish daydreams about a handsome shipbuilder. Hadn't she learned her lesson about love once before? But Luke seemed so different. . . .

"Then I believe that tonight is the perfect remedy for your doldrums." Aunt Clara reached out to adjust Rebecca's hair clip. "There's nothing like a party to lift one's spirits."

Rebecca's lips curled into a slight smile. "I suppose you're right. I've always loved parties."

"And you look beautiful. I'm quite certain you'll capture the eye of at least one or two young gentlemen this evening."

Rebecca shivered. "I think I'd prefer to be a simple wallflower than attract the attention of some interested suitor."

"Plenty of young men regard marriage in a higher light than Jake did, you know."

"Yes, but if a man is always going to add such complications to my life, I don't know if I ever want to get married."

"The right man is worth the extra complication." Aunt Clara rested her hands against her hips and tilted her head. "Who is it?"

"Who is it?" Rebecca started at the question. Surely her unsolicited yet seemingly irrepressible interest in Luke hadn't been obvious. "It's no one. No one important, anyway."

"Luke Hutton, by any chance?"

Rebecca felt her cheeks flush at the mention of Luke's name. "How did you know?"

Aunt Clara rested her forefinger against her chin. "Let's see. If I recall correctly, his name has been mentioned at least once over dinner most nights, and—"

"I was simply—simply sharing with you the events of my day." Rebecca stumbled over her excuse. "He often dropped by to leave messages from his mother regarding the work I'm doing for her. Nothing more." *Nothing more intended on his part, that is.*

"And that's the other thing," Aunt Clara began with a twinkle in her eye. "How many of your other clients require a personal carrier to deliver messages to you regarding their slipcovers and draperies?"

"None, but—" Rebecca closed her mouth, feeling caught.

"I've known his family for years, and he's a good man." Aunt Clara reached out and squeezed Rebecca's hands. "Take your time and get to know him. Maybe something will come of it. On the other hand, maybe he'll never be more than a good friend. Just don't let the past stop you from finding out."

Rebecca stood and wrapped her arms around the older woman's waist. If only forgetting the past could be easier. Still, she knew Aunt Clara was right. She'd never find out what could happen between her and Luke, or any other man, if she let Jake's actions stop her from trusting her heart again. "I know why Michaela loves you so much. She told me how wise you are."

"I'm just an old woman who's thankful to have been blessed by love twice in a lifetime."

Rebecca closed her eyes and wondered if she had any chance at all to find true love—just once.

❦

Classical music played in the background as Rebecca sipped the tangy citrus-and-tea-flavored punch from a crystal cup. A number of elegantly dressed guests mingled along the outskirts of the room, but for the moment, Rebecca enjoyed studying her surroundings. Mrs. Hutton had chosen to hold the party in a large room that led to the outside terrace and well-manicured gardens below. Like the rest of the house, the room held a collection of fine furniture: rosewood tables with carved grape motifs and marble tabletops, chairs with balloon-shaped backs, and a sideboard with ivory inlay. A pair of gas chandeliers with cut-glass prisms reflected dancing shadows on the pale pink wallpaper and added to the festive ambiance of the evening.

Across the room, Aunt Clara and Uncle Ben stood talking to Mrs. Hutton beside a table laden with corned beef, seafood, pies, and other tempting delights. The gracious hostess had greeted Rebecca warmly at the door, but she'd yet to catch a glimpse of Luke. She scanned the room and tried to convince herself it didn't matter if she had the chance to speak to Luke tonight. Surely he'd be far too busy playing host for his mother to pay any attention to her. Regardless of the fact that their families had been longtime friends, she was, in reality, only someone his family had hired. But her heart felt different. She did want to see

Luke tonight. Wanted him to seek her out and make her heart quiver the way it did when he was near.

Spotting a friend from church across the room, Rebecca edged past an arrangement of shelves filled with a number of pieces of glassware, framed daguerreotypes, and other unique curios, then stopped at the light touch of someone's fingers against her elbow.

"You look lovely tonight, Rebecca."

Turning slowly, she found herself facing the object of her daydreams. "Luke?"

"I'm sorry if I startled you—"

"No, it's just that—" *It's just that I can't seem to stop thinking about you, and now here you are.*

Her heart fluttered out of rhythm. This time her nervousness left her uncharacteristically tongue-tied. Clean shaven and elegant in his matching charcoal-gray coat, vest, and trousers, he looked as if he'd come straight from the tailor rather than from a day's work at the shipyard.

Luke cleared his throat. "Do you like the punch?"

Rebecca stared at her empty glass. "Yes. It's quite refreshing."

The corners of his eyes crinkled in amusement. "I believe the recipe comes from Mrs. Lincoln's *What to Do and What Not to Do in Cooking*."

"And I believe you're teasing me." She felt her cheeks flush, something that was becoming too frequent when in Luke's presence.

"Far from it." He stared back at her. "You have an unreserved passion about everything that goes on around you, from Mrs. Lincoln's recipes to things of much weightier importance, like the quilts you're making for the orphans. You know my mother's eager to get involved with the project."

If she'd been the delicate type of female, she was sure she would have swooned by now. Could it be that her instincts were correct and Luke Hutton was interested in her?

Another man, with bright red hair and dressed as elegantly as Luke, stepped up behind him and slapped him on the back. "Luke, why haven't you introduced me to your beautiful companion?"

Luke flashed his friend a look of amusement. "Rebecca, this is Raymond Miller. He's an old—and ornery, might I add—friend of the family."

"Shameful, isn't he? And a pity for you, Luke, that the *Liberty* leaves in a mere two weeks," Raymond said with a wide grin. "I don't suppose I could steal her away for the next dance now, could I?"

Before Rebecca could come up with an excuse to decline the invitation graciously, Luke grasped her forearm lightly with his fingers and drew her toward the dance floor. "Not a chance, sailor."

The music stopped then, and Luke placed her empty cup on one of the tables. "Shall I have the honor of dancing the next waltz with you?"

"Of course." She smiled at his protective manner.

Before she could take another breath, she was in his arms and floating across the room. For a man who worked with his hands and spent most of his time outdoors, he was an excellent dance partner. The intent way he looked down at her left her with no more doubts about his intentions. Clearly he wasn't simply being polite.

☙

Luke rested his gloved hand lightly against Rebecca's waist and breathed in the sweet scent of her perfume. He'd promised himself one dance with her before telling her the truth about his upcoming voyage—before he was caught up even further by her charms. Unfortunately, he was fully aware he had already lost his heart to her.

While the small orchestra played the three-quarter tempo piece, Luke kept his gaze focused on Rebecca. At least a dozen other eligible young women were in the room, each dressed in their finest silks and many showing obvious interest in his status as a wealthy bachelor. But for now Rebecca had his full attention. Despite the fact that etiquette required that he mingle with the other guests throughout the evening and avoid dancing with the same partner, he planned to find a way to prolong their time together.

"Whose idea was this party?" Light from the chandeliers caught the flecks of gold in Rebecca's eyes as she posed the question.

"Originally the idea was mine." Luke drew her slightly closer. "My mother would never have arranged something like this for herself. I'd wanted to surprise her with a few friends over, but those friends, deciding it was a wonderful idea, took matters into their own hands. Before I knew it, half of Boston had been invited."

Rebecca's soft laugh chimed like one of his mother's crystal pieces. "And the surprise part?"

Luke grinned. "Mother found out about it weeks ago. It's impossible to keep a secret from her."

"Why is it that mothers never seem to miss a single detail of what's going on around them?"

The musical piece would come to an end soon, and he knew he had to talk to her. Ignoring the reality of the situation wouldn't change anything. In fact, it would only make matters worse. He'd realized that when he'd introduced her to Raymond, who'd almost given the situation away when he brought up the

Liberty. He was thankful he'd been able to distract her by asking her to dance. She'd never forgive him if she found out the truth from someone else. And he'd already waited far too long to tell her.

Still, his heart told him to pull her closer in his arms and beg her to wait for him until he returned. But he'd never do that to her. If only things were different and he wasn't leaving. If only he wasn't facing months of solitude at sea without the sweetness of her face to brighten his day.

"Rebecca, there's something I need to talk to you about. I was wondering if we could stroll in the garden for a few minutes."

Her eyes widened.

With interest? He hoped so.

"You're the host tonight. What if your guests need you?"

"I'm sure they can spare me for a few minutes."

"All right, then."

❧

Rebecca took Luke's arm and let him escort her across the floor. With scores of beautiful women filling the room, she couldn't help but feel a thrill that he wanted to spend time with her. And a walk in the garden meant he wanted to prolong their time together. Aunt Clara had been right in her advice. Rebecca couldn't let what Jake had done stop her from finding love again. It was certainly too early to know if Luke was the one God had chosen for her, but it was time to take a chance and find out.

And if he wants to ask if he can call on me formally. . . Rebecca glided beside him toward the open terrace doors and smiled at the thought of getting to know him better.

An older woman, dressed in a fashionable navy and cream pin-striped silk, stood in the breezeway and greeted them with a pleasant smile. "Luke, darling, let me compliment you on the party. What a wonderful occasion this is for your mother."

"Thank you, Mrs. Lewis. May I introduce you to Rebecca Johnson. Her grandparents have been longtime friends of my mother."

"So you're the young lady in the room who has managed to steal the attentions of our host."

"Knowing Mr. Hutton the little that I do, I'm certain he will strive to make everyone feel at home tonight." Rebecca laced her fingers together, unsure of how else to respond to the woman.

"Don't worry, my sweet. Just be sure to enjoy his company before he leaves."

"Excuse me?" Confused, Rebecca turned to Luke, whose face had paled whiter than a Boston winter.

"Luke," Mrs. Lewis continued, "don't tell me you haven't yet informed this young woman that you set sail in a few days."

Rebecca stood speechless at the announcement, and Luke didn't seem to be faring any better if she was reading correctly the horror-struck expression on his face.

"We're all proud of him. As one of the top officers of the *Liberty*, he's destined to become the captain of his own vessel one day."

Rebecca choked out an unladylike cough. Luke was leaving on a whaling voyage? Surely this woman was incorrect. Luke would have told her something as significant as the fact he was leaving on such an extended expedition. Wouldn't he?

"I hadn't yet. . ." Luke stuttered out his reply. "I was planning on telling her everything now. . .in the garden."

So it was true. He was leaving and had never intended for their relationship to continue.

"If you'll excuse me, I—" The room began to swirl around Rebecca, and her stomach clenched as she ran onto the terrace and into the night air.

Chapter 6

Rebecca knew she shouldn't care. Shouldn't care that Luke Hutton was leaving on a whaling voyage that would take him away from Boston for the next three years. Shouldn't care that she'd more than likely never see the handsome sailor again. And why should she? She'd known him a mere few weeks, and in all that time he'd never spoken of his interest in her or said he wanted to call on her. He had no claims on her, nor did she on him.

But he still ought to have told her. How could she dismiss the look in his eyes as he held her in his arms tonight? She'd been so sure of his intentions. Now she knew how wrong she'd been. She was nothing more than another pretty face to him. Someone who could amuse him with animated conversation and other such pleasantries before he had to run off to sea without any thoughts to the future or further commitment. He'd poured on the charm, never once caring that she'd lost her heart in the process.

Drawing back into the shadows of the garden to gain a few moments of privacy, Rebecca took in a deep breath. The sweet scent of the rosebushes did nothing more than remind her of what she'd carelessly dared to dream of having with Luke. A house with a garden, a family. . . How could she have been such a fool to lose her heart again?

And no doubt that was exactly how he saw her—a fool who had mis-interpreted his intentions. Didn't Luke Hutton have the choice of every girl here tonight? Their mothers were inside right now, plotting how to get him to notice their little darlings, their sights set on his substantial inheritance. What were a few years of waiting when it came to marrying into a good family with financial stability?

She, on the other hand, had no intention of waiting for months on end for someone like Luke. She wasn't the kind of woman who would pine like a lovelorn maiden for her sweetheart's return—that is, if he'd ever had any plans to ask her, which he obviously hadn't.

"Rebecca?"

She leaned into the flora at the sound of Luke's voice. She never should have run away from him. What kind of undignified behavior had she displayed? Fleeing his mother's party and hiding in the garden were certainly not the actions of a proper lady and only showed him she cared for him. Her heart, though, wasn't acting in a rational manner tonight. Her heart was breaking.

"Rebecca, are you there?"

Swallowing her pride, she knew facing him would be wiser in the long run. "Luke—"

Something pulled against the back of her bustle as she tried to take a step toward him.

"Before you say anything"—he stepped in front of her—"I need to apologize about what happened inside. There are some chairs on the terrace where we could sit, and I could explain—"

"I can't—" Momentarily distracted, she struggled in the dim light to discover what her dress was caught on.

"I never meant for things to turn out this way." He reached forward and brushed his fingers down her sleeve. "I never meant to fall in love with you."

She jerked to face him and heard the ripping of fabric behind her. "You're in love with me?"

Luke was proclaiming his love for her, and she was stuck in the bushes. Of all times for something ridiculous like this to happen. "I think my dress is caught on a thorn—if you could help me."

"Of course."

He reached around to unhook her bustle from the cluster of roses. He was so close she could smell the woodsy scent of his cologne and feel his warm breath against her neck. She tried to steady her rapid pulse. This couldn't be happening. Just when she had decided to take a chance with her heart, she discovered he was leaving. Was it true he wasn't the cad she'd assumed him to be and he really loved her?

"I'm afraid your dress is torn slightly." He picked up a perfect red rose that had fallen to the ground and, after breaking off the thorns, handed it to her.

"Thank you." With the rose in one hand, she stepped into the silvery light of the moon to inspect the garment, but a tear in her dress seemed insignificant at this point. "It's only the bustle and shouldn't be that noticeable."

"Perhaps I shouldn't have spoken so openly," he began, "but I meant what I said. I didn't think it would happen, but you've captured my heart."

She squeezed her eyes shut for a moment and tried to make sense of her jumbled emotions. "I—I don't know what to say."

"Tell me you feel something, too?"

A woman's shrill laugh erupted from the terrace, competing with the soft strains of a violin. Snippets of conversation floated past them. Dogs barked in the distance. Crickets chirped. Each sound gained intensity in her mind, throwing her normally organized thoughts into further confusion.

She wanted to ignore his question, but she couldn't. "How can I let myself continue to care for you now that I know you're leaving?"

"So you feel it, too."

Picking up the hem of her dress, Rebecca escaped toward the terrace. Being alone in the shadows of the garden wasn't proper. And besides, she wasn't sure she could handle his nearness. Not when she knew how much he affected her—and what it meant to her heart to know he was leaving.

She chose a padded bench in the corner of the stone terrace and sat down. Music continued to filter out the French doors and into the night air. On any other summer evening, the verdant garden would have been a sight that took her breath away. But tonight the willows and rhododendrons and the lilacs and roses blurred before her tear-filled eyes until they disappeared, like the sweet scent of the honeysuckle that was evaporating into the night air.

Luke slid onto the bench beside her.

"Why didn't you tell me you were leaving?" she asked, breaking the awkward silence that gathered between them.

"I was wrong not to."

"But why didn't you?" Her heart ached with the realization of how much she'd come to care for him. "Wait—you don't owe me an explanation. You never said or did anything to state your feelings."

He moved toward her, allowing the glow from the gas lighting to illuminate his face. She wanted to reach out and smooth a lock of his dark hair away from his forehead. To trace the curve of his strong jawline. But those were intimate things she would never do.

"I wanted to tell you how I feel," Luke began. "Every time I saw you at the shop or at the house, I had to stop myself from coming to you and asking you to wait for my return."

Rebecca stared at her hands. "Why didn't you?"

"It wouldn't have been fair to you. I won't be a man who leaves his family behind for years at a time. And besides that, I know how you feel about sailors."

Catching the sadness reflected in his eyes, she raised her brow in question. "What do you mean?"

"Do you remember when I walked you back to the shop shortly after we met? You told me—"

"That I'd never live that way." She nodded at the memory. "I could never wait year after year for the one I love to return."

That's why he'd left her so abruptly that day in front of the shop. He'd known she would never agree to wait for him. Tonight the words seemed harsh and insensitive. Nevertheless, they still rang true. She'd never have the courage to wait, wondering if he'd return to her or if the sea had swallowed him into its depth. No, living like that would be far too painful. It was better to put a stop to anything that might have started between them right now.

He caught her gaze. "Do you ever wonder what God's will is for your life?"

His question surprised her. Pulling off the velvety rose petals one at a time, she pondered the issue. Hadn't she asked God the same thing dozens of times? "It seems to be a constant question of mine lately. I want to follow His will, but more often than not I can't seem to see clearly what His will for my life is."

"Then maybe you can understand how I feel." His eyes seemed to plead with her. "I've spent my life trying to follow God's will, but more often than not I find myself pursuing the plans laid out by my parents. My father was the captain of a ship, and now my mother expects me to take the same path. Money might not be an issue, but following in my father's footsteps has always been of first importance to her."

"What do you want?"

"To work with my hands building ships."

Rebecca let the last petal fall to the ground. Building ships would mean he would no longer have to spend years at a time away from home. Instead of being a career officer at sea, he'd have time for a wife and a family. . . .

"What about this upcoming voyage?"

"I'm committed to this last trip, but after that I won't go back to sea. My mother will have to understand that I'm not my father, and what was a proper occupation for his life's work isn't the right choice for me."

A couple waltzed out onto the terrace, the woman's blue satin dress flowing in the gentle wind. They looked content and carefree as they laughed about something together. Rebecca had grown up believing God's will for her was to marry and raise a family. If that were true, then why had God put Luke in her life only to lose him so quickly? Could it be that God's will was bigger than she'd imagined?

"What if God's will is simply to live completely for Him wherever we are?" She pondered the implications of her own question. "Following Him in whatever situation we find ourselves?"

"Like your work with the orphanage?"

She nodded. "Exactly. In helping to get the quilts made for the orphans, I feel as though I'm serving God with my talents, and for the first time in a long time, I feel a deep satisfaction in what I'm doing."

☙

Luke studied Rebecca's face in the amber light. He heard the passion in her voice and saw the obvious joy she felt in what she was doing. It was easy for him to see why he'd fallen in love with her. The difficult part was in knowing he shouldn't have.

"What about when God gives you more than one choice?" he asked. "But you can't have both." *Like the woman I love and the job I'm obligated to finish.*

"Two choices don't necessarily mean one has to be wrong. But when they conflict with each other. . ." Her smile faded.

There were no easy answers. He could speak to Captain Taft and tell him he wasn't going. Many a sailor had backed out at the last minute, knowing the hardships ahead of them. Life on a whaling vessel was grueling. Not only was the pay for the crew minimal; a good fourth of them would never make it home because of death or desertion. But no matter what was ahead, he always strove to be a man of his word. A man whose word could be counted as an unqualified guarantee. And Captain Taft was counting on him to be his first mate on the upcoming voyage.

He sat up straight and tried to loosen the tense muscles in his back. Surely God's will didn't include his losing the woman he loved merely because he'd given his word to someone else. There had to be another way. Three years would seem like an eternity, knowing he'd lost her. She'd go back to Cranton and find someone else to marry who would give her a home and a family.

The thought was sobering. Would he regret it if he never asked her if she would wait for him? Surely he had nothing to lose.

"Rebecca, I—"

"Please don't ask me to wait for you." She laid her gloved hand gently on his arm, and he flinched at her touch.

He'd known she couldn't make that kind of promise, and he wouldn't ask it of her. "Just know that if the circumstances had been different or if the timing of things would have been different—"

"I know."

He watched as she stood to leave and caught the glisten of tears against her dark lashes. What a fool he had been. He'd never meant to hurt her. If only he'd kept silent, then maybe the pain of his leaving would have been lessened. Without knowing how he felt, surely she would have quickly forgotten him.

"I'm sorry, Rebecca."

"So am I."

His hands balled into tight fists at his sides. Was it really God's will for him to lose her forever? With one last fleeting look, she hurried into the house—and out of his life.

Chapter 7

It had been only three days, and Luke already missed Rebecca. He missed her bright smile and their stimulating conversations. Missed the sparkle in her eyes when she looked at him. She'd cared for him, and in turn he'd broken her heart. If only he could make her understand that he'd never intended to hurt her. That he'd never intended to come to care for her. But he did care for her, and now he was faced with the knowledge that he'd lost her forever.

Still, he wanted to see her, even if it was only for one last time. But was it worth the pain it would inflict on both of them? He knew the wisest thing for him to do was to set sail on that whaling vessel without ever seeing her again.

His shoes clicked against the hardwood floors as he strode down the hallway of his mother's home. The overcast sky created morning shadows that merged into the cream-colored walls, causing the darkened corridor to echo the gloom in his heart. Finding his mother writing letters in the parlor, he first glanced at the Baltimore clock that had characteristically stopped.

"What time is it, Mother?"

"Eight thirty," she said, glancing at the jeweled watch pinned to her dress. "I'm expecting Rebecca any minute now. She's coming with fabric samples for my bedroom. She's done such a fine job in here."

"I'm glad she's helping you, but I can't stay. I'm on my way out."

He reached down and kissed her on the cheek, wanting to escape not only a possible confrontation with Rebecca, but the constant reminders of the parlor as well. Like an artist, she'd managed to brighten the room with her sense of style and color. But he barely saw the intricate details of the room. He just saw Rebecca.

"Don't forget to mail your letters," he said, turning to leave. More than once he'd found a pile of his mother's unsent letters. Attention to detail was not her forte.

"You're avoiding her." His mother dipped her pen into an ink bottle and signed her name in elegant pen strokes to the bottom of the letter she'd been writing.

"I'm not avoiding her. I'm just. . ." *Just what?* He shook his head, realizing that in trying to avoid her, he was trying to avoid his own guilt. Nothing he could say or do, though, could take back the events that had transpired the night of his mother's party. "Could we please not talk about this right now?"

The narrowing of her eyes made him feel like a schoolboy who'd been chastised for stealing a handful of penny candy. "It was no way to treat a lady, you know. Leading her on with no intentions of furthering your relationship."

"That was never my objective, Mother, and you know it."

"Maybe not, but how do you think she views the situation?" She smoothed out the silky folds of her blue morning dress. "You visit her numerous times at the shop with an obvious hidden agenda and then bring her flowers. She couldn't help but interpret your actions as interest in her. Then, without warning, she finds out you're leaving, and in a most unscrupulous way, I might add."

Luke let out a long sigh. Reviewing the facts did nothing to relieve his guilt. "Then what do you propose I do? I have no doubt that at this point she wants nothing more to do with me."

"Why don't you invite her to tomorrow's baseball game?"

"What?" Surely his mother was losing her mind. How could she, in good conscience, even suggest he do such a thing after all that had transpired between the two of them?

"We'll invite her aunt and uncle and make an enjoyable time of it."

Luke leaned his palms against the top of his mother's secretary. "And why would she agree to something like that?"

"Why wouldn't she? If nothing else, the two of you can work things out so that when you leave you won't have this vast barrier between you."

He ran his fingers across the smooth grain of the wood and shook his head. "What has come between us can't be erased with one afternoon at a ballpark. Besides, by the time I get back from the voyage, she'll more than likely be married with a couple of kids in tow."

"You don't know that. Rebecca's a fine woman, and you'd do well to mend the situation between the two of you. She has more passion and integrity than the majority of those empty-headed girls who are always chasing after you."

Luke squeezed his eyes shut for a moment, trying to grasp what his mother was implying. "Is that what you think? That I can somehow make things right between us and she'll change her mind about me? She won't wait for me, Mother. She's already made that quite clear."

"Your father and I—"

"I'm not my father." He struck his hands against the table. "Can't you see that? You expect me to live out my life the way the two of you had planned, but—"

The front door slammed shut, and he looked up to see Rebecca walk through the doorway of the parlor. His stomach churned as he drank in her beauty. She wore her hair in its normal fashion, parted in the center and secured at the nape of her neck. Her short, curly bangs framed her face and gave it a gentle softness. He had no doubt that the image of her dark brown eyes and heart-shaped face would remain etched in his memory. The same way it haunted his dreams at night.

"The housekeeper let me in. I hope you don't mind," Rebecca said.

"Not at all. I'm glad you're here." Luke's mother picked up a stack of lavender-scented sheets of paper and slipped them into the top drawer. "We were just speaking about you."

"Really?" She smiled at Mrs. Hutton but avoided Luke's gaze. Her hesitation at seeing him at home was obvious.

"We were wondering if you, along with Ben and Clara, of course, would like to spend part of tomorrow with us watching the Boston Beaneaters play."

"Oh?" Rebecca's eyes widened at the suggestion. "You like baseball, Mrs. Hutton?"

Luke's mother's laugh was light and playful as if she didn't feel an ounce of the tension that hung between them. "Surprised that a society woman involved primarily in charity work would enjoy such a sport?"

"Well, no, but—"

"I've found it to be a pleasant distraction from time to time."

"Really?"

Confusion marked Rebecca's face, and Luke couldn't help but wonder if it was due to his mother's invitation or the fact that he would be there.

"Say you'll come. This will be a splendid occasion for all of us."

Luke's heart felt as if it were about to be torn in pieces. If she agreed, it would mean that much more time he could spend with her, something he longed for desperately. But any time they spent together would make it that much harder to leave her. Could it give him a chance to make things right between them? He knew she wouldn't change her mind and wait for him. Especially after he'd foolishly waited too long to tell her the truth. But if he could be assured of her forgiveness, he wouldn't leave with the mountain of guilt that threatened to consume him.

Surely there's a way for us to be together, Lord.

Instead of a measure of reassurance for the impossible, the physical emptiness inside engulfed him like a tidal wave. The crew of a vessel always faced the threat of lost lives in the midst of a storm, but as far as he was concerned, he'd already lost his heart.

❧

Rebecca adjusted the tilt of her wide-brimmed hat to block out the sun. She'd been surprised at the invitation and even more surprised that Luke had gone along with the request. After what he'd done to her, surely he had more sense than to think she would want to go anywhere with him. Hadn't he hurt her enough? But because it was Mrs. Hutton who'd asked, she'd agreed, not knowing how to reject the invitation politely.

Luke was obviously behind the idea, but she wasn't sure why he wanted to spend time with her. Hadn't she made it perfectly clear she had no intentions of waiting for him? Sitting on the row of bleachers that had been built for the spectators, she tried to focus on the grassy field and not the fact that Luke was sitting beside her. It wasn't as if the thought of his leaving didn't pain her. Far from it, but she knew he was someone she needed to forget. If only part of her didn't long to confess that her feelings toward him matched his own toward her.

No matter how much she wished things were different, she knew she couldn't wait for him. If he would decide to stay, they might have a chance of finding out what the future held, but she knew that would never happen, either. Too much could change in three years, and they still had a great deal to learn about each other. It was better to say their good-byes and end things before it got any harder.

"This is the Beaneaters' seventy-sixth game," Luke said, turning toward her.

"Pardon?" Drawn out of her contemplation, Rebecca stole a glance at him.

"The Beaneaters," he repeated. "It's the seventy-sixth game of this year's season."

"Oh. I'm sorry. My mind must have been elsewhere."

While Aunt Clara chatted away with Mrs. Hutton and Uncle Ben dozed in the warm sun, no one seemed to notice the discomfort she felt with the situation. In fact, seating her and Luke next to each other seemed more like a matchmaking strategy.

Trying to return her focus to the events at hand, she watched as the Boston Beaneaters made their way out onto the South End Grounds. With their red stockings and padded gloves, they lined up in front of a lively crowd of spectators who stood to root for their home team. The opposing team, the Cleveland Blues, received a far less warm welcome.

"Is this your first game?" Luke asked.

"For the National League, yes."

Rebecca chewed on her bottom lip. She hated the awkwardness that had come between them. She wanted so much to forget Luke, but how could she when he sat mere inches from her?

"I assume you've watched a few of the local games in Cranton?"

"Watched? I've played dozens of those country games with my father and brothers."

"You've heard of the women's teams, haven't you, like the Philadelphia Blue Stockings?"

Playing on her father's farm after a church social was one thing. Parading around the country for the sport was another matter altogether. "I've heard that women's teams have stirred up a good bit of controversy in the past few years, even to the point that they were once labeled a dreadful demonstration of impropriety."

"And do you agree with that statement?"

At first she thought he was mocking her with his question, but with one glance, she knew he wasn't. Instead, he appeared genuinely interested in her opinion. And he wasn't the kind of man who would berate women and their roles in society no matter which side of the issue she stood on.

She flashed him a slight grin. "It should suffice to say that you'll never find me being paid to run around a grassy field."

As Luke chuckled in response, the Beaneaters scored another run. With Luke's attention back on the game, she let her gaze linger on his clean-shaven face. While many men wore moustaches and beards or even drooping moustaches without beards, she rather preferred the trim look. It made him look like quite the distinguished gentleman.

As the crowd settled down, he turned back to her. "May I get you something to eat from the concession stand?"

She shook her head. "I'm fine, thank you."

"Are you sure?"

"Of course." The concern on his face seemed to stem from something far weightier than wondering if she needed something to eat. "Why wouldn't I be?"

"I. . .because I never had the chance to apologize properly for what happened at my mother's party."

"You don't have to—"

"Yes, I do. Even my mother thinks I'm a cad."

In spite of the severity of his expression, she wanted to laugh at the term. He might have displayed a lack of good judgment regarding that particular situation, but he was certainly not without gentlemanly instincts. "You never acted improperly or said anything that suggested you were interested in me."

"Nevertheless, the implications were there, and I can't stand the thought of my leaving with this hanging between us."

She glanced at the rest of their party, thankful none of them appeared to be listening to their conversation. "Of course I forgive you."

Smiling, she turned back to the game. Luke Hutton was like no man she'd ever met. He certainly wasn't perfect; his omission in their conversations of his upcoming voyage was proof of that. But she could also see his strengths in the fact that he wanted desperately to make things right between them. And something told her his need for her to forgive him held no ulterior motives. He might still wish she would agree to wait for him, but even more important, he wanted to do the right thing.

By the end of the game, Rebecca had all but forgotten the wall that had been erected between the two of them. She'd laughed at his commentary of the game and enjoyed his constant humor as he told her stories from his own childhood growing up in Boston.

With the final crack of the bat, the Boston Beaneaters won against the Cleveland Blues, four to zero. Watching Luke's handsome figure stand up and cheer for the home team, she was struck with the reality of their situation. Life wasn't a game of points scored, declaring winners and losers. Life, with all the joys and accomplishments one encountered, could never be measured in home runs.

Turning away from him, she knew what she had to do. If she were smart, she would protect her heart, walk away, and never see Luke Hutton again. But what if her heart was right and he was worth waiting for?

Chapter 8

Rebecca wiped away the beads of perspiration from her forehead, then took the porcelain teapot out of the icebox. Earlier this morning she'd brewed a mixture of black and green tea so it would be at its peak flavor in the sultry afternoon heat. Mid-August had brought with it a number of sizzling days, and if it hadn't been for the cool breezes given off by the Atlantic, the heat would have been unbearable.

Caroline sat on the other side of the kitchen–sitting room combination of her and Philip's apartment above Macintosh Furniture and Upholstery. The pleasant room was full of detailed black walnut furnishings Philip had handcrafted, and Caroline's fabric designs gave an added cheerful feel despite the tight quarters.

While the residence was small by most people's standards, Caroline continually reminded everyone this was simply a temporary arrangement that allowed close access to the shop while their new house was being built. Despite a number of unscheduled delays, their two-story dwelling was expected to be finished before winter arrived, something Caroline seemed to anticipate almost as much as the coming baby.

"What would I do without you?" Caroline asked.

Rebecca let out a soft giggle. "You'd be suffering through this heat without the health benefits of Mrs. Lincoln's iced tea."

"All I can do is thank the good Lord that I have only five weeks left." With her feet propped up on an upholstered stool, Caroline leaned back in her Boston rocker while Rebecca finished preparing the iced tea. "Do you realize that if one has a dozen children, like Susan Parker, one is pregnant an entire nine years of her life?"

Resting her hands against her hips, Rebecca shook her head. "I do believe you have far too much time on your hands."

Caroline laughed. "Maybe, but if I don't do something, I'll go crazy. I've already told Philip that having one child will more than likely keep me plenty occupied and there is simply no reason to have another one."

"I have no doubt that once this little one comes into the world, you will completely change your mind. And as for me, someday I'd like at least three or four."

Rebecca closed her mouth and busied herself by filling the goblets full of crushed ice, wondering why she'd made that last ridiculous statement. Adding two cubes of block sugar and a slice of lemon to each glass, she tried to ignore the fact that, at the present anyway, the very possibility of children in the near future was out of the question for her. Especially since the one man she'd finally decided to take a chance with was now out of her life forever.

"Do you think I made a mistake?" Rebecca poured the chilled tea into the goblets then crossed the room to join Caroline.

"In making the tea?"

Rebecca frowned at Caroline's flippant response as she handed her one of the drinks. "Of course not. I'm talking about my decision not to wait for Luke's return."

"Honestly? I can't say I blame you."

"Really?"

Caroline took a long drink of the tea. "Too much could happen in three years, and it's not as if you have known each other for a long time. You could meet someone else, or what if he finds someone at one of the ports during the trip?"

Rebecca frowned. "Luke is not that kind of man."

"I never meant to imply he is anything but honorable, but what about the dangers of the voyage? The life of a whaler isn't easy, whether he's the captain of the ship or the lowest crew member. The sea's never choosy about whom it decides to take."

Rebecca sat down on the end of the sofa and studied the peaceful, wintry scene of a Currier and Ives print hung on the wall across from her. The people pictured seemed to live an existence of perpetual contentment. A stark contrast to her own life. "A few weeks ago you implied it was romantic to be the lovelorn bride waiting anxiously day after day for her husband to return from sea."

Caroline ran her hands across her swollen abdomen. "As a woman close to her hour of delivery, I claim the right to change my mind on whatever subject I want and as often as I like."

"You're absolutely incorrigible today." Rebecca shot her friend a wry grin.

"You miss him, don't you?" Caroline asked.

"I don't want to, but yes." She swirled the glass of tea in her hand and watched the ice clink against the sides. "And the sad thing is, he hasn't even left the harbor yet. He still has another few days before the ship leaves."

"You'll forget him, because life always goes on. You'll find someone who will fill the void you feel right now, and before you know it, Luke Hutton will be nothing more than a vague memory."

"You make it sound so simple." *And sad.*

"Love is never simple, but for me anyway, it helps to remember it won't hurt forever."

"I suppose you're right."

Rebecca took a sip of her tea and savored its sweetness. If only life could so easily be sprinkled with a dab of sugar to make everything work out. But as much as Caroline's words made sense, it wasn't enough. Luke wasn't just another acquaintance she could quickly forget. There was something different about him, and she wasn't convinced she'd find someone else who made her feel the way she did when she was around him.

Even what she'd felt with Jake didn't begin to compare with the deepening feelings she had toward Luke. Every time she saw him, he made her laugh, and when he was away from her, her heart felt empty. She loved the way he encouraged her to pursue her dreams for the orphanage and never made her feel she was less important because she worked as a seamstress and didn't have the wealth of so many of the girls who ran in his circles. He cared about her because of who she was, not where she came from.

Caroline leaned forward slightly. "What is it?"

Rebecca lifted her head from her contemplations. "Is my brooding that obvious?"

"I've never seen it take longer for you to drink your tea than for the ice inside the glass to melt."

Rebecca glanced down at the nearly full goblet. Today even the refreshing flavor of the tea was doing little to restore her spirits. "What if I tell him I'll wait for him?"

"You're serious about him, aren't you?"

Rebecca nodded slowly. "I don't want to lose him."

"I think you're setting yourself up for a heartache. You need to forget him. Maybe his parents did all right marrying a short time before his father left for sea, but how often do you think a situation like that works out for the good?"

Rebecca ran her finger around the rim of the glass. "I don't know."

"None of us can say what will happen between now and the time he returns. Maybe you won't have found someone else by then, and the two of you will be able to continue your relationship. Just don't close off all your options."

"I was right, you know, when I said romance with a whaler was bound to end in tragedy." Rebecca brushed back her bangs and let out a deep sigh. "Except in my situation it's a tragedy no matter what I decide to do. If I choose never to see him again, I'm afraid I'll regret my decision for the rest of my life. But on the other hand, I don't know how I could ever handle waiting so long for him to return. I'm afraid that would only bring me more heartbreak."

"I'm sorry, Rebecca. I really am. And I know none of this is easy for you. I guess all we can do at this point is pray that God shows you what to do."

"Sometimes I wonder if He cares which choice I make. He seems so far away from me lately."

"Of course He cares." Caroline set her tea on the small table beside her then leaned forward. "My mother used to quote from First Peter five, where it tells us to cast all our cares on Him, for He cares for us."

Rebecca contemplated her friend's words. "If that's true, then why does He make it so difficult to know what's best? Why is it so difficult to give up my fears and let Him take them?"

"All I can do is encourage you with the fact that He is in control and that He does love and care about you. Never lose sight of that reality."

❧

Time was running out. With only a handful of days left until the *Liberty* departed, Luke spent the majority of his time getting both the crew and the ship ready to sail by week's end. The grueling schedule of working with Captain Taft, as well as helping Dwight Nevin put the finishing touches on the boat, gave him little time to dwell on the fact that Rebecca was forever out of his life.

Refreshed from his bath and clean change of clothes, he opened the door from his room, eager for a hot meal. Already he could smell the pungent aroma of clam chowder coming from the kitchen. Stepping into the hallway he heard the familiar sound of Rebecca's laugh coupled with his mother's.

Luke froze. His mother had told him Rebecca was coming over this afternoon, but he'd been sure she would be gone before he returned, so he hadn't worried about running into her. It wasn't that he didn't want to see her again. Not at all. But he had the memory of seeing her for the last time at the ballgame etched in his memory, and he didn't want to take the chance of spoiling it.

She'd worn a sunny yellow dress that brought out the flecks of gold in her eyes, along with a fashionable hat that had been tilted slightly to the side, giving her an elegant look. After the first few awkward minutes of watching the Boston Beaneaters play, they'd relaxed until even he had almost forgotten he was leaving.

After the baseball game, they'd had no opportunity for any private goodbyes between them, but he'd known that was best. He didn't want a drawn-out scene that would only bring both of them heartache. Still, he'd wanted to kiss her, to hold her in his arms and hear her say she'd wait for him; but since that could never happen, that was the way he wanted to remember their final moments together.

Knowing he shouldn't see her again, he decided to step back into his room and wait until she left; but before he could shut the door, the laughter increased, and Rebecca and his mother emerged from the bedroom.

"Luke, I didn't realize you were home. You simply must come see what Rebecca has done with my bedroom. She's just finished the slipcovers, and they look absolutely divine. They're the most stunning navy-blue and cream combination. . . ."

He barely heard his mother. All he could see was Rebecca. She stood in the doorway, her gaze firmly set on him. While a slight smile rested on her lips, he didn't miss the look of sadness in the depths of her eyes. This was what he hadn't wanted—for her to be hurt any more than she had been already.

"Rebecca, how are you?" he asked.

"I'm doing fine, thank you." Her voice sounded formal and lacked its normal passion. "Business at the shop is very good right now."

"That's wonderful."

Suddenly he knew he wanted that private good-bye he'd missed with her. Maybe it was a foolish sentiment but one he was afraid he would regret later if he didn't at least ask. "Have you ever been up on the widow's walk on the roof of the house?"

She shook her head slowly, as if she didn't understand what he was really asking.

"The view of the ocean is incredible. I'd love to show you. . . ."

"Go ahead, Rebecca," his mother encouraged. "We're finished for the day."

Rebecca turned back to him, and he tried to read the expression on her face. Longing yet hesitation. Anticipation mixed with grief? He'd been foolish to speak so hastily.

"I'm sorry," he began. "If you need to leave—"

"No, it's fine. I'd like to see it."

As he made his way up the narrow staircase to the roof, Rebecca followed slightly behind him. He could feel the awkwardness growing between them. It was as obvious as the sound of her skirts swishing against the stone walls and the rickety steps beneath his feet. No longer could they ignore his imminent departure.

Once they were at the top of the house, he led her to the railing that secured the edge of the small widow's walk.

"The view is breathtaking." She brushed a number of loose wisps away from her face, then took a deep breath of the sea air.

"This was always my favorite place to come when I was a boy."

A brisk wind blew in from the ocean, which from this point one could see for miles. An endless movement of blues and grays that met the cloudless sky in the distance. The shoreline spread out beneath them, like one of John Banvard's famous panoramic paintings that made it possible for viewers to see the world in colored detail. Waterfront businesses lined the harbor, the tide lapped against the coast, and in the distance, the American flag flew proudly at the bow of a yacht.

"My father once told me about the widows' walks where the sailors' wives could come watch for the ships of their husbands to come into the harbor." Her fingers grasped the railing.

"I remember finding my mother here countless times as she watched for the *Annabella* that was to carry my father home on that last voyage."

She turned toward him. "It must have been hard for her, raising you alone for all those years he was out at sea; yet it seems to me she was content with life."

"It was always a happy life. For years my grandparents lived with us. My grandfather had acquired a sizable fortune by owning his own vessel in a time when whale cadavers were at a premium."

"Where is the *Annabella* now?"

"My father was her captain until she went down in a horrible storm off the coast of Nantucket Island."

"Is that when he died?"

Luke nodded. "A handful of men were able to make it to shore, but he went down with the ship. It was a horrible loss of life."

"I'm sorry."

"I miss that I wasn't able to know him really. He died when I was quite young."

Just as he'd never understood as a child why God took his father, he didn't understand today why God had brought Rebecca into his life only for him to lose her. But if nothing else, he would try to be thankful for the times they'd shared. It would have to be enough.

"I'm thinking about going home for Christmas," she said, seeming to try to fill the silence that hung between them.

"Do you plan to return to Boston?"

"I don't know. We just received a letter, and my stepmother, Michaela, is expecting a baby sometime in January. I'd like to be home to help. And then there's my brother Adam's maple farm. They'll be harvesting the syrup early next year."

"What about your work here?"

She shrugged, and he hated the sense of despondency that had come over her. "I've already begun training a well-qualified seamstress to help with the workload. I don't think it would take much to find a second person if I decided not to come back."

"My mother will miss you." His words were foolish, and he knew it. Why couldn't he come out and say exactly what was on his heart? "I'm going to miss you."

"I'll miss you, too."

He watched her as she stared out across the ocean, and for the first time, he understood why she couldn't wait for him. He'd seen his own pain mirrored in her eyes as he spoke about the loss of his father. She feared the same fate would happen to her. It had been wrong of him to hope she might agree to wait until he returned. She was young and had her whole life ahead of her. Standing on the widow's walk waiting for him was a place where she should never be.

She shivered beside him. As much as he longed to extend their time together, he knew he couldn't.

"Why don't we go back down to the house now? Once the sun drops, the temperature will fall, as well."

She looked up into his eyes, her lips parted slightly. He couldn't think. He couldn't process the reality that this was more than likely the last time he'd ever see her.

"May I kiss you good-bye?" He spoke the words without thinking, but even as he asked the question, he didn't regret it.

Nodding, she took a small step toward him. He gathered her into his arms with a passion he'd never felt before. When his lips met hers, the regret over his leaving intensified, until he lost himself in the softness of her kiss.

With tears in her eyes, she pulled away to look up at him one last time, then turned toward the steps and was gone.

Chapter 9

Trying to concentrate on the final seam of the colorful quilt top, Rebecca pushed the needle into the cream-colored fabric and winced as the sharp end jabbed her index finger. A tiny pool of blood soaked through the center of the material, ruining the square.

She let out a sigh of frustration, then carefully ripped off the spoiled square. While it wasn't yet her usual hour to retire for the evening, she knew she needed to stop. The sun that had filtered light into her bedroom for the past two hours had now slipped below the horizon, so she turned up the wick slightly on the kerosene lamp. For a week she'd thrown herself into her work. During the day she ran the shop's showroom and worked on slipcover orders. By night she sewed diligently to transform the boxes of scraps into colorful quilt tops that would grace the beds of the orphans this winter.

With the involvement of Mrs. Hutton, as well as a half dozen other women from church, they'd already managed to complete five quilts for the children, leaving another fifteen to make. With the cold-weather months upon them, they couldn't afford to fall behind on the project. If only she wasn't so tired.

Yawning, she folded the quilt top, then set it on the small table beside her bed. Agnes had been thrilled to hear about the upcoming donations for the children in her care, but despite the excitement she felt about the project, Rebecca still couldn't shake the restlessness inside.

Staying busy wasn't helping at all. By next week her work for Mrs. Hutton would be complete, but she had plenty of other orders that needed to be finished. Still, it seemed that as much as she tried to stay occupied, she couldn't erase the image in her mind of her last moments with Luke.

As they'd stood at the edge of the widow's walk facing the ocean, she'd been sure he was going to ask her one last time to wait for him. And at that moment, despite her earlier hesitations, she would have said yes. But instead, he pulled her into his arms and kissed her, proving to her how much she was losing. When she pulled away and looked into his eyes, she knew he wasn't going to ask her to wait.

He'd only been thinking of her, and he'd been right in his decision. But being right didn't fill the emptiness in her heart. Not marrying Jake had been her decision. In the end, she'd faced the situation head-on, knowing that what she was doing was best despite the fact it had been painful to let him go. With Luke things were different. It had never been her choice to end things between them, especially when she'd decided to open her heart again and take a chance on finding love.

Rebecca shoved back the chair she'd been working in, then walked to the open window. Outside the moon shone brightly in the darkening sky, competing with the hundreds of stars that were making their nightly appearance. A cricket chirped below her. A dog howled in the distance. The *clip-clop* patter of a horse's hooves kept time with the lively piano tune coming from a neighbor's home. Normally she enjoyed the nightly symphony of music that played out between nature and the bustling city around her, but tonight her eyes were focused on the darkened waters of the Atlantic. Through a small clearing in the skyline, she could see the silhouette of a boat entering the harbor. A fisherman coming home to his family after a day's work, or maybe a rich businessman returning in his yacht from a relaxing day at sea.

Luke had left three days ago. That afternoon she'd watched the tips of a ship's white sails flutter in the breeze from this window and wondered if it was the *Liberty*, the very vessel that was taking him away from her.

Her fists gripped tightly at her sides, she felt the wetness of a tear travel down her cheek. *It isn't fair, Lord. Why should I finally decide to give my heart away only to have it shatter into a million tiny pieces?*

Except for the rumbling of thunder in the distance and the normal nightly sounds, silence greeted her instead of the reply she longed for. It wasn't as if she expected God to appear before her and give her the answers, but she needed something. Some obvious sign that letting go of Luke had been God's will.

Her Bible lay on the bedside table, and she plopped onto the feather mattress and picked it up. Where was the verse Caroline had mentioned to her last week? Flipping through her Bible, she finally found the fifth chapter of First Peter. "Casting all your care upon him; for he careth for you."

She closed her Bible and hugged the book to her chest. Cast all your cares on Him. Why was it so easy to know the truth of a matter and so difficult to take it to heart? She knew God cared about her. Hadn't He created her? She knew He loved her to the point where He knew how many hairs were on her head and even counted the steps she took. Her father had made sure she knew these truths from a young age. That the God they served was not one who lived far from them but had given His Holy Spirit to live within those who followed Him.

Lord, help me to give up my fears and frustrations and learn how to follow You with all my heart. I want to find contentment in You.

Walking back to the windowsill, she watched the display of lightning brighten the distant sky. Billowing clouds had covered up all but a sliver of the moon as a storm blew in across the water. Somewhere, out among the crashing waves and endless miles of expanse, Luke was more than likely studying this very sky. How many ships now lay at the bottom of the sea from the spectacular handiwork being displayed tonight?

She pushed back a loose wisp of hair from across her face and shuddered at the thought. All she could do now was pray.

୧

The air in the captain's cabin hung heavily around Luke. Sunlight shone through the small window, but with the dark storm clouds rolling in, the last rays of light would soon disappear. Captain Taft sat at his desk across from Luke, his elbows resting against the solid oak desk that separated them. A matter of discipline had presented itself in the early stages of the voyage. An unschooled sailor thought his philosophies of running the ship were superior to the captain's. After a fight that ended with the same young chap getting his nose split down the middle, the man had attempted to throw one of his fellow crewmen off the bow of the ship. The captain quickly took over the situation and sent the man to the brig for a couple of days of solitude. While the captain was a just and honorable man, he ran his ship with a firm hand, something Luke knew was essential for the survival of the crew.

The ship rocked beneath them, and the captain's pen rolled across the table. Lightning cracked in the distance like a whip, flashing its brilliance against the cabin walls.

"The storm's increasing in velocity," the captain said, picking up his pen and setting it into the top drawer of his desk. "This will be a good first test of how the crew works together."

Luke nodded, then let out a knowing chuckle. "I'm thankful most are experienced, with the exception of our brig occupant, Mr. Lawrence. This will no doubt be a test of strength for him."

The captain rubbed his graying beard, then leaned back in his chair before catching Luke's gaze. "This is going to be your last voyage, isn't it?"

Luke raised his brow in surprise at his superior's question. "To be honest, sir, the lure of the sea has never lessened for me, but I find it hard to imagine myself spending the rest of my life at her mercies. It's my parents' dream to see me captain of my own vessel, not mine."

"Then you hide your emotions well."

"Maybe, but no matter what my decision about future voyages might be, I assure you my commitment to this voyage, this crew, and to you as my captain has not diminished in the least. Nor will it until we step back on land at the end of our journey."

"I never thought it would." There was a twinkle in the older man's eyes. "Who is she?"

Luke leaned forward. "I beg your pardon?"

"Who is she? Only one thing can snatch a man from the lure of the sea—a woman."

Sensing the amusement in his voice, Luke relaxed. "There was someone, but she's not the reason for my reevaluating my future."

"Are you sure?"

"Yes, sir. My mind was pretty well made up before I met her, though I will admit she's going to be hard to forget."

"Hasn't she agreed to wait for you?"

"No, sir." Speaking the word aloud caused Luke's heart to plummet. "I couldn't ask that of her."

"Then I suggest you forget her." The captain slapped his hands against the desk. "We have a voyage ahead of us such that if our focus isn't 100 percent on the job at hand, we'll all suffer. Lives are at stake, something I know you realize, but I know the effects women can have on my men. Unfortunately, none of us is immune to their charms at all times."

"Yes, sir. I won't forget."

After a couple of more suggestions from the captain regarding the crew's schedule, Luke made his way up onto the deck, where the winds continued to pick up. It was time to forget about Rebecca Johnson. Time to forget her captivating smile and her laugh. Besides, the captain was right. He knew if they didn't find a way to stay on the outskirts of the storm, they were in for trouble. And even if they did manage to miss the worst of the torrent, he had no doubt this was going to be a long night.

By the next morning, instead of the storm abating, it had increased in its fury. The headwinds had grown stronger, and visibility was limited as the ship fought against the unseasonably strong winds. The ship's compass had been affected by the relentlessness of the storm, a serious fact considering celestial navigation was impossible because of the heavy cloud cover. Hour after hour found the crew attempting to avoid the brunt of the storm that raged around them. Luke struggled at the wheel, every muscle in his body exhausted from fighting against the winds.

The captain was worried. Luke had noticed the tension in his jaw when he'd left the bridge to supervise the rest of the crew in their endeavors to keep the ship afloat. Pounding waves continued to lash against the sides of the ship, flooding the deck with several inches of water. Luke had read plenty of accounts of shipwreck disasters and had imagined the horror of taking one's last breath of air before being swallowed into the depths of the sea. He had no desire to die that way. It had always been a reality he chose not to consider. But today things were different. It was a possibility he couldn't ignore.

Water dripped down his forehead and onto his clothes, which were already soaked from the constant barrage of waves hitting the ship. Shivering, he wiped the back of his hand across his mouth. The cup of lukewarm coffee he'd inhaled earlier had been his only source of nourishment all morning, if it could even be considered that. His stomach grumbled in complaint, but he couldn't give in to the strong desire to escape to the galley for a meal. That would come later. If it came at all.

A sharp crack ripped through the morning air as if the helm of the ship were being split in two. The vessel shuddered beneath him as it struck something. Men shouted above the commotion as they fought to save the ship. Moments later Luke saw the bright lights of a red flare being shot into the murky sky. . .then nothing.

Chapter 10

S he's so beautiful." Rebecca sat down on the featherbed beside Caroline and ran the back of her thumb across the soft cheek of the newborn who lay nestled peacefully in her mother's arms. "I'd forgotten how small babies are."

"She is tiny, but thank the Lord she's healthy despite her early arrival." Caroline's face beamed with happiness, all the complaints of her condition forgotten with the arrival of the baby. "What smells so wonderful?"

"Hungry?"

"Famished, actually."

"Good, because I made you a thick beef stew."

Caroline's brow narrowed. "And wherever did you find the time to cook something for me?"

"Somewhere between Mrs. Kendall's slipcovers and Myra Potter's lined draperies."

"And don't forget the quilts for the orphans. I know you've spent hours of your own time on that project." Caroline reached down and kissed the baby gently on the forehead. "You know I'm going to be spoiled before long. Susan Parker came by last night and told me several women at church would be bringing meals for the next few days. I don't think I've ever eaten so well."

"Then I won't even mention the mince pie Aunt Clara made for dessert."

Caroline groaned, but the delight was obvious in her eyes. "I just can't get over the miracle of this little one's entrance into the world."

"So," Rebecca probed, "you've decided not to stop at only one?"

"Despite a long and strenuous labor, I can't believe how in love I am with her. I don't know if three or four will be enough to satisfy my longings of motherhood."

"So Susan's twelve doesn't sound so bad after all?"

"I wouldn't go quite that far."

Rebecca laughed but couldn't ignore the stirrings she felt inside.

"Do you want to hold her?" Caroline asked.

Nodding, Rebecca gently took the baby, then went to sit on the cushioned rocker that had been moved into the bedroom from the living area. The small bundle of pink whimpered softly in her arms and opened her eyes briefly. After a moment, she was sleeping peacefully again.

"Have you and Philip decided on a name?" Rebecca looked up at Caroline, who still had her gaze fixed on her daughter. "It's been two days, you know."

Caroline shook her head. "The problem is that Philip has the most atrocious tastes when it comes to names. The only thing we've agreed on so far have been boy names. Of course, that was after I convinced him we couldn't name a child Milborough or Perine—family name or not."

Rebecca chuckled over Philip's awful tastes. "I would have to feel sorry for your child if given one of those names."

Caroline nodded in agreement. "The problem is, now that the Lord has blessed us with a daughter, we can't seem to come up with anything that suits us both. His first choice is Bertha after his mother. I told him that while I'm sure his mother was a wonderful woman, I have no intentions of giving my darling baby a name that sounds more like the name of a whaling vessel than a little girl."

Rebecca's smile vanished at the reminder of Luke, and she lowered her head so Caroline couldn't see her fallen expression. Reminders of him were everywhere. From the sea itself to the bouquets of flowers the street vendors sold. She'd spent half the night praying God would help her forget him, but if anything, her feelings toward him had strengthened.

Rebecca took her gaze off the baby and glanced at Caroline. She was thankful her friend seemed so wrapped up in her new daughter that she didn't appear to notice Rebecca's sullen mood. She pasted on a grin. "What name had you chosen if it was a boy?"

"John. Plain yet strong. For some reason that wasn't nearly as difficult, but names for a girl. . ."

"What about Johnna for a girl?"

"Johnna." Caroline reached over and grasped the baby's hand between her fingers and smiled. "I like that name. I'll have to see what Philip thinks once he comes up from the shop for lunch. Have you thought any more about your plans for leaving?"

Rebecca glanced down at the infant, who had inherited her mother's fair skin and plump cheeks. "I think it's best for me to go home, but not until right before Christmas. That will give me a chance to help you with the baby and make sure there are competent staff to continue making the slipcovers until you're ready to take over things again."

"I'm certainly going to miss you. Michaela did well in marrying your father and bringing you into her family."

"Don't think you've gotten rid of me forever," Rebecca said, trying to lighten the somber mood that had fallen over her. "I'll have to come back and visit the baby, as well as see my grandmother someday."

"When is she due back?"

"Unfortunately, Mrs. Hutton informed me last week that she's postponed her return until late spring at the earliest."

"Well, I for one don't know what I'm going to do without you. I've enjoyed having you here."

Rebecca felt a stream of guilt course through her. "You understand why I'm leaving, don't you?"

"Of course I understand. I just hope you're not leaving Boston to escape memories of Luke."

Rebecca cringed at the statement but knew Caroline's words held a hint of truth. If only forgetting Luke was as easy to do as loving him had been.

⁂

Rebecca set the feather cushion onto the coverlet and sighed with relief. The satin, with its floral needlework pattern and lace trim, was the finishing touch in Mrs. Hutton's bedroom. Rebecca had carried the dark blue and cream theme throughout the room, including floor-to-ceiling draperies with tiebacks and accents in the padded ottoman and throw pillows on the sofa. The overall effect was simple but stylish.

While she had no doubt she would see more of Mrs. Hutton in the coming weeks before her departure, since they worked together on the orphans' quilting project, today was the day she planned to say good-bye forever to Luke in her mind. No more would she be obliged to visit the Hutton home to measure the length of a divan or panels that would hang gracefully from cornices. No more would she have to be surrounded by the constant reminders of him that filled the house.

"Rebecca, I'm glad you're still here." Mrs. Hutton stood in the doorway, her hands clasped behind her back. "I wanted to catch you before you left."

"Is everything satisfactory?"

"Of course," she said, stepping into the room. "You've done a splendid job. I wanted to make sure I had the chance to thank you again. I'm so pleased with the way the room turned out."

Rebecca smiled with relief. "I'm glad. I've enjoyed the time I've been able to work here."

Mrs. Hutton smoothed back the same strand of silver hair that seemed to fall habitually from the neat pile atop her head. But even that didn't take away from her beauty. It always amazed Rebecca to see how elegant the woman appeared no matter what the occasion.

"Mrs. Hutton, I was wondering. . ." Rebecca paused. She wanted to do one last thing before leaving the house.

"What is it, Rebecca?"

"Would you mind if I went up on the widow's walk? The view is so beautiful. I'd like to see it one last time." *And I need to say good-bye one last time.*

"Certainly, but are you all right? You seem a bit pale today."

"I'm fine. I just—" What should she say? Would Mrs. Hutton understand the feelings Rebecca felt so strongly for her son? Would she understand why she couldn't love him?

"You miss him, don't you?" Mrs. Hutton drew Rebecca onto the narrow settee that lined a section of the bedroom wall.

Rebecca nodded, determined not to shed a single teardrop. "I wish the circumstances had been different. That we'd had more time together before he left."

"And I wouldn't have minded having you for a daughter-in-law." Mrs. Hutton smiled. "I told Luke more than once that you were a good catch for a sailor like him, unlike those empty-headed girls always chasing after him."

Rebecca felt the heat rise in her face at the admission. She looked up at the wall covered with framed daguerreotypes of Luke's parents, grandparents, and other relatives. At one time she'd foolishly dared to imagine her and Luke's wedding photo gracing this very wall.

Mrs. Hutton took Rebecca's hand and squeezed it gently. "Letting go of love is never easy, even if it's the best thing."

"But was it the best thing?"

"I don't know, but I can tell you this. Right now you need to lean on God's strength. Allow His Spirit to work through you and use this situation to make you more like Him. In sixty years, I've learned that life isn't always easy, but it's the experiences that have been the most painful that have taught me the most. They gave me perseverance and in the end strengthened my faith."

Rebecca laced her fingers together, pondering the advice. "That's what I want, but instead of growing in my faith, I seem to be at a standstill. I can't hear God's voice anymore. I don't feel His presence. I'm like a raft being swept along by the tide with no real direction."

"Sometimes we can find God only in the quiet. Go on up to the widow's walk where you can see the power of His creation and just listen for His voice."

Rebecca took the narrow staircase slowly, running her hand across the cool stone walls. At the top of the house, the endless sea spread out before her. A crisp wind whipped around her face, bringing with it the signs of the coming winter. Leaning against the railing, she watched wave after wave make its way toward the shore. The ocean churned before her, and she couldn't help but wonder how Luke was faring today. But she wasn't here to daydream about him.

Instead, she closed her eyes and, one by one, began erasing the memories of the two of them together. The first day they met at Macintosh Furniture and Upholstery. Their walk along the boardwalk. The bouquet of flowers he brought her. The night he told her he cared for her. The baseball game. And then the last time she saw him. Wiping her mouth with the back of her hand, she attempted to wipe away the burning memory of his kiss.

She opened her eyes again and watched as a large schooner made its way into the port. Women would be standing on their own widows' walks right now, waiting for the men they loved to return to them. Children waiting to see a father they barely remembered. Mothers ready to embrace the boy who had become a man.

But not her.

She wouldn't be here waiting when Luke returned from the sea. She wouldn't be here to welcome him home with her kisses and words of love. Instead, she'd be in Cranton where she belonged, surrounded by her brothers and sisters and parents who loved her. And maybe someday she'd find a man who loved her unconditionally and whom she could love the same. Someone who shared her beliefs and passions. Someone she could grow old with.

Rebecca gripped the edge of the railing, knowing only One would never let her down.

Help me give my burdens totally to You, Lord. To let You be my strength in my weakness. Help me find You again.

She'd spent her entire life trying to be strong and handle things herself. From the time she was eleven years old, when her own mother had died, she'd been thrust into running much of her father's household. Not that she'd ever complained. It came naturally for her to care for her younger siblings, and despite the ache she'd carried in her heart from her mother's death, she'd blossomed with the responsibility.

But it had always been her own strength she'd relied on. Even with Jake she'd made the decision to call things off and move to Boston. Had she spent her life confusing her own will with God's will?

Rebecca closed her eyes again, but this time she worked to quiet her mind and focus on God and His power. To understand God's will for her life, she needed to know God. Of course she knew He cared for her, loved her, and wanted her to follow Him, but did she grasp the significance of who He was in her life? Not just her Savior, but her Lord and Master? She'd been so busy doing things that would please God, such as the quilting project, but she'd devoted little time to getting to know her heavenly Father.

And it was time to change all of that. Opening her eyes, a wave of peace washed over her. She'd taken the first step.

"Rebecca?"

Turning around, she saw Mrs. Hutton standing at the top of the staircase. Her normally calm presence had vanished, and her face had paled to the color of ashes.

"What is it?" Rebecca asked.

Mrs. Hutton leaned against the door frame. "A courier's just arrived. The *Liberty* was caught in a storm and is lost at sea."

Chapter 11

Rebecca's hands covered her mouth as she tried to grasp the news regarding the *Liberty*. She'd listened to the storms that had riveted the coastline and watched the lightning rip through the sky the past few days. Through it all she'd prayed that God's hand would protect Luke and his crew. But the *Liberty* had gone down. Surely it wasn't true. Surely this was some kind of mistake. The reality of the situation gripped her like the dark shadows of a nightmare. They'd been gone long enough that the chances of surviving that far out on the sea were too slim to expect any survivors.

The cold wind whipped around her, and she could hardly breathe. In spite of knowing it was over between her and Luke, she'd still held on to a sliver of hope that one day she'd see him again. Now every thread of hope was broken. Closing her eyes, she could see him standing beside her as he'd done the afternoon they gazed out across the sea together. She could feel his lips on hers as he kissed her good-bye. A part of her had dared to dream he would come back for her. Now she'd never know what might have happened between them.

Her eyes filled with tears. As she looked across the choppy waters, the emptiness in her heart swelled. *I miss you so much, Luke, and I'll never be able to tell you. . .*

Rebecca felt Mrs. Hutton's fingers grasp her arm, drawing her back into the present. The older woman opened her mouth, but no words came out.

"What is it?" Rebecca's heart pounded in her throat. "Is there news about Luke from the survivors?"

Mrs. Hutton nodded slowly, her breaths coming in short spurts. Rebecca didn't want to know the details of how he had died. Surely being swept into the ocean had been terrifying beyond imagination. If he'd been injured and had suffered during his last moments alive, she'd rather not know.

"Luke was—" Mrs. Hutton's fingers grew tighter around her arm. "He was rescued by another vessel."

"What?" Rebecca's eyes widened at the life preserver of hope Mrs. Hutton had thrown her.

"He's injured but alive. I've arranged for him to be brought here to the house immediately."

Tears of relief flooded down Rebecca's cheeks as she clung to Mrs. Hutton. Luke was alive! After a moment, Rebecca pulled away, her ears still ringing from the news. He might be alive, but how badly was he injured? Surely God wouldn't save him from the sea only to take him from them now.

"Has he seen a doctor?" Rebecca asked.

"Only aboard the ship that rescued him. I've sent someone to go and get Dr. Neil, who is an old family friend."

Rebecca blinked, not knowing what to think. If he was alive, she had to see him. "What can I do to help?"

"Could you stay here for a while? I have no idea of his condition, and if it's life threatening—"

"Of course I'll stay. Please, just tell me what you need me to do."

While relieved at the older woman's response, Rebecca realized the request had nothing to do with her and her feelings for Luke. Patience Hutton was a mother awaiting the return of her injured son with no real clues yet as to his condition. She'd lost a husband to the sea and now was faced with the possibility of losing a son, as well.

Rebecca sat in an oval-back chair in the upstairs hallway while Mrs. Hutton paced the tan plush carpet. It had been over an hour since Luke had been brought into the house, then whisked away behind the closed door of his bedroom. Rebecca had begged God for Luke's healing while struggling to read through a number of the Psalms. For now she had no more tears to shed. Only a quiet desperation that filled every corner of her heart. He might have been rescued from the sinking ship, but whether he would survive the night was still in question.

At half past four the doorbell rang. The housekeeper had already dealt with a number of callers, and Rebecca was certain that news regarding the sinking of the *Liberty* had spread quickly across Boston.

One of the maids appeared at the top of the stairs. "I'm sorry to bother you, Mrs. Hutton. We've thanked and sent away the other callers, but this gentleman says he's the captain of the vessel that rescued your son."

"Tell him I'll be down immediately." Mrs. Hutton clutched her hands to her chest and turned to Rebecca. "Please, come with me."

Rebecca's stomach churned as she followed Mrs. Hutton down the stairs, anxious for more details of what Luke had gone through. She'd only caught a glimpse of him, and from his colorless features, it was obvious his condition was serious. Assurances that Dr. Neil was one of the best physicians in Boston did little to relieve her fears, as she was convinced that only a miracle could save

Luke now. And a miracle was exactly what she was praying for.

As they entered the parlor, an older man dressed in a simple black suit stood waiting to greet them. "Mrs. Hutton? My name is Vincent Sawyer, captain of the *Marella*."

"Mr. Sawyer." Mrs. Hutton grasped the balding man's outstretched hand. "Thank you for taking the time to stop by. May I introduce Rebecca Johnson, a family friend."

"It's a pleasure to meet you, Miss Johnson."

"Thank you." Rebecca shook the captain's hand, then took a seat on the sofa, anxious over the impending news.

"Won't you please sit down, Mr. Sawyer?" Mrs. Hutton motioned to a chair for the captain before sitting down on the sofa next to Rebecca. "Am I correct in assuming you've come with news regarding my son and the loss of the *Liberty*?"

Mr. Sawyer leaned forward in the chair. "Your son is one of the fortunate few who were able to survive in the open sea."

Mrs. Hutton held a handkerchief to her lips and exhaled deeply. "Please tell me everything. What I've heard so far has been extremely vague."

"Apparently the *Liberty* sailed into the storm a couple of days ago. Details are still sketchy, but I was on my way back from England to the Boston harbor when we came across five men who were holding on for their lives on one small lifeboat."

"How long was my son out there?"

"I can't be sure of the time line, ma'am. A number of unseasonable yet vicious storms have swept through the area these past few days, and any one of them had the potential to damage a ship."

"And my son's injuries?"

Rebecca leaned forward, listening intently to the man's words. She could hardly stand the fact that Luke lay upstairs fighting for his life and there was nothing she could do.

"I'm not a medical expert, ma'am," the captain explained, "but our ship's doctor did care for him on our return. I know his leg is injured, and he's been unconscious off and on since he was first hauled aboard our ship."

"And the other men?"

"While we were able to rescue only five of the crew, I believe they will all pull through. I've just been to see Captain Taft's wife. Unfortunately, the captain didn't make it."

Mrs. Hutton stared out the window. "I lost my husband over twenty years ago. I've always feared I'd lose my son, as well."

"Then you're fortunate God chose to save your son this time."

~

Two hours later Rebecca stared at the bowl of vegetable soup the cook had set before her at the dining room table. Mrs. Hutton had insisted Rebecca eat something, but so far she'd been able to take only one bite. On any other occasion, she would have enjoyed the simmering bouquet of nourishment, but not today. Instead, it was tasteless as her stomach churned from the morning's events. The doctor's report had been far from encouraging. At some point during the storm, Luke's left leg had been crushed. It was a miracle he'd survived the open sea for any length of time. She'd overheard whispers of amputation and shivered at what that would do to Luke. He was a man who thrived on physical work. What would the loss of an extremity do to him?

Rebecca looked up as Mrs. Hutton entered the room, her face thin and pale. Fear tightened the muscles of Rebecca's stomach as she dreaded news of Luke's worsening condition.

"How is he?"

"He's still asleep." Mrs. Hutton said. "I'm worried, Rebecca."

Rebecca worked to hold back the tears, wanting to stay strong for Mrs. Hutton's sake. Inside, though, she felt anything but strong. The doctor had left an hour ago with assurances that he'd return before nightfall. For now, they could do nothing else but wait. And the waiting was excruciating.

"Why don't you have the cook get you something to eat?" Rebecca pushed back her bowl of soup. "You need to eat to keep up your strength."

"So do you." The older woman grasped the back of the mahogany armchair at the end of the oval table. "I don't think I can stomach anything to eat, but a cup of hot tea might help calm me."

"I can't eat either." Rebecca stood from the table. "Why don't you let me sit with Luke while you rest for a while? You're exhausted and won't be of any help to him if you become ill."

She expected an argument, but instead, Mrs. Hutton nodded. "You wouldn't mind?"

"Of course not. I promise to call you if he wakes up."

Rebecca headed for the doorway but stopped when Mrs. Hutton continued. "Have you ever lost anyone close to you?"

"My mother died giving birth to my sister." Rebecca leaned against the door frame, feeling the stinging pain from dredging up the old memories. "I was eleven years old."

Mrs. Hutton pulled out a red and gold porcelain cup and saucer from inside the reed-inlaid sideboard. "Then you know how it feels to lose someone you love. Someone you can't imagine living without."

"Like your husband?"

"I still miss him." Mrs. Hutton laid the delicate pieces on the table and sat in one of the chairs. "Our marriage wasn't perfect, of course, but we did love each other deeply."

"I'm sure he was a wonderful man."

"He was, but marrying a sailor brings its own difficulties. I would never have admitted it to Isaac, but there were moments when I wanted him to leave on the next voyage and never come back. Our time apart was so difficult."

"All marriages have their own set of adjustments, but what you went through had to be extremely hard."

Mrs. Hutton nodded slowly, not bothering to sweep back the strand of silver hair that had once again fallen out of place. "The last time I saw him before he left on the *Annabella* was early on a misty autumn morning. I was mad at him over some silly misunderstanding we'd had the night before, but at the time, I was stubborn and didn't want to believe our argument was partly my fault. When he kissed me that last morning, I let him walk away without saying good-bye to him. How could I have been such a fool? I never saw him again."

The room was silent for a moment. Rebecca bowed her head and studied the intricate pattern in the Oriental rug. She'd seen the pain of past mistakes etched into the creases around the older woman's eyes, but what could she say that would make a difference?

"I've never forgiven myself for wishing he wouldn't return," Mrs. Hutton continued. "For months after his death, I blamed myself, somehow thinking God heard my grumbling and decided to teach me a lesson."

"God doesn't work that way."

"I know He doesn't, but sometimes my heart has a hard time accepting what I know is true."

"How well I understand that." Rebecca let out a deep sigh. She had no doubt that God had never left her, yet how easy it was to feel the void of His presence when things became difficult and the answers seemed so far away.

Mrs. Hutton traced her index finger around the rim of the empty cup. "I told you earlier that life isn't always easy, but it's the painful experiences that have taught me the most. Realizing Isaac wasn't coming back after the horrid things I said to him was one of those instances that took me years to work through. I think that's why I've always encouraged Luke to follow in his father's footsteps—maybe too much—but I haven't wanted the guilt from my own past to stop him from doing what he wants to do."

"I'm so sorry you had to go through that."

"Luke's accident brings it all back to me. I'm so afraid of losing my son. You understand, don't you, because you love him?"

"Yes," Rebecca said, squeezing her eyes shut at the admission. "I love him."

ॐ

Fifteen minutes later, Rebecca sat in a chair at Luke's side, a weathered Bible open in front of her. But with her eyes filled with tears, she couldn't focus on the words. If she hadn't heard the doctor's diagnosis, she could almost believe Luke was simply sleeping peacefully. Instead, she feared that each breath he took might be his last. And she couldn't lose him now.

Shutting the Bible, she looked around the room at signs of the boy who had turned into a man. A pupil's copy of *McGuffey's Eclectic Reader* lay beside Ralph Waldo Emerson's *Nature* and James Fenimore Cooper's *The Last of the Mohicans*. A pair of hardened steel skates sat precariously on the floor. On his desk perched a brightly painted cast-iron bank, cleverly engineered so that the little mechanical dog would leap through a clown's hoop and drop a penny in the barrel for safekeeping.

Realizing Luke was alive had made her feel as if God was giving them a second chance to find love with one another. A second chance to let go of their fears and trust in Him completely to show them what direction He would have them take. But was this truly a second chance? She tried to pray, but her words seemed empty. Mere words seemed insignificant when searching for God's will in her life—and when begging for God to save the life of the one she loved.

ॐ

Luke felt a piercing pain rip through his leg and struggled to open his eyes. Why did it hurt so much? A shiver swept over him, reminding him of the dark, cold waters. The ship had hit something, then he'd felt the sea pull him under. But he wouldn't let it win. He wasn't ready to die, so he'd clung to something until—

"Luke?" He could hear Rebecca's voice, but he couldn't find her. "Are you awake?"

He groaned and forced his eyes open. The room swirled around him like a dark fog. It was his room. He recognized the mechanical bank his grandfather had given him. In the distance. . .a shelf of books. . . When had he returned home?

"Luke, it's Rebecca."

He turned his head toward her voice, gritting his teeth at the intense pain that refused to leave him.

"You're home now. It's going to be all right."

Too exhausted to talk, he closed his eyes again. Despite the searing pain, only two things seemed to matter. Rebecca was with him, and he knew he loved her.

Chapter 12

Rebecca set the worn copy of *The Golden Trail* in her lap and smiled across the small stretch of green lawn toward Luke's sleeping form. Six days after his rescue, he was still confined to a wheelchair, but the color in his face was back, and on most days his spirits had been high. Leaning against the rough bark of the oak tree that majestically towered above her in the Hutton garden, she let out a contented sigh of relief. Only God knew what the days ahead of them would hold, but for the first time, a life spent with Luke seemed possible.

Only one dark shadow hovered in the recesses of her mind. While the doctor had decided against the necessity of amputating the injured extremity, full use of the limb was still questionable. Because of the uncertainties that lay ahead, Luke spoke little about the future, except for telling her that his days spent on a whaling voyage were over. He seemed to accept this without remorse, and she hoped his acceptance of the matter was because of her. With him now free from the obligations of the sea, they had been offered the chance to pursue a future together. Whether he still wanted to take that chance, she wasn't sure.

Luke's eyes opened halfway. "Why did you stop reading?"

"You were asleep."

"I was not."

"You were snoring." Rebecca laughed. "You know, between the cook's succulent dishes and your orneriness, you might actually recover."

Luke folded his arms across his chest and frowned. "So what did I miss?"

"In the book?"

He nodded, appearing disinterested in the story, but she knew that was far from the truth. He'd had to spend most of his time lying in bed for nearly a week, and she knew he enjoyed the hours she spent reading to him from either the Bible or the dozen dime novels she kept tucked away in her mother's wooden trunk.

She hugged the yellow-spined book to her chest. "Cassidy Walker, the wicked villain of the story, was sent to jail for robbing one of the transcontinental railroads. Max Crane, on the other hand, was heralded a hero for his daring role in saving the town's fortune of gold. And in the end, of course, the beautiful

Bessie was so awed by his bravery that when he asked to take her hand in marriage, she swooned, but not before saying yes to his proposal."

Luke's gaze shot to the sky, and he shook his head at her dramatic rendition of the story's ending. "Perhaps it's time you tried a new profession. You could let your imagination run wild while teaching lessons in morality, like how being honest has its rewards."

Her eyes widened at his teasing. "You can't be serious. My dull imagination would have people closing the covers before they reached page two."

Luke laughed. "Maybe, but I still can't believe you got me to listen to one of those dime novels."

"You're bored silly, and you know it. Besides, what's so horrible about them?" She held up the book and pretended to be miffed. "Evil is punished, and virtue is well rewarded. And you enjoyed every minute of this tale, didn't you?"

"Something I certainly would never admit." He winked at her. "One thing I have noticed, though, is in the end, the hero always gets the fair maiden."

Rebecca sucked in her breath and held it as he looked at her. His eyes glistened like tiny fireworks as they caught the last rays of the setting sun. The dark outline of a beard covered his strong jaw. All she wanted to do was sit and watch him, hardly able to believe he was alive and with her again. But he was here, and each day she spent with him, she found herself falling deeper and deeper into his charms.

"It seems a lifetime ago that you let me kiss you on the widow's walk." His words came out huskily as he spoke of the very moment she'd dreamed about for days.

"For me, as well."

Fiddling with a blade of grass between her fingers, she stared at it and longed for him to tell her of his intentions toward her. Longed for him to take her in his arms as he had that moment when they'd overlooked the sea, knowing he was leaving. He'd captured a part of her heart the way no man ever had. And a part of her never wanted to take it back.

But one question haunted her. She'd seen the way he stared across a room or the garden when he didn't know she was watching him, his eyes full of pain and grief. It was obvious the accident had changed him. Had it also changed things between them? Was it possible, despite his teasing, that now that he was here to stay, he regretted his impulsive actions toward her?

She twisted the thick blade until it split under the strain. She'd come to the Hutton home every day since the accident, telling herself it was simply to help Luke's mother deal with the difficult recovery. But she knew that wasn't true. She'd come because of Luke. Because she longed to see him and be near him. It was as if letting him out of her sight might mean she'd lose him again forever.

"Everything seems different now, Rebecca."

Her chin darted upward, and she cringed at his words as she waited for him to continue.

"I don't know why God let me live while most of the other men on that ship lost their lives."

"You know the accident wasn't your fault."

"I know." He shrugged his shoulders. "But I also know things will never be the same again."

"You're right." She leaned forward and rested her palms against the cool grass. "Those men's families will never see them again—children who lost their fathers, women who lost their husbands. There's an emptiness that will never be filled. And as for your own injuries. . ."

She watched as his fingers gripped the bulky blanket on his lap. He was right. Things would never be the same again. Life might go on, but it was clear that a part of him had died when the *Liberty* went down.

"Is it crazy to want to know why God saved me and not the others? Captain Taft was a good man with a wife and three children. Williams, our cook, had a son born three months ago who will never know him." His jaw tensed, bringing out the veins in his neck. "How could God let something like this happen?"

"I don't know, Luke."

She swallowed hard, praying that God would help her to know what to say. The pain in his eyes flashed before her, his grief obvious from the tone of his voice. She couldn't even imagine the things he'd seen and heard during those fateful moments when the sea swallowed his friends and crewmates into its depths. It was a tragedy, the consequences of which would be felt for decades by those left behind.

"I've been struggling lately with the feeling that God is so far away and not knowing what He wants me to do with my life." Trying to formulate her words, she stared at the last streaks of color from the sunset as they faded into the darkening skyline. "I haven't been able to feel His presence, and when tragedies like this occur, it leaves me questioning His role in my life.

"I found a verse in Hebrews that I've clung to these past few days. It tells us to hold fast the profession of our faith without wavering, because He's faithful. Life is full of difficulties, but in the end, if we persevere, we have victory through Christ and will be with Him forever in the place He's preparing for us."

" 'In the world ye shall have tribulation: but be of good cheer; for I have overcome the world.'" He shot her a half smile. "My mother used to quote that verse to me frequently."

Rebecca smiled back, despite the deep conviction the verse brought her. "It's still hard putting the words into practice, though, isn't it?"

"I definitely feel caught between what I believe to be true and knowing how to put it into practice."

"Trust me—you're not the only one."

He leaned back in the chair and looked at her. "I'm sorry to have switched to such a serious subject."

"I'm not. I, too, have so many questions regarding the matter. I guess I just have to cling to the truth that He is faithful."

"And the other subject we started talking about? The one about you and me—"

She glanced away from Luke, momentarily distracted as Philip, Caroline's husband, stepped down from the terrace and onto the lawn. "If the two of you are ready to come in, the rest of us can start eating dinner."

With her heart still pounding at Luke's last comment, she stood and managed a polite nod. What had Luke wanted to say? Had he finally planned to ask if he could court her, or had he changed his mind and wanted only to tell her the truth about his new feelings?

"You're fortunate Mrs. Hutton invited you for dinner tonight, Philip," Rebecca said with a forced laugh as she maneuvered Luke's chair toward the house. "I do believe that all you men think about is food."

Luke cleared his throat and looked back at her. "I have to confess, now that my appetite is finally back, I always seem ready to eat."

Rebecca pushed Luke to the bottom of the stairs, where Philip waited to help maneuver the chair into the dining room, wondering all the while what tomorrow might hold.

❦

Luke felt the light breeze filter in from his open bedroom window and wheeled his chair closer so he could look out over the silhouette of a city preparing to sleep for the night. Familiar sounds of dogs barking and the occasional raised voice played against the softer sounds of the incoming waves of the nearby sea, that vast churning beast that seemed to take life as easily as it provided for it. How strange that the very sea that had taken him away from Rebecca had been the same sea that now sent him home.

He let out a deep sigh, both out of frustration and out of longing. Life seemed so full of uncertainties. Not that he doubted God's presence in his life, but that didn't change the fact that He often seemed farther away than the distant shores Luke visited on his last voyage. Still, Rebecca's words had reminded him of his Creator's constant care despite the dreadful events he'd somehow survived. But even that knowledge didn't erase the pain burning within his soul.

He didn't understand why he lived when the majority of the crew, including his captain, had perished in the accident. How could he not question the purpose of his survival? God might have a plan for his life, but at the moment, with a useless leg, he had no idea what it might be.

Like Rebecca, their minister had come by and assured him any guilt he felt over his crewmates' deaths was normal, but instead of feeling absolved, he fought against feelings of remorse. He longed to find the reason why God pulled him out of the depths of the sea. Being thankful for his survival wasn't always easy, in spite of the fact that he knew he had a lot to be grateful for. Friends, family. . . Rebecca.

He'd seen the glimmer of hope in her expression as she spoke about God's unfailing care and love and wished he could feel the peace she exhibited despite her confessed uncertainty at times.

All week her smile had given him a reason to fight. The doctor might not be sure how far his recovery would go, but with Rebecca's encouragement, he'd made significant progress. His biggest hurdle now was getting out of the chair to which he was temporarily affixed. But he was determined to walk. He'd overcome numerous obstacles in the past, from a life-threatening case of measles as a child to the sun-scorched conditions on a whaling vessel. His own fortitude of mind refused to allow this newest barrier to stop him. The doctor had managed to save his leg. It was up to him to get out of the chair.

Luke stared out his window as a shooting star streaked across the blackened sky. Higher on the horizon the moon hovered like a brightly lit whale-oil lamp. He knew that the God who displayed His majesty in the heavens above as well as the earth below could bring healing to his battered body, but would He bring peace to his troubled soul, as well?

Turning away from the window, Luke edged his way toward the bed as fatigue took over his body. Philip's presence in the house tonight at dinner had affected him, as well. As Philip spoke about his wife and new daughter, Luke could vividly imagine the joy he hoped to feel one day about his own family. Isn't that what he wanted at some point? A wife, a family, and a place to call their own? And he was certain he wanted to spend that life with Rebecca. Before Philip had interrupted them in the garden, he'd planned to speak to her about his intentions. He yearned to tell her it was time they took a step forward with their relationship if she would agree to allow him to court her officially.

He gripped the arms of his chair as the reality of his situation rushed over him. Maybe it was good he'd missed the chance to say anything. Certain questions haunted not only his waking hours, but also his dreams at night. What if he was never able to walk again? How could he, as a cripple, support Rebecca? He'd always felt that God's will for him revolved around the bounty of the sea, both through his past whaling voyages and his dream of building ships. Without his legs, though, finding a purpose for his life seemed hopeless.

Parallel to the edge of his bed, Luke stifled the urge to call for the man his mother had hired to assist him. A week had already passed, and while he felt somewhat stronger, it was time to push his physical limits. He refused to rely on this chair or other people for the rest of his life.

Forcing his tired arms to push his body out of the chair, Luke felt his muscles burn with the effort, but he refused to give in to the pain. He set his good leg on the floor and stood slowly. He swayed with the effort, then caught his balance. One step was all he needed to take. One step and the exertion would be over. He felt a spasm in his leg, and it refused to move.

Struggling to fill his lungs with air, he let his other foot touch the ground. Tiny beads of perspiration broke out across his forehead. Closing his eyes, he could envision Rebecca's face before him. She would tell him to keep on no matter how much his body revolted against the effort. And that's exactly what he planned to do.

His injured leg brushed against the floor, shooting a wave of fire through the extremity. Clenching his teeth, he fought the swelling pain that surged within him and tried to regain his balance. But determination wasn't enough. With a loud groan Luke crumpled into a heap on the rug.

Chapter 13

Y ou haven't heard a single word I've said, have you?" Rebecca sat back in the padded wicker chair on the Huttons' terrace and frowned at Luke's somber figure.

For the past few days, she'd managed to juggle her time between fulfilling her responsibilities at the furniture shop and staying up late into the night to complete the remaining quilts for the orphans. In addition, she'd continued to keep Luke company in the afternoons. While spending time with him was something she'd come to enjoy during his recovery, his sullen attitude these last couple of days had tempted her more than once to send her regrets that she would not be available to stop by. If he simply wanted someone to be around, the maid could do that.

Matching her frown, he said nothing as he slid his knight across the wooden chessboard.

She folded her arms across her chest. "I didn't come to sit and talk to the wall."

"Then why did you come?" He looked up, exposing the pair of atrocious muttonchops he'd allowed to grow along the sides of his face. Others might contend that such a look was fashionable, but she did not.

Rising from the table, she glanced into the house, wishing Mrs. Hutton hadn't gone out. Luke's mother had assured her the daily afternoon visits lifted his spirits and had invited her to continue coming until he was walking again. It was something she'd done with pleasure. Until today.

At the moment, she wasn't even sure why she had come. Not once had he made further mention of his intentions toward her, leaving her at a loss as to where their relationship, if there even was one, was headed. In fact, the conversation they'd begun the other night regarding their future had seemingly vanished along with the fading daylight.

"It's your turn." Luke's fingers gripped the armrest as he rocked his chair back and forth.

The slight squeak coming from the left wheel was enough to drive her mad, and while she hated venting her own frustrations on him, she was tired of his unpleasant moods. "I'd rather not play anymore."

"Would you prefer reading to me?"

"Reading to you?" Rebecca plopped back down in her chair, exasperated. After his long-winded complaints about the ending of the last dime novel she'd read him, she was surprised he had the gall to ask. "You want me to read to you?"

A fire blazed in his eyes as he looked at her. "Honestly? No. I don't want you to read to me. I want to go down to the harbor and start building another boat. I want to wear my ice skates and spend the afternoon at the indoor rink. I want to—"

"Luke—" She clenched her teeth together.

"What? What do you want to say? That I can't do any of those things now?" He leaned forward in his chair. "Don't you know I'm fully aware of what I can't do anymore?"

With one long brush of his hand, Luke swept the chessboard onto the stone floor of the terrace, its wooden armies scattering in every direction. The following silence was deafening. Rebecca stared at the jumbled pieces strewn across the ground and was overcome with a sense of guilt. He may have lost his temper, but she'd helped drive him to it. Who was she to judge his unpleasant attitude when he'd been through so much? On top of watching the horrendous deaths of his crewmates, he'd possibly lost not only the use of one of his extremities, but his dream to be a shipbuilder. Didn't the man have a right to go through a time of mourning?

"I'm sorry." Their apologies came at the same time, bringing a slight grin to Rebecca's lips.

Luke ran his fingers through his wavy hair. "You have nothing to regret. I'm the one who's been truly horrible these past few days. I really am sorry."

"Wanting to quit the game because I was irritated at you wasn't exactly model behavior either."

He tilted his head slightly. "Why do you keep coming every day to see me?"

"What do you mean?"

"Look at me." He lifted the blanket off his useless leg. "The doctors aren't sure I'll ever walk again on my own. I'm grumpier and ornerier by the minute. Why do you bother coming at all?"

She picked up one of the chess pieces that had fallen into her lap and rolled it between her fingers. Why did she continue to come, day after day? Why did she put up with his cantankerous attitude and his impossible disposition? It wasn't as if she had to come. She had no claims on him.

You've come every day because you still love him, Rebecca Ann Johnson.

Rebecca swallowed hard at the confession. As afraid as she was to love him, it was an emotion she couldn't ignore. And she realized now the question she had to ask despite the searing pain his rejection would bring.

"I need to know your intentions by me, Luke. I know the accident changed you. If you want me to walk out of your life today, then I'll never bother you again. But if what you said to me that night in the garden is still true. . .I need to know."

"I've been such a fool." He shook his head slowly, then squeezed his eyes shut for a moment.

Her heart thudded as she studied his solemn expression, dreading his response. She was the one who had been the fool. He didn't love her anymore. She could see it in his face. His head dropped as he avoided her gaze. He may not want to tell her the truth, but she had to know.

Besides, she should have known that now that no excuses stood between them—no three-year voyage saving him from having to make a commitment—his true feelings would eventually surface. She'd seen what she wanted to in the situation, not the true reality of what was. Had she believed Luke Hutton cared about her when he could have any woman he wanted? Nausea washed over her. They lived in two different worlds, and she'd been childish to believe their relationship could have a happy ending like one of her cheap dime novels.

He leaned forward in his chair. "I told you the other day that everything has changed for me, but one thing I don't think ever will, and that's how I feel about you."

Her brow wrinkled in confusion. "I—I thought—"

"I still love you, Rebecca."

Any traces of anger or frustration vanished from her face. She couldn't breathe. Had he really told her he still loved her? A smile broke out across her face as the reality of his words began to sink in. Luke Hutton loved her. But as a shadow crossed his face, she knew there was more.

"What is it?"

He pressed his fingertips together before speaking. "I don't know if I'll ever be able to walk again. I might have a nice-sized inheritance from my father, but I don't know if I can survive that way. Living day after day in this chair, being forced to rely on others for everything I want to do. You deserve more than a man who's an invalid."

Tears sprang to her eyes, and she shook her head. "When you left on the *Liberty*, I thought I'd lost you forever. I was the foolish one who refused to wait for your return even though I knew I loved you. If you really love me, please don't let this get in the way of us."

CZ

Luke felt the tension grow along his jawline. His first impulse at her question had been to tell her a lie. If he told her he didn't have feelings for her, it might make it easier for her in the long run. She'd go home to Cranton and forget about the washed-out sailor who'd more than likely never navigate another ship again, let alone build one. He didn't want to be a burden to her.

But as much as he'd wanted to lie, he knew he had to tell her the truth. How could he deny his feelings to the one woman who had completely stolen his heart? No matter what he did, he felt trapped.

"What if I never walk again, Rebecca?"

"What if you do?" A look of determination flashed in her eyes. "It hasn't been that long since they dragged you out of the ocean, clinging to a dilapidated lifeboat. You're going to walk again someday—I know it."

He laughed aloud as all the frustrations from earlier melted away. "Now I know why you've been coming."

"And why is that?"

"To give me the swift kick of motivation I need each day. You're right for me, Rebecca Johnson. I need you in my life."

He noticed the crimson blush that crept up her ivory skin, giving her a radiant glow. A smile lingered on her lips. "Then we'll have to take things slowly so I can make sure you're going to behave."

"Yes, ma'am."

Fumbling with the pawn in her hand, she laid it on the chessboard, then knelt on the ground to pick up the other escaped soldiers.

I don't deserve her, Lord. But whatever Your will is for my life, after all that's happened, she's the one thing that still makes sense.

But would she decide to stay? She was close to her family, and the desire to be with them was pulling her away from Boston. It was something he understood, but would she stay long enough for them to see if a relationship between them would work? And what about after that? Could he move to Cranton, leaving behind his mother and the sea that still called him? He seemed to have far more questions than answers.

"What about your going home to Cranton?" he asked.

"I'd still like to go and visit my family, but now I'd have a reason to return to Boston." She looked up at him. "And if you're up and walking by Christmastime. . ."

He couldn't help but hope her subtle invitation was one offered in all seriousness. Throughout the time they'd known each other, he'd enjoyed numerous stories of her six brothers and sisters, from how Samuel presented their stepmother, Michaela, with a frog the first time they met her, to how they had adopted little Anna from the Mills Street Orphanage. While he had never met any of them, he could picture them clearly in his mind. Sarah, who loved to talk almost as much as she loved her animals; Adam, who dreamed of running his own maple syrup farm. . .

All his life he'd longed for a big family, and while the thought of meeting Rebecca's relations might be a bit overwhelming, he wanted to be a part of them.

Luke watched the hem of her purple dress sweep against the stone flooring as her slender fingers scooped up the remaining pieces. He'd never noticed how her lips pressed together when she concentrated on something or how when she tilted her head she gnawed on her lip.

Trying to ignore the throbbing pain in his knee, he thought about the night the *Liberty* sank. He'd thought she was there with him. He remembered now. He'd heard her voice as he clung to the board. She told him not to give up. Not to let go of hope. Frigid waters had swirled beneath him, threatening to ravage his weakened body. He remembered the warmth of her kiss and the taste of her lips, and as he prayed for deliverance, he somehow found the strength to hold on.

Slowly he rolled the chair around the table and across the terrace. Even from where he was, he could smell the flowery scent of her perfume captured by the afternoon breezes. He moved until he was mere inches from her.

"You know you need to grease your wheel." She turned to him, her hands filled with the last of the chess pieces.

"Really? I didn't notice." How could he when she was all he noticed?

She moved to stand, then stopped at the sound of ripping fabric. She let out a sharp breath. "Luke, my dress—it's caught beneath your wheel."

Unable to stop himself, he laughed aloud but made no attempt to move the chair. "I seem to remember another time you were entangled by my charms."

"It was a rosebush," she said with a giggle, examining the front of her dress.

Resting her hands on one side of the chair, she pushed it back slowly until the garment was free. He leaned toward her until he could feel the whisper of her breath against his cheek.

"You're going to have to be more careful with this contraption." She let go of the chair but didn't move away. "You're liable to catch some poor girl in it."

"There's only one girl I have any desire to capture."

"And who would that be?"

"You."

Laughing, she tried to pull away, but not before he caught her in his arms. Lightly he brushed his lips across hers before letting her go.

The sun spun a halo of gold above her. "What happens next?"

"I believe I have some hard work ahead of me." He squeezed her hands between his fingers. "If I'm ever going to court you, I have to be able to walk again."

※

Rebecca ambled up the brick walk toward Aunt Clara's home, a lazy smile across her face. The two-story home loomed ahead of her with its corbeled brick exterior and arched windows, obstructed only by the giant oak trees whose yellow leaves fluttered to the ground around her. Back in Cranton, Michaela had recounted dozens of stories pertaining to her growing-up years in Boston with Aunt Clara. Fond memories of Christmases spent in front of the stone fireplace, evenings singing carols and drinking hot chocolate, and especially the fact that the house had been filled with love. In the short time Rebecca had lived here, she'd come to feel as if she'd known Aunt Clara her entire life. She was the grandmother she'd never known.

Taking the porch steps two at a time, she wondered if maybe God's will for her life had always been right in front of her. She hadn't known how much she cared for Luke until she lost him. Now that he was back, she knew she never wanted to let him go.

Aunt Clara opened the door, and Rebecca wrapped her arms around the older woman, content with the way her life had turned. After a moment, she stepped back, but before she could say anything, she caught the quiver in the older woman's chin and the white pallor of her face.

"Aunt Clara? What's happened?"

Aunt Clara squeezed Rebecca's shoulders and didn't let go. "We received a telegram from your parents a short while ago."

Rebecca's hands covered her mouth. Her parents had never sent anything but letters. If something was wrong with a member of her family. . .

"Come inside, Rebecca, and sit down."

Obeying, she followed her aunt into the parlor. The normally cheery room turned gloomy. Even the pale rays of sunlight spilling across rose-colored walls couldn't brighten the impending despair she felt.

Sitting next to the older woman on the flowered slipcovers, Rebecca leaned forward. "What is it, Aunt Clara? Please tell me."

Aunt Clara gathered Rebecca's hands between her wrinkled fingers. "The telegram was brief, so we don't have all the details, but your brother Samuel was involved in a serious accident."

Rebecca worked to slow her breathing. He'd sent her a letter a few weeks ago telling her about a girl he'd met. At seventeen he might not be ready for the responsibilities of starting a family, but from his penned words, he was quite smitten with the girl.

Please, God, whatever it is, let him be all right.

"What happened? How is he?"

Aunt Clara shook her head slowly. "Apparently his injuries were quite severe. I'm sorry to have to tell you this, Rebecca, but Samuel died this morning."

Chapter 14

Rebecca stepped onto the stone terrace behind the Hutton home, unsure how she was going to tell Luke she had a ticket for the afternoon train to Cranton. Had it been less than twenty-four hours since he'd kissed her in this very place and told her he still loved her?

I don't understand, God. Just when I thought things might work out between Luke and me. . .

He sat in a patch of sun at the edge of the terrace, reading his Bible. She watched him unobserved for a moment, unable to stop wondering how long it would be until she would see him again. In the midst of her sorrow over Samuel's death, the darkness of last night had brought with it the old seeds of doubts over God's will for her life. Surely her brother's death hadn't been a part of God's perfect will. A cloud of confusion weighed her down as she struggled to hold on to the fibers of her faith.

But despite the gnawing uncertainties that plagued her over her family's loss, she knew that whatever the future might bring, she loved Luke. She wanted him to hold her. To tell her everything would be all right. To tell her this was nothing more than a horrid nightmare and when he kissed her she'd wake up and discover it had all been a terrible mistake—

"Rebecca?" He looked up, his smile revealing how happy he was to see her. He closed the Bible in his lap and pushed the chair toward her. "I hadn't expected to see you until this afternoon."

"I needed to speak to you about something."

"Why don't you come and sit by me?" He paused for a moment and furrowed his brow. "What's wrong?"

She knew she looked dreadful. Before she left Aunt Clara's home, she'd glanced into the beveled mirror in her room. Her eyes were red from crying, and her normally rosy complexion had turned into a chalky shade of white. In her losing Samuel, one of the bright lights in her life had been snuffed out forever.

Ignoring the pain in her heart, she tried instead to focus on memorizing every detail of Luke's face before she left. His cleft chin, eyes the color of maple sugar, his broad shoulders and solid form. Her heart thudded, reacting to his nearness. He'd even shaved, ridding himself of those horrid muttonchops. She noticed another change in his countenance as well. It was as if the anger and frustrations he'd been experiencing had all but disappeared. Would what she was about to say change that?

"Rebecca, what is it?"

She clutched her hands together and sat down on the padded chair beside him, wondering where to start. How could she tell him she was going away and had no idea when she planned to come back to Boston? How could she tell him about her brother?

"Samuel's dead." She hadn't meant for it to come out so blunt—so cold. Saying it aloud made it final.

"What?" She saw a flash of pain in his eyes, a look of shock that mirrored her own feelings. He reached out and took her hand. "I'm so sorry. What happened?"

She shook her head, trying to steady her breathing. "I'm still not sure about many of the details. Samuel's always been a bit of a daredevil, but this time someone else was involved. Samuel threw the first punch and must have pushed him too far, because the other boy. . .he. . .he had a gun."

"And he shot your brother?"

Rebecca nodded, fighting back the sting of tears. "Adam was there and tried to stop it but couldn't. They don't even know the other boy's name."

She thought she'd cried until her heart was dry the night before, but she was wrong. Tears began to stream down her cheeks, bringing another measure of soul-wrenching grief. She was angry at Samuel for taking an unnecessary risk and losing his life over a stupid argument. Angry because now she'd never see him again.

Luke rubbed the backs of her hands with his fingers. She felt comfort in his touch but realized that even in his presence he could do nothing to take away the pain she was experiencing.

"He was seventeen years old," she began between sobs. "He dreamed of becoming a doctor someday. I can still remember so vividly when he and Adam spent countless lazy summers fishing along the Connecticut River. Samuel was always the first to pull pranks on the rest of us."

She smiled at the memory, wishing she could bring back those carefree days before one tragic moment had changed everything so drastically. "He used to sit in the parlor with Adam and my father, devouring copies of Orange Judd's *American Agriculturist* for information on scientific farming while planning out their own ideas on how to better develop the land. Samuel's the one who encouraged Adam to expand his maple syrup farm."

Now her brother had been killed for no reason.

Luke lifted her chin and turned her head toward him. "You're going home, aren't you?"

"Uncle Ben's waiting for me outside, but I couldn't go without saying good-bye to you."

Her lip quivered. She was only inches from his face. So close she could read the sadness in his eyes and see the tremor of pain in his expression. She could hardly stand being so close to him and knowing that in a few minutes she was going to walk out the door. She didn't want to make things any more difficult than they already were.

And she felt torn. Torn not only by the conflicting emotions surrounding Samuel's death, but also by the fact that she was leaving. Luke's physical recovery wasn't going to be easy, and she wanted to be here to encourage him; yet she knew she needed to be with her family, as well. If only Luke could come with her—

"Do you have any idea how long you'll be gone?" Luke asked.

She shrugged. "I don't know. With Christmas barely three months away, I thought it might be best to stay at least until after the New Year, but then Michaela's baby is due in January. And Adam is not taking this well. I'm hoping I can be there for him. We've always been close."

She stopped, not knowing how to say the remaining thoughts that lingered in her heart. Samuel's death had spun her world into a mass of confusion. She would miss her grandmother's return and Luke's recovery—

"Go home to your family." He leaned forward and wiped away her tears with his thumbs, then brushed his lips across hers. "Before long I'll be walking again and waiting for you as long as it takes."

She leaned into the warmth of his arms and prayed he was right.

༄

Rebecca shoved the heel of her hand into the smooth bread dough, then flipped it onto the floured board. Returning to Cranton had been dreamlike for her. While a few new stores lined the town's wooden sidewalk, it appeared little had changed. As they'd pulled in front of the gray-shingled farmhouse where she grew up, she'd been greeted by not only the familiar acres of farmland, bordered with stone fences and tall elm trees, but also the subdued welcome of her family.

Only one thing had undeniably changed. Samuel would never be with them again.

Beside her, Michaela worked on rolling out a piecrust, seeming to know instinctively that Rebecca needed the quiet. Her stepmother may not have given birth to Samuel, but the love she had for him was clear in her eyes. It mirrored that of her father's and the rest of Samuel's siblings. A part of all of them was gone.

"I still can't believe what happened," Rebecca said, breaking the silence between them.

"None of us can, dear."

Feeling restless, Rebecca paced to the window and looked out over the familiar landscape where summer was now giving way to autumn and its golden woodlands. They'd buried Samuel beside her mother's grave in a quiet ceremony yesterday, and with him she'd buried a part of her heart. Even knowing she'd see him again in heaven did little to ease the ache in her heart.

"How could Samuel have done something so foolish? He'd just written me with plans to go ice skating together this Christmas, and he was going to introduce me to Mattie." Leaning against the counter, Rebecca folded her arms across her chest and tried to blink back the tears. "Instead, I met her at his funeral."

"She's such a sweet girl." Michaela wiped her flour-dusted hands on her apron. "I hope you get a chance to spend some time with her while you're home. This has been rough on her, as well."

Throughout the train ride to Cranton and during the following nights in her room, Rebecca had searched the Bible for scriptures that spoke of God as her strength and of clinging to her faith no matter what was happening around her. *Let us hold fast the profession of our faith without wavering (for he is faithful that promised). . . Be ye steadfast, unmovable. . . Blessed is the man that endureth. . . Be strong in the Lord, and in the power of His might. . . .*

She'd played them over and over in her mind, longing to find that measure of peace that comes only from Christ. *I'm trying, Lord, but there is still so much I don't understand.*

Luke had asked her many of the same questions she was asking now. He wanted to know why God had allowed the *Liberty* to go down, saving some and letting others die. She wanted to know the same things concerning her brother.

"Why does God allow things like this to happen? Samuel was taken while a killer lives." Rebecca's hands balled into fists at her sides. "How can murder be part of His will?"

"Sin is never part of God's perfect will." Michaela built the pie dough up around the rim of the pan, then began pleating the edge into scallops, her face tense with emotion. "I'll never forget the night I lost Ethen and Leah. For weeks I couldn't believe they were gone. I can't begin to tell you how many times I asked God that very same question. It was one of the hardest things I ever lived through.

"But the Bible says that death's sting has been defeated by the amazing love of Jesus, who conquered it through His own death on the cross. I finally came to realize they were resting in the everlasting arms of our merciful Savior, something far better than life here on earth could ever be."

Rebecca retraced her steps across the kitchen to finish kneading the bread dough. "Knowing Samuel's in heaven doesn't take away the emptiness of not having him here with us. . .or the questions."

Michaela stopped pouring the prepared Marlborough pudding into the piecrust and turned to Rebecca. "What questions?"

"Questions of God's will for our lives. When I heard that Luke's ship went down at sea, I knew I'd lost him, but for some reason God saved him." Pounding her fist into the elastic dough one last time, she set it into a bowl, then placed a cloth over it. "Why did God choose to save Luke but not Samuel?"

"I don't think that's a question anyone can answer," Michaela said. "The truth is, death is not something any of us can avoid. What we have to remember is that God has already conquered death, and we don't have to fear it. For the believer it's just a pause until we see each other again."

Rebecca placed her hands on her heart. "But it still hurts."

"I know." Michaela bridged the short distance between them and gathered Rebecca into her arms. "I'm so sorry you're having to go through this."

After a moment, Michaela pulled back but kept her hands on Rebecca's shoulders. "It took a long time before I could freely let go of Ethen and Leah. Finally, I realized the truth that they now sit enwrapped in peace and happiness at the feet of Jesus instead of in our temporary world of pain and struggles. They've seen the glory of God. And so has Samuel."

"It is an incredible thought, isn't it?" Rebecca wiped away her tears with the back of her hand. "I want to follow in His will, but even though I know heaven is a reality, it is still hard to imagine."

"That's because God's plans are always higher than our own. And it's only in following Him with all our heart that we can learn to discern what His will for our lives is."

"But how can I know for sure?" Rebecca gnawed on her lip, trying to formulate what she wanted to ask. "Like with Luke, for instance. I thought everything was so clear, but Samuel's death has brought up questions concerning my relationship with Luke. At times I'm just not sure what God wants from me."

"You knew you had to end things with Jake, didn't you? Maybe not as soon as you would have liked to have known, but I have no doubt God was the one who stepped in and intervened in your life."

"I'm not sure Jake would agree with that." Despite the somber subject, Rebecca let out a soft laugh.

"I spoke with his father not too long ago. Jake's doing well. He's living in Oregon, where he's a foreman of a ranch. And he's met someone. . . ."

"It's all right. I'm glad. I want the best for him."

"And God wants the best for you, Rebecca. If Luke is the one, you'll know. Trust Him."

Luke forced himself to make the final two strokes through the water, then pulled himself out of the pool.

Peter Watkins threw Luke a towel. "She must be some girl."

"What do you mean?" Water dripped from his hair as he mopped the droplets off his face and regarded his friend out of the corner of his eye.

"You beat your record from last week."

"It's not enough, though. My upper body might be gaining strength, but the rest of me has a long way to go."

"Don't worry—it'll happen. Come on."

Luke frowned. "Haven't you pushed me enough today?"

"Remember, champ—today you're taking your first step."

Peter helped him to a pair of wooden parallel bars, then waited beside him as Luke struggled to find his balance. Standing there, his arms supporting his weight, he tried to remind himself why he'd been pushing himself so hard the past two and a half weeks. He could still see Rebecca clearly when he closed his eyes, and at night she floated through his dreams. The tilt of her mouth when she smiled, the soft cadence of her laugh. . .

But he had seen the look of hesitation in Rebecca's eyes as she'd kissed him that final time before leaving on the train for Cranton. So far she'd sent him two letters full of news about what was happening in the small town and with her family, but she'd written little regarding her feelings for him. It wasn't as if he doubted her love. No, it was something else. Something he'd seen in her expression that he couldn't put a name to or understand. Though he longed for her to confide in him, he had the feeling it was a personal matter she had to work out on her own. All he could do at this point was wait—and pray.

He'd promised her he'd be here for her when she returned, but he wanted to do more than that. As soon as he got his strength back and was able to walk, he was leaving for Cranton to be with her. The thought was like a bolt of energy shooting through him, and he willed his mind to focus on the task at hand.

Slowly he worked to ease the weight of his body evenly onto both of his legs.

"One step at a time, Luke. That's all you have to think about."

It was as if Rebecca herself had spoken the words. Ignoring the dull ache that spread through the limb, he focused on the mechanics of moving his leg. He set it down in front of him, and as he gritted his teeth from the pressure of his weight, Luke took his first step.

Chapter 15

Rebecca played the mellow chords from one of Mozart's pieces, then stopped as the ivory keys began to blur. Even music didn't bring her the joy it had when she first learned to play. But how could it when her heart was miles away from her parents' farmhouse? She missed Luke.

The last time she'd heard from him had been almost five weeks ago. He'd been struggling to gain his strength back. Now yet another week had passed without a letter. She ran the back of her thumb down the keys, then pounded out a dissonant chord. A lone tear made its way down her cheek, and she wiped it away with the palm of her hand.

Trying to hold back the flow of tears, she pulled her lacy shawl closer around her shoulders and stepped outside. Winter had already begun to settle into the valley. The red, yellow, and orange leaves that had burst into color during the month of October had all but vanished from the woodlands. In their place were patches of white from last week's snowstorm.

She leaned against the wooden rail of the porch. In the distance, Sarah and Anna hurried along the path toward the barn, swinging their metal buckets beside them. Their laughter, ringing through the cool evening air, brought a slight smile to Rebecca's lips. Familiar images like this helped to keep a degree of normality in her life. So much had changed since that night Aunt Clara told her Samuel had been killed. So many things she wished she could go back and change. But life didn't work that way.

She'd stayed in Cranton partly for her own need to be with her family, but also because of Adam. Her younger brother had witnessed the last seconds of Samuel's life and still struggled to let go of the guilt over the fact that he hadn't been able to stop the tragic event. Maybe he never would completely forget that fateful moment when Samuel's life was taken, but if she could help his heart and mind to mend, she'd stay as long as she was needed.

Drawing in a deep breath, she shivered under her light wrap. Before long the sun would drop below the horizon, leaving brilliant streaks of pink and gold behind. Then night would settle into the valley, wrapping a blanket of darkness across the rambling farmlands and forests. After Samuel's death, nighttime had brought with it a myriad of doubts, reminders of her ongoing search for God's will and the occasional uncertainties about her relationship with Luke.

For the first time in months, though, her doubts toward God were beginning to dissipate. She'd taken Michaela's advice to heart. How could she follow God with all her heart if she didn't really know Him? His ways were higher than her own, and the more she tried to learn those ways, the hungrier she'd become to know His Word better and experience a deeper sense of His presence in her life.

The front door slammed shut, and Rebecca turned to see her father stroll across the porch toward her. Except for a slight graying around his temples, he'd aged little in the past few years. She was sure it was because of his marriage to Michaela. Love seemed to keep him young.

"I was enjoying your playing." He bent over and kissed the top of her head. "Up until the last chord, that is."

"Very funny."

Rebecca drew her arms around her father's waist and laid her head against his shoulder, wishing she were a little girl again. As a child nothing had really mattered, because her father had always been able to make everything right. It didn't seem quite so easy anymore. Spilled milk was much easier to mop up than a broken heart was to mend.

Her father rubbed the back of her head with his hand. "You miss him, don't you?"

"Samuel?"

"Actually, I was thinking about Luke." He wrapped his arm around her shoulder. "I know we all still miss Samuel. Always will for that matter."

"It still hurts." Rebecca frowned. "There's a hole in my heart that will never be filled."

"I know. I feel it, as well. Sometimes I wake up in the morning, and I've forgotten he's not here anymore. Then it hits me that he's never coming back."

"At least I'm not blaming God for Samuel's death anymore."

Her gaze drifted across the snow-laden landscape to where the lacy boughs of the elm trees stood in all of winter's glory. The flowers had faded away with promises to return in the spring. God had created this world full of beauty and goodness. It was man who had corrupted it with evil.

"What about Luke? You haven't spoken of him lately."

Rebecca nudged her father with her elbow. "You're persistent, aren't you?"

He squeezed her shoulder. "When it comes to my children, I am."

She wished she knew how to put her feelings into words. She had no doubt that the stress of the past few weeks had altered her sensibility. "I haven't heard from him for weeks."

"There could be a number of explanations. Recovering from an accident isn't easy." He smiled. "Besides, I don't know a man alive who would win a blue ribbon for letter writing."

Her father's positive outlook did little to change her somber mood. She'd tried to justify Luke's lack of communication without avail, yet there had to be an explanation. "If nothing else, he could dictate a letter to his mother or send me a telegram."

"That's true, but I'd hate for you to make any snap judgments without knowing exactly what's going on." Her father turned her head toward him, then looked into her eyes. "Because of my pride I almost lost your mother. Don't shut a door because of fear. Trust is a decision, Rebecca."

He was right, and she knew it. It just seemed like forever since she'd told Luke good-bye. Sometimes she was certain he'd only been a dream. Her mind tried to make sense of the storm of emotions raging within her. Her feelings might be irrational, but that didn't keep the lingering doubts from intruding.

Rebecca shrugged. "Whatever happens, this has all been good for me in one sense."

"How is that?"

"I've decided to stop second-guessing God." She pressed her fingers against the edge of the rail. "In talking to Michaela, I've realized that I've been looking for fulfillment in life through marriage and a family. I think what God truly wants is for us to seek Him with all our hearts, no matter what is happening around us."

Her father smiled again. "Those are pretty wise words coming from my eldest."

"I don't know how wise they are, but they do make sense. At least it's something I'm working on."

"And what about Boston? Are you planning to go back?"

"I think so." Gazing out across the white farmland, a part of her wondered how she could ever leave this place again. The other part longed for something more. "I was making a life for myself there. While I missed you terribly—"

"You'd better have."

Rebecca laughed, enjoying the light banter with her father. He was the one person in her life who always made her feel safe and secure. "As I was saying, while I did miss you, I really enjoyed working with Caroline. Plus, making the quilts for the children at the orphanage helped me feel as though I was finally doing something useful with my life. And then there's Luke. . ."

"So you've discovered God's will for your life?"

"I've discovered that serving Him is His will for my life."

She'd have to wait and see how Luke fit into that plan.

Luke stared out across the choppy gray water from the edge of the widow's walk, watching as each ripple followed its intended path to the shore. It was one component of life that never changed. The sea worked in one continuous rhythm, pressing wave after wave toward the shore. It was like the plan for summer to turn into autumn, and autumn into winter. It was all part of God's design.

If only life were that simple. But it wasn't. Luke had spent his entire life doing the predictable, but now he was finally ready to break away. Leaning against the wooden rail, he watched the white sails of a ship make its way toward the harbor. There would be no more voyages for him. No more rush of adrenaline as his whaling boat slid into the surf, prepared for the hunt. The only trip he had plans to make was one to Cranton—and Rebecca.

She'd been on his mind since the moment he had kissed her good-bye. He dreamed about their starting a life together—something that had been impossible before the accident. Only one obstacle hung between them. Her letters were full of colorful anecdotes of her family. The joy she felt being with them again was obvious. Once she decided to stay in Cranton for good, it would be only a matter of time before Boston would become nothing more than a faded memory.

It was something the two of them would have to discuss. While he had no longings to captain his own vessel, his desire to build ships had grown stronger. Dwight Nevin assured Luke that as soon as he recovered from the accident, he would have a job at the shipyard. What he ultimately dreamed of, though, was having his own shipbuilding company. Something he could never do in Cranton.

He'd found a verse in Romans chapter twelve that had become pivotal in helping him answer the lingering questions. It was so significant that he'd committed it to memory. *"And be not conformed to this world: but be ye transformed by the renewing of your mind, that ye may prove what is that good, and acceptable, and perfect, will of God."* The verse was clear. In order to find out what God's will was in his life, it was necessary for him not only to be unconformed to this world, but also to be transformed by His Spirit.

For the past few weeks, he'd done more than simply work to restore his physical condition. He'd taken the time to delve deeply into God's Word. He realized how he'd always done what was expected of him—and that God might have something else in mind for his life. It was time to trust fully in Christ for everything he needed. Even if that meant going against a long-standing family tradition. It was time to tell his mother how he felt.

Turning, he made his way slowly across the balcony and down the narrow stairs into the house. The muscles in his leg burned beneath him, but he refused to give in to the pain. The past few weeks had brought about remarkable progress. Three days ago he'd thrown away the wooden walking stick. Now he worked to make sure each step was steady so he didn't shuffle across the floor.

He found his mother in the kitchen, fussing over a simmering pot of soup. Bowls and pans lay strewn across the countertops. His mother's interest in cuisine was nothing new but remained a fact that amused Luke, considering she had a full-time cook and seldom ate what she prepared.

"Where have you been, Luke?" She glanced up, a marked look of frustration across her face. "Vincent Sawyer and his family will be here in less than thirty minutes for dinner. He's looking for some new men for his crew, and now that you're walking again—"

"Mother, I'm not going on another voyage." The words came out sooner than he intended, but he wasn't going to put off telling her his decision any longer.

"Of course you are." She waved the wooden spoon in the air, seemingly dismissing what he'd said. "Your leg is almost healed, and by springtime, when the *Marella* pulls out again, you'll be as good as new. This isn't an opportunity to pass up—"

"This has nothing to do with my leg. It has to do with what I plan to do with the rest of my life." He took a step forward so he could lean against the counter and take some of the weight off his leg. "Being a whaler isn't my dream."

The spoon clattered against the tile floor as she turned to him. "What are you saying?"

"I'm not going on another voyage." His jaw clenched with determination. "Not with Captain Sawyer. . .not with anyone."

Her face paled. "You're serious, aren't you?"

Instead of the bout of frustration he expected, a growing sense of peace settled over him. "I'm very serious."

His mother's shoulders slumped. "I always thought it was your dream. That's why I've encouraged you."

"It was your dream. Yours and Father's." Reaching deep inside, he worked to find the words that would help her understand that he needed to follow his own dreams. "The future isn't in whaling anymore, and—"

"I've heard all the arguments, Luke." Her face softened, and he detected the hint of a smile behind the wonder in her voice. "What I want to know is how much of this decision has to do with a certain young lady you've been pining over the past few weeks."

Luke shook his head. "I made this decision before the *Liberty* ever took sail. It was going to be my last voyage. It just ended a bit sooner than I expected."

"Why didn't you ever tell me this was how you felt?"

He'd expected her to put up a fight, but instead she sounded surprisingly relieved with his decision.

"You've always told me you wanted me to carry on the family tradition like my father and his father before him. Letting you down has never been easy for me."

"I've been told a time or two that I'm a hard woman to please." She took a step toward him and gathered his hands between hers, the grin across her face broadening. "I thought it was what you wanted, so I was determined to ignore my own fears. You can't imagine how much I dreaded your going off to sea each time. Losing your father was so horrid. I can't imagine losing you, as well."

The change in her countenance astonished him but brought a measure of relief at the same time. "Your life has always been so caught up in the sea and family tradition. I was afraid you'd regret my decision."

"All I've ever wanted was for you to be happy." She drew him into her arms for a moment, then pulled back and caught his gaze. "There's still one question you need to answer."

"What's that?"

"What are you still doing in Boston when the woman you love is in Cranton?"

Chapter 16

Rebecca lifted the hem of her heavy wool dress and stormed into the barn, where her brother saddled up his black stallion. She hadn't meant to overhear the conversation between Adam and Jethro Wright, but their shouts had been loud enough for the neighbors to hear. Jethro's claims that he had a lead on Samuel's killer turned her stomach sour, considering she was convinced Jethro simply wanted to get his pudgy fingers on the reward money. He knew Adam well enough to realize her brother would jump at the chance to take revenge into his own hands, which is exactly what Adam had told Jethro. Adam planned to go after the man—alone.

She scurried into the darkened stall, stopping only to catch her breath. "Adam, I heard you and Jethro talking about going after Samuel's killer. You can't do this!"

"You can't stop me, Rebecca." He finished cinching the girth beneath the horse's belly, then turned to face her. "Have you forgotten this man killed our brother? No one else seems willing to do anything about it—"

"That's not true. There's a reward out for his capture, and Sheriff Briggs is following any leads he has." Desperate to stop him from doing something foolish, she gripped the sleeve of his leather coat. "He's a killer, Adam, and you're going to end up his next victim if you're not careful."

Jerking away from her clutch, he led the horse into the pale afternoon sunlight. Dark storm clouds were gathering in the east. If he went ahead with this ridiculous quest, the weather might prove just as dangerous. And there was no telling how long it would take to track the man down.

She followed him, not finished with what she had to say. "You're not thinking straight because you're too angry. Bounty hunters are already looking for him. We can increase the reward—"

"I'm going after him, Rebecca." His cheek twitched as he slid into the saddle, grasping a loaded rifle in his hands. "Tell Father I'll be back when the job is finished."

"Adam, please. . ." *Lord, I don't know what to say to convince him.*

Adam pulled back on the reins, and the horse whinnied, ready to go. "I have to do this."

226

She felt a surge of anger rip through her as she watched Adam head south on the road toward town. How could he be dim-witted enough to go after a murderer by himself? Stomping the heel of her boot against the ground, she weighed her options. Her father had gone into town, and her stepmother had taken the girls to visit one of the neighbors. By the time either of them arrived home, Adam could be miles away.

She glanced at the barn, where the rest of the horses were corralled. She could hear one stamping in the stall, ready for such a task—and she had no time to waste. Running inside the barn, she saddled one of the horses. If she went after Adam herself, she might be able to overtake him and somehow convince him to leave the settling of scores to the bounty hunters.

Moments later she mounted the horse, thankful for the warmth of the wool coat she wore. The horse responded to her urgency and tore off down the winding road. She'd have to keep a steady pace to catch up with Adam.

Please, Lord, protect him from his foolishness. If anything would happen to him. . .

The thought sent a chill down her spine. She didn't know her brother anymore. Adam had always been quiet and reserved, but since Samuel's death, all he'd thought about was revenge. Revenge, though, wouldn't solve anything, and in the process, more lives might be taken—possibly Adam's. She couldn't bear the thought of losing another brother. The wound from Samuel's death was still too raw and painful, and she was determined not to live through something like that again if she could help it.

And nineteen years old was far too young to deal with the likes of an experienced gunman. They knew little about Samuel's murderer, except that he was an immigrant. This fact had given rise to a growing prejudice in Adam's life and had been further inflamed by men like Jethro who worked to pass on their racist beliefs that never did anything but cause trouble. She knew how deadly the consequences of unrestrained anger and prejudice could be, and the thought of what might happen if Adam carried through on his threats was sobering.

The wind whipped against her face as she followed Adam's tracks. Just past the Carter homestead, the tracks veered off the main road. She pulled on the reins and slowed the mare. The horse stamped beneath her, not content to stand still. If Adam were headed for the town of Hayes as she thought, cutting across the valley would take a good bit of time off the ride. It would also make him harder for her to track.

The squeaky wheel of a wagon ahead caught her attention. She glanced up the road and sighed with relief as her father's wagon headed toward her.

Nudging the mare with her knees, Rebecca galloped up the road, desperate to lose as little time as possible.

She caught a glimpse of a dark-haired man sitting beside her father, then pulled sharply on the reins. The stress of the day was causing her mind to play tricks on her. She'd imagined seeing Luke in the distance a dozen times, but this time. . .

"Rebecca?" Luke jumped out of the wagon and with a slight limp, ran toward her.

She slid down from the horse, certain she was dreaming. It had been so long since she'd heard from him.

"I missed you so much." He lifted her off the ground and swung her around.

"I can't believe you're here." Tears of joy streamed down her face at seeing him again. "And you can walk."

Still holding her hands, he pulled them against his chest. "I wrote and told you. Didn't you get my letter?"

"No, but that doesn't matter anymore. I'm just glad you're here." A sharp wind whipped against her face. She hadn't forgotten the urgency to find her brother. "Something's happened, Luke."

"What is it?" His fingers pressed against her arm.

She grabbed the reins of her horse, addressing her father as his wagon stopped beside them. "Adam's left. He heard a rumor that Samuel's killer is working north of here. He's left to go after him."

A shadow crossed her father's face. "How long ago did he leave?"

"Ten minutes. Fifteen at the most."

"Where's he headed?"

"North toward Hayes, and he won't stop until he finds the man. You could go into town and get a posse together."

Her father adjusted the brim of his hat as he considered the choices. "Going back into town will lose valuable time."

Luke took a step forward. "I'll be happy to go with you."

"You can't go." Rebecca shook her head. "What about your leg? You're still limping, and it could be days before you return—"

"I'll be fine. I've faced worse situations before."

Don't go. Not just when I've got you back. . .

This time Rebecca didn't try to hold back the tears. The strain from the past few weeks, along with Adam's leaving and the emotional shock of seeing Luke, was more than she could handle. His notion to chase after Adam was as foolish as her brother's quest to bring in a murderer single-handedly. One of them would get himself killed.

"I just want to help." Luke's hand gripped her shoulder. "I'll be fine—"

"You can't make me a promise like that."

"Shh." He touched her mouth with his fingertips, then wiped away her tears.

All she could do now was pray she didn't lose another man she loved.

Luke leaned back in the saddle, trying to stretch the weary muscles in his back. It had been almost thirty-six hours since they'd left the Johnson farm, and still they'd seen no sign of Adam. He and Rebecca's father had been able to follow Adam's tracks until last night, but now a fresh layer of snow covered the ground. All they could do was rely on what Rebecca had heard and hope they were continuing in the right direction.

He'd hated to leave Rebecca. The two months they'd been apart had seemed like an eternity, and then to see her so briefly before his unexpected departure to find Adam had been torture. At least he was sure of one thing. While he knew she was upset about his decision to go after Adam, he hadn't missed the obvious joy in her eyes when he'd arrived.

His ride on the train to Cranton had given him plenty of time to think. One thing had become clear. He wanted to marry Rebecca, even if that meant giving up his dreams of having his own shipbuilding business. There were always other opportunities. Boats ran along the Connecticut River, and surely there would be a need for someone with his skills. If not, he'd dreamed of raising horses as a boy. Maybe that was something he could learn to do.

With Rebecca's father beside him, he kept a steady pace, staying on the main road toward the town of Hayes. He knew it was important to join in the search, but a part of him wished he hadn't volunteered to come. His leg ached in the cold, reminding him he needed to take things slowly. He was thankful he'd been able to keep up so far, but he wasn't sure how much longer he could continue the rigorous pace.

A chickadee perched in a nearby tree, attempting to entertain them with his cheerful call. A flock of migrating birds beat their wings above them in the cloudless gray sky. He was amazed at how calm and peaceful the valley was. Except for the crunch of snow beneath the horses' hooves, it was surprisingly still—and beautiful. Snow glistened like tiny jewels in the morning sunlight. The landscape was a gentle combination of ridges and valleys, where meadows intermingled with thick woodlands, making a patchwork pattern like one of his mother's quilts. He could see why Rebecca loved this part of the state so much.

"Thanks for coming with me," Eric said, breaking the comfortable silence that had settled between them.

"I'm glad to be able to help, sir."

"How's the leg?"

Luke massaged the top of his thigh with his gloved hand. "It aches in the cold, but I'll make it. Compared to some of the situations I've found myself in at sea, I certainly can't complain."

Eric's rich laugh reminded Luke of Rebecca. "You'll have to tell me a story or two while you're here. I remember countless nights sitting around the fire, listening to my father-in-law speak of his adventures on the high seas."

Already Luke's memories seemed a lifetime ago. "I have a few of my own good tales to spin, I suppose. Stories of mutiny and legends of the monsters of the deep that at times rang true."

"Have you ever thought of writing your own chronicles?"

Luke chuckled at the thought. During his convalescence, Rebecca's constant reading to him of adventures of heroes and heroines had been enough to discourage him from the idea. "I think I'll leave that to men like Herman Melville, who no doubt have a better grasp on weaving such tales."

A bough snapped beside Luke from the weight of the snow, reverberating like the muffled crack of a rifle. His horse started beneath him, and he pulled back gently on the reins to settle him. Scanning the horizon, he shivered in the wind, thankful for his wool coat, but selfishly longed for the roar of a warm fire. And for Rebecca.

"How many miles away do you figure the town of Hayes is?" Luke asked.

"I don't think we have much farther. Another mile or two at the most. We'll stop and talk to the sheriff to find out if he's seen Adam or if he knows about the reward poster. If we can't find him there, I think we'll have no choice but to turn back."

"Unfortunately, I have to agree." Luke picked up his pace beside Rebecca's father, still feeling awkward at calling him by his first name as requested. "Finding Adam in this vast wilderness will be difficult without a clear idea of which direction he's gone."

"Samuel's death struck all of us hard," Eric said, his jaw taut. "Adam's never forgiven himself for not being able to stop it. In his mind, bringing in the killer is the only way to absolve himself for what happened."

"Right or wrong, I think I'd feel the same way."

Luke remembered the overwhelming feelings of guilt he'd experienced over the loss of the *Liberty*. He still had moments when he relived the experience. Moments when he questioned God as to why he survived and others perished.

He had no doubt Adam was struggling with many of the same questions. As he'd experienced in his own life, it was a difficult journey to go through. Until he'd stopped trying to fight God at every turn, he'd seen no relief in his future. Maybe God had brought him here for reasons beyond his relationship with Rebecca.

Eric lowered the brim of his hat to block out the rising sun. "We've never talked about your intentions toward my daughter."

Luke wrapped the leather reins around his hand and slowed his pace. He'd been looking for an appropriate time to ask Rebecca's father for her hand. Now was as good a time as any. "I'd like to marry your daughter, sir."

"I had a feeling you'd say that."

Luke caught the slight grin on Eric's lips and breathed out a sigh of relief. The past day and a half spent alone with her father had been surprisingly amiable, but that hadn't erased Luke's feelings of concern, considering he was a virtual stranger to Rebecca's family and wanted her hand in marriage. "I realize you haven't known me long, but I love her and promise to take care of her."

Eric wrapped his scarf around his neck, then stuffed the ends into the front of his coat. "My wife knew your mother back in Boston and speaks highly of her."

"I'm glad to hear that. My mother's a wonderful lady."

"Rebecca speaks favorably of you, as well, except for the fact that your letter writing leaves a bit to be desired."

Luke cringed. "Unfortunately, my mother has a habit of writing letters then forgetting to post them. I have a feeling she did the same thing with the letters I wrote while I was recovering; though, I confess, letter writing has never been my strong point."

"I'd say that's true for all of us men." Eric's laugh was quickly replaced by a look of concern. "Do you plan to take her back to Boston with you?"

Luke had expected the older man's question. He could only imagine how he'd feel when the day came for him to face the same thing with his own daughters. "I plan to leave that decision up to Rebecca, sir. Far as I'm concerned, as long as she says yes, I'll be happy wherever we live."

"Then I'll give you my blessing and hope Cranton wins out."

Luke smiled at his words as they topped another ridge and found the settlement of Hayes dotting the valley below them. Ten minutes later they rode into the sleepy town, dismounted, and tethered their horses a few yards down from the sheriff's office. The ache in Luke's leg was intensifying, but he worked to will the pain away. Stepping onto the boardwalk, he turned as two men flew out of the saloon and clattered onto the boardwalk beside him. The blond man landed a solid punch to his opponent's jaw before stepping into the street. The other man, his lip bleeding, staggered down the steps after him.

"Adam!"

At the sound of his father's voice, Adam hesitated, giving his blond adversary time to pull a gun out of his holster. Luke threw himself onto Adam, knocking him off his feet as the crack of gunfire split the morning air. The burning sensation of the bullet knocked the wind out of Luke as he slammed into the hard ground; then everything went black.

Chapter 17

Rebecca knelt on her hands and knees and worked in monotonous circles to finish scrubbing the living room floor. She focused on the straight grain pattern of the wood with its occasional knots, trying to control the fear she felt in the pit of her stomach. Four days had passed without news of Adam—or Luke and her father. She should have gone with them. At least then she wouldn't have been left to imagine what was happening. As much as she loved Luke, she was still furious he would risk his entire recovery to go after Adam. More than likely, he was going to end up deathly ill from exposure to the cold because of his weakened condition.

Rebecca rubbed the floor harder, knowing she shouldn't worry about something she could do nothing about. It certainly wouldn't bring them back any sooner, and all it had accomplished so far was to give her a headache.

She glanced up as Michaela stepped into the room from the kitchen, her hands resting against her bulging stomach. Despite the tension she must have felt, an expression of peace crossed her face. "You're going to scrub away all the floor polish if you're not careful."

Rebecca wiped away the beads of moisture from her lip. "Sorry."

"Don't worry. I'm not complaining." Michaela smiled, then skirted around the edges of where Rebecca worked. "Every time I turn around, you're a step ahead of me. I haven't had to do a thing to prepare for Thanksgiving dinner, and everything is ready for tomorrow. I really appreciate it."

"I've needed to keep busy." Rebecca leaned back on her heels and balanced her arms against her legs. "Do you think they'll be back in time?"

Michaela rested her hands against the wooden sill and stared out the window overlooking the front yard of the farmhouse. "If they're not here by tomorrow, then we'll wait and celebrate once they return. The girls will be disappointed. They're upstairs right now making decorations for the table."

Despite Michaela's optimistic front, the lines beneath her eyes were evidence she was also worried. Winter's fury had held off so far, but any day could bring signs of another storm.

With the back of her hand, Rebecca wiped the moisture off her forehead. "The pies and other dishes we made today will last only so long."

Michaela turned away from the window to face her.

"Is anything else bothering you?"

Rebecca let out a long sigh, then began scrubbing again. "I'm frustrated at Luke for leaving when he has no business being out there in this weather. How could he risk his life when he doesn't have to?"

"He did it because he loves you, and Adam is your brother."

"I know." Rebecca stood and dumped the rag into the bucket, sloshing water down the sides. "But it seems foolish for him to risk his life to go after Adam when he's still recovering from his accident."

Michaela shook her head. "Luke's not Samuel, Rebecca. He's not out there because he's trying to prove something to you. Samuel made a bad decision and unfortunately paid for it with his life. I don't think that's what Luke's doing."

"I'm still scared." Rebecca gnawed on her bottom lip. "They've been gone so long."

"Love makes you vulnerable, and it even hurts sometimes; but when you find the right person, it's worth the risk." Michaela pushed back the edge of the red-checkered curtain and looked out the window. "And I'd say your prayers have been answered, Rebecca. Your father and Luke have just arrived with Adam."

"They're here?" Rebecca looked down at her stained dress and moaned, wishing she had time to change. "I'm an absolute mess."

Michaela smiled and reached out to take Rebecca by the hand. "You look fine."

Rebecca stepped onto the porch, a clatter of footsteps behind her. The girls must have been watching from their upstairs bedroom window, because Sarah, Ruby, and Anna ran ahead of Rebecca to welcome the men home.

She watched as her father got off his horse, then reached down to toss Anna into the air. Even Adam looked glad to be home. For the first time in weeks, a smile covered his face. Rebecca's shoes crunched against the snow as she walked toward Luke. For the moment, he was the only person she wanted to see. The scene faded around her until only she and Luke existed. All that mattered now was that he was here with her—and safe.

He slid off the horse, wincing as his boots struck the ground.

She reached out to grasp the edge of his sleeve. "What's wrong?"

"It's just a flesh wound—"

"What?"

The wind whipped against them as Luke pulled his coat back to reveal the bandaged shoulder. "I'm going to be fine."

Anger welled within her. "You should never have gone—"

"Luke saved my life, Rebecca." Adam stepped up beside her. "I found Samuel's murderer. Before he escaped, he took a shot at me, and Luke pushed me out of the way."

"I'll be fine." Luke grasped her hand, his eyes pleading with her to believe him.

Blinking rapidly to stop the flow of tears, she watched as her father pulled Michaela into an embrace and nuzzled his face in her hair. The look of love in her father's eyes was unmistakable. Rebecca had always longed for a love like theirs. They faced life with God as the center of their relationship. And they trusted each other completely.

This was what she wanted in a relationship with Luke. He spent his life facing danger. It was a part of who he was and a reality he had learned to cope with. But his risk taking wasn't based on pride or even revenge. Her parents had been right all along. If she wanted her relationship with Luke to blossom into what they had, she would have to trust him.

❧

Rebecca finished scrubbing the last kitchen counter and listened to the happy chatter coming from the parlor. Thanksgiving dinner had been wonderful, but the biggest blessing was that they were all together. The girls had worked hard at setting the table with their homemade decorations, as well as helping her clean up after the meal so Michaela could rest. The one thing she'd had little opportunity to do, though, was speak to Luke. While his wound was healing, the trip had worn him out, and he'd spent the past twenty-four hours resting.

Adam strode into the kitchen and kissed Rebecca on the top of her head. "Dinner was fantastic, Sis."

"I'm glad you approve." She flicked her rag at him and chuckled, thankful for the subtle changes in his attitude since his arrival home. She wasn't sure what had happened to put the smile back on his face, but whatever the cause, she was grateful.

"And I have to tell you another thing." Adam leaned back against the counter and crossed his legs. "I really like Luke. Promise me you'll marry him."

"That's none of your business." Her brother reached for another piece of pumpkin pie, and she slapped the top of his hand. "How many have you had?"

"It's Thanksgiving. I'm not counting." He swiped a piece of the dessert. "So are you going to say yes?"

"He hasn't asked me to marry him."

"He will."

"How do you know?"

"If ever I've seen a man in love, it's Luke." He popped a bite of pie into his mouth and grinned. "Remember—I spent a lot of time with him the past couple of days."

The reminder of that ill-fated quest sent a shiver down her spine. "You almost got him killed."

"I know. And I'm sorry." All signs of teasing vanished as Adam leaned back against the counter again. "On the way home, Luke said some things that made a lot of sense. He shared with me his feelings of guilt when the *Liberty* went down."

"You still feel guilty over Samuel's death?"

Adam shrugged his shoulder. "Maybe I always will—I don't know. But at least now I've decided to try to let go of the guilt. And let God in."

Rebecca fiddled with the towel between her fingers. "The same way I'm realizing I need to let go of my fears and let God reign in my life."

She'd begun seeking God with all her heart but had still allowed a web of fear to cover her. God didn't want her to be a woman steeped in worry. He had called her to rely on Him.

Wrapping her arms around her brother's waist, she squeezed him tightly. "I'm proud of you. I know this has been hard for you."

"In case you hadn't noticed, there's someone waiting for you outside."

Rebecca peeked out the window at the snow-covered terrain, where Luke was harnessing the horses to the sleigh. "What's he doing?"

"What does it look like he's doing? I'd say he's taking you for a sleigh ride."

❧

Luke's breath caught in his throat as Rebecca stepped out of the house. She'd put on a hooded brown cape that covered most of her head but didn't hide her bright smile. Delicate flakes of snow had begun to fall, draping the countryside in their grandeur. She stopped in front of him, her breath leaving short vapors in the frosty afternoon air.

"You look lovely." He smiled at her and wiped away the snowflake that had landed on her cheek before it melted.

"Thank you." She took his hand and allowed him to help her into the sleigh. "How's your shoulder?"

"Sore, but I'm on the mend." The soft feel of her gloved hand left his senses spinning.

Once Rebecca was settled on the narrow seat, he joined her, then wrapped a thick quilt around her. It had been too long since he'd been this close to her. The scent of her perfume tantalized him, and he longed to feel the sweet touch of her lips against his.

The horses started out at a slow pace away from the farmhouse and down the winding road through the valley. A cloudless sky hovered above them, and he could hear the muffled plodding of horse hooves as the snow crunched beneath them. Their sleigh bells jingled through the stillness of the day, a *clang-y* melody never to be written down.

He glanced at her profile. "Are you still angry at me for going after your brother?"

She shook her head and smiled. "But you did scare me. I've been so mad at Samuel for making a foolish choice that cost him his life. Then when Adam ran off, I couldn't believe he was doing the same thing. Putting his life at risk unnecessarily. When I found out you'd been shot, it scared me. I was so afraid I'd lose someone else I love."

He wrapped the lines in front of him so the horses could continue their leisurely pace down the road without a driver; then he caressed the back of her hand with his thumb. "You know my motivation was never to take a risk. I've always wanted a brother, and with all the stories you've told me about your family, I feel like I know them. I want to be a part of that. I want to be a part of your life."

A tear trailed down her cheek, but her mouth curved into a wide smile. "For so long I was afraid of the risk of loving you. I've realized now, though, that I'm more afraid of the risk of losing you."

"That's why I came—because I love you." Luke cupped her face in his hands, wiping away her tears with his thumbs. "I promised I'd wait for you as long as it took. I just couldn't go any longer without seeing you." He leaned over and kissed her gently, silent assurances of what was to come. "And there's one more thing."

"What is it?"

He reached into his pocket and pulled out a thin gold band, his heart beating with anticipation. "Rebecca Ann Johnson, will you do me the honor of becoming my wife?"

She nodded, wrapping her fingers around his hands and pulling them toward her heart. "I've found what I've always been looking for, Luke."

"What's that?"

"A man who could capture my heart completely."

The beauty of the snow-covered fields surrounded him. Towering pines reached to the heavens beside apple orchards and maple sugar farms. But at the moment, he concentrated his attention on only one thing: the woman he loved.

"And your heart, Rebecca, is something I'll never let go of."

Epilogue

Ten months later

Rebecca smoothed down the front of her cocoa-colored wedding gown and took in a deep breath to calm the butterflies of anticipation. The day had finally arrived. The day she would become Mrs. Luke Hutton.

Sunlight filtered through the stained-glass window in the front of the church, casting a muted hue of color across the floor and echoing the warmth she felt in her heart. In a few short minutes, her father would walk her down the aisle to where Luke waited for her.

Rebecca fingered the lace trim on the front of her fitted bodice, knowing her father had been right all along. She'd almost given away a lifetime with Luke because of pride—and fear—until she'd learned to put her full reliance on God. Her heavenly Father's timing was always best, and in the end, He'd shown her that true fulfillment could only come through Him. Finding love with Luke had been an added blessing, and one she never planned to take for granted.

Laughter erupted behind her where Sarah, Ruby, and Anna whispered among themselves near the back of the entrance, careful to keep their pink, starched dresses neat until it was their turn to march down the narrow aisle of the church. It was hard to believe how much the three had grown the past year. She was going to miss them deeply. With her family's blessing, she and Luke had decided to return to Boston to live after the wedding. Luke had finally convinced Mr. Nevin to shift their business to the private sector, giving Luke a chance to do what he'd always dreamed. In return, she'd never have to pace the widow's walk waiting for him to return from sea, and would have the chance to continue to work with Caroline at the shop.

Her father brushed up beside her with a broad grin on his face, pulling her from daydreams of the future. "I can't believe my little girl's getting married today."

Rebecca laughed. "Your little girl grew up."

"Yes, she did." He tilted up her chin with his thumb and caught her gaze. "Your mother would have been so proud of you. And Michaela's as pleased as if she'd given birth to you herself."

She felt her heart swell at the compliment. "She's a wonderful wife and mother. I'm glad she's a part of your life. A part of all of our lives."

"Rebecca, I've watched you grow into a mature young woman who's about to become a wife to a wonderful man." He paused for a moment before continuing. "I know you often had a heavy burden to carry in helping me raise your siblings, but you were always there for me. I couldn't be prouder of you than I am at this moment."

"Thank you." Rebecca reached up to hug her father as the music started.

She felt her breath catch in her throat. Her father squeezed her hand before leading her toward the doorway into the small sanctuary. Luke stood at the front wearing a new gray suit. As on the first day they met in the front showroom of Macintosh Furniture and Upholstery, his piercing brown eyes caused her heart to tremble.

Her father squeezed her hand. "Are you ready? There's a very handsome young man waiting for you."

Rebecca felt a wave of peace flow through her as she slid her hand through the crook of his arm. "I'm ready."

Tears formed in her eyes as she looked up at her father one last time. She'd dreamed of having a marriage like that of her parents. One filled with love and respect and centered on God. There would be difficulties, no doubt, but at the moment, that didn't matter. She was marrying the man who had captured her heart, and spending the rest of her life with Luke was all she needed.

Adam's Bride

Dedication

To my sweet, sweet Jayden.
May He give you the desire of your heart and make all your plans succeed.

Chapter 1

A cold February wind ripped through Adam Johnson's coat as he hurried down one of Cranton's wooden sidewalks. The crunch of snow beneath his heavy boots brought a smile to his lips. Instinctively, he checked the direction of the wind with the tip of his finger. He was pleased with the strong westward direction that would ensure a good run of sap from his sugar maple grove.

While the majority of the townspeople huddled in front of their fireplaces, he had no complaints about the frosty weather. An early spring meant disaster for him, because without a hard freeze at night, his syrup would take on a leathery taste, something he couldn't afford with this year's crop.

Jingling the bag of nails in the palm of his hand, he whistled a nameless tune he'd heard his father sing a hundred times. Last year Adam harvested thirty gallons of syrup. This year he planned on setting out five hundred buckets for an even bigger yield.

A boy whose back was hunched against the wind bumped into him as he walked. Adam struggled to keep his footing on the icy path. His bag of nails hit the ground and scattered across the boardwalk as he watched a scrawny boy take off with his wallet.

"Hey!" He lunged for the kid, but the wiry figure slipped from his grasp.

The guttersnipe was fast, but Adam was faster. Months of hard work on his farm had turned his boyish stature into that of a man. In contrast, the thin youth in front of him looked as if he could use a good hot meal. At the edge of the alleyway beside the First Bank of Cranton, Adam gripped the boy's collar and held on tight.

"I believe you have something of mine."

"Please, mister. . ." The boy threw the wallet onto the ground, then slithered out of Adam's grasp, leaving his threadbare coat behind.

Immigrants.

Irish, Poles, and Italians had poured into the area, bringing crime with them. Granted, he'd heard of the horrid conditions many of these foreigners had escaped from in Eastern Europe. Those who hadn't settled in the big cities like Boston and New York had made their way across the eastern states to find work in the dozens of mills where life was strenuous, but at least they had food to eat and a bed to sleep in at night.

Regardless of how much compassion a God-fearing man like himself ought to feel toward these people, his brother had been murdered in cold blood by one of the immigrants. That was something he could never forget—or forgive.

Adam snatched up his wallet and opened the soft leather pouch. Empty. How that cavorting thief had managed to clean him out in such a short time, he had no idea, but he wouldn't let this go. Something had to be done. He crossed the street with broad, determined steps in search of the sheriff. The wooden door of the jailhouse slammed against the inside brick wall as Adam stormed into the office.

"Sheriff Briggs, I've got a complaint to lodge."

"Get in line." The balding lawman waved a pudgy hand at a chair. "You're the third person this morning who's come in here unhappy about something."

"Why are you still sitting here?"

"I didn't want to miss listening to your rambling complaints." The sheriff scowled from behind his desk. "How much money did the boy take from you?"

Adam gripped the back of the offered chair with his hands. "How'd you know I was robbed?"

The sheriff's jowls jiggled as he laughed. "Like I said, you're not the first person to come here in a rage."

Adam didn't see the humor in the situation. "The young ruffian stole five dollars, and that's not including the bag of nails that he scattered across the boardwalk."

"Wilton Hunter lost seventy-five dollars."

Adam stepped around the chair and slammed his palms against the top of the sheriff's desk. "So what are you going to do about it?"

"The boys' names are Edward Malik and—"

"He's Polish," Adam interrupted, feeling the tension in his jaw tighten. "I've said before, if we don't do something about the number of—"

"I said *boys*. Plural, meaning there's more than one. We're pretty sure the second is Simon Miller's boy."

"Figures." Miller was a well-respected member of the Cranton community. Adam had never heard of any problems with the storekeeper's youngest son, but spending too much time with the wrong crowd could easily change that. "Doesn't the Good Book say that bad company corrupts good morals?"

"So you're automatically assuming that Edward Malik's to blame?"

"A Pole murdered my brother, Sheriff. Why would this one be any different?" Adam turned toward the wanted posters and ripped the familiar sketch off the wall before tossing it down in front of the sheriff. "What other proof do you need?"

"One bad egg shot your brother, Adam. It was a tragic event, but don't let the past cloud your judgment toward an entire group of people. You'd see that we have some fine immigrant families in the area if you could get beyond what happened."

"You weren't there, Sheriff. You didn't see the look of hate in this boy's eyes." Adam jabbed his finger at the poster. "Samuel might have thrown the first punch, but he didn't deserve to be shot down."

"Samuel's death hit us all extremely hard." The sheriff scratched his bald scalp. "But nothing you or I can do will ever bring him back. Don't let one man's foolish actions leave you with a lifetime of bitterness, son."

Adam didn't want the advice, and he sure wasn't through with their conversation. "Why haven't you found his killer yet?"

"Bounty hunters are still looking for him, but we aren't even sure who the murderer is. All we have is a first name and a sketch based on your description."

Adam slammed his fists against the desk. "It's been seventeen months, and you don't even know the killer's last name!"

Was it so wrong for him to want justice for his brother's death? His family seemed to have accepted what happened, but he couldn't. Not when he knew there was a lunatic on the loose who might kill again. Adam had considered taking the law into his own hands. The only thing stopping him was a promise to his sister Rebecca. He'd never been one to take his promises lightly.

"You know I'll contact you as soon as we get another lead," the sheriff said. The front legs of the sheriff's chair hit the floor with a thud. "As for the thieves, my deputy's out looking for them right now. I'll let you know when we've brought them in."

Five minutes later, Adam set out in his buckboard down the snow-covered lane toward his farm. He tried to erase the last vivid image of his dying brother. He loved all six of his brothers and sisters, including little Anna, who had been adopted into his family, but Samuel had also been his best friend. They'd spent countless lazy summer mornings fishing for bass along the Connecticut River, afternoons playing ball or pulling pranks on their other siblings. Besides the fun they'd had together, it had been Samuel who helped him get through his first maple syrup harvest.

His brother had wanted to go to Boston to study to become a doctor but had decided to stay in favor of experimenting with more efficient ways of planting and producing higher yields for the farmers in the area. Together, he and Adam had devoured copies of the Orange Judd's *American Agriculturist* for information on scientific farming while developing their own ideas in the agricultural arena.

One malice-driven bullet waylaid those dreams forever.

A deafening shriek brought Adam out of his bittersweet memories. A grungy mutt at the base of a tree growled at whatever—or whomever—he had cornered in its branches. Adam glanced up and saw a patch of dark blue fabric peeking through the thick tree. Something wasn't right. Picking his rifle up off the buckboard, he reined the horses a safe distance from the dog, then stepped onto the frosty ground.

The dog turned toward him, ignoring for the moment his treed prey. He growled, showing his teeth. Adam took a step forward, shouting at the dog to get away, but even his animated gestures didn't scare the mutt. Taking aim at the dog, he inched across the snow. Regarding the animal out of the corner of his eye, he squinted against the midday sun to see who was in the tree. Probably some boy playing hooky from school and looking for a bit of adventure. The victim sat precariously on one of the lower branches, partially hidden from view by the thick growth, but far enough up that the vicious dog couldn't get him.

"Watch out! I think he's rabid."

Adam froze at the sound of the female voice coming from the tree. He'd never seen a lady suspended that high up on the branches of a tree. How had she managed to climb so high in a dress?

The dog growled, and Adam turned his attention back to the snarling creature. A dog in such a state was dangerous. If it attacked a person, the consequences could be fatal. And if she'd been bitten. . .

The dog, drooling at the mouth, shifted its gaze back and forth between him and its prey and bared its teeth at Adam, convincing him of the woman's diagnosis of rabies. "I'm going to have to shoot the dog; then I'll help you down."

Taking aim, he pulled the trigger and cringed as his shot echoed across the valley, signaling the end to his grim deed. He felt sorry for the beast, especially if it had been some boy's best friend. But one didn't take chances with rabid animals.

"Name's Adam Johnson," he said, stepping over the motionless animal and moving toward the base of the tree to get a better look at the dog's intended victim.

"I'm Lidia."

"Are you hurt?"

"No, just scared half out of my mind."

Adam rested his hand against the rough bark and looked up into the darkest pair of mahogany eyes he'd ever seen. Her long, auburn hair was pulled back neatly, with one tendril having escaped during the ordeal. Fair skin, rosy cheeks from the winter chill, and her petite stature reminded him of a fairy straight out of a storybook.

A clump of snow fell from the branch and hit him in the nose, knocking some sense back into him. He shook his head and laughed.

"I'm sorry," she said.

"Not your fault at all, ma'am. Can I help you down?"

With Adam's arms around her waist, Lidia slid onto the ground and tried to catch her breath. After a moment, he let go, but she could still feel the warmth of his hands through her thin coat.

Frankly, she found the entire situation utterly ridiculous and certainly embarrassing. Being chased up a tree by a rabid dog was no proper situation for a lady to find herself in, let alone a suitable backdrop for a romantic encounter with a well-built hero. Not that she expected such a silly event to occur. Things like that only happened between the pages of a dime novel or in her imagination.

Her grandmother, her sweet *babcia*, had first planted such wistful yet foolish notions in her head. While she remembered little about the country she left when she was six, she'd never forget memories of cold nights cuddled up with her babcia under a thick quilt, listening to her enchanted stories. But true romantic champions were saved for legends like Lajkonik, the renowned horseman who rode into Kraków to warn the citizens of the impending Tartar raids, or other such tales of bravery her people had passed down for centuries. But she was an American now, she reminded herself. If she was going to make it in this new land, she had to put aside such outlandish ideas.

"Can I take you somewhere?"

Lidia jerked her head up at Adam's question. His hair was as black as coal, and his eyes, while dark, had glints of gold in their depths. She'd never been as scared as she had the few moments before he'd arrived. While the rabid dog chased her across the frozen terrain, she'd been quite certain her short life was over. If it hadn't been for a small flock of birds that distracted the aggressive beast, she wouldn't have had the time to make it up the tree.

Then he'd come along.

"You want to take me somewhere?" Lidia glanced at the motionless form of the dog and tried to clear her head. "No. I'm fine, really, and I doubt I'll run into a rabid animal twice in one day. Besides, I'm not going far."

"If you're sure. . ."

She nodded, and despite the frigid wind, she felt a warm blush creep up her cheeks. There was something about him that made her want to stop and take a second look. But he must think her to be the most unconventional lady, or perhaps not a lady at all, for hoisting herself up in a tree—no matter what the circumstances.

Quickly saying good-bye, she shoved her hands into the pockets of her threadbare coat and hurried down the icy lane toward the mill, determined to forget this Adam Johnson. She still had a full day's work ahead of her, and there was certainly no time in her life to fantasize about handsome heroes and their legendary conquests. Not when she had a brother to take care of. No. Thankfully, she'd more than likely never see her gallant rescuer again.

⚒

Adam reached down to pick up the gun he'd propped against the side of the tree and tried to shake the strange feeling that had swept over him when he'd looked at Lidia. Of course, he was imagining things. Just because it had been months since he'd seen anyone quite as lovely as her was no reason to let his mind wander. Teasing from his older sister, Rebecca, didn't help, either. She might have run off to Boston and snagged herself a husband, but that didn't mean Adam was looking to settle down.

A flash of color in the snow caught his eyes. He bent for a closer look. After sweeping away a layer of powdery snow, he picked up a small Bible with gold lettering on the cover. He opened it to the front page and felt his heart plummet. He hadn't noticed her accent, but the name was evidence enough. Inside the front cover in neat script was the name Lidia Kowalski. The truth struck him like a second bullet to his brother's heart. The beautiful girl he'd just rescued was Polish.

Chapter 2

Y ou never told me what Lidia's like."

Adam leaned back in one of the hotel dining room chairs and frowned at Rebecca's pointed statement. "I didn't tell you, because I don't know. I only spoke to her briefly, then offered to take her home. When she refused, I left. That was all."

He pulled off his thick wool gloves, then laid them beside his hat on the restaurant table. Normally it was his younger sister Sarah who was full of nosy questions, but lately Rebecca had become just as probing. He hadn't planned for anyone to discover that he'd rescued the young woman. If it hadn't been for Rebecca noticing the small, gold-lettered Bible in his coat pocket after church on Sunday, no one ever would have found out. That was when all his troubles began.

Instead of forgetting the incident as he'd wanted, he'd suddenly become some heroic champion ripped straight from the pages of one of those dime novels Rebecca read when she thought no one was looking. And Sarah also found it terribly romantic because he'd "rescued a beautiful maiden in distress," as she'd exclaimed more than once during the past week.

The waitress brought their hot drinks, giving him a reprieve from answering more of Rebecca's questions. He busied himself with adding three teaspoons of sugar to the steaming coffee, then settled back in the wooden chair to take a sip. With the bright yellow and orange flames crackling in the large stone fireplace beside them, it was easy to forget how quickly the temperature was dropping outside. If the cold spell lasted another week or two with its hard freezes at night and temperatures warming up during the days, the conditions for harvesting the sap from his maple trees would be perfect.

"You're telling me that you didn't notice anything about her?" his sister persisted.

Adam groaned inwardly. He hadn't planned to stay in town long today, but Rebecca had convinced him to join her for a cup of coffee at the hotel. While he normally enjoyed spending time with her, he wasn't so sure it had been a good idea with her mind obviously on matchmaking.

Trying to stifle a sneeze, he frowned. "I thought you promised not to bring up a subject even remotely related to matchmaking again."

He took another sip of his coffee and watched his sister out of the corner of his eye. Rebecca's marriage to Luke Hutton last fall had reaffirmed her belief in true love and made her a staunch believer in the institution of marriage. Her efforts to find the same marital bliss for her brother were. . .well. . .in a word, annoying. And it wasn't the first time one of the female members of his family had taken it upon themselves to set him up with someone.

It wasn't as if he didn't love his family, or that he was in any way opposed to the idea of marriage, but at the present he viewed the issue as personal. When it was God's timing to marry, he had no doubts that he'd know it and act upon it. So far, he hadn't found the person he intended to spend the rest of his life with. And until then, he was content to wait.

"It was just an innocent question." Rebecca tasted her drink, then added another dash of milk. "You are considered one of the most eligible bachelors in town by most of the single women, and you saved someone's life, so. . .I'm interested."

Adam knew his sister well enough to know that her questions ran far deeper than simple curiosity. He was quite certain that if he'd rescued his neighbor's plump and prim daughter, who was well past the age of marrying, the subject would not have been worthy of resurrecting again.

He strummed his fingers against the table. "She's beautiful—is that what you want me to say?"

"That's a good start." Rebecca leaned forward, a calculated smile on her lips. "What else?"

He squirmed under her scrutiny. How could he admit that he'd dreamed about Lidia every night for the past week? That he'd seen her face every time he closed his eyes. Those soft brown eyes framed with long lashes. . .creamy white skin. . .captivating smile. . .

Then he would remember she was Polish, and his foolish daydreams would vanish. That was something he could never forget. It was why he intended to forget her.

He shoved his hands into his coat pocket, only to be reminded of her Bible that he'd been carrying with him all week. "Her last name is Kowalski."

"I know. I saw it on the Bible."

"She's Polish." He hated the way his clipped words sounded, but that didn't take away the truth—Samuel had been killed by a Pole. Rebecca hadn't seen the vacant look in their brother's eyes as Adam had held him, his chest covered with blood—

"Adam?"

"I know what you're thinking." His stomach clenched at the memories. "Why can't I get over Samuel's death? Why can't I forgive those involved? You weren't there, Rebecca. You didn't watch him take his last breath."

His sister's eyes reflected his own pain. "We all miss Samuel, but Lidia's not responsible for his death. She wasn't the one who took his life. If he'd been named Rudolpho or Tazio would you hate all Italians?"

The muscles in his jaw tensed. "That's not fair. It's not that simple—"

"Sure it is." The intensity in her voice increased. "You've let your hatred for one man spread to an entire nationality."

He shook his head and let his hands coil into tight fists as a searing rage rippled through him. "You just don't get it, do you?"

"I want to understand. We all do."

Why was it that when this vein of conversation erupted, he always ended up being the bad guy?

Adam worked to relax his muscles but found it impossible. "You don't know how many times I've begged God to take away this anger that burns inside me, but I'll never forget what happened."

And that I never stopped it.

The thought was sobering. None of them had this mountain of guilt to carry the rest of their lives. He closed his eyes, trying to erase the scene he knew would be forever imprinted on his mind. It had all happened so fast that he hadn't even seen it coming. He hadn't seen the gun until it was too late and Samuel lay dying in a pool of his own blood.

Adam wrapped his fingers around the smooth cover of the Bible and drew it out of his pocket. "I'm not sure what to do with this."

"Don't you plan to return it?"

"I don't know where she lives." He had a dozen excuses ready to throw at her. He had too much work to do at the farm, and the weather was getting worse. . . .

"It can't be too complicated to find her, Adam. After all, Cranton isn't Boston." Rebecca's eyes lit up, and he could see an idea formulating in his sister's mind. "She was walking from town, which means she can't live very far away. Maybe she lives on one of the nearby farms."

Rebecca sounded like a detective out to solve a mystery. She had definitely been reading too many of those dime novels. Life was different. It didn't always have a simple story line that neatly wrapped up at the end of the book. Look at Samuel. Sometimes things went wrong in real life that would never turn into a happy ending.

Clearing his throat, Adam glanced at his pocket watch. He needed to get back to his farm before dark. "Can I take you home?"

"Thanks, but I'll wait here for Luke." Her brow puckered when he changed the subject, but thankfully she seemed ready to leave it alone. "He's planning to meet me here in about twenty minutes." She leaned across the table and took his hand. "I'm glad I ran into you. With you not living at home anymore, I don't see you nearly enough when I'm back for a visit."

"You're the one who moved to Boston."

She squeezed his hand. "Thankfully, Luke's willing to bring me home once or twice a year."

"That's not enough." Despite her constant prying, he still missed her when she was gone. He laid a few coins on the table to cover the drinks, then leaned over and kissed her on the cheek.

"I'll see you Friday night?"

It had become tradition for the family to get together on Friday nights. And the family was growing. His father had married Michaela, Rebecca married Luke, and before long, no doubt, there would be other spouses and grandchildren.

Adam picked his hat and gloves up off the table. "Promise not to bring up the subject of Lidia or any other female you think might make the perfect match for me?"

"We just want you to be happy, Adam."

"Promise?"

"I promise."

He couldn't help but smile at her insistence. It felt good to be cared about. "I'll see you Friday night."

Adam said good-bye, then stepped out into the cold wind, thankful for the warmth of his coat and heavy gloves. Snow began to fall, the thick flakes covering the icy ground with a white blanket. His sister was right about letting go, and he knew it. But knowing what was right and actually doing it were simply not the same thing.

Sneezing twice, he tried to ignore the growing ache that was beginning to spread across his body. He didn't have time to be sick. Tapping his sugar maples was going to take every ounce of energy he had. He could ask for help from his father and his younger brother, Matt, but this was something he wanted to do on his own to prove to himself that he was capable of running this farm.

The silhouette of a familiar figure yanked him out of his thoughts. He stopped abruptly in front of the sheriff's office and stared at the young woman leaving the mercantile. The hem of her dark blue dress fluttered in the wind beneath her threadbare coat as she hugged a thick package to her chest. Even before she turned, he knew for certain it was Lidia. He wasn't sure how, but he'd memorized every detail of her face after their one brief encounter. The slight lilt in each step and the way her smile lit up her face. He'd seen her over and over in his dreams at night, but today he was awake, and this was real.

Her gaze met his, and she narrowed the distance between them until she was standing in front of him. "Mr. Johnson, how good it is to see you again."

"Please, you can. . .you can call me Adam." He didn't get tongue-tied in front of women. It had to be all the nonsense of Rebecca's matchmaking attempts. Lidia didn't affect him that way. She couldn't. She was Polish.

"I was hoping to run into you again." Holding the package with one hand, Lidia pushed back a long strand of dark hair the crisp wind had blown into her eyes. "I wanted to thank you again for coming to my rescue."

"It was nothing, really." He kept his sentences brief, determined not to notice her wide brown eyes or the sweet curve of her smile. "Nothing any decent person wouldn't have done for someone else."

She frowned, and he wondered what he'd said to take away the sparkle in her eyes. Just because he was attempting to keep his distance from her didn't mean he had wanted to be rude. Besides the fact that they were strangers, what he'd said was true. Any decent man, or woman for that matter, would have done exactly the same.

He pulled her Bible out of his pocket. "I almost forgot. You dropped this in the snow. I discovered it after you'd left, and I didn't know where to find you."

He handed her the book, feeling like an awkward schoolboy. A part of him had wanted to find her again, but now that she was here, he felt as if his emotions were piled in a jumbled heap around him. If only he could see her in a different light. If only being Polish didn't matter to him.

"I can't thank you enough." Her smile broadened as she took the book. "It was a gift from my parents. I thought I'd never see it again. I guess I'm doubly indebted to you now."

"It was nothing, really." Adam fidgeted, not knowing what to say. Maybe there was nothing else that needed to be said.

"All the same, I do appreciate it."

He tipped his hat and took an awkward step back. "I'm on my way home, so if you'll excuse me."

❧

Lidia nodded solemnly, her stomach churning as she continued toward the outskirts of town. Fingering the smooth cover of her Bible that she'd stuffed inside the pocket of her coat, she felt tears well up in her eyes. She wiped them away with the back of her hand and took a deep breath, determined to control her spiraling emotions. She'd been a fool to let herself daydream about the handsome stranger who'd rescued her from that rabid mutt. Adam Johnson had been right. He'd done nothing more than any other person in the same circumstance would have done. She foolishly misread the looks of attraction in his eyes as he'd helped her down from the tree.

The fact was he was no different than any other man she'd met. Either they wanted her for affections she'd never give a man until she was properly married, or they wanted nothing to do with her because of her heritage. The same was true with most of the women. Both the well-to-do immigrants and the Yankees looked down at girls like her who were forced to work because of their financial situation. She'd seen the same condescension reflected in Adam's eyes. It was a look that made her feel like a second-class citizen. As if being Polish meant that she wasn't a true American. But she *was* American—she would show everyone that Poland was nothing more than a distant memory to her. A story like her babcia's stories. Nothing more.

Pulling her coat closer around her, she shivered against the icy wind. For years, she'd worked to ensure that she never spoke with an accent. She strived to demonstrate the refined characteristics of a lady. Her hard work had paid off—she'd made a few friends who hadn't noticed how different she was. Life had become almost normal. Then her parents' death a year ago changed all of that. No longer was there time for fancy frivolities like tea parties with her friends and picnics on lazy Sunday afternoons. She had to support not only herself but her brother, as well, and the only time she was allowed to escape the confines of the mill was for church or when her boss, Mrs. Moore, sent her to town on an errand.

Hurrying through the snow, Lidia let the tears run freely. Her brother had just turned thirteen. God hadn't meant for a boy his age to be raised by his older sister who had yet to turn twenty. He needed a mother to love him and a father to teach him the Word of God and how to act like a man—something she could never do for him.

Sometimes it's just so hard, God.

She tried to swallow the lump of pain in her throat. When she'd met Adam Johnson, something about him had reminded her of all she yearned for in life. Foolish notions of falling in love and living happily ever after were not luxuries she normally allowed herself to indulge in. They were nothing more than silly dreams of being rescued from the life she was trapped in. That would never happen to her.

Instead, she would spend her days working long hours at the mill. Every spare moment was used reading from the Bible or works of poetry, such as that of N. P. Willis and John Greenleaf Whittier, graciously lent to her by dear Mrs.

Gorski from church. If she wasn't reading, she spent those brief moments filling the pages of her blank notepad with her own poetry, wondering all the time if anything better lay ahead of her. Wasn't there more to life than tediously attending to the looms for ten hours each day?

For a moment, Adam had made her forget. Her breath had caught as she'd looked into his dark eyes, and when he smiled at her, he'd left her speechless. Lidia's foot plunged into a crusty pile of snow, bringing her back to reality. She shivered as the icy crystals tumbled into her boots. It was a chilling reminder of the truth of her situation.

Obviously Adam was no different from the scores of folks who disliked her simply because she was Polish, and now, without a family of her own, she had little interaction with others like her who had emigrated from her homeland. No matter what she did or how hard she worked to be a true lady of quality, things would never change. There was simply no place for her to find love in this New World.

Chapter 3

The eighty-foot maple soared above him. Adam pressed the palms of his hands against the ridged bark of the tree and smiled, ready to continue the tradition of harvesting sap that had been done by men and women for centuries. A brisk westward wind blew, ruffling the hair on the back of his neck. Above him the sun shone bright, warming the day, but not enough to thaw the ground. The conditions were perfect.

For five winters he'd worked beside Old Man Potter, a no-nonsense codger who'd taught Adam everything he knew about the tedious process of gathering sap and the final process of turning the sap into syrup. After suffering from a bad case of pneumonia, Mr. Potter hadn't made it through the winter. To Adam's surprise, he had left the entire farm to him.

This was the second year Adam worked the sugar bush alone. By next year, he hoped to be able to afford to hire a handful of men to gather an even larger amount of sap. And that wasn't all he planned. He was studying the profitability of using a portion of the land for horse breeding or perhaps dairy farming. Something that would make the acreage self-sustaining.

Water dripped from an icicle at the top of the sugarhouse, then slid down the side of Adam's face. He shivered, not certain if it was from the cold or from the infection he'd been fighting for days. He simply didn't have time to be sick. He'd spent the past month repairing the furnace, vats, and other supplies at the sugar camp that was situated beside a small stream. Now that those preparations were finished, it was time to begin tapping the maple trees. Already he'd placed the taps into the trunks so he'd be ready for his first run tomorrow. The only thing left to do was to finish hanging the buckets that would collect the maple sap.

He could almost taste the spread of sweet treats his stepmother would serve at the upcoming sugaring off, the annual celebration of the maple sugar harvest signaling the end of winter. Maple sugar on pancakes, maple cream, and caramelized sugar on snow would be plentiful as long as the weather cooperated. A bird chirped in the distance, and Adam sent up a short prayer that the Lord would hold off the warm weather this year. Spring might be coming, but not before his harvest had been collected.

He grabbed the last of the buckets from the back corner of the sugarhouse, pausing when he noticed a scrap of paper lodged in a crack in the wall. Curious, he knelt to pick it up. His heart sank when he realized what it was. Fingering the tattered photograph of Mattie was like a jolt from the past. He could still see the faraway look in his brother Samuel's eyes the day he'd sat on the stump down by the creek, the image of the girl he loved in his hands.

"I think I'm in love, Adam." Samuel had gazed at the photo like an infatuated schoolboy.

"You're too young to be in love." Adam's voice rang sharp with a note of truth, but he couldn't disguise his amusement. At sixteen, Samuel's head was in the clouds more often than not—and Mattie helped to keep it there.

"What about your dreams of becoming a doctor?" Adam leaned back against one of the maple trees, its flaming scarlet leaves reflecting its Creator's glory.

Samuel shrugged. "Mattie and I've talked about staying right here in Cranton and farming a bit of land once we're married—"

"So you've already talked about marriage?" Adam teased.

Samuel jumped from the stump, tackling Adam to the ground in one swift motion. Adam might have had the advantage of height as well as ten extra pounds, but Samuel was quicker. They rolled down the embankment, stopping only when they slammed into the side of a tree.

A wave of nausea swept over Adam, jerking him from the memories of carefree days that were no longer. With the image of his brother's lopsided grin still fresh in his mind, familiar feelings of anger seared through Adam's body as he stuffed the photo into his pocket.

Why did You let him die, God?

He pounded his fist against the wall of the sugarhouse. It was the question he longed to ask God face-to-face. If anyone should have died, it should have been him. As the eldest son in the family, he was responsible for his siblings. Failing to save his brother's life was worse than losing his own life.

Trying to ignore the growing dizziness, he yanked the last four buckets off the ground and headed for the maple grove where he would hang them. He had no choice but to make it though the next few weeks of the harvest. Maybe it was pride, like his father said, that had stopped him from accepting help from his family, but this was something he needed to do. A chance to prove to himself that he could succeed.

Five minutes later Adam hooked the last bucket onto one of the spouts he'd tapped into the tree. He took a staggering step, his vision blurring as he stumbled up the slight rise toward his cabin. He rubbed his eyes with the back of his hands, then stared into the distance at the glistening snow. Maybe if he went to lie down for a few minutes he'd feel better. He shouldn't be surprised at how tired he felt. Besides preparing to harvest the sap, it had taken weeks of backbreaking work to make Old Man Potter's two-room cabin livable, and there were still a dozen things he planned to do once the harvest was over.

Like make it livable for a wife and a family.

The thought caught him off guard and brought with it vivid images of Lidia. Her long auburn hair and those sad eyes that made him long to find out what heart-wrenching secrets they held. Trying to erase the memory of holding her in his arms at the base of the tree, he tugged at the collar of his shirt and made his way up the hill. The temperature had gradually warmed throughout the afternoon, but not enough to cause him to break out into a sweat. If he could just get to the cabin. . .

He stumbled toward the porch and tripped on a scrap piece of wood. Falling onto the ground, he felt the sharp impact of something hitting his head. He cried out in pain and watched the flow of crimson spill across the white snow.

℃

Lidia shivered as she tramped through the snow, wondering what she could say to Koby that would knock some sense into him without deepening the silence that separated them. Her brother shuffled beside her, a sullen expression on his boyish face. At thirteen, he was as tall as she and noticeably heavier. No longer a boy yet still not a man.

She watched as he kicked the ground with the toe of his shoe. White powder flew in every direction. He might be mad at her for making him return to the mill, but she was furious that he'd run away. After a coworker informed her that Koby had left his work post in a huff, she'd spent two hours searching the surrounding woodlands. Just before the last curtain of night had fallen, she'd found him trudging down a narrow road.

Lidia worked to control her unsteady breathing. She was angry with him for jeopardizing their jobs. Angry with him for putting her in the position where she had to risk her life searching for him. The incident with the rabid dog had proven to be a reminder that it wasn't safe to wander these roads alone. It was time he thought about someone besides himself. Life might not be easy, but they were family. In order to survive, they were going to have to stick together.

"Why did you leave?" she asked, breaking the silence between them.

"What does it matter to you?"

She decided to ignore his defiant tone for now and worked instead to keep the frustration out of her own voice. "We're family. We have to be there for each other."

"I'm sorry."

"Sorry?" She stopped, choking back the stream of tears that threatened to flow. "Is that all you have to say? You scared me, Koby! If anything ever happened to you—"

"What do you want me to say?"

Lidia squeezed her eyes closed. *I don't know what to do anymore, God.*

Continuing her prayer for wisdom, she ran to catch up with him. His hands were stuffed in his pockets, and his head hung low. She'd heard him threaten numerous times to leave the strict confines of the mill, but she had always believed he realized the foolishness of such an act. Apparently, she'd been wrong. Still, part of her couldn't blame him. A boy his age ought to be out fishing with friends after school, but instead his lot was ten hours of manual labor every day.

Lidia paused at a fork in the road. Darkness hung over them, with only the glowing light of the full moon to lead their way. She didn't know the outlying areas, and it was obvious they were lost. At some point they had veered off the main road. The chilling howl of a dog broke through the night air, enveloping her in a cloak of fear. The snow had begun to fall, and she knew she'd never find her way back to the mill in these conditions. She had to find shelter.

Ten minutes later, with the snow flurries increasing, she caught sight of the silhouette of a cabin a couple hundred feet ahead of them. On a cold evening like tonight, smoke should be billowing from the chimney, but there wasn't even a hint of light shining though the windows. If no one was home, at least they could use it as a temporary shelter. It wasn't worth walking in circles all night trying to find their way back to the mill. They could freeze to death before morning.

She motioned to her brother, who solemnly followed her. As they came closer to the house, she noticed the dozens of buckets set up in the surrounding sugar bush, ready to collect the year's harvest of sap. For years, her father had spent the final weeks of winter working for various sugarhouses helping with the gathering of the sap. It was one of her favorite memories of her family. After the maple crop had been harvested, they gathered together for the sugaring off, where the children had been allowed to eat as much of the sweet syrup as they'd wanted.

Her foot struck something solid in the middle of the path, and she nearly stumbled.

Koby caught her, then knelt in the snow. "It's a man, Lidia."

She stopped, gazing down at the crumpled figure. More than likely the cad was drunk, but this man had made the unfortunate mistake of choosing the wrong place to consume his spirits.

Lidia bent to see if he was breathing, then jerked back in surprise. Even in the darkening shadows of night, she recognized Adam. He was alive, and there was no smell of alcohol on his breath. After ripping off her gloves, she touched his forehead with the back of her hand. Fever raged through his body.

"Quick, Koby. Help me carry him into the house."

Grunting his disdain, her brother leaned over to grab Adam's shoulders. Lidia struggled under the weight of his limp body. Somehow they managed to move him past the slick steps and into the only bedroom of the cabin.

They laid him on the wool blanket that covered the bed, then, after lighting a lantern, she instructed her brother to get a fire going. The first thing she had to do was determine the severity of the head wound, then warm him up. Searching the confines of the small cabin for fresh water and a cloth, she was surprised at how orderly the room was. While simply furnished, each piece was solid and well built. All it needed was a few extra touches that only a woman could provide. Curtains to grace the windows, colorful rugs to adorn the floor, and perhaps a handmade quilt to cover the bed. . .

And you foolishly dare to imagine that you could ever be that woman?

Frowning at the unwanted thought, she took the wet cloth and sat beside Adam, carefully wiping the wet blood from his forehead. He groaned and opened his eyelids.

"Li. . .Lidia?" He smiled at her, but his voice was unsteady. "I was dreaming about you." Clearly he was delirious.

"Be still. You're burning with fever, and I need to clean your wound."

"No, I'm not, it's just. . ." He struggled to get up.

She eased him back down on the bed and finished washing away the blood. While he was going to have quite a lump, it didn't look too serious. More worrisome were his fever and the fact that he had likely spent several hours lying on the cold ground. If they hadn't come along when they had. . .

"You don't understand." This time Adam fought harder to sit up. "I have to check the buckets. It's time for the sap to run."

From the pale light of the lantern, she could see splotches of red across his face from the cold. He was in no condition to get out of bed, let alone work. She laid him back against the pillow. Thankfully, he was too weak to resist her any longer.

"Don't worry about your sap collection." She wrung the cloth into a bowl. "You're not getting out of this bed."

It was a choice between her employment and the livelihood of this man, but as soon as she'd spoken, Lidia knew she'd already made her decision. With weather conditions the way they were, she didn't dare try to go for help. And that left her with one option.

She knew how grueling the process was. Harvesting the sap was only the beginning of the timely process. Once collected, the fresh sap had to be boiled immediately into syrup. Winter would not wait for Adam to recover. She and Koby would have to harvest the sap.

Chapter 4

Lidia ran her finger down the rough bark of the maple tree, then across the tip of the spout where a clear liquid dripped into the bucket below. The bulge of an icicle remained on the tap, confirming that the conditions for the harvest of the sweet sap were perfect. At first, Adam had tried to fight her decision to begin the gathering in the maple grove, insisting he was well enough to do the work himself. She watched as he stumbled across the room in search of his boots, until he finally conceded that he wasn't well enough to get up, let alone work out in the chilly March afternoon. In his feverish state, he'd been forced to lie back down and, within minutes, had fallen into a restless sleep against his thick feather pillow.

Now the wind whipped through the grove, leaving a stinging sensation in Lidia's cheeks. The snow glistened beneath the pale sun, shimmering like tiny crystals through the maple grove. It wasn't cold enough to freeze the sap, but it was cold enough for the wind to make its way through the threads of her thin coat.

Balancing the half-full bucket between both hands, she tromped through the crusty snow toward the next tree. By nightfall, the buckets would be heavy with sap. How Adam had ever thought he could collect then boil the sap while keeping the fires going by himself, she had no idea.

In the short time she'd been around him, he'd reminded her of her father. Stubborn, yet enthusiastic at the same time. Her father had possessed a passion for freedom. This deep emotion had sustained him through difficult times in his native country, through the long crossing of the Atlantic with their family, and to the new life they started together in America. She wasn't sure what drove Adam. Part of her wanted to know what lay behind those dark eyes. Another part of her wanted to run.

Koby labored without complaint, a feat considering his normal attitude at the mill and the work that still lay ahead of them. Once they collected the sap and transferred it into the large vats at the sugarhouse, the liquid would have to be constantly stirred as it boiled, making sure it didn't run over or form a skin on the surface. With the furnace burning strong, the entire process would have to be repeated tomorrow and the next day—as long as Adam needed them or until the weather cleared enough for one of them to go for help.

Lidia was used to hard work. She hung an empty bucket, swapping it for the fuller one. For a moment, Mrs. Moore's birdlike nose and thin, wrinkled face flashed before her. While the woman who ran the factory where they worked wasn't as stern as many of the overseers she'd heard about, Lidia knew she wouldn't tolerate their absence. But neither could Lidia ignore the fact that Adam needed her. A good run of sap wouldn't wait for the deep snow to melt from the roads or for Adam to regain his strength.

Her brother struggled beside her as he strained to lift the wooden sap yoke that carried the two buckets across his shoulders. "Do you remember the last sugaring off we went to?"

"I remember how you ate so many sour pickles we all thought you'd turn green." Lidia set down the bucket, then leaned against one of the sturdy trees, smiling at the memories.

The pickles were said to cut the sweetness of the sugar so one could eat plenty. Koby had never had any problem eating a generous amount of the waxy, taffylike treat that had been boiled then cooled into strips on the snow and eaten with a fork.

She wrapped her arms around herself and let out a slow sigh. "We had some good times together as a family, didn't we?"

Her brother kicked one of the buckets with the tip of his foot. "I miss them."

"I miss them, too, Koby."

Her brother's pained expression sifted though the recesses of her heart. *What do I say to make things better for him, God?* She longed for her mourning to turn into joyful dancing, as David once wrote in the Old Testament. Longed to see a carefree smile cross her brother's lips. But it was something she hadn't seen for months. Or felt in her own life.

"Do you ever think what life might be like if they hadn't died?"

Lidia cleared her throat at her brother's question, unable to stop the sudden flood of emotions that overtook her and brought the sting of tears to her eyes. "You know thinking like that won't bring them back. All we can do is make the best of what we have."

Koby folded his arms across his chest, his chin set in fierce determination. "You could always marry someone like the mister inside. He might not be rich, but he's got all this land. Maybe he wouldn't mind having a boy like me around if I was extra good. I'd work hard so he wouldn't have any reason to send me away. It would almost be like having a family again—"

"Koby!"

"What's wrong with my dreaming about having something gooder?"

"Something better." Lidia frowned. She couldn't blame him for wishing things were different. It was something she did, as well. But in reality, sometimes life handed you a plate of sour pickles instead of a huge iron vat of sweet maple syrup. No gallant hero was going to sprint from the pages of a legend and into her life to change her situation.

"What about you?" Koby took a step forward. "Don't you want more out of life than working ten hours a day for some overseer who doesn't care anything about us, except that we can get the work done so they can make more money?"

"Koby, you—"

"Well, it's true, ain't it?"

"Isn't it?" Lidia shut her mouth at the attempt to correct her brother's grammar. Perfect speech and fine manners would never really change who they were. She'd found that out firsthand. Their parents had worked for a dozen years to establish themselves as hardworking American citizens who could provide for their family in ways they never could have in the old country. And they had achieved much of what they'd dreamed.

She'd seen the look of pride in her father's eyes when he returned from work with a piece of penny candy for each of his children. Her mother would scold him for spoiling them, but her eyes couldn't hide her own feelings of thankfulness for the blessings God had showered upon them. Life had been good.

But all that had changed. It had only taken the dreaded cholera a matter of days to rob her parents of life and in turn change Koby and Lidia's future forever. With the loss of her father's income, she and her brother had become nothing more than immigrant factory workers. It was useless to spend her life dreaming about things changing. Someone like Adam would never choose a girl like her. Fairy tales like that didn't happen in real life.

"It's time to get back to work, Koby." Swallowing the lump in the back of her throat, Lidia picked up her bucket, stiffened her shoulders, and resolved to forget the past and concentrate only on the matter at hand. Saving Adam Johnson's maple crop.

⸎

Adam rolled over onto his side, then winced at the sharp pain that splintered behind his eyes. Reaching up to feel the throbbing knot on his head, he struggled against someone's hand pressing down on his shoulder.

"Please. Lie back, and I'll get you some broth to drink."

He opened his eyes and let them adjust to the fading shadows in the room. Something simmered on the stove, making his mouth water. How long had it been since he'd eaten? He focused on the figure leaning over him. The final rays of the evening sun filtered into the room, bathing Lidia's face in the soft light and causing him to wonder if he was simply dreaming about the fairylike girl who fluttered in and out of his dreams.

Adam pushed his elbows against the bed and tried to sit up again. The pain that seared through him confirmed he was awake.

"Not so fast." Lidia felt his forehead with the back of her hand. "Your fever broke a couple hours ago, but that doesn't mean you can get up."

"I feel fine. Just a bit achy."

She rested her fists against her hips and frowned. "You might be feeling better, but after three days in bed with a raging fever and a bump the size of Massachusetts on your head, I think—"

"Wait a minute." Adam studied the swoosh of her skirts as she moved away from his bed. At times he'd been aware of her presence as she hovered around him with a cool cloth and cups of water for him to sip. But he thought he'd been dreaming. "What did you say?"

"You've been sick."

"I know, but how long?"

She paused beside the rickety table he needed to refurbish. There were so many things he'd intended to do.

"My brother and I found you lying outside on the ground three days ago. I'm not sure how long you were sick before that."

Adam's stomach clenched. A few more hours lying against the frozen ground and more than likely he wouldn't have made it. But three days passing meant that three days of harvesting his sap was lost.

Struggling to ignore the ache that engulfed every muscle of his body, he forced himself to sit up. Sick or not, he had work to do. "I've got to get up. My maple crop—"

"My brother and I have been harvesting the sap in the mornings and afternoons." Lidia stopped in the doorway of his room and turned to face him. "The run slowed down a bit last night as the temperatures dropped too low, but the sun was out today and the taps ran well again. You're going to have a great crop this year."

Adam's jaw tightened. It wasn't as if he didn't appreciate the effort, but there was so much more to gathering the sap than simply emptying the buckets. A novice trying to do the work would ruin the entire season's production. "You don't understand, the sap has to be boiled—"

"Of course." Lidia tilted her head. "Koby's kept the fire going strong. Thankfully you had plenty of wood for fuel."

"But do you know how to test the density of the sap when you're boiling it?

Once the sap begins to drip off the end of the dipper in sheets—"

"Then it's syrup. It's called aproning." He watched through the doorway as she busied herself in the kitchen, then returned with a cup of the broth he'd smelled simmering on the stove. "My father used to work in the maple groves at the end of every winter, and I helped him."

The room seemed to spin around him. "I don't understand. Why are you doing this for me?"

"There wasn't much of a choice. Since I don't know this area well, I was afraid I wouldn't find my way back to town with the snowdrifts and the weather being the way it is. Once it clears, my brother and I can go and find a few men to help, but until then, we couldn't let your sap go bad, now could we?"

He fingered the edge of his worn blanket. "It's not that I don't appreciate what you've done, but I can't have you and your brother working my maple crop for me."

"And why not? You'll never get well if you don't get your strength back, and either we do the work or buckets sit full of wasted sap." Lidia's eyes brightened with her smile. "Drink some of this broth and stop worrying. Fretting over things you can't do anything about will only make you grow old quicker, as my babcia used to say."

"Your who?" Adam took a sip of the broth and felt the warmth of the liquid run down his throat.

"My grandmother. You'd have liked her. She was almost as stubborn as you are."

He shook his head at the comment, then winced as the pain returned. Whether he wanted to admit it or not, it did seem as if his stubbornness had once again gotten him into trouble. If he'd listened to his father, he would have the help he needed instead of having to rely on a young girl who barely weighed more than a feather. The days might be warming up, but she had no business working out there. Harvesting a maple crop was hard work.

Ignoring the guilt that surged through him, he tried to stand, determined to get out of bed. He crossed the wood-planked floor in uneven steps.

Lidia grabbed his arm. "You're too weak to get out of bed."

"I'm fine." His jaw tensed. "Just let me sit in the other room for a while, then I promise to go back to bed."

"Suit yourself."

He watched as Lidia bustled around his kitchen. He had plans to sand the cupboards and replace the stove, but time hadn't allowed it. There had been so much work to do, and the kitchen had never been a priority. Suddenly, he wished he'd made it a priority.

Lidia pulled a pan out of the oven, and the yeasty aroma of freshly baked bread wafted to him. It and the fragrant broth were much more alluring than the smells of burnt biscuits and stale coffee that normally filled the room. He had no problem fixing beans and overdone biscuits in his kitchen, but he'd certainly never stopped to consider what a woman might think about his living conditions.

"I'm sorry about the kitchen." He cleared his throat. "It wasn't exactly built with the needs of a woman in mind. The supplies are a bit low. . . ."

"I've managed to make do." She waved her hand in his direction. "Once you're up and around, you'll need something hearty to eat, like a steaming pot of *bigos*, though you're right. Your store of food is completely inadequate, even if it is just for one man."

"*Bigos*?"

"Stew. My father could never understand how a man could survive without a steamy bowl of stew on the table at night. It's full of different meats and vegetables." She dried her hands on a dishcloth. "I'll make you a huge pot one day, and you can taste it for yourself."

She must have realized how intimate her comment might be interpreted, because Adam caught her sheepish expression after she'd said it. Her cheeks reddened as she turned away from him, pushing a strand of auburn hair out of her face. Once he got out of bed, she would leave and there would be no reason for her to ever make him another meal. His pulse quickened despite his earlier resolve to forget her.

"Tell me about your family," he said.

Lidia shrugged as she finished washing the dishes. "There's not much to tell. My parents emigrated from Poland to America when I was six. I never saw my grandmother again."

He could hear the marked sadness in her voice. "And your parents?"

"They died during a cholera outbreak a little over a year ago. Now it's just me and my brother."

"I'm sorry."

"There's no sense in dwelling on the past." She shook her head, as if trying to erase the memories inside. "What about your family?"

"My parents live a few miles from here on a farm where I was raised with my brothers and sisters." He cleared his throat. "There's seven of us now. Samuel was killed last fall."

"I'm sorry. You must miss him tremendously."

"I do."

As much as he appreciated Lidia's and her brother's help, he couldn't help thinking of his own brother. The deafening sound of a gun firing. His brother lying dead on the street. Anger welled within him at the memories. He knew his sister Rebecca was right. It wasn't fair to blame an entire people for one man's wrong, and he knew Lidia had nothing to do with his brother's death. But knowing the truth and stopping the anger inside him had proved to be two different things.

Part of him wanted to reach out and comfort her for her own losses. To tell her that everything was going to be all right despite the horrible heartache she'd lived through. The other part of his soul still grappled over what he'd lost. There was no way around it. Seeing Lidia only reminded him of his own pain and his own guilt in allowing it to happen.

Struggling to remain sitting up, he fought against the growing nausea. While he appreciated Lidia and Koby's help, he needed to find a way to finish the job—alone.

Chapter 5

Adam shoved his boots on before stepping out onto the porch. The morning sun greeted him, a pale circle against a white sky. He pulled up the collar of his jacket against the wind, not needing to look at a thermometer to know the temperature wasn't rising fast enough. And if he was reading the sky correctly, a storm was coming in. Though it wasn't unusual for cold snaps or warm days to temporarily stop the run of sap, he was anxious that the weather conditions hold for at least another two weeks so he could collect his entire run this year. He already had a buyer lined up for his syrup, and he would need every bit of cash he could earn in order to continue with his expansion plans for the land.

He rubbed his hand against the side of his head, thankful that the swelling had gone down. After another two days of recovering, he'd made no promises to Lidia that he would stay in bed as she and her brother had slipped outside to begin another day of harvesting. Even if the sap weren't running, there would still be plenty of work to do. Supplies needed to be scalded to prevent the syrup from spoiling; necessary repairs to the buckets and other equipment would need to be made, as well as extra wood chopped for the fire.

Lidia rounded the corner of the house with two buckets in her hands, stopping when she saw him. "Adam. I thought you were sleeping."

"I couldn't stay in bed another minute." He read the look of concern in her eyes as her brow furrowed, and he forced a grin. "I'm fine. Really. And I'm ready to get back to work. A man can only stay cooped up in that cabin for so long."

"You're still weak." She set the buckets on the porch and started up the steps. "And you need to eat something."

"I already did. I found the leftover biscuits you made. Tasted as good as my stepmother's, which is saying something. She's a fantastic cook."

"I'm glad you liked them." He caught her familiar blush as she spoke and couldn't help but warm at her smile. "I'm sure you felt the cold snap last night, and the temperature's not warming up like it needs to. I'm not sure how much we'll be able to collect."

He'd expected her to tell him that he needed to march back inside the house and get back in bed, but apparently she'd decided not to argue with him today. He was glad, even though she'd probably be right.

He leaned his palms against the porch rail. "A break in the weather will give me a chance to get caught up."

Lidia picked up the empty buckets and started across the snow toward the grove of stately maple trees. He followed her through the sugar bush, amazed at her endurance. He had poured so much of who he was into this land and knew the backbreaking effort it took to harvest the sap.

The buckets hung from each tree, waiting to collect the sweet liquid. Some of the trees spanned almost four feet in diameter. Others were much smaller, but Old Man Potter had told him they were all at least forty years old.

"Did you know that as the tree grows, the bark doesn't expand with it? You can see how it keeps splitting open." Adam ran his hand across the shaggy bark. "These trees are as individual as people."

She came to stand beside him. "Meaning?"

"One might produce sap that is consistently sweeter than the others while another's sap might taste like water. And their sap runs differently, as well. Some manage a good run every year, and others might produce a lot less."

"Who taught you about the harvest?"

"Old Man Potter owned this property. I started working for him when I was about fourteen, and while he was a bit of a codger, he became like a grandfather to me." Adam smiled at the memory of the gray-haired man who had been an active part of every harvest until the year he died. "He taught me the science of tapping a tree for the best results, how to study the bark as well as the new growth, and where to set the buckets. When he died, he left me the land."

"That's quite an inheritance."

"I suppose I was the grandson he never had. While he never told me, rumor has it his only son was killed in a gunfight back in Kansas in the '50s."

"You must have meant a lot to him, then."

"He meant a lot to me, too." He fidgeted, uncomfortable with the way the conversation had turned. "You know, if I close my eyes, I can almost taste the syrup."

Lidia's eyes lit up when she smiled. "This has always been my favorite time of the year."

"Mine, too." As he lifted one of the buckets off the tree, he was surprised at how much he enjoyed her company. "It's crazy, I guess, but while my brother dreamed of being a doctor, my dreams always centered around God's good earth and the things I could produce with it."

"That's not a crazy dream. I think that's why I love poetry. Much of it describes nature so beautifully."

"Do you write your own?"

"Poetry?" Lidia lowered her gaze at the question. "When I find the time. I have a book where I write down thoughts and ideas, though my attempts certainly couldn't compare to some of the great poets of our time."

"Who said they had to?"

Adam tried to ignore the stirring of his heart when he looked at her, but he couldn't. What was it about Lidia that set his senses alive when he was around her? From the first time he'd looked into her dark mahogany eyes and caught the rosy blush that swept across her fair cheeks, she'd affected him like no woman ever had.

The wall he'd put up around him was beginning to crack. He was now able to see Lidia as an individual person, not simply a Polish immigrant.

"What's your favorite kind of maple syrup?" Lidia's abrupt change in subject amused him. While she emitted a certain confidence, at the same time he sensed a streak of vulnerability within her. And that only made her more captivating.

Adam smiled at the question. "Without a doubt, maple cream. Spread it on a piece of hot bread and it's like a bit of heaven right there in your hand."

"That's my favorite, too. That and a tall stack of pancakes dripping with hot syrup. Then there's the music and singing at the annual sugaring off."

"While I've never been much on social gatherings, you do have a point."

Lidia laughed, then picked up one of the buckets filled with sap. "Do you feel like walking to the sugarhouse? Or would you rather take the wagon?"

"It's not far. I'll walk."

Five minutes later, Adam stepped out of the chilly breeze that blew through the maple grove and into the warmth of the sugarhouse. The aroma of hot syrup lingered in the air from the sap that was being boiled down. Taking in a deep breath, he felt his body relax. There was something about this first rite of spring that always invigorated him. Looking at the bubbling vats, he saw that everything had been done exactly as needed.

"I don't know what to say. I'm amazed at how much you've accomplished."

Koby stood in the corner of the room stirring the sap.

Adam reached out his hand toward the boy. "I don't think I've thanked you properly for what you've done, young man."

Koby shook his hand and cracked a smile. "It's better than working for the old crow at the factory—"

"Koby!" Lidia's eyes widened.

"Well, it's true." The boy went back to stirring the hot liquid in slow, circular strokes. "She's not exactly the friendliest overseer in the world."

"She's always been good to us, Koby, and you know it."

Adam paused, confused. "You work in one of the factories?"

Lidia played with the folds of her skirt and nodded.

Why should he be surprised? A majority of immigrants worked in the factories. Adam swallowed hard, realizing for the first time that their sacrifice to help him ran far deeper than just the physical strain involved. "They'll fire you for this."

"Probably." She bit her lip.

Koby took a step toward him. "Trust me, it's no great loss, Mr. Johnson. There are other factories looking for workers, unless you'd like to hire us for the rest of the season. There's plenty of work that could be done here—"

"Koby, that's not appropriate for you to ask." Lidia kept her words low and steady, but there was an obvious hint of pride behind her statement.

"Fine." The boy's dark brow puckered. "Like I said, there are other factories in the area willing to take advantage of us like the old. . .I mean Mrs. Moore."

"I wish I could offer to hire you both." Adam cleared his throat, not knowing how to respond to the boy. "I'm just not sure how I could pay—"

"Of course not." Lidia whispered something to her brother before moving to empty one of the buckets into the vat. "We would never want to put you in such an awkward position. We'll be fine. Right now, all we need to worry about is the work before us."

Adam cringed. He'd never given a second thought to the conditions of the surrounding factories that dotted the state. Even with new laws that limited the number of hours children were allowed to work, he knew that the labor was hard, rules stringent, and the pay minimal. It wasn't the kind of place he wanted to see Lidia working in—or Koby. But he knew that even if he wanted to hire them for the rest of the season, he simply didn't have the means to pay them. If they lost their jobs on top of everything else. . .

"Let me speak to Mrs. Moore on your behalf." Adam caught her troubled gaze. "Once I explain what happened, I'm sure she'll be sympathetic."

Lidia shrugged a shoulder. "It might make a difference, but please don't worry about us. We'll be fine."

She smiled at him, and his heart pounded. She looked small and vulnerable beside the large iron vat. He shouldn't feel this way. Something inside him made him want to protect her. To gather her into his arms and promise her everything would be all right.

A wave of nausea swept over him, and he leaned against the wall for support.

Lidia grabbed his arm and led him to a wooden bench in the corner of the room. "You're not strong enough yet."

"I'm fine. It's just a dizzy spell."

"No, it's not. You've overdone it." Lidia glanced up at her brother. "If the snow melts enough by morning, we'll go into town for help."

છ

"Didn't you know? All Polish fairy tales have at least one dragon." Lidia laughed as she leaned closer to the fire that crackled in the stone fireplace of Adam's small cabin.

He sat across from her, his eyes twinkling with mischief. "And like the story you just told, are the princesses always rescued by handsome heroes?"

"Of course, just like the stories you tell in this country."

Two more days had passed, and Lidia found herself wanting to suspend their time together indefinitely. Tonight the stars loomed bright overhead, signaling an end to the gray, overcast skies and below-normal temperature that had stopped the flow of sap.

While they had waited for the daytime temperatures to rise, Lidia spent the long days scalding the utensils for the sap harvest, while her brother ensured there was plenty of wood to keep the vats of sap boiling. Adam had worked intermittently as he slowly regained his strength, repairing the handles of several of the buckets when he wasn't resting or engaging in snowball fights with her brother.

Adam's cheeks had lost their pasty appearance, and it was becoming clear he wouldn't need her much longer. Besides that, now that he was up and around again, it wouldn't be proper for her to stay even with her brother beside her.

It was time to go into town to find someone to help Adam with the rest of the harvest. Then she would return to the factory where she could only pray Mrs. Moore would graciously agree to keep her and her brother on as employees.

Koby snored softly beside her on the small couch. She put her arm around him and pulled him close. In spite of the hard work he'd accomplished, she hadn't missed seeing how he'd thrived this past week. Being outside in the fresh air, away from the demanding labor of the factory, had done wonders for him. She'd seen him smile for the first time in months, something even she hadn't been able to get him to do before.

Adam had a way with him, as well. Lidia was convinced he'd gotten out of bed sooner than he should have, but even in his weakened state, he seemed to find the energy to encourage her brother. And now she would have to take Koby away from all of this.

Something cried out from the darkness beyond the cabin.

"What was that?"

Adam cocked his head. "Sounded like an owl."

"No." She leaned forward and put a finger to her lips.

She listened carefully as an animal rummaged in the trees. "Are there animals that might get into the buckets?"

"Might be. I'll go check it out."

"I'm coming with you."

The front door creaked open, and she followed Adam across the porch and down the steps, careful not to slip on the remnants of ice that encrusted the wooden boards as she worked to stay in the light of the lantern he held above his head.

"Could be a wildcat," he whispered. "But I doubt it."

Lidia shivered and wondered if she should run back to the safety of the cabin.

Adam shone the light up into one of the trees and caught the reflection of two round eyes. "I was right. It's an owl."

"Are you sure?" She still wasn't convinced. "What I heard sounded much bigger."

Adam laughed. "There's nothing to worry about. We get a few wild animals around here, but none of them have ever made a menace of themselves so far."

"I hope not."

"Look at the stars." Adam blew out the lantern and gazed toward the heavens. The night sky was so bright the extra light wasn't needed. "My father and I used to lie out in the fields in the summertime where he'd teach me the names of many of the great constellations."

"It is beautiful." She looked up at him and tried to ignore the flutter of her heart over his nearness. "Maybe we should go in now. You must be exhausted after today."

Adam drew in a deep breath. "I do need to shake this lingering fatigue. If the temperatures rise like I think they will after I get you off to town, I'm going to have a busy day tomorrow."

The reminder that she wouldn't be a part of his days anymore saddened her. "We could stay longer, my brother and I. . ."

"I wouldn't ask that of you. I'm already worried about your job at the factory."

He was right. She knew they had to leave, but the thought left her sober. Tomorrow she would be gone. She wasn't sure when she'd ever see him again.

Lidia turned and twisted her ankle on a broken limb. Struggling to keep her balance, she felt his strong hand envelop her arm and hold her upright. "Thank you. I'm fine."

She caught his gaze, and for a moment, time hovered motionless around her. She had no right feeling what she did toward him. They lived in two different worlds. She was a second-generation immigrant. A factory worker. He came from a successful family and owned his own land—

"Lidia. . ."

Before she could say anything, his lips pressed against hers. She felt breathless and light-headed. Hadn't she daydreamed of him holding her and telling her he cared for her? And now his arms surrounded her.

He stepped back abruptly. "I'm sorry. I don't know what I was thinking. I had no right to kiss you."

She smiled up at him. "It's all right. Really."

Heat rose in her cheeks, and she was certain he could read her thoughts. While he'd been in his feverish state, she'd dared imagine what it would be like to care for him as his wife. Dared to imagine that something could ever come about between them, and now wasn't that very possibility looming before her? Surely this wasn't really happening.

"It's late." He ran his thumb down her jawline. "We'll talk more in the morning."

Following closely behind him, she stepped into the cabin and watched as Adam entered his room and shut the door behind him. With a smile on her face, she sat down beside her sleeping brother, wondering all the time what tomorrow might bring.

❧

Lidia arose early the next morning, careful not to disturb her brother as she went about the morning chores in the small cabin one last time. She smiled as she chopped up the potatoes and fried them, remembering her dreams filled with Adam and the softness of his touch. She longed to know more about the man she'd diligently nursed back to health over the past few days. It seemed unbelievable that he might care for her.

Standing in front of the kitchen window that overlooked the maple grove, she flipped the last of the pancakes in the hot pan as the morning sun began to peek above the horizon. Not only had she decided to prepare a decent breakfast for Adam, but she also wanted to make sure everything was in order before he took them to the mill this morning. It was the least she could do.

Or maybe it was simply because she wanted to prolong her time here. But the dark clouds that had hovered above them the past few days had vanished, and with Adam's health returning, there was no excuse for her to stay.

With the pancakes cooked and the potatoes nearly finished, she quickly worked to tidy up the room. Dusting the wooden bookshelf, a small stack of newspaper clippings fluttered to the floor. She picked them up, then froze as she glanced at the familiar face.

"Jarek."

She hadn't spoken the name of her older brother for almost a year and a half. Her family hadn't known anything until her father had happened to see the sketch of his eldest son in the post office—wanted for murder. Jarek had been missing for weeks and had a bounty on his head; none of her family believed they'd ever see him again.

She scanned the paper, which told briefly about the incident. Here, in black and white, were the details she'd tried to forget during the months that followed her father's discovery. Then her parents died, bringing another fresh wave of grief. A name caught her attention. One of the details she'd apparently chosen to forget. But this time the named burned across her heart. Her brother, Jarek, had murdered Samuel Johnson.

Chapter 6

Lidia crinkled the paper between her fingers and let the sketch of her brother drop to the floor. It was happening again. Feelings of panic, grief, and helplessness washed over her in a single wave. She remembered the day they learned the truth about why Jarek had run away. Father had sat her and Mother down and told them what he'd seen in town, revealing the awful truth that a thousand dollars was being offered for the capture of her brother.

Her mother had refused to believe the accusations that Jarek had killed someone. Lidia hadn't wanted to believe them either, yet she'd seen the way his temper flared, time and time again, with little provocation. Then there was the fact that her father's gun was missing. Her father hadn't told her mother, but Lidia had opened the empty case and at that moment, realized the accusations were true. Her brother was a murderer.

Until today, she'd never really stopped to think about the family of the young man Jarek killed. At the beginning, she'd felt sorry for them, wishing she could go back in time and change things, but all she'd known was that someone had died. He'd been a nameless person she couldn't put a face to, and her own grief in losing her brother was still too new. Now the family had a name. Her heart ached for Adam.

Lidia straightened the papers and shoved them back inside the cabinet. She'd seen the pain in Adam's eyes when he spoke about his brother. Even after almost a year and a half, the pain ran deep. She could sense the closeness the two men had shared. It hurt her to know how much he'd lost. She could imagine that feeling all too well. Because on the day Jarek took Samuel's life, she lost her own brother, as well.

The smell of something burning filled her nostrils. She hurried across the room, barely scooping the pan off the stove in time to save the potatoes from scorching. She shoved the buckwheat pancakes and salvaged fried potatoes onto a pan and into the oven to warm, letting the door bang shut.

The crude drawing of her brother's face was etched in the back of her mind. That wasn't how she wanted to remember him. She wanted to destroy the newspaper article and the heated accusations and put it all behind her as if it had never happened. Nothing, though, could change the reality of what had taken place between Jarek and Adam's brother.

There had been a time when things had been different with Jarek. Before he'd started running around with the wrong crowd. Before Lidia began to notice his anger simmering under the surface. Maybe if her parents had been stricter with him, he would have realized what he was doing, or if she had found the right words to say to him... But she knew that wasn't true. Jarek had been eighteen. The choices her brother made were his choices, not hers or her parents'.

She began washing the table in vigorous circles, remembering how her father decided not to tell the sheriff that he knew the once-innocent lad portrayed on the wanted poster. "What does it really matter?" he'd asked her mother as he wiped away her tears. They didn't have any information as to where he was. Even if they did, how could a father turn his eldest son over to a hangman's noose?

As much as it hurt, she'd known deep inside that she'd never see Jarek again. He was on the run from the law. Coming home wasn't an option. She didn't even know if he was alive. Had he somehow heard about the sudden death of their parents, or even begun to understand the tragedy he'd caused the Johnson family in losing their son?

Why did it have to be Adam's brother, Lord?

The truth was impossible for her to deal with. Glancing across the small living quarters, she felt as if the room were mocking her. There was no chance for her and Adam. She'd lost him before ever really getting to know him. She'd seen the way he looked into her eyes in the moonlight. The wide grin that crossed his face as he dared to steal a kiss. In her amazement over it all, she knew without a doubt that she felt the same way. She'd dared to wonder if there was a chance for him to fall in love with her.

But now it didn't matter what Adam felt toward her. All that was about to change. He would never look at her that way again once he found out the truth about her brother.

Running the back of her hand across her lips, she could still feel the sweetness of his kiss. It had been wrong to think there could ever be anything between them.

❦

Wondering where Lidia and her brother were, Adam stepped out of his room and into the kitchen. The appetizing smells of buckwheat pancakes and fried potatoes filled his senses as he peeked into the oven at the breakfast Lidia had prepared. How she'd managed to transform his meager supplies into such a mouthwatering meal, he had no idea. He'd never had the opportunity to eat with her during his recovery and didn't intend to lose this chance to be with her one last time before she left.

Sighing, he shut the oven door. All he could think about was the unsettling truth that he had to take them back to the mill this morning. He cringed at the thought of Lidia working day after day for some calloused overseer who didn't care when she got tired or hungry or if she simply wanted to spend an afternoon reading poetry. She didn't deserve to live such a harsh life. She needed a home and a family where she could feel safe and secure. But it was more than just the conditions of the factory that bothered him. After their kiss, he realized how much he didn't want to see her go. And how much he was going to miss her.

He'd never intended to kiss her, but even in that brief moment, he'd delighted in her touch and her closeness. Yet he'd realized something else, as well. Lidia was an honorable woman with high moral standards. A stolen kiss in the moonlight wasn't the way to win a lady's heart. He wanted to proclaim his feelings to her, then ask permission to court her properly.

Adam stepped out onto the porch where he finally caught a glimpse of Lidia carrying buckets across the edge of the maple grove. He'd never expected her to work this morning. For the first time since the day she found him in the snow, he felt strong and ready to finish the job at hand. He wanted to take care of her. Not have to depend on her hard work for the survival of the farm.

He took the porch steps two at a time, realizing that Rebecca had been right. His anger toward one man shouldn't have anything to do with his feelings for Lidia. He sensed that she was uncomfortable with her position in life, but the fact that she worked in a mill didn't matter to him. There were so many things about her that amazed him. He'd watched her take a chance at losing her own means of livelihood for a stranger, seen her care for her brother, and witnessed her faith in God. This was the kind of woman he wanted to spend the rest of his life with.

He had no way of knowing if Lidia would be the woman he brought home as his wife one day, but he at least wanted the opportunity to find out. Before he took her in to town, he would make an opportunity to talk to her and see if there was a chance she felt the same way toward him.

Feeling a resurgence of energy with each stride, Adam crossed the open yard that separated the cabin from the maple grove. "Lidia, there's no reason for you to work this morning. Have you eaten?"

She nodded her head, her gaze trained on her work. "I left plenty for you in the oven."

"I saw what you made. Thank you. It looked wonderful. I thought we could eat breakfast together. The three of us, of course."

Lidia nodded, but again she didn't look at him. "I'm sorry, but I'm not hungry. Koby's already down at the sugarhouse. We wanted to do what we could before you took us back to the mill. There's so much to—"

"Wait a minute." They'd laughed under the stars last night. He'd felt the warmth in her voice as they'd talked to each other, but now her greeting seemed colder than the frozen ground beneath them. "What's wrong, Lidia?"

Her eyes widened. "Why do you ask?"

"I don't know. I just thought. . ." Adam paused. Perhaps he'd read her wrong last night and her response to his kiss had been nothing more than a figment of his imagination. Or worse, he'd offended her by presuming she was interested in him.

He lowered his voice. "It's about the kiss, isn't it? I'm sorry. I never should have assumed that you—"

"That I'm interested in you?"

"Are you?" He closed his mouth.

"That doesn't matter anymore."

"You're not making any sense, Lidia. I know now that I was presumptuous in kissing you without stating clearly my intentions toward you, and I do apologize."

She shook her head and squeezed her eyes shut. "You're only going to make things harder—"

"I was wrong." He took a step forward, longing to take her into his arms and make things right again. "That's what I wanted to talk to you about. I don't want today to be the last time I see you. I want to call on you and get to know you better."

"That will never happen, Adam."

"Why not? I don't understand."

"It's your brother Samuel." Lidia leaned against one of the trees. "I know who killed him."

"What?" The sugar bush began to spin around him. How could she know who Samuel's murderer was?

This time she looked him straight in the eye. "I never told you that I have another brother. His name is Jarek."

"What does he have to do with Samuel?"

She took a deep breath, then blew it out slowly as if trying to steady her nerves. "Shortly after we moved here, he disappeared. All we could do was pray that God would protect him and bring him back to us. Then one afternoon my father saw a sketch of my brother on a wanted poster, and we found out that he was wanted for murder. I never heard the name of the boy he was accused of killing until I saw one of your newspaper clippings this morning while I was cleaning." Lidia clenched the material of her dress with her fists. "He's wanted for the murder of Samuel Johnson."

Adam felt as if he'd been punched in the gut. Surely he'd misunderstood what she said. It didn't make sense. Maybe he was sicker than he thought. Fever often signaled delirium. He ran his hand across his brow and felt the heavy beads of sweat. That's what it was. He was simply having a bad dream. Maybe if he closed his eyes and relaxed, he would dream about their kiss instead. That had been real. She'd been so close, so real. It had happened. He knew it, but this. . .

"Adam, did you hear what I said?"

"There must be some mistake." Adam shook his head and took a step back, not wanting to believe her.

"There's no mistake. My brother killed your brother."

He looked up at her. Her eyes were rimmed with tears and her cheeks were blotchy as if she'd been crying. He'd never meant to make her cry.

"His name is Jarek."

"Jarek." The earth spun faster. That had been his name, but. . . "No, Lidia, you're mistaken. It couldn't have been your brother."

"I've seen the sketches. There's no doubt. They look just like him." She picked up her bucket and headed for the wagon. Her tears had been replaced by a vacant expression. "We never saw him again after that day. At first, my mother believed he'd simply gone back to Boston where we'd lived. She'd hoped he'd return for Christmas, but when my father saw the drawing and the reward of a thousand dollars on his head, we knew we were wrong. He wasn't ever coming home again. At least not alive."

Adam stopped beside her at the wagon. "Lidia, I'm so sorry. . ."

He choked on the words. Anger seeped through his pores. For a moment he was there again. In the past. He squeezed his eyes shut, praying that the haunting memories would leave him, but they wouldn't. Instead, they replayed over and over.

Samuel throwing the first punch. The other boy returning the blow. Adam had tried to stop them, but Samuel wouldn't listen as he ran out the back to the side street and across the deserted field. There hadn't been time to pull them apart. There was nothing he could do but watch as the boy drew a pistol from his holster, aimed it at his brother, and killed him.

Adam tried to steady his breathing as he looked at her, but his heart raced out of control. It shouldn't matter. The fact that Lidia's brother had been the one to kill Samuel had nothing to do with her or who she was. She hadn't pulled the trigger. She was only guilty of being his sister, a fact she certainly couldn't control.

He looked into her eyes and saw tears brimming in the corners. Her gaze begged him to understand. Begged him to forgive her for what had happened in the past between their brothers. He could forgive her, because in truth there was nothing to forgive. But the fact that her brother had been the one to take Samuel's life would always stand between them. How could it not?

Chapter 7

Lidia stood and watched Adam stride toward the cabin, all the while willing her tears to disappear. The door slammed shut behind him and caused a thin layer of snow to slide off the roof and cascade onto the porch.

She'd known the moment she read Samuel Johnson's name in the paper that no matter what Adam's feelings toward her might be, nothing would ever be the same between them. And how could she blame him? Every time he looked at her, he would be reminded of what he'd lost.

She'd seen the pain reflected in Adam's eyes as he'd fought to take in the truth of what she told him. The flash of anger that crossed his face might not have been directed toward her, but she'd felt it all the same.

Why, Lord? Why do You allow things like this to happen?

She grabbed one of the buckets by its handle, not caring that the sugary liquid sloshed over the sides. Her breath rose in frothy waves in front of her, the coldness of the morning penetrating her lungs. All around her lay the fading beauty of winter. Trees reached toward the heavens, their limbs proclaiming praises to their Creator. Birds chirped in chorus around her, singing their sweet songs that would soon usher in the coming spring. It was a scene she never tired of. God's white blanket had covered His earth, keeping it dormant, but soon He would bring it to life again in a blaze of color with the vast arrangement of spring's flowers, green grass, and azure skies.

But today, in spite of the beauty around her, she couldn't sense God's presence.

"Lidia?"

Turning, she saw her brother coming toward her, his feet crunching though the last of winter's snow. "Is Mr. Johnson all right? I thought he'd be up by now."

She didn't want to feel anything, but her heart skipped a beat at the sound of his name. "He's in the house. I'm sure he'll be out to work soon. Remember he's still recovering from his illness."

She wouldn't mention the real reason he was in the cabin. Whether or not it had been the right thing, their parents had tried to shelter Koby from Jarek's actions. Koby knew his brother had run away, but he had no idea about the details surrounding his disappearance. He had enough to deal with in life without knowing his brother was wanted for murder.

"I need to get him back for yesterday." Koby leaned against the side of the wagon, a mischievous grin on his face. "The weather's warming. I thought we could have one more snowball fight before we leave and it all melts away."

"Not today." She shook her head. "I was just coming to get you. We need to be leaving now."

"Come on." Her brother's lips curled into a pout. "We have time. It's not like Mrs. Moore will let us come back anyway. Why can't we just stay until the harvest is over and then figure out what we're going to do?"

"I said it's time to go." She winced at the sharpness in her voice. "I'm sorry, but it wouldn't look right. Now that Adam is out of bed, we're not needed here anymore."

"He does need us." Koby folded his arms across his chest. "You're worried about going back to the mill, aren't you?"

She jutted her chin upward at the question. "I'm responsible for you, and with the strong possibility that helping with the harvest has cost us our jobs—"

"He likes you."

"What?"

"Adam."

Lidia picked up two buckets that were full of sap and headed toward the wagon. "I really don't want to talk about him."

"Why not? Did you have a fight?"

"Yes—no." She closed her eyes, wishing her brother wasn't quite so curious. . .and right.

"So which is it?"

She spun around to face him. "It's complicated, Koby."

"What's so complicated about two people liking each other? You could marry him, and we could stay here and forget the past and that awful Mrs. Moore."

Lidia frowned. He was right about one thing. It was time for her to forget the past. And that meant leaving her feelings for Adam behind, as well. While she didn't regret helping him, the reality was she had probably lost her job. Still, staying here was not an option. There was always the possibility of answering an ad from the local paper for a mail-order bride, but the very thought of marrying for anything but love made her blood run cold. A better option would be if someone in town agreed to hire her, but that still left them needing a place to stay.

Adam wasn't the answer to her prayers as she'd briefly dared to hope, but perhaps their situation would turn out better for them after all. If she could get a position in town, it would give her brother an opportunity to go to school, something she desperately wanted for him.

Koby stepped beside her and draped his arm around her shoulder. "Leaving the mill would mean no more of the cook's dinners. I love your cooking, and it's obvious that Mr. Johnson agrees—"

"Koby." Despite his persistence, she had to laugh. Leave it to her brother to say the right thing to make her smile. The food at the mills did leave much to be desired. She and her brother had come up with their own names for the bland, often unidentifiable dishes—mysterious macaroni pie, seafood surprise, peculiar pastries. . .

"Do we really have to go?"

Lidia glanced up at the cabin and swallowed the feelings of regret that threatened to surface. "Yes, Koby, it's time to go."

❧

Adam stared at the thin pile of newspaper articles he'd kept after his brother's death. He shouldn't have walked away from Lidia, but he'd been so afraid of losing control of his emotions. His reaction was far from godly, but at the moment, he didn't care. He knew he should bury the incident and leave it in the past. He should even be relieved to find out who was responsible for Samuel's death. But nothing would bring Samuel back, and nothing would erase the pain or the guilt he felt over what happened.

Trying to hold back thoughts of revenge, he pulled his leather-bound Bible out of a drawer. The pages fell open to the Sermon on the Mount in the book of Matthew. He'd underlined the verses on forgiveness in chapter six, but as many times as he'd read them, forgiveness still seemed impossible to find.

Forgiveness toward Samuel's murderer? Or forgiveness toward myself?

Adam slammed the book shut at the question. He hated the feelings of guilt that plagued him. Wasn't it easier to lay the blame at the feet of the boy who killed Samuel?

And his entire family, as well?

Again the unwanted stab of conscience haunted him. At Lidia's confession, he'd run like a frightened animal. It had been her brother who'd killed Samuel. He couldn't deny that truth.

The uninvited image of Lidia filled the recesses of his mind. Her wide, brown eyes and soft smile had touched something inside of him that had never been awakened before. He could hear the entertaining lilt of her voice and the tinkling sound of her laughter. But most of all he could feel the feather touch of her lips against his. He'd wanted that moment to last forever and had even wondered if she might be the one person he needed to make his life complete.

A fire blazed in the hearth, taking off the chill of the morning. He threw the papers into the fire and watched the orange flames lick hungrily at the added fuel. As the articles disintegrated before him, crackling into black ashes, he wondered if it were possible for his emotions to do the same. To not only forgive and forget, but to put the past and its horrible mistakes behind him. Wasn't Lidia worth taking a chance on? Wasn't she worth taking the time to get to know better despite what her brother had done to his family?

I just don't think I can do it, Lord.

The squeak of a wagon wheel broke into his thoughts and drew his attention to the window. His father stepped out of the flatbed wagon in front of the cabin.

Adam took a deep breath, wondering what he should tell his father. Knowing the identity of Samuel's murderer should make it easier for the sheriff and his men to find him. But in the process, it would break Lidia's heart. That was something he didn't want to happen no matter what his conflicting feelings toward her were at the moment.

Adam opened the door, then paused in the entrance as his father took the porch steps two at a time to greet him. He'd been told a dozen times how closely he resembled his father with his coal black hair and dark eyes with their hints of gold. He'd always longed to emulate his godly character, as well, something that at the moment was proving difficult to do.

"I know you've been busy harvesting the sap, but we've missed seeing you." His father enveloped him in a hug. "Michaela insisted I come out and check on you."

Adam took a step back and forced a smile. "You can tell her I'm fine, though I've been sick for the past week. That's why I haven't stopped by."

His father's brow narrowed in concern. "If we'd known you were sick, we'd have come to help earlier. You've just been so insistent on handling things alone—"

"I know, and you were right."

"Never thought I'd hear you admit that." His father smiled and squeezed Adam's shoulder. "What about the sap?"

He glanced toward the maple grove, but there was no sign of Lidia or Koby. They must have taken the wagon, full of the morning's harvest, down to the sugarhouse.

Adam cleared his throat. "I've had some help."

His father leaned against the porch railing, a smile playing on his lips. "So you finally took my advice and hired workers?"

"Not officially." Adam's gaze dropped to study the rough boards of the porch. As much as he knew he needed to tell his father the truth, the very idea sent a wave of nausea coursing through him. "There is a problem, though. We need to talk."

"What is it, son?"

"Why don't you come inside and sit down. I'll get you some coffee."

He was avoiding the issue, and he knew it. He studied his father's puzzled expression as they entered the house. Adam wasn't sure how he did it, but the past year and a half had produced a deeper strength in his father. He'd seen the tragedy draw him and his stepmother, Michaela, even closer together as they rallied around the family for support. Their spiritual lives had taken on deeper meaning, but none of it made sense to Adam. It seemed to him that God had played favorites between Samuel and Jarek—and Samuel had lost.

"Something smells good." His father made himself at home on one of the two chairs Adam had to offer. "Don't tell me you've taken up cooking?"

"Hardly." He handed his father a mug of the hot coffee, then took a seat across from him. "I told you I've had some help. About a week ago I passed out in the snow and hit my head rather hard. Lidia Kowalski and her brother Koby were looking for shelter from the weather and stumbled, literally, upon me. They both work at one of the mills, but with the weather so unpredictable Lidia was afraid she wouldn't find her way back. I was in and out of consciousness, so she decided to stay and begin harvesting the sap."

"I wish we would have known. Thank God you're all right."

"I'm feeling fine now, and in fact, I planned to take them back to the mill this morning so I could explain to the overseer what happened. I don't want them to lose their jobs over this. But. . ." Adam paused to take a sip of his coffee. "I found something out this morning about Lidia and Koby."

His father leaned forward, resting his elbows against his thighs. "What is it?"

Adam worked to formulate his words. There was simply no easy way around it. "Lidia's brother Jarek is the one who killed Samuel."

The color drained from his father's face. "How do you know this?"

"She was cleaning the room and found some newspaper articles I'd kept. She knew her brother was wanted for murder but never knew who he'd killed until she saw Samuel's name. She put two and two together. . . ."

His father set his coffee on the small table beside him and rubbed his chin with his hand. "I'd given up ever knowing who had pulled the trigger, so much time has passed."

"Lidia has no idea where he is, but we have a name now, which will help. Knowing who it is means we might be able to narrow the scope of the search.

They moved here from Boston, so it would make sense for him to go back to the place that is familiar to him."

"I suppose you're right, but what about Lidia? She must be quite upset."

"Of course she's upset, but so am I." Adam marched across the room to the window before spinning around to face his father. "The last thing I want is for her to get hurt, but didn't you hear me? We know who killed Samuel, which means we can go after him and find him."

"It's been a year and a half. Sometimes I think it might be best if we simply let things go."

Adam raked his fingers though his hair, fighting the emotions that battled within him. "Answer this question. Why would God allow Samuel's life to be taken and let a murderer go free?"

"I know it doesn't make sense, and don't think I haven't asked myself the very same question a thousand times." His father pressed his palm against the smooth wooden arms of the chair. "All I know is that our God is not unjust. He might not work the way we want Him to, but that doesn't change who He is. Read through Romans chapter nine when you get a chance. It talks about God's sovereign choices toward man."

Stopping at the window, Adam's hands gripped the sill. He didn't want to hear about God having the right to be compassionate toward a murderer. He wanted answers. He wanted revenge.

The last days of winter were fading in front of him. Already the changing weather had left dry patches on the ground, warmed by the morning sun. Before another week passed, his run of sap would be over. He wouldn't even have a harvest if it hadn't been for Lidia and her brother. He owed them everything, and yet all he could think about was the fact that their brother had destroyed Samuel's life. His father was right. He needed to put the past behind him and forgive, but putting one's words into action had proved to be nearly impossible.

His father stood and walked toward him. "I can't work through this for you, but you're going to have to come to terms with what happened if you ever plan to go on with your life. It wasn't Lidia's fault her brother took Samuel's life. And it's not your fault you couldn't stop it from happening."

Adam's stomach clenched. "It *is* my fault. Samuel shouldn't have died."

His father wrapped his arm around Adam's shoulder. "You have to stop blaming yourself. You're not responsible."

Adam stared out the window. Lidia walked beside her brother toward the maple grove. Her normal smile was missing. Instead, her brow was furrowed with worry. Did she hurt as much as he did? He was a coward, but he couldn't face her again. At least not today.

He turned to his father. "Would you mind taking Lidia and her brother back to the mill? If there's any problem with them keeping their jobs, I'll make a trip out to talk to their overseer."

Chapter 8

Lidia swung her leg over the thick branch of the elm tree and worked to untangle the rope that had caught on one of the limbs. More than likely, it was one of the Miller boys who managed to rig the seat of the swing so it hung lopsided, though none of the young neighbors would own up to the offense.

"Be careful, Miss Lidia."

Lidia looked toward the ground from her precarious position in the tree at Adam's younger sisters, Ruby and Anna Johnson. Only two adorable little girls would compel her to temporarily disregard all attempts at being a proper lady to scale the rough trunk of a backyard tree. Well, that and a rabid dog, she supposed, but at the moment, thankfully, she felt perfectly safe from any such threats. Something she hadn't felt for a long time.

It never ceased to amaze her how God worked in such marvelous and mysterious ways. Adam once saved her life from a rabid mutt, and now his parents were doing the same thing. Not that her life was in danger now, but she still felt as if they had saved it. Instead of leaving Koby and her on their own to find jobs after Mrs. Moore dismissed them, Mr. and Mrs. Johnson had hired them to work on the Johnson farm.

Lidia untangled the rope, careful to keep her balance in the process as she teetered on the edge of the branch. She had no idea what Adam would think now that she was living on his parents' farm. She'd seen his face the day she rode away from his cabin with his father barely two weeks ago. The hurt in Adam's eyes had been clear, as though she'd betrayed him with the truth. He might have had feelings toward her at one time, but they had vanished with her confession.

She shook her head. Adam Johnson and his maple grove weren't her problems anymore. She refused to pine after a man who couldn't put the past behind him. She was dreadfully sorry for what her brother had done, but nothing she could ever say or do would change what had happened. The rest of the Johnson family, in giving her and her brother employment, had decided to move on with their lives. Something she could only hope and pray Adam would one day do, as well.

She gave the rope one more tug, and it broke loose. "All right, girls. I think it's fixed."

Dropping the rope, she watched the swing fall to its proper position. Pleased at her accomplishment and the giggles now emanating from the girls, she allowed herself a moment to enjoy the patchwork of rich earth that spread out before her. With spring clearly on its way, the acres of farmland were beginning to wake from their winter sleep. Soon mayflowers, hydrangeas, and a vast array of flowers would bloom. The apple orchards would begin to bear fruit. Pastures with their stone fence borders were dotted with grazing cattle, and in the distance, the banks of the Connecticut River rose from the water.

Taking in a deep breath, she relished the fresh scent of spring that hovered in the air like a bee ready to take nectar from a blossom. It had been a long time since she'd felt so free and happy, and she had no intention of losing this feeling.

Dust rose in a hazy cloud to the north. A horse and rider galloped across the dirt road toward the Johnsons' house. Not wanting to be found in such an awkward position, Lidia began to make her descent. She felt a sudden tug at her waist. Reaching behind her back with one hand, she felt the material that had caught on one of the branches, but it was too taut for her to loosen it. She tried squirming free, but the fabric only pulled tighter. If she wasn't careful, she would rip a hole in the dress. With only three dresses to her name, she certainly couldn't afford ruining one of them.

"Hurry down, Miss Lidia. Adam's coming."

Lidia froze. Ruby and Anna jumped with excitement below her. For the first time all morning, Lidia regretted agreeing to watch the girls while their parents went into town. Surely she hadn't heard them correctly. Adam was supposed to be on his farm finishing the sap harvest. Not here. Not now. The girls continued squealing with delight as they watched their older brother and his black stallion approach the back of the gray-shingled farmhouse.

Her jaw tensed as he drew closer. He looked so handsome wearing Levis and a tailored work shirt with his Stetson pulled low across his forehead to block the sun's warming rays. He pulled on the reins as he approached the tree, then jumped off his horse, his eyes lighting up as his sisters enveloped him with their hugs, greeting him with more excitement than a fireworks display on the Fourth of July.

The wind ruffled his hair when he took off his hat, and she could see the shadow of stubble covering his jawline. This wasn't the Adam who kissed her in the moonlight beneath a blanket of stars. That man had vanished, taking with him a piece of her heart. She fought against the sense of panic that swept over her, not knowing what he would think when he realized she was hovering above him. She'd known he would show up eventually, but she planned to be ready to see him at that point. Not perched in the top of a tree with her skirt caught on a branch.

She tugged on her dress again, but the material wouldn't budge—and neither could she. Lidia closed her eyes. He hadn't noticed her yet. Maybe if she couldn't see him, he would disappear.

"Lidia?"

Facedown on the limb, she peeked through her lashes, her stomach feeling as if it were lodged in her throat. Adam shook his head, his eyes widening with surprise.

Oh Lord, how do I manage to get myself into such embarrassing situations? And just when I think I've finally got things in my life under control.

"Adam. Hello." Swallowing hard, she pulled on her dress again, but no matter what she did, it wouldn't release its grip.

He folded his arms across his chest and looked up at her. "If I remember correctly, this isn't the first time I've seen you in this position."

Lidia sighed. "It does seem that climbing trees has become somewhat of a habit for me, doesn't it?" *And a rather unladylike habit at that!*

"Are you coming down?"

She gnawed at her lip. "I can't."

"What do you mean you can't?"

Ruby jumped up on her brother's back, her arms firmly around his neck. "I think she's stuck."

"She was fixing our swing for us," Anna added, sitting on the wooden seat. "The Miller boys broke it."

"Is it true?"

Lidia tried to slow her quickened breathing. "That the Miller boys broke the swing?"

"No, that you're stuck."

"I'm afraid so." Lidia closed her mouth and tried not to let the irritation sweep over her. She could see the smirk that covered his face. "It's not funny, Adam."

"I'm sorry." He held up his hands. "I'm not making fun of you, it's just that. . ."

"That what?"

"Never mind." His smile melted into a solemn look. "Do I need to climb up and help you?"

"I think it might be necessary since I can't reach the spot where my skirt is caught without falling off the branch."

"Did you know you can see all the way to the Connecticut River on a clear day from there?" Adam set Ruby on the ground, then easily shimmied up the trunk of the tree. "My brothers and I used to spend hours up here."

She tried to ignore the way the familiar sound of his voice pulled at her heart. Why did it have to be today, of all days, for Adam to decide to visit his family? She'd played out the moment in her mind a hundred times. He'd arrive at his parents' farm surprised to see her, but one look into her eyes and he'd realize that he'd been wrong. Nothing would stand between them and their future together. She shook her head. What had happened to her resolve to forget the man who couldn't forgive her? Daydreaming was going to get her nowhere except in trouble. At least where her heart was concerned.

Adam perched beside her on one of the branches and worked to unfasten the fabric. "I think this will fix things, and it's not even torn."

"Thank you."

Finally free, Lidia sat up. His face was only a few inches from hers, and her heart beat ferociously at his nearness. She was afraid to look at him, though, knowing she'd never again see the look of interest in his eyes that she'd once seen. Instead, she'd see the pain and know that her brother was responsible for putting it there.

Avoiding his gaze, she studied the intricate pattern of the bark and waited to follow his descent down the tree. As soon as he was on the ground, he reached up to help her. His arms encircled her waist. She was sure he could hear her heart as she worked to steady herself once her feet hit the grass. Raising her face toward his, she forced herself to look him in the eye. For a moment, she found what she was looking for. They were back under the winter stars in his maple grove, before everything had gone so wrong. The world around her disappeared until it was only the two of them.

"Lidia, I . . ."

Her pulse quickened. "What is it?"

He took a step away from her and shook his head. Whatever she'd seen in his eyes was gone. She could hear the girls playing again and feel the warm sun pressing against her face.

Anna sat in the swing while Ruby pushed from behind. Lidia tried to focus on the girls, but all she could see was Adam. In spite of what passed between them, she could feel the tension dissipate.

"The girls are happy. Why don't we talk?" He motioned her toward the back porch, no doubt wanting to converse in private as to why she was still here at his father's farm.

"All right." She matched his long stride, trying not to notice the strength of his profile. Instead, she sent up a prayer that God would help him understand what she was about to say.

"I'm surprised to see you here." Adam stopped at the bottom step and leaned against the wooden railing. "I assumed because I didn't hear from you that everything was fine at the mill."

Lidia swallowed the lump that was growing in her throat.

"I don't know what you're going to think about this. . . ." Lidia fought to keep her composure. "When your father learned that my brother and I had lost our jobs at the mill, your parents decided to hire us both to help out on the farm."

Adam raked his fingers through his hair, not sure he'd heard Lidia correctly. "You're working for my parents?"

Lidia nodded. "The crop was so good last year that your father is planning to turn some of the pasture into additional fields, and with little Daria, your stepmother needed some extra help around the house—"

"My father never told me he was planning to expand his planting this spring or that he was hiring new workers." He shook his head, working to keep the anger out of his voice. Had he been so caught up with his own projects that he'd failed to listen to his father's plans? He was the eldest son. If his father needed help, he should be the one filling in the gap. He would have found a way to make it work.

He kicked a pebble with the toe of his boot and watched the thin wisps of dust fill the air. When he'd first glanced up to see Lidia perched above him in the tree, he'd almost forgotten the last dark moments that had transpired between them. Instead, the warmth of her kiss lingered in his memory and with it, the feelings he'd tried to forget.

But that wasn't enough. He appreciated all that Lidia and her brother had done for him and admittedly owed them a lot, but how could his father consider hiring the siblings of the man who killed Samuel? He understood the need to forgive, but to go out of his way to give them jobs? It simply didn't make sense to him.

"I was afraid you'd be upset when you found out." Lidia's voice broke into his thoughts.

Upset didn't begin to describe his feelings. "My father. . .where is he?"

"He went into town with your stepmother. They asked me to watch the girls while they were gone."

He gripped the porch railing with his hand. "I don't understand. You lost your job at the mill? Why didn't you let me know? I would have gone and spoken to your overseer for you."

"It wouldn't have mattered. They'd already replaced us and made it clear that what we had done wasn't acceptable."

"I'm sorry. I. . ." He wasn't being fair to her, and he knew it. He should have stopped by the mill on his own accord.

She looked up at him with those big brown eyes that were now rimmed with tears, and he cringed inside. When he'd watched her leave his farm with his father, he'd convinced himself that he could forget her. But now she stood before him even more beautiful than he remembered. Some of her hair had come undone from its braid, leaving auburn wisps of curls that framed her face. He didn't want to feel this way toward her—this attraction. No matter what feelings she invoked inside him, nothing would change the fact of who she was.

"And the harvest?" Lidia asked.

Adam raised his brow at her question. "I finished yesterday. I wanted to stop by and talk to my father about the sugaring off celebration. I haven't seen him since. . ."

"Since the day you found out my brother murdered Samuel."

"I guess there's nothing more for us to say then, is there?"

Lidia picked up the hem of her skirt and strode away from him, toward Ruby and Anna.

An hour later, Adam felt his shoulder muscles burn as he swung the ax into the log behind the wooden shed on his father's property. The weather was still a bit chilly, but he was drenched in sweat.

His father rounded the corner of the structure and stopped beside him. "We'll have enough wood to last us until the turn of the century if you keep up this pace."

Adam threw the log onto the pile before plunging the blade into another thick piece of pine. "I wanted to talk to you before I went home."

"So your sisters said. Didn't expect to find you hiding out behind the shed, though."

"I'm not hiding."

"Then what is it?"

The blade cracked through the wood, splitting it down the middle. "I've been to the sheriff's office. I gave them the information I have on Samuel's killer."

"You mean Lidia's brother."

Adam wiped the moisture off his forehead with the back of his hand. "Why did you hire them?"

"They needed work, and I needed extra help around the farm."

"Don't make me feel guilty. I've tried to put the past behind me, but that doesn't mean I have to accept them into our family. For you to go and hire them. . ." Adam swung the blade to finish splitting the piece he was working on. "How could you even consider such a thing?"

His father tossed the fallen section onto the woodpile. "I don't understand your reaction, Adam. Lidia and her brother lost their livelihood because they helped you save your maple harvest."

"So now we owe them?"

"Yes! But I wasn't doing them a favor. Michaela and I had already decided we needed extra help around the farm. I want to expand this year, and with Daria taking up a lot of your stepmother's time, it seemed to be an answer from God that helped all of us."

"But why *them*?" The wood groaned as the blade forced it apart. "There are dozens of other people in town who could use the work."

"If you could forgive, you might be able to see that Lidia is a wonderful, godly woman."

"I know she's a wonderful person." The confession left an ache that radiated deep within him. That was the very reason why he had to stay away from her.

"I convinced the sheriff to raise the bounty on Jarek," Adam confessed.

"Why?"

Adam pounded the ax into the side of a stump. "Because I want him to pay for his crime."

His father took a step toward him. "And what about Lidia?"

"Her brother deserves justice."

"Yes, I suppose you're right, but how do you think she feels knowing that her brother will likely be sentenced to death?"

Adam shrugged, unable to answer.

"You're willing to lose Lidia?"

Adam cringed at the question. It was the very thing he was afraid of. That one day, he was going to regret just how much he'd lost in his search for justice.

Chapter 9

Lidia let out a deep sigh of contentment as she watched the festive scene unfold before her from the Johnsons' front porch. The social gathering of friends and neighbors during the annual sugaring off had always been one of her favorite times of year. Laughter from the children mingled with the spirited sounds of a fiddle playing the chorus of yet another lively tune. Tonight's activities reminded her of good memories from the past with her family. And that God had blessed her with hope for a future again.

She watched Koby dip a paddle into the vat of maple syrup, then lick it clean. The grin on his face told her she had made the right decision in accepting the Johnsons' generous offer of employment. While she still considered herself merely one of the hired help, the Johnsons treated her as if she were a part of the family. It was a feeling she'd missed since the deaths of her parents.

"Are you enjoying yourself tonight?"

Lidia drew her gaze from the mesmerizing dance of the bonfire that crackled in the crisp night air and smiled at her new employer. "Very much, thank you, Mrs. Johnson."

It was hard to believe that Michaela Johnson would soon be a grandmother. Her eldest daughter, Rebecca Hutton, who now lived in Boston with her husband, had recently announced that she was expecting the Johnsons' first grandchild. Even with one-year-old Daria in tow, Mrs. Johnson always looked lovely with her pinned-up hair full of reddish highlights and her glowing fair skin. But it was more than her outward beauty that had impressed Lidia. It was what radiated from the inside—her contentment with life and generosity toward others as she managed a household of five children still living at home. Mrs. Johnson leaned against the rail beside her. "I was afraid it might be too cold, but it turned out to be perfect weather."

"Yes, ma'am, you're right." Lidia gazed at the cloudless sky. Above them, the stars glimmered in all their brilliance, covering the festivities in a canopy of lights. "I know I've said it before, but I can't even begin to express to you how much it means to me and my brother that you and Mr. Johnson took us on. I know it couldn't have been easy, with what happened with Samuel—"

"That's not true." Mrs. Johnson laid a reassuring hand on Lidia's shoulder.

"You've been an incredible help already. I must have told Eric a dozen times that I don't know what I'd do without you."

"Still, I do appreciate it."

Mrs. Johnson smoothed down the front of her lavender dress, its design simple yet elegant—perfect for the festivities. "There's plenty of food and no excuses not to indulge tonight."

Lidia glanced at the wooden table that was laden with meats, salads, sandwiches, and doughnuts, as well as the customary pickles to counteract the sweetness of the syrup. "I promise to make myself a plate in a little bit. For now, I'm just enjoying watching all that's going on."

A short distance across the lawn, Adam walked up to the table and began filling his plate. Lidia felt her jaw muscles tense. So far she'd managed to avoid him, something she knew she wouldn't be able to do forever. Of course, more than likely he had no desire to see her either, but she refused to have her evening spoiled by him.

He looked up, and his gaze swept past her before returning to linger on her face. Her breath caught in her throat, and she wondered if she would ever forget him. But there was nothing in his eyes tonight that hinted that he still cared. Sadness filled his expression. Was he sorry that he'd changed his mind about calling on her? When he turned away without saying a word to her, the answer was clear.

Lidia turned back to Mrs. Johnson. "Why do you think Adam still hangs on to so much guilt regarding his brother's death? It wasn't his fault."

"And it wasn't your fault either, Lidia."

Her fingers gripped the wooden rail. "I know, but it's hard not to feel responsible. Jarek is my brother."

"I learned a long time ago that bitterness will only bring you pain and heartache. Adam has his own lessons to learn, but don't torture yourself over things you can't control."

"Still, I can't imagine how he must feel, and. . ." Lidia paused, not sure she should reveal her feelings toward Adam.

"What is it?"

"I don't know. I shouldn't even bring it up, but before Adam found out who I was, he looked at me differently. Maybe nothing would have ever come from it, but there was something in his eyes. Sometimes I wish. . ."

"That he still cared for you."

Lidia nodded. "He was a complete gentleman while Koby and I were at his place, but one night. . .there was something romantic about the frosty air and the brilliance above. When I looked into his eyes, I knew he cared about me. He kissed me and told me he wanted to call on me once I was back at the mill. But all that changed when he found out the truth about my brother. Then nothing mattered anymore except that I was Jarek Kowalski's sister."

"I'm so sorry, Lidia." Mrs. Johnson turned toward Lidia, her eyes filled with concern. "Unfortunately, I don't think Adam even talks to his father much anymore. He's done a good job of closing himself off from people."

Lidia fingered the soft fabric of her skirt. "I'm praying he can someday put the past behind him and give me a chance, but I know that can never be."

"I wouldn't say that. Give him some time. Adam's a fine man who needs to deal with what happened, but we're praying there will come a day when he finally lets go of his guilt. Then he'll be ready for love."

"I'm not naive, Mrs. Johnson." Lidia shook her head. "Loving me would never be enough motivation for him to forgive Jarek."

"Don't be so sure about that. God has ways of bringing healing that we could never imagine. I'm always here for you if you need to talk. I know I can't take the place of your mother, but I can certainly be a friend."

Sensing the genuineness behind Mrs. Johnson's words, tears welled in Lidia's eyes. Things might never work out between her and Adam, but that didn't diminish the gratefulness she felt for God putting them together with this family.

Baby Daria cried from inside the house, and Mrs. Johnson moved toward the front door. "She was supposed to be asleep. If you'll excuse me—"

"You have guests." Lidia followed behind. "I don't mind checking on her."

"Are you sure?" Mrs. Johnson turned to her.

"It's no problem at all."

"Very well, then." A grin crossed the older woman's face. "I do need to check on Mr. Wentworth. Widow Sharp has her mark set for him, and last time I saw him, his face was as flushed as a ripe tomato."

Lidia laughed. In her short time on the farm, she'd heard of the Johnsons' nearby neighbor, Widow Sharp, who even at the age of eighty-two was determined to marry again despite the fact that she'd already buried four husbands.

"One more thing before you go inside." Mrs. Johnson grasped Lidia's hand and squeezed it gently. "You're a lovely young woman. I have no doubt that not only did God bring you into our family for a purpose, but also that He has something, maybe even someone, very special in mind for you and your future."

Lidia wanted to believe her, but she had no illusions that life always ended happily ever after. Still, the Bible did promise that God could work all things together for good. All she could do was to pray that was exactly what He was doing.

Adam set his empty plate down on the table and scanned the lively crowd for Lidia. Social events like this made him want to get out his fishing pole and find a quiet spot away from it all. Having Lidia here made him even more uncomfortable. The sight of her talking to his stepmother earlier had caught him off guard. No matter how his emotions spun inside, he couldn't deny how beautiful she looked tonight. The pale green dress she wore, while modest, accentuated her figure and left him with an impulsive longing to gather her into his arms and kiss her once again beneath the silvery moonlight.

He didn't understand the intense draw he felt toward her. He knew plenty of pretty women, even beautiful ones, but they'd never caused his heart to race at such a rapid pace or his dreams to be constantly flooded with their presence.

Standing in the shadows beyond the reach of the light from the bonfire, he watched his sister Sarah's face light up with laughter as she ate another pickle. Sometimes it seemed that his own carefree days had vanished forever. Life had become all too serious. He missed the times when he had been able to laugh for no reason at all. When he didn't feel as if he carried the weight of the world on his shoulders.

Mr. Wentworth, with Widow Sharp on his arm, ambled in Adam's direction. Judging by the firm grip Widow Sharp had on Mr. Wentworth, there was no doubt that she had set her sights on yet another potential husband. Adam quickly slipped around the edge of the festivities and into the house. Perhaps he should have tried to rescue the timid farmer, but such attempts would no doubt do little to discourage Widow Sharp. And listening to her rambling talk of the weather and her seventeen grandchildren wasn't something Adam felt up to at the moment.

Inside, the house was quiet compared to the events going on outside. Everyone, it seemed, was content to enjoy the crisp night air and the festivities and food that went along with the annual sugaring off.

Away from the laughter and the serenade of the fiddle, a quiet lullaby reached his ears. Across the open living area, his littlest sister cooed contentedly, and he could see the silhouette of someone sitting in the rocking chair, gently lulling her back to sleep.

"Mother?"

The figure turned toward him. "Adam?"

A yellow glow from the crackling flames that radiated within the stone fireplace caught Lidia's profile and like a magnet drew him a step closer. "I. . .I didn't know you were in here."

The rhythmic sway of the rocking chair squeaked softly beneath her. "Daria was crying, and I told your stepmother I'd come check on her. I think she's about to drift off again, though with all the noise filtering in from outside, it's hard to believe she's able to sleep at all."

He shuffled his feet, the awkwardness growing between them, then cleared his throat. "Are you having a good time tonight?"

She ran her thumb across the back of the baby's head. "It brings back many good memories of when my parents were alive. The annual sugaring off was one of our favorite times of the year."

"Tell me about them." He perched on the edge of an upholstered stool across from her, thankful that the shadows of the room masked her expression. He was afraid of what he might find within the depths of her eyes.

"My parents?"

"You've told me about how they died, but there must be much to tell about how they lived."

The woodsy scent of the burning logs filled his lungs as he stared into the yellow and orange flames. "Where we come from in Poland is very poor and overpopulated." Her voice sounded surprised at his question, but not as surprised as he was at himself for drawing out their conversation. "My parents were blessed to be literate, but the majority of my people are not. They saw this country as a place where they could give their children a better life. And not simply material things, but freedom." She paused a moment, as if she wasn't sure he really wanted to hear what she was saying.

"Go on. Please."

The creaking of the rocker slowed as she began to speak again. "My parents were hard workers who took whatever jobs they could find. While we lived in Boston, my mother worked as a seamstress, and my father, who had been a farmer in Poland, did everything from carpentry work to manual labor. They loved us, taught us to work hard and to put God first."

Lidia's voice quivered, and he wondered if she wasn't thinking of how her brother had rebelled against their parents' belief system. It must have hurt her family deeply to know what Jarek had done when all they'd wanted was a fresh start in life.

One of the logs burning in the fireplace popped, and Daria started crying. Lidia drew the toddler toward her and started singing again. Adam fidgeted with one of his cuffs as he listened to the sweet clarity of her voice.

His little sister took a deep breath and settled peacefully in Lidia's arms. If only Lidia didn't have an effect on him. Then his heart wouldn't have to wrestle with letting her go.

"I'd better leave." He stood quietly, not wanting to wake the child—or deal anymore with his own roiling emotions. "I need to go and find Ruby and Anna. I promised them I'd sample the syrup with them."

"Adam, wait."

He turned back around to face her.

"I know I have no right to say anything to you about what has happened between us, but I can't help it."

"Then don't, please." He couldn't bear to hear her say that she cared for him, because no matter what his own heart might feel, there would always be a wall between them. He didn't want to hurt her, but neither could he allow himself to continue something that he knew would never work.

Lidia shook her head. "This isn't about you and me and what might have happened between us if the circumstances were different."

His jaw tensed. "Then what is it about?"

"It's about what happened between our families. It's about you getting on with your life and letting go of the bitterness you feel toward me, my brother. . . toward all of us. My people are no different from yours. While some of us make mistakes, all we want is what is best for our families—political and religious freedom, and a place to call *home*."

At that he simply turned and left. His heels thudded against the wooden floor. He wanted to lash back at her, tell her that she was wrong. That he wasn't prejudiced toward her or her people, but in his heart he knew she was right. He longed to be the man God would have him be, but the emotions raging within him were like consuming fires as his conscience battled against the truth.

What would she think if she knew he'd talked to the sheriff about her brother? No doubt she'd feel betrayed. But he still believed he was right to seek justice for his family.

What if my desire for justice in turn ruins another family?

He cringed at the unwelcome thought and wondered when life had become so complicated. But there was more to the story than Lidia knew. More than anyone knew. That was why he couldn't let go of the past and be with Lidia. And why he would never forgive himself for what had really happened the day his brother Samuel was killed.

Chapter 10

Adam pounded the last nail into the roof of the sugarhouse, then climbed back down the wooden ladder. Last night's storm had managed to loosen a number of the cedar shingles from both the sugarhouse and the roof of his cabin. Thankfully, the damage had been minimal, saving him from losing valuable time on more repairs.

Stepping off the last rung of the ladder, he paused to look out across his land. Winter's snow had melted away, leaving behind a green collage of ridges and valleys that blended into the woodlands in the distance. Besides the damage to the roofs and a few broken limbs, there were no obvious signs of the spring gale that had passed through overnight. Instead, the sun's rays bathed the land in its brilliant light.

He reached up to adjust the brim of his hat against its glare. His dreams for this farm went far beyond the sugar maple grove that stood in anticipation of next winter's harvest.

He had plans to expand the brick foundation of the house, adding extra rooms with hardwood floors and a large window to capture the view of the sloping hills that eventually led to the Connecticut River in the west.

To the east, he wanted to build a twelve-stall horse barn with a riding ring, as well as fenced-in pastures for cattle. With horses as the principal means of transport, breeding would ensure a steady source of income in addition to cultivating the rest of his acreage. Working the maple grove had given him his first real taste of what hard work could accomplish, and he knew he wanted more.

Already the crystallized blocks of maple sugar that would later be broken up or shaved had been poured into wooden molds, ready for the buyer who would arrive tomorrow. Glass syrup jugs were lined up, as well, filled to the top with the sweet liquid and ready to be sold in the surrounding stores all the way from Cranton to Springfield.

He had decided to give Lidia and her brother a portion of the profits, knowing if it weren't for their hard work he would have lost the majority of this year's harvest. While her financial standing had no doubt improved because of her new position on his parents' farm, he knew that the extra savings would help.

At the thought of her, Lidia's image flashed in front of him. Try as he might, he hadn't been able forget her. Seeing her face in the recesses of his mind reminded him of something else. What good were all his plans if he couldn't share them with someone? Were his anger and guilt worth the price of living alone? Without Lidia?

Hooking the ladder back on the wall of the sugarhouse, he bit back the questions. There were plenty of other women who would be more than willing to share a life with him. Two Sundays ago he'd been introduced to Silvia Dolny. From his short conversation with her, she had not only seemed to be intelligent but possessed a sense of humor, as well. She certainly wasn't lacking in good looks, either. Her hair was the color of honey, her complexion perfect. . .and not once had he thought of her until today.

Why hadn't it been that easy to forget Lidia. . .and the anger that separated them? Tool bucket in hand, Adam made his way back toward the house. Last night at the sugaring off, Lidia's pointed words had struck their mark somewhere deep inside him. Who was she to confront him when she knew little of what had really happened that day?

The wrath of man worketh not the righteousness of God.

The toe of his boot struck a rock, and he kicked it off the dirt path. He'd read the verse from James last night, knowing that he'd lived far too long wrapped up in his own anger and bitterness. He felt like Jacob who in the Old Testament had wrestled with God as he fought to lay aside his own anger, hurt, and guilt. Adam had lain awake half the night trying to come to terms with not only his own prejudices toward others but his guilt, as well.

He'd also read through the ninth chapter of Romans as his father had suggested. The passage had opened his eyes to another side of God's character. Paul said that God was not unjust, but instead, in order to make the riches of His glory known, He chose whom to be merciful to and whom to have compassion on. Had God, who saw beyond Adam's own human viewpoint, had a greater plan in mind when He chose not to save Samuel that day?

"Adam!"

Pulled from his heavy thoughts, Adam glanced up the windy road that led into town. Thirteen-year-old Sarah drove the wagon toward him, sandwiched in between Ruby and Anna, who were bouncing in their seats. Living alone on the farm had taken time to get used to. The church he attended had blessed him with a number of friends, but hard work on the surrounding farms made socializing for many of them few and far during the busy times of the year. While he enjoyed the peace away from his younger siblings' squabbles, it was always a treat to have visitors—especially family.

Ruby clasped her hands together once Sarah had stopped the wagon in front of him. "We brought you something, Adam."

Adam swung Ruby down from the buckboard, then proceeded to help Anna. Sarah had already climbed down on the other side, a sly grin on her lips.

"It's a surprise." Anna jumped up and down, hardly able to contain her excitement.

Ruby grabbed both of his hands and spun him around. "Guess."

"Guess what?"

"What we have for you."

Sarah picked up a large basket, then joined them beside the wagon. The forlorn howl of a puppy sounded from the basket.

"No fair." Ruby stomped her feet. "Now you know."

"And all this time I'd thought you brought me lunch."

Sarah handed him the basket. "Be glad I didn't cook anything for you."

Adam laughed. Sarah was known in the family for her love of animals, not her domestic qualities.

Ruby leaned in beside him. "Daisy had puppies a few weeks ago, and we decided you needed one. No farmer can be without a dog."

Adam cautiously opened the lid, not sure of what he was in for. The yellow dog, with ears almost as big as his head, jumped up and licked him across the side of the face.

The girls broke out into a chorus of laughter.

"He likes you," Anna cooed.

"I don't know if I've got time for a puppy." Adam stared out across the open field waiting to be plowed and planted, but the grin never left his face.

"Of course you do." Ruby buried her face in the puppy's coat and wiggled her head as it continued licking.

"I thought puppies were a lot of work," Adam said. "And trouble."

"Only when they chew on Pa's shoes."

Adam ruffled Ruby's dark hair. "Sounds like words from experience."

The girls began to spew out their defense, sprinkled with words of advice for caring for a puppy.

"Hold on here." Adam took the puppy out of the basket and held it up in front of him. "I suppose we ought to come up with a name for him if I decide to keep him."

"What about Fluffy?"

"That's not bad." Adam mulled over Anna's idea. "He definitely is a ball of fur."

"What about Max?"

"Or Matilda."

"Matilda?" Adam choked back a laugh at Ruby's suggestion. "Reminds me more of someone's portly aunt than a puppy."

Anna reached up to scratch the dog's ear. "Lidia suggested Star. She adores puppies, just like we do."

Adam's jaw tensed. Had she remembered the night he kissed her under the stars when she suggested that name, or had she managed to put what had happened between them behind her? Judging from the admiration shining in Anna's brown eyes, Lidia had obviously captured the hearts of his family.

"Look at his back end." Ruby turned the dog around despite its nipping at her hand. "There's a spot that looks like a little white star."

"It's a nice name," Sarah said. "I think you should pick that one."

Adam swallowed hard, wishing that he could forget Lidia but doubting that was possible. "Sounds like you've got a name then, Star. But you're not going to be any trouble now, are you?"

Star simply yipped, then proceeded to wet down the front of Adam's freshly laundered shirt.

❧

Lidia closed her father's worn copy of *Nature* by Ralph Waldo Emerson and filled her lungs with the fresh spring air. With her regular morning chores complete in the house, Mrs. Johnson had insisted Lidia go outside to enjoy one of the season's first warm days until it was time to start preparing the evening meal. Glancing at the small watch pinned to her dress, she stood up quickly. She'd been so engrossed in the book, she hadn't realized how much time had passed, and the last thing she wanted to do was take advantage of her new employer's generosity. There was always plenty of ironing and washing needing to be done at the house, and frittering the day away wouldn't help to accomplish any of it.

Even though the distraction had been pleasant, it hadn't been enough to rid her of her thoughts of Adam. The girls had gone to his farm this morning to take him one of Daisy's new puppies and had insisted she join them for the excursion. The thought of seeing Adam again made her uneasy, so she had managed to find a way to persuade them to go without her.

She had, though, gone along with their naming game and threw out the first suggestion that came to mind. Star. It was true that the tiny ball of fur had a white star on his back, but there was a deeper meaning to the name. The brilliant stars shining overhead would always remind her of Adam and the night he kissed her.

There was another incident that continued to bother her. Last night at the sugaring off, she'd seen the look of torment in Adam's eyes. How she could have been so bold as to blatantly tell Adam he was prejudiced she had no idea. She only wanted to encourage him so he could find peace. No doubt her unladylike forwardness had done little good and instead had widened the gap between them.

She headed toward the house, the memory of Adam walking away from her still fresh in her mind. If only he knew that she'd never meant to hurt him. The past two weeks had shown her what true forgiveness was. She knew she didn't deserve the Johnsons' forgiveness over their son's death, let alone for them to hire her and Koby on as help. Yet they had gone beyond merely voicing their forgiveness. They had acted upon it.

This acceptance of her for who she was had made an imprint in her life that could never be erased. Claiming to be Christian was something she'd seen dozens of people profess. Actually living the life of one called to follow Christ had always been harder for her to find. It was something she had begun to pray that she could implement into her own life.

"Lidia?"

Sarah emerged from the barn with three of Daisy's puppies yipping at her heels. The sight of the frisky animals couldn't help but lighten her somber mood.

"They're adorable, aren't they?" Lidia shoved her book under her arm, then scooped up the little brown and white runt and began scratching him behind his ears.

Sarah shoved a loose piece of her blond hair out of her eyes and nodded. "I hate the fact that we have to give them all away, but my father would never allow for us to keep them all."

Lidia laughed as the puppy licked her chin. "Maybe he'll let you keep one."

"It is worth a try, but I know my father. As much as he loves animals, he believes firmly that they were made to help mankind, not the other way around." Sarah picked up one of the puppies. "At least I can visit Adam's puppy when I'm over there."

"What did Adam think about your present?"

Sarah's eyes sparkled with amusement. "While he probably won't ever admit it to me, I'm convinced he loved it."

"I'm glad." Lidia set the puppy back down, watching as it pulled at the black laces of her boot.

"Adam liked your suggestion and named him Star."

Had he thought of her at all when he agreed to the name? Lidia shook off the ridiculous thought. "The name did seem to fit the pup."

"I think Adam likes you—"

Lidia frowned at the comment. "I don't think so."

She'd heard of Sarah and even Rebecca's attempts to play matchmaker between her and their brother, but this was a game she had no intention of being a part of. She knew all too well that she would be the one who ended up hurt.

"Don't be so sure. There's something in his eyes when he says your name." Sarah let the pup nuzzle against her neck. "Despite his ornery side, he's really a wonderful person. Besides, I think it would be horribly romantic if the two of you got together. Just think of the stories you could tell your grandchildren about how you met when he saved you from a rabid dog."

Lidia brushed an imaginary piece of lint off her skirt and took a step backward. "I really need to get back to work. Your stepmother will think I'm shirking my duties."

Sarah frowned, then reached out her hand to touch Lidia's sleeve. "I didn't mean to upset you. I wouldn't have said anything if I didn't think you liked him, as well. I just thought. . ."

Lidia bit her lip. Had her emotions been that transparent? Except for her bold confession to Mrs. Johnson last night, she'd been careful to keep her feelings toward Adam to herself. "I think your brother is a very nice man who will make a fine husband for someone one day. But not for me."

"I'm sorry." Sarah's cheeks reddened to match the narrow trim of her dress. "I just want my brother to be happy, and you're perfect for him—"

"No, I'm the one who's sorry." Lidia pressed her fingers against her temple as a headache started to throb. "I didn't mean to snap at you. Your family has been so wonderful to my brother and me. I just know that because of what happened, there can never be anything between Adam and me."

"So you do care about him."

"I didn't say that. . .I. . .I don't know." One of the puppies nipped at her leg, and she shook her skirts to shoo him away.

"I just think if two people really care about each other, there has to be a way for them to work it out."

Lidia couldn't help but smile at Sarah. "You're an incurable romantic, aren't you?"

"Yes, and someday I'll find my own true love."

Lidia headed toward the house, wondering if there was any chance that Sarah and her stepmother could be right. It would be easy to dream that everything was going to turn out fine. Lidia's grandmother's stories had always had happy endings, but life had proved very different. She didn't blame God for the losses she'd experienced, but that didn't keep her from wondering why He didn't do anything to stop them.

She gave her head a shake. Dwelling on the past would never help. Instead, she was going to put everything she had into her work. Maybe someday she'd find the right man with whom she could spend the rest of her life, but for now she was determined to be content being exactly where God had placed her.

Mr. Johnson stood on the porch, his hands stuffed into his jeans' pockets. "Lidia, I wondered if you would come inside for a moment. Michaela and I need to speak with you."

"Yes, sir." Lidia's mouth went dry as she made her way into the house. She knew she'd been taking advantage of the Johnsons' generosity by enjoying her book outside all afternoon. After all they had done for her, she should have known better. Losing herself in a book was no excuse.

Mrs. Johnson entered the room from the kitchen. Despite the apron that she wore, there were several patches of flour sprinkled on the sleeves of her coffee-colored dress. "Lidia, please have a seat."

Lidia perched on the edge of the sofa determined to hold her composure whatever they might say. She could always try to find work in town or even at one of the other mills if worst came to worst.

Mr. Johnson sat down beside his wife and squeezed her hand. "I've just come back from town where I spoke to the sheriff about your brother."

Lidia's eyes widened. She hadn't even imagined that they wanted to talk to her about Jarek. Had her brother finally been caught? A lump began to form in her throat. For over a year she'd known that someday this moment would come, but even the tempered joy of being able to visit him in jail wasn't enough to take away the apprehension she felt. After what he had experienced, Jarek wouldn't be the same boy who used to play tag with her in the summertime and help her with her math homework.

And there was another distinct possibility, as well. If a trial came, the Johnson family would have to relive their son's death in court, opening old wounds. They wouldn't want her and Koby staying with them anymore. Forgiveness could only go so far.

Mrs. Johnson leaned forward, and Lidia was surprised to see compassion in her eyes, not judgment. "We're so sorry to have to tell you this, Lidia, but Jarek was killed three days ago by a bounty hunter."

Chapter 11

Reuben Myers was not someone Adam wanted to mess with. The burly businessman jumped down from his wagon in front of Adam's place, his thick arms bulging at his sides. Thankfully, Reuben had become one of Adam's best customers.

"Afternoon, Adam." The man's voice bellowed in the crisp air.

"Good to see you, Reuben." Adam walked over to where he'd placed the sugar crates in neat stacks so they were ready to be loaded onto the man's wagon. "I think you'll be pleased with the quantity from this year's harvest."

Reuben eyed the season's production of sugar that Adam had laid out on half a dozen solid wooden containers. "Would love to see another year like 1860. Maple sugar production was at an all-time high that year, but at least the demand is still fairly strong."

"Good, because next year I'm planning to expand the harvest even more."

"I'm assuming you've heard the news from town?" Reuben began hoisting one of the heavy crates of maple sugar blocks onto the wagon, while Adam followed suit.

"Haven't gotten away from the farm for the past few days. Things around here have been too busy."

Reuben rested his fists against his wide girth. "Hope you don't mind me being the one telling you then, but bounty hunters killed the man who shot your brother."

"What?" Adam dropped his load against the wagon's lowered tailgate.

"Clean through the heart, I heard. Just like he deserved."

Adam closed his eyes for a moment. Instead of feeling relief as he'd expected, all he could see was Lidia's face. No matter what her brother had done, Lidia had never stopped loving him. Wouldn't he feel the same in her place? Nothing one of his brothers or sisters would ever do could break the bond of family he felt with them.

"Adam?"

"Sorry, it's just that. . ." Adam shoved the crate into the wagon bed, then went to pick up the last load.

"I know it must be a relief. I keep telling the sheriff that they are going to have to start turning away them immigrants from coming into our country." The purple veins in Reuben's neck began to bulge. "I say we send them all back to where they come from."

The wrath of man worketh not the righteousness of God.

Adam stood still. Not long ago he would have made the same fiery speech that Reuben was making right now. But today all he could hear was the prejudiced ring that marked every word.

". . .should hang the lot if you ask me. What do you think about that?"

Adam swallowed hard. His attitude had been no different from men like Reuben who liked to spread their hatred to the rest of the town. Yet he realized Jesus came to earth to change all that. To make people think differently. Hadn't all mankind been offered redemption through Christ no matter who they were? German, Italian. . .Polish. Adam certainly wasn't perfect, and yet he'd claimed Christ's forgiveness. Because of his heavenly Father's great love, Christ's death on the cross now covered Adam's many sins.

Adam took a slow, deep breath. "Reuben—"

"I even told the sheriff that if we gathered some of those men together and—"

"Reuben, thank you for telling me about Jarek, but I was wrong. It's time I forgave him for what he did and stopped blaming an entire people for one man's wrongdoing."

Reuben's laugh shook his bulky torso. "He can't accept your forgiveness now, Adam. If you've already forgotten, the man's dead."

Adam stared at the ground. "I know, and I'm sorry."

"You're sorry he's dead?" The man's eyes flashed with antagonism. "I never thought the day would come when you'd be defending these intruders that have come into our towns and—"

"I've heard enough, Reuben. Jarek Kowalski did a horrible thing, but he also left behind a younger sister and brother who have had to struggle to support themselves—"

"Isn't that the exact point I've been trying to make?" Reuben grasped the edge of the wagon with one hand. "Life would have been better off for all of us if they'd never left their mother country in the first place."

It was no use and Adam knew it. Adam hoisted the final crate into the wagon bed, then slammed the wooden tailgate shut.

He avoided the older man's penetrating gaze. "I'll expect the second half of the payment in full by the end of the month," Adam said.

"You'll get it." The irritation that laced Reuben's words was impossible to miss. "I don't understand what's come over you. Of all the people involved, I assumed you'd regret not being the one to tie a noose around that murderer's neck. In the least, be thankful someone else did it for you."

Adam straightened his back and stood tall. "I was, until I took a look at my own life and realized I wasn't any better than he was."

"You're a fool, Adam Johnson, if you believe that. Nothing more than a fool."

With a sullen shake of his head, the man climbed into his wagon and drove off. Adam sat down on a stump and rested his elbows against his thighs. He wanted to pray but wondered if God would even want to listen to him. How had it come to this?

There was no arguing the fact that his brother's death had been a violent wrongdoing, a horrid crime that could never be undone. Nor could the pain of that night ever be erased. But he'd let that one violent act completely change him. Bitterness had become a poison in his veins that had spread into his relationships with his family, with friends. . .and with Lidia. What kind of man allowed the ruthless acts of another to overcome every aspect of his being? He'd ended up no better off than the criminal who'd wronged him.

Adam combed his fingers through his hair. "God, I don't even know where to begin. How can I come before You, the Maker of this universe, when I don't even deserve another breath of air?"

❧

The sky loomed above him as darkness began to settle across the wide expanse. Minutes slowly passed, but he didn't move from the stump. One by one, the stars made their nightly appearance, lighting up the sky like a million fireflies. It was a testimony of God's power. He had no doubt that the heavens—and all of creation—were proof of God's existence.

The heavens declare the glory of God; and the firmament sheweth his handiwork.

Adam felt small as the words from Psalms spun through his mind. The glory of God's universe surrounded him completely. Everything God had created was for a purpose. The sun, moon, and stars gave light to the earth. The nearby stream that trickled in the night air gave life to the vegetation. The maple trees that reached toward the heavens beside him were full of intricacies he would never completely understand. Yet he knew how to watch the gradual changes in the seasons and wait for the right temperature that would in turn give him the sought-after liquid from its depths.

It was one thing, though, to believe that he had a Creator. But the reality that the Maker of this world had sent His only Son to pay the ransom for Adam's sin was more than he could grasp.

His hands clenched together. "You knew the choices I would face from birth, God, yet I know I've failed You. How could You still love me enough to sacrifice Your Son for someone as worthless as I am?"

"Because I chose you from the beginning. You're Mine, and I love you."

Adam froze. The words whispered quietly into the recesses of his mind shook him to the core of his being. How could his Creator truly love him?

"I have chosen you, and you are Mine. I love you."

Adam wanted to cry out at the repeated words. To scream that he didn't deserve God's love... Instead, they began to wash over him like a healing balm.

"Forgive me, Lord." He fell face down onto the ground. Dust blew into his nostrils as he pulled his hands across the loose dirt. "I want to be a man who can persevere in the face of trials and come out stronger because of them. I want to be a man who keeps his faith no matter what happens around me."

An unexpected peace began to envelop him. He might have stumbled through the fires of this trial and made a mountain of mistakes along the way, but his God had forgiven him. It was a forgiveness he didn't deserve—no one did—yet God offered it freely to anyone who would accept His unfailing love and follow Him. Strange how he'd heard sermons preaching the same lesson dozens of times since he was a boy, and yet it had taken this long for the words to pierce his heart.

Star ran up beside him and licked the back of Adam's neck. He sat up and rubbed the mutt's ears. "How are ya doing, boy?"

In spite of the seriousness of the moment, Adam laughed out loud. God must have a sense of humor.

"I guess God created you for a reason, as well, you little rascal." He gathered the pup into his arms. "While it might be hard for me to admit it, I've enjoyed your company. Especially the fact that you listen and never argue with me."

Emotionally drained, Adam felt a wave of fatigue overcome him, but he knew that there was something left he had to do. He'd finally found it within himself to forgive Jarek for what he had done to his brother. Forgiving himself for what happened that day was something he knew he'd continue to struggle with, but come daybreak he'd head out to his parents' house. It was time to ask Lidia for her forgiveness.

❧

Lidia stood on the front porch of the Johnson family home and watched the stars dance in the heavens above her. Since a girl, she'd been mesmerized by the beauty of the night sky. Like precious pearls strung out across a velvet mantle, they left her to wonder about what lay beyond Earth's landscape. Discoveries, like Maria Mitchell's finding of a new comet, or Asaph Hall's more recent detection of two satellites circling the planet Mars, had always fascinated her.

Tonight, though, it was hard for her to find the beauty in anything around her.

Jarek was dead.

Somewhere, deep inside her, she'd managed to hold on to the sliver of hope that things would turn out differently. That all of this would be nothing more than a horrible mistake. That Jarek really hadn't killed Samuel, and any day now he was going to come riding back into her life as the boy she used to know.

But none of that would ever happen.

She'd never again watch Jarek play baseball in the dusty field behind her parents' row home. Never see his eyes light up when he laughed or pulled a childish prank on her or Koby.

Shivering at a gust of wind that swept across the open land before her, Lidia pulled her shawl closer around her shoulders and went inside the house. The living area was empty, though she could hear ripples of laughter coming from the lighted kitchen. The normally pleasant scents of cinnamon, brown sugar, and homemade bread wafted into the dimly lit living room, but tonight it only made her stomach churn. Food was the last thing she was interested in. Picking up a newspaper, she sat on the rocking chair beside the fireplace and creased the paper's folded edges.

The smoky light from the lantern that lay on the mantel above her fell across the page as Lidia thumbed through. She had no interest at the moment in editorials or fashion advice. A fancy dress to "sweep him off his feet" as the article promised would do nothing to bring back her brother. About to set the paper on the hearth, a small notice on the back page caught her eye.

Wife Wanted

*Decent hardworking rancher is looking for a good Christian woman
to join me on my large homestead in New Mexico.
No drinkers or smokers. Seeking companionship and help on ranch.
Suitable candidates please respond to the following address.
Sincerely, Jonathan Washington Smith*

Lidia ran her finger across the newsprint. She'd glanced at similar ads in the personals column of newspapers and never given them another thought besides wondering what kind of desperate woman would have the nerve to answer them.

Now she knew.

For the first time in her life, agreeing to marry someone she'd never met seemed far from ridiculous. In fact, it just might be the answer to her prayers—a way to completely start over. Laughter rang out from the kitchen, but she ignored the happy sounds. Surely she could find a good man who was in need of a faithful companion and who would be willing to take in her brother, as well. As long as he was treated kindly, Koby would earn his keep.

Pulling the paper to her chest, Lidia let out a deep sigh. How exactly did such an arrangement work? A short courtship by correspondence followed by a loveless proposal? The thought was far from appealing. Her childish dreams of her romantic champion coming to her rescue, falling in love, then living happily ever after would have to be forgotten. Romance wouldn't be a factor in such a formal transaction.

But what other option did she have? What would the people of Cranton think now that they knew her brother had murdered one of their own? No, she had no option but to leave, and while the very idea made her sick to her stomach, becoming a mail-order bride did hold a solution.

Engrossed in her thoughts, Lidia started as someone entered the room.

"Hello." Michaela dipped her head to gaze into Lidia's eyes. "How are you doing?"

Lidia shrugged her shoulders. Michaela handed her a plate with a gooey cinnamon roll, then sat on the brick hearth across from her. "I need your expert opinion. How is it?"

The newspaper slid to the floor as Lidia forced herself to take a small bite. "It's wonderful as always."

Michaela reached out to pick up the fallen paper, then balanced it on her knees. "I was afraid I might have added too much brown sugar this time."

Lidia couldn't help but reveal the hint of a smile at the comment. Michaela had already found out that brown sugar was one of her weaknesses. "That, as you know, would be impossible."

"Are you all right?" Michaela leaned forward, and the light from the lantern captured the reddish highlights in her hair.

"I will be."

"Let me know if you need anything. I'm here for you. We all are."

"Thank you." The reassurances from her employer helped, but they still weren't enough to bring Jarek back.

Michaela glanced at the paper, a puzzled furrow lining her brow. She held the paper up in front of her. "Don't tell me you've been reading advertisements for mail-order brides."

"I. . ."

What could Lidia say? She wouldn't lie, and yet such an admission would only hurt Michaela and her family if they knew that not only had she been reading them but also seriously considering such an option.

When did life get so complicated, God, that I've begun to see the benefits in becoming a mail-order bride?

Lidia chewed on her bottom lip. "I've always thought them quite. . .amusing." That was true, at least.

Michaela reached up to tame a curl that had escaped the confines of her hairpins. "My best friend, Caroline, and I used to read these every week, trying to read between the lines."

"What do you mean, read between the lines?" Lidia set the plate in her lap, unable to take another bite of the sweet bread, no matter how delicious it might be.

"Think about it." She tapped her fingernails against the paper. "A man, or woman for that matter, can say anything they want in a personal advertisement or letter. For all you know, Mr. . . . ." She glanced again at the wording. "Mr. Smith is twice your age and lives in a run-down shack in the middle of the scorching New Mexico desert."

"How do you know—" Lidia choked out a laugh at the realization. "That's reading between the lines?"

Michaela nodded. "And no doubt he wants companionship, but more than likely he wants someone to cook his dinner and wash his clothes."

"Slop the pigs and can vegetables?"

Michaela's grin widened. "You're getting the picture."

"I don't know." Lidia shrugged a shoulder and let her fingers play with a loose thread on her skirt. "Jonathan Washington Smith. . .it's a nice name. He might really live on a huge ranch and simply be lonely—"

"And you might simply be trying to run away from your problems."

The truth hit hard. "My brother's dead, and I know people aren't saying good things about him. . .about me and Koby."

"It's not fair, is it?" Michaela rested her hand on Lidia's shoulder and caught her gaze. "There will always be those who find reasons to look down on others. I know how bad it hurts to lose someone you love so much, no matter what the circumstances. I've had my times of grieving, and it was never easy. Cry, scream, do whatever you need to do, but don't run away from the people who love you and care about you."

Lidia felt the tears begin to swell in the corners of her eyes. "I don't know if I can stay."

"Listen." Michaela reached out and gripped Lidia's hand as Koby's distinct laugh rang out from the kitchen, filling the recesses of her heart. "Your brother's thriving, and both of you are surrounded by people who love you like family. Don't throw it all away because you're afraid of what tomorrow might bring.

"Let God's Spirit work within you to bring you the strength you need for today. Then let Him help you again tomorrow and the next day. You can't do it alone, Lidia, and I can promise you that Jonathan Washington Smith doesn't care for you the way our family does."

Lidia squeezed her eyes shut to stop the flow of tears. She crinkled the edge of the paper and bit her lip. She understood Mrs. Johnson's concerns that answering an advertisement for a mail-order bride might not be the solution to her situation, but surely it wouldn't hurt to write Mr. Smith a letter.

Chapter 12

Adam rounded the bend of the road that led to the Johnson farmhouse and let the warm spring air fill his lungs. The wagon jostled beneath him as he followed the uneven lane past lush farmland that spread out beyond a row of towering pines. Evidence of the new season was noticeable wherever he looked. Grazing cattle wandered throughout green pastures, content to feed off the land's rich substance. Before long, a brilliant display of flowers would be in bloom, from the white blossoms of the hydrangea bush to the colorful rhododendrons that edged his parents' home.

The gray-shingled farmhouse, with its large front porch, came into view. Adam pulled on the reins to slow the horses' gait. This was the home where he'd been born and where he'd watched his brothers and sisters grow up beside him. Memories of afternoon baseball games, picnics, and church socials filtered through his mind. Those happy memories, though, were paired with vivid images of his mother's death and the emptiness he'd felt knowing she'd never be there to help him with his schoolwork or kiss him good night. Sometimes the memories still left a hole in his heart. Michaela's unexpected entrance into their lives had helped to draw him out, but life didn't stay static for long. It had hit him with one more punch. No one had expected Samuel to die so young.

The sun brought out trickles of moisture across the back of his neck, and he reached up to wipe them away, wishing he could just as easily wipe away his melancholy mood. Life wasn't always fair—he'd discovered that early on. But he'd learned an even greater lesson lately. God saw beyond the outer surface of a man. He saw into the very heart. But having the willing heart that God wanted wasn't always easy.

Drawing in the reins, he stopped the wagon in front of the house and jumped down. The yard was quiet except for a plump hen that had somehow managed to escape the confines of her coop. Even her annoying squawking wasn't enough to distract him from the real purpose of his visit. Adam's heart throbbed at the thought of seeing Lidia again. The last time they'd been together, he'd been nothing like the gentleman he should have been and far from the Christian example he yearned to be. He could never make up for his actions. Just as he would never be able to make up for the pain she was feeling over her brother's death. That was one thing they had in common. They both understood the deep pain of loss. It might not ever bring them together as he'd once hoped, but it might help erase some of the uneasiness between them.

Reaching into the bed of the wagon, he pulled out a small basket he'd secured on the side. He'd brought Lidia a peace offering. He couldn't help but wonder what her reaction would be to seeing him again. Hopefully, between the jar of maple syrup and his heartfelt words of apology, she'd find it within her to forgive him.

Michaela walked out of the house with baby Daria partly hidden in the folds of her skirt. God had known what He was doing when He brought his stepmother from Boston to Cranton. She could never completely take the place of the mother he lost, but there had never been any doubt of her love for him or any of the other Johnson children.

"It's been too long since we've seen you." Michaela leaned against the porch railing. "Your father was starting to worry that maybe you were sick again."

Adam shook his head and smiled as he took the stairs two at a time, then embraced his stepmother with a warm hug. "Nothing of the sort. Just needed some time to come to my senses is all."

He pulled a shiny red ribbon out of his pocket for the dark-eyed toddler. Daria might be shy, but Adam found that a treat every now and again went a long way in gaining her affections. He tousled the child's hair, watching in amazement as she manipulated the shiny fabric between her fingers, her eyes lit up with joy.

"I've come to talk to Lidia." Adam cleared his throat. "I need to apologize to her. Blaming her for Samuel's death was wrong."

Michaela raised her brow. "What changed your mind?"

"I was forced to look at my own life and realize I wasn't any better than Jarek."

"That's a powerful conclusion to come to." Daria started to whimper, and her mother lifted the child onto her hip. "There's. . .there's something else you should know."

Michaela glanced away, and Adam's heart skipped a beat. If something had happened to Lidia. . .

His stepmother pulled Daria against her chest as if trying to shelter the young child from the expected ups and downs she would face throughout her lifetime. "Lidia's brother was killed by bounty hunters a few days ago."

Adam let out a sigh of relief. "I know. Reuben Myers told me yesterday when he came to pick up his load of sugar."

A frown spread across her face. "I'm sure I wouldn't like to hear what he had to say about it."

"No, you wouldn't, but listening to him made me see what a fool I've been."

"Lidia's taken it hard. I'm pretty sure she thinks the town, and maybe even our own family, are going to turn against her now that they know it was her brother who killed Samuel."

Adam's gaze swept the sanded boards of the porch, and his stomach knotted together. "I was one of those people."

"And now?"

"I once blamed her for Samuel's death simply because they were kin. Now I realize how hatred and bitterness can affect the truth."

"You're right, but that still doesn't change how she feels, or how she believes people see her." Michaela gently rocked the young girl who looked almost asleep against her shoulder. "I hope you can make things right with her and help her see that what happened doesn't change the way any of us feel toward her."

Still pondering his stepmother's words, Adam made his way through the farmhouse toward the backyard where Lidia was hanging out the laundry. Stepping into the kitchen's outer doorway, he stopped at the sight of her. The fabric of her beige dress billowed in the morning breeze as she reached up to secure a white sheet to the line. She'd gained some weight, which only accented her gentle curves. Several tendrils of her long auburn hair spilled across her shoulders, and the sun reflected a bit of color on her fair cheeks.

He couldn't deny the truth. From the very first moment he'd found her treed by that rabid dog, something within him had known that in meeting her, his life would change forever. In many ways it had. She'd shown him what real sacrifice meant, and what it meant to truly love one's fellow man.

Then there had been their kiss beneath the stars—

"Adam?"

The sound of her voice startled him.

"Lidia. . .I—" He stopped, suddenly uncertain of what to say.

"Did you need something?" Her voice rang cold and void of any emotion.

"I came to see you," he started again. "How have you been? I mean, I'm sorry. I'm sorry for. . ."

He stepped outside and hurried down the stairs, closing the distance between them so he could look into her eyes. He hated the sadness he saw in their depths.

She held her head high. "Sorry for what?"

"For everything." *Give me the words, Lord. Please.* "I'm sorry for the loss of your brother."

He had to start somewhere, but he wasn't sure he'd chosen the right place. Her eyes misted over, and she turned away from him, grabbing the next sheet from the basket in a quick, jerky movement as she flung it over the line.

Adam swallowed hard. "I know how much it hurts to lose someone you love."

Her gaze avoided his. "I thought you'd be happy now that your brother's murderer has paid with his life for his deed."

Her words pierced like a poisoned arrow to his heart. "I might have been—would have been—a few weeks ago, but not today."

"What's changed?" She kept her back to him.

This wasn't going the way he'd planned at all.

"Everything's changed for me, Lidia." He came around to the other side of the clothesline to face her. "When I see what you've gone through, it—"

"You don't have a clue what I've gone through." She flung a clothespin at him and struck him on the forehead.

Adam took a step back, not sure how to react to her display of emotion. "That's not what I meant."

Another wooden pin bounced off his shoulder.

Deciding he had nothing to lose, he set the jar of maple syrup down on the grass and continued, "Lidia, I've seen how you respond to life in a godly way no matter what happens. That's what you've taught me."

He ducked at the third clothespin. *Okay, maybe not in every instance.*

She looked up and caught his gaze. He expected to see anger in her eyes, but all that was left was pain.

"Lidia, don't you see? I've been so blinded. You've shown me what true sacrifice is, and what it means to love someone through God's eyes."

Her head bowed and her shoulders shook as sobs racked her body. Adam moved toward her and gently took her hands, drawing them toward his chest. "I'm sorry, Lidia, for everything. I'm sorry your brother died, and I'm sorry I treated you the way I did."

Lidia leaned into his chest as he wrapped his arms around her.

This is where you belong, Lidia.

With his arms still around her, he led her to the porch stairs where they could sit down. She wiped her face with the back of her hands before looking up and searching his eyes.

"I'm sorry about the clothespins."

He stifled a laugh. "I knew you had a bit of spunk in you, but I never imagined I'd have to defend myself from a fleet of flying clothespins."

A smile formed beneath her rounded eyes, and Adam felt his heart pound within his chest. No. Now wasn't the time for him to express his feelings toward her. Lidia had just suffered a horrible loss. He needed to be there for her without any hint of an ulterior motive.

And there was something else he had to do.

"I need to ask for your forgiveness." He tilted her chin so she couldn't look away from him. "I've let bitterness over Samuel's death run my thoughts and emotions. Not only did I blame your brother for what he did, I blamed you, Koby, and anyone else who got in my way."

Adam paused, trying to find the right words to say. "I. . .I guess there's nothing else I can really say, except that I'm sorry."

☙

Lidia drew in a deep breath, her mind spinning at Adam's confession. She'd waited for so long to bridge the gap that hung between them. Their kiss had stirred something within her she'd never felt before, but she'd finally realized that any hope of a relationship between them had long passed. Saying sorry would never change that.

She laced her fingers together, trying to ignore the effect his nearness had on her. "Your reaction was no different than the dozens of other people in town who won't want anything to do with me once they find out that Jarek was my brother. You, of all people, had an even greater motivation. Samuel was your brother."

"That's no excuse." Adam shook his head and rested his forearms on his thighs. "Not that I didn't have the right to be angry and hurt over what happened, but the way I acted was no better than Reuben Myers and his blatant hatred for immigrants. As for the rest of the town, most of them are good, upright people. I don't see them blaming you for what your brother did."

She leaned away from him. "Don't try to sugarcoat things for me, Adam. I've lived in this country long enough to recognize the expression on people's faces once they hear my last name. I've tried so hard to be an *American*, but no matter what, I'm still an immigrant. At least to everyone else I am."

Shoving her hand into the pocket of her dress, she fingered the folded letter she'd written to Mr. Jonathan Washington Smith. This morning it had seemed to be the only way she could escape to a place that would take her away from all of this. She looked out across the land, past the newly tilled garden and toward the orchards and pasturelands. There would never be any escape from who she was.

Lidia Kowalski.

She couldn't deny it. Polish blood ran through her veins. Grandmother had always taught her to be proud of her heritage and who she was. Besides the Bible, her sweet babcia had charged her to remember the stories from her mother country. Stories she could in turn pass down to her grandchildren. In the end, she'd betrayed her grandmother by trying to hide who she was.

I'm sorry, Grandmother. In betraying who I am, I've betrayed you. . .and Mother and Father. I've betrayed my very existence.

Crumpling the soft fabric of her skirt between her fingers, she looked up at Adam. "I always thought if I could talk like a lady without any accent, no one would know who I really was, and I'd be accepted. I constantly corrected Koby over his grammar, and for myself, I read everything I could get my hands on so no one could ever accuse me of being ignorant. But I was wrong."

Adam leaned back against the porch rail. "There's nothing wrong with trying to improve one's self."

"But that wasn't my reasoning. I was trying to become someone I never could be. There's nothing I can do to change who I am. Nor should I ever want to." She held her head up high. "I'm an American *and* I'm Polish, Adam Johnson. It's time I started to be proud of who I am."

A deep feeling of peace flooded through Lidia's heart. Like cool, healing waters, it ran into the tiny holes and crevices that had been chipped away like broken pieces of pottery. For a moment, she sat still beneath the warmth of the morning sun, working to push aside the pain from her past.

Adam broke the silence. "You never answered my question."

She raised her gaze to meet his. "What question?"

"I need you to forgive me, Lidia. I'm not sure I'll ever be able to forgive myself, but I need to hear it from you."

Something stirred within her. It was like the first time she met him. For a brief moment, she'd stood in the shelter of his arms knowing he was the one who'd rescued her from the rabid dog. Today his coal black hair glistened in the sunlight. The gold glints in his eyes seemed to plead with her to forgive him.

"I do forgive you. What my brother did was horrible, but that still doesn't change the fact that I. . ."

"You what?"

Tears glistened in the corners of her eyes. "I miss Jarek so much. I know what he did was wrong, but. . .I can't help it. He was my brother."

"You have every right to miss him."

A strand of her hair blew across his face, and he pulled her closer. "I've forgiven your brother for what he did to Samuel."

"I wish he could have heard your confession, but at least I have—"

"Lidia!"

Lidia turned to see Koby running toward her at full speed. "What is it, Koby?"

"Aren't you ready to go yet? The wagon's loaded."

She lifted her fingers to her mouth. "I'd entirely forgotten."

Adam turned to Lidia. "Forgotten what?"

"We're supposed to go to a barn raising for the Nowaks. They're a Polish family who live nearby."

"I suppose I'd better go then." Adam stood, shoving his hands into his pockets. "I have plenty of work to do on the farm—"

"Why don't you come along, Mr. Johnson?" Koby piped up. "Your entire family's going, and the food's going to be wonderful. Hunter's stew, noodles and cabbage, cucumber beet soup—"

"Cucumber beet soup?" Adam wrinkled his nose.

"Come on. It will be fun."

Lidia saw a flicker of hesitation register in Adam's eyes. Did he wish that they could prolong their time together? Did she? Despite all that had transpired between them, she couldn't ignore that her heart didn't want things to end this way. Still, sharing a kiss beneath a starlit sky didn't promise them a future together. Just like asking for one's forgiveness didn't erase the pain. Adam might feel bad about the way he had treated her, but so much heartache had transpired between them. Nothing could ever change that fact.

"Please come," Koby begged.

"Would you mind, Lidia?" Adam shifted uncomfortably beside her.

Her breath caught in her throat. She couldn't determine if she was more nervous or excited with the opportunity to prolong their time together. "Of course not."

"I'm not much on socials, and I don't promise to try any beets. . ."

Koby laughed. "Then, if we're all going, we'd better hurry."

Lidia followed them into the house and tried to untangle the web of confusion she felt tugging at her. Part of her longed for Adam to acknowledge that he cared for her. Another part wanted to run away and forget that she'd ever met him.

I don't know what to do anymore, Lord. Please, show me Your will for my life.

Stopping at the threshold of the living area, Lidia reached into her pocket and fingered the one-page letter she'd written to Mr. Smith. The thin paper crinkled between her fingers. All she had to do was send it in the mail, and if Mr. Smith agreed, she and Koby could be on the next train to New Mexico. Surely she and Mr. Smith would be able to find a way to make a marriage work.

If that was true, though, then why was her heart begging her to stay?

Chapter 13

Lidia watched Koby mingle with a group of friends on the other side of the newly constructed barn. He was eating a plate of noodles and cabbage and laughing as if the world were free from any cares.

Adam, on the other hand, stood beside Lidia looking uncomfortable in his starched white shirt and black pants. He seemed to have enjoyed working with the other men during the barn raising, but now that the celebration had begun, he'd grown quiet and reserved. Standing rigid, he pulled at his collar, then shoved his hands into his pockets. He didn't have to say anything for her to recognize that he felt like a frog in a bees' nest.

The structure bustled with activity around them. A dozen couples stomped their feet on the rough wooden floor in the center of the barn as they danced to a Polish folk song played by a group of fiddlers. The vivid colors of the women's skirts swished before her, while smells of sawdust mingling with savory meats filled the air.

Lidia looked up at Adam, her hands behind her back. "Are you sorry you came?"

"Of course not." He tugged on his collar again and chuckled. "Though to be perfectly truthful, I could have done without the beet soup."

Lidia laughed. He'd finished off two bowls of Hunter's stew with relish but had sampled the cucumber beet soup under protest. "I don't suppose it's a crime to dislike beets."

"I hope not. I've always tried to avoid that and squash."

She smiled, reminded of what she liked about him. He might not be one for social gatherings, but he was handsome and honest, and he made her laugh.

"I hate liver and cooked spinach," she confessed, enjoying the festive spirit around her and the growing camaraderie between them. Only a few short hours ago, she'd been ready to take the next train out West in reply to Mr. Smith's advertisement. But with Adam standing beside her, she felt the now familiar tugging of her heart begging her to stay and at least see what might happen, if anything, between them.

The fiddlers stomped their feet and picked up the tempo a notch. Lidia loved celebrations like today. The music lifted her spirits and set her heart soaring. If she closed her eyes, she could imagine her father's wide hand on the bow of the violin and her mother's smile as she swayed to the music from Poland.

Jarek's image flashed before her.

Jarek murdering Samuel. . .His face on the wanted poster. . .Jarek running from the law. . .Jarek killed at the hands of a bounty hunter. . .

Guilt overwhelmed her.

I shouldn't be here, Lord. I shouldn't be smiling. There's too much pain to laugh again.

The music closed in around her, but this time the beauty had vanished. The room moved in slow motion. Someone laughed. Voices buzzed in the background.

It's time to turn your mourning into dancing.

Lidia gripped the edge of the wooden table beside her and attempted to keep her balance. How many times had she prayed that God would turn her sorrow into joy? That she would hear laughter once again in Koby's voice? That she would be able to dance with joy?

Dance, Lidia. Dance for joy, for I will make you whole again.

"Lidia. Are you all right?" Adam's fingers brushed her elbow.

She stared up at him. "I don't know."

Another song started, and her foot tapped automatically to the familiar rhythm.

"Let's dance." Lidia blurted out the words before realizing how forward she sounded, but for once she didn't care. "It's a traditional *mazurka* from Poland. You'll be able to catch on—"

"No, I'm sorry. . . ." He took a step backward. "I can't. I'm sorry. . . . I'm not much for dancing."

Lidia swallowed her disappointment.

I came to set you free, Lidia. Dance for joy!

She glanced up at Adam, who gave her a weak smile. Lidia stepped out onto the floor with the other dancers and quickly chose a partner. She let the music fill her senses, her heart racing as she kept up with the quick tempo of the fiddler. She slid her foot sideways, then clicked her heels together, following the basic steps her mother had taught her as a young girl.

The music grew louder. How long had it been since she'd felt this free? Free to forget all the pain and loss she'd experienced the past two years and to simply live. This was a day for celebration. A day for new beginnings. Wasn't that what God was trying to tell her? Of course she'd never be able to forget Jarek. He'd always be a part of who she was—just as she'd never forget her parents. She couldn't change the past, but it was time to move on.

Give me a clean start, Lord.

She glanced at Adam, who still stood on the sidelines.

Is it too much to ask for a new start with Adam, as well?

Her feet kept time to the beat. She held her head high and let her arms move gracefully until the final note. The song ended too quickly. Trying to catch her breath, she moved away from the center of the floor.

Adam held up two glasses of punch in his hands. "I thought you might like something to drink."

"Thank you." Lidia took a sip, then placed her free hand on her heart, not sure if its rapid beat was from the exertion or Adam's nearness. "What did you think?"

"That I'm glad I didn't let you twist my arm into joining, though the dance was beautiful." His voice was barely above a whisper. "And so are you."

Lidia felt the heat in her cheeks rise. "It's a traditional dance that my people have done for centuries. It's a celebration of who we are."

He took a swallow of his drink. "You. . .you seem happier tonight."

"Being here today has confirmed who I am. It's reminded me that God can still give me happiness despite what's happened."

"Adam." Eric Johnson's voice broke into their conversation. "We could use your help over here for a moment."

Adam turned toward a group of men talking in the corner of the barn. "I'm sorry, Lidia. If you'll excuse me."

"Of course."

Lidia finished her punch and watched Adam join his father and several other men. The entire Johnson family had worked hard to finish the new barn for their neighbors. Sarah, Ruby, and Anna danced in circles along the side. Michaela, with little Daria clinging to her skirts, visited with several of the married women. It amazed Lidia that God had used this family to teach her so much about love, family, and true forgiveness.

"I didn't know you were such a talented dancer, Lidia."

"Silvia?" Lidia turned to her old acquaintance. She'd seen the young woman only a handful of times since her parents' death.

Silvia swayed to the music, letting the bottom of her dark green dress swish beneath her. "You looked as if you were enjoying yourself."

"I did. It's been quite a while since I had so much fun."

"That is a shame. I heard that you're working out at the Johnson farm now. A bit better, I suspect, though, than working at the mills."

Lidia stood up straight, determined to ignore the obvious jibe in Silvia's remarks. "I've always considered it a privilege to be able to provide for my brother and me."

"You are fortunate in that sense, I suppose." Silvia twirled the long sash that hung at her waist. "Adam Johnson is quite a good-looking man, isn't he? I know I certainly wouldn't mind working around him."

Lidia nearly choked. "Yes, I suppose he is. Good-looking, I mean."

"You suppose? Don't tell me you've never noticed."

Lidia sighed, wondering if there was a way to escape without being rude. She'd forgotten how annoying the woman could be. Still, she couldn't deny the obvious. "He's very good-looking."

"So you have noticed." Silvia smiled, and Lidia wondered what her motivation was with the personal questions. "I understand he even owns his own farm. A decent, hardworking man. You can't ask for much more than that, can you?"

"I suppose not."

"I saw him talking to you. Don't tell me you actually think he's interested in you."

"I don't know. I. . ." The question caught her off guard.

"You are interested, though, aren't you? I saw the look you gave him right before he was called away." Silvia leaned forward. "Don't fool yourself, Lidia. If it weren't enough that you're an immigrant working out in his father's home, your brother murdered his brother—"

"That's none of your business."

"Maybe not, but no matter how hard you try, nothing can change the fact that you're not a native-born Yankee girl. Or that the people of this town will never completely accept you. You know how they think about girls who work outside the house. That's why my mother would never allow her girls to participate in such an undignified occupation."

"I'm an American, I'm Polish, and I'm proud of both." A lantern dangled above her, casting eerie shadows across the barn wall. Lidia's stomach felt queasy despite her bold stance.

"Being an American is easy to talk about, especially when you stand here surrounded by music from the motherland and more Polish food than an army could eat in a week. But you can't deny the fact that people look down on girls like you who work out on the farms. Manual labor is something no proper lady would ever be caught doing."

Lidia refused to back down. "There's nothing wrong with what I do, and besides, Adam's different."

"He's not different, Lidia. You just want him to be different. The reality is he'll settle with someone like me who comes from a well-to-do family and who would never lower her standards to be a servant."

Lidia held her breath as Silvia spun on her heels and walked away. The woman was incorrigible. Silvia held her head high as if she'd just done some noble deed by putting Lidia in her place.

Lidia pressed the fabric of her dress between her fingers. She couldn't argue with what Silvia had said. No Yankee or prosperous immigrant family would ever hire out their daughters to do housework at the local farms or in town. The jobs were given to impoverished girls like Lidia, most of whom were more than willing to help out their families by working outside the home. Still, Lidia knew what the women in town thought. All girls wanted to be ladies, and it was degrading to be hired help.

Needing some fresh air and a chance to gather her thoughts, Lidia escaped through the large doors of the barn into the moonlight. Silvia had only confirmed something she'd known all along. The Johnson family had taken her in and treated her like family, but that wasn't enough. She would never be like Adam. She would always be the hired help. She'd wanted Adam's confession to change things between them, but was that even realistic? He'd tolerated the food and passed on the dancing, things that were so much a part of who she was. Would being born a Yankee have made him see her differently?

You were chosen to be who you are from the beginning, Lidia. You're Mine, and I love you.

Lidia slowed her steps as she continued along the path toward the house. Words from her Savior filled her mind once again. They were words she wanted to believe, yet—

Lidia, I chose the exact time you would come into existence, and the exact place where you would live.

She stopped beside a fallen tree, stepping over it so she could sit on its trunk and overlook the valley below. She clung to the words, knowing that they were true. Her heavenly Father loved her. What had the psalmist written about her existence? God had created her, knit her together in her mother's womb, and every day ordained for her had been written down before she breathed her first breath.

The thought was too incredible for her to comprehend.

Music filtered into the night air. . .a million stars hung above her. . .a gentle breeze tugged at the base of her neck. . . . For too long, she'd lost her joy in the beauty of God's world and in His creation that surrounded her. Yet slowly, God was working to restore her joy.

No matter what happened around her—death, prejudice, injustice—she had to hold to one truth. Her existence wasn't a mistake. Men might live their lives full of hatred, but that would never change the fact that she'd been created in God's image. And He loved her.

She ran her fingers against the smooth bark of the fallen log. Silvia's words played in the back of her mind. She glanced up the hill and into the lighted barn. There was no denying that she'd seen the haughty expressions on people's faces when she'd gone into town. They might never consider her to be as good as they were, but she wasn't going to believe the lies anymore. What she'd told Silvia was true. She was an American and she was Polish. And she was proud to be both.

There was one other thing that was true, as well. If anything were ever to happen between Adam and her, he was going to have to accept her for who she was.

❧

Adam scanned the crowd, wondering where Lidia had gone. He felt as if he'd let her down. He'd never been much for parties and felt out of place tonight. He'd enjoyed working on the construction of the barn because he was good with his hands and knew he'd contributed significantly to the project. It was another story, though, when it came to dancing. He might as well try to swim across the Atlantic. He'd attempt that before trying to keep up with Lidia in one of the traditional Polish dances. And he'd never told her about what had really happened the day Samuel died. He knew now that nothing could ever happen between them if he didn't tell her the truth.

Grabbing another cup of punch, he took a sip, frustrated because he couldn't find her. She'd looked so beautiful tonight, wearing the pale green dress he'd admired several times before. It might not have been as fancy as some of the other young girls', but its simplicity had only managed to set her apart. Her long hair had been pulled up, leaving tiny curls that framed her face and ran along the base of her hairline. He couldn't deny it anymore. He was in love with her.

He'd also seen something change within her tonight. He knew she still grieved over the loss of her brother. It was an emotion he understood all too well, but he hadn't missed the joy in her eyes as she'd stood beside her friends and danced. He loved to see her smile and wished that he had been the one to make her smile.

"Are you looking for someone?"

Adam turned around and tried to place the young woman who stood beside him.

"I'm Silvia Dolny. We met at church recently."

"I'm sorry. Of course."

"I only ask because you were looking a bit lost."

"Actually, I was looking for Lidia. Lidia Kowalski. Do you know her?"

"Of course." The young woman pushed a strand of her honey blond hair away from her cheek and smiled. "I've known Lidia for years."

"Have you seen her recently?"

She rested her fingers on his forearm. "I saw her slip out with someone a few minutes ago. Rufin, I think his name is. He's a tall redhead. You might have seen him tonight. He's quite a dancer."

"No. I don't think I've met him." Adam shook his head and tried to follow the young woman's implications. "I've been introduced to so many different people."

"Rumor has it they're engaged, or about to be anyway—"

Engaged?

Adam swallowed hard.

"I don't understand. How can Lidia be engaged?" It was a stupid question. He had no claims to her. Every time he'd been with her, he'd only managed to push her away. She certainly didn't owe him an explanation. He'd just thought. . . What had he thought? That saying he was sorry would erase all the pain that had piled up between them?

"Well, they're not technically, I suppose, but she just told me she was expecting Rufin to ask for her hand any time. Perhaps even tonight. It's the perfect setting, you know, so romantic. Apparently Rufin's been in love with her for years, but it's only been recently that he had the courage to tell her how he felt. Lidia's a sweet girl and all, but unfortunately she's been forced to work out—"

"I know. Lidia works for my parents."

"Well, of course you know, then. I suppose they'll have to find someone to take her place before long, unless Rufin doesn't mind her working out. Some men don't mind their wives taking in menial jobs to help support the family, though personally—"

"If you'll excuse me." Adam ignored the shocked expression on her face and hurried to the other side of the barn.

He'd been a fool for so long. Pride had stopped him from forgiving Lidia's brother. It had caused him to turn against Lidia and her people. Pride had even stopped him from dancing with her tonight, afraid he'd make a fool out of himself. Now he was afraid that because of his pride, he might have lost her forever.

Chapter 14

Adam strode out of the confines of the barn and stared into the darkness. A light breeze blew across his face but did little to erase the beads of sweat forming on his brow. He felt sick to his stomach. Surely there was nothing to the rumor that Lidia was engaged. . .or practically engaged to someone else. He should be the one courting her.

Lively music continued to play in the background while he scanned the path that meandered toward the Nowaks' darkened home. He looked for signs of Lidia and the redheaded Rufin, but there was little movement outside save the slight swaying of the trees that lined the walkway.

Shaking his head, he leaned against the side of the barn. Why should he be surprised if Lidia had given her heart to someone else? He didn't deserve her. She needed someone who wouldn't let her down the way he had. Someone who wouldn't make the same mistakes. Knowing he'd changed simply wasn't good enough.

"Adam?" His father stepped outside to join him, a bowl of stew in his hands. "I saw you leave. Trying to escape the celebrations?"

"You know I've never been much for parties. I needed a bit of fresh air." The spicy scent of the rich broth would have been tempting any other time, but at the moment, the thought of food soured his stomach.

His father took a bite of the thick stew. "Your leaving seems a pity with all those pretty girls inside, not to mention the great food."

Adam tried to laugh, but his voice rang hollow and empty. There was only one girl he cared about, and more than likely he'd lost her. He studied the other end of the yard where a number of tall trees were scattered over the terrain. If he ever did find this Rufin fellow, he had a few choice words he planned to say to the chap.

Adam's jaw tensed. "What do you know about a man named Rufin?"

"Rufin?" His father shook his head. "The name's not familiar. Who is he?"

"I don't know him personally, but I thought you might have seen him around the house. He's courting Lidia."

"What?" His father dropped his spoon into the bowl. "That's news to me. There haven't been any young men around our place looking for Lidia that I

332

know of—except a certain son of mine."

Adam kicked the toe of his boot into the dirt. Why hadn't he done things properly from the beginning? He could have been the one courting Lidia. He could be the one holding her in his arms beneath the glow of the full moon. Instead, he'd let her slip away.

"I just spoke to Silvia Dolny." Adam folded his arms across his chest. "She told me that Lidia was being courted by this Rufin. That he was going to ask her to marry him."

"Marcus Dolny's daughter?"

Adam shrugged. "I think so. I met her a few weeks ago at church."

"And are you sure she was telling the truth?"

Adam's brow rose in question. "What reason would she have to lie to me? I don't even know her."

"Has the thought ever crossed your mind that you're one of the area's most eligible bachelors, Adam Johnson?" His father cocked his head. "Don't tell me you haven't noticed the way Silvia and the other single women look at you."

He hadn't noticed anyone since he met Lidia.

"I could be wrong," his father continued, "but from what I've heard about Silvia, I wouldn't discount the idea that her comments regarding Lidia were nothing more than a ploy to get you to turn your affections away from Lidia— and onto her."

Adam frowned. "That's ridiculous."

"Maybe not. I just know that if I were in love with someone, I certainly wouldn't gamble my future on the words of a stranger."

His father was right.

Adam tugged on the collar of his shirt. "If you'll excuse me then, I'm going to find her."

His father nodded, and not sure where else to go, Adam followed the path toward the house. Whether or not Rufin's intentions were valid didn't matter at the moment. He wasn't prepared to lose Lidia without a fight.

Adam stopped when he caught sight of her in the distance. She stood beneath the canopy of a large tree with Rufin, he presumed, who had his arms around her waist. Adam's fists clamped together at his side, and his teeth clenched together. Silvia had been right all along. Lidia was going to marry Rufin.

❧

Lidia tried to push Rufin's hands off her waist; then she took a step backward. She never should have agreed to allow him to walk her toward the house to get her coat and bag. Lidia shoved against the man's broad chest with all her might, but the stocky man was too strong.

"Come on." His grip tightened around her waist. "I've seen the way you look at me. We could sneak down to the river and have a little fun tonight—"

Bile rose in her throat. "I have no intention of doing any such thing."

She could still hear the lively strains of the fiddle, but they were far enough away that she feared no one would hear her if she screamed. She'd been a fool to leave the celebrations alone. Rufin pulled her tighter, then pressed his mouth against hers. She jerked her head back and screamed.

Please, God. . .

Lidia closed her eyes and swung a fist upward hard.

"Ouch!"

"Adam?" Her eyes opened at the sound of his voice, and she sucked in her breath in horror.

Rufin's grip on her loosened.

With one hand nursing his jaw, Adam drew back his other fist and hit Rufin square in the chin before the thug had a chance to react.

Adam watched Rufin slide to the ground. The man was out cold and hopefully wouldn't awaken anytime soon.

Rubbing his jaw, Adam turned to Lidia. "I never imagined you'd have such a solid swing."

"I can't believe I missed him and hit you instead." Lidia shook out her sore fingers, and from the look on her face, Adam wasn't sure if she was going to laugh or cry. "How did you find me?"

"I was out looking for you and saw you struggling to push him away. I thought I could pull him off from behind. That's when I got in the way of your punch."

This time she chuckled. "I really am sorry. I didn't see you at all."

"It doesn't matter. He'll wake up and hopefully have learned a lesson. What were you doing out here with him?"

"I was talking to Silvia, and. . ." Lidia paused.

She'd been talking to Silvia? He didn't like where this was going.

"I needed some fresh air and decided to go to the house to get my coat. Rufin offered to walk with me. I've talked to him a few times at church, and he'd always seemed decent enough—"

"Until he decided to take advantage of you." Adam frowned.

"I was such a fool—"

"No, I've been the foolish one." He reached out to push back a strand of her hair that had fallen into her eyes. He wanted to pull her into an embrace and never let her go, but instead, he tucked her arm into his and guided her back toward the festivities. They left the stirring Rufin to manage on his own.

"What do you mean you've been the foolish one?" She looked up at him as they headed back toward the barn, her eyes wide with question.

"Silvia had a talk with me, as well. She told me that Rufin had been calling on you."

"What?" Lidia stopped midstride. "That's ridiculous. I barely know the man."

"So there's no chance that you're engaged?" The question might be absurd, but he had to know for sure.

"Of course not. I wouldn't have let the man court me."

Adam let the music wash over him like a soothing balm. He'd already waited too long to state his intentions.

He took a deep breath and gathered her hands into his. "I haven't been the same since I kissed you that night beneath the stars. I've made a mountain of mistakes, but I have to know one thing." He stopped, trying to gather his courage. "Is there any way you'd give me a second chance? Give us a second chance to see what might happen."

"I. . ." She pulled away from him.

"Lidia, please." He strode after her, wishing he could read her mind. "I can't deny any longer how I feel about you."

"It would never work, Adam." She looked straight ahead, avoiding his gaze. "I appreciate your saving me from Rufin, but we're two different people. I saw you in there tonight. You'll never be comfortable with who I am."

"That's not true."

"Isn't it?"

Surely he'd heard her wrong. He hadn't come this far to give up now.

"Lidia, stop for a moment. Please." He gently grasped her shoulder and turned her toward him. "If it's Samuel—"

"No." Lidia shook her head but this time didn't move away from him. "You don't understand, do you? It's not about Samuel anymore. It's about who I am and how you see me."

"What do you mean?"

"Close your eyes and listen."

Not sure of why she wanted him to do it, he complied. The upbeat strains of a fiddle met his ears. Laughter and shouts radiated from the barn as people kept up with the traditional Polish folk dance. The smells of freshly cut wood and sawdust drifted through the night air, competing with the faint scent of her perfume.

He opened his eyes. The moonlight cast a ray of white light across her face and caught her pained reflection. He couldn't let things end between them this way.

She reached out and touched the edge of his sleeve before drawing her hand away, as if she was hesitant of what she was about to say. "This is who I am, Adam. I'll never be like your sisters or any other Yankee girl. People will always look down on me because of my heritage, and nothing you can say or do will ever change that."

"That's not true, and even if it is, it doesn't matter to me anymore."

"It matters to me." She took a step back. "I've spent my entire life trying to be someone else—an American. I've finally realized that I don't need to be like them. I'm proud of who I am. God's been speaking to me lately. Reminding me that He chose me from the beginning—"

"And that He loves you for who you are." Adam finished her sentence with a half smile.

Lidia nodded. "Yes. How did you know?"

"God's been telling me the same thing lately."

"Really?" Her gaze penetrated his soul. It was more honest, searching, than anything he could think of. He could feel its pull.

Adam dug his nails into the palms of his hands. He'd almost decided not to tell her the truth. But there would never be a chance for anything to happen between them until he did. "There are things that took place the day Samuel died that I never told you. Things I've never told anyone."

"It's not too late. Tell me now."

Adam tugged on his earlobe and forced himself to tell her. "I doubt if you heard about it at the time, but there was a series of events that happened right before my brother was killed. The sheriff had to handle more than the usual number of petty thefts, vandalism, and looting of stores. A Polish man named Artur was arrested for breaking into several of the stores in town, and most of us began to blame the incidents on the immigrants who had been flooding into town during the previous months."

He cleared his throat before continuing. "The day Samuel died, he and I had gone into town for supplies. On the boardwalk I overheard your brother saying something offensive to one of the shopkeepers. Jarek's accent made it obvious that he wasn't an American, and I made the comment to Samuel that...that it was high time the immigrants were sent back to Europe on the next cargo boat."

Adam winced at his own harsh words. How long had he prayed that he could erase the past? Yet it was something that could never be done.

Lidia's eyes darkened. "Tell me the rest of what happened."

"Your brother overheard what I said and pulled me into one of the side streets where he shoved me against the wall. Samuel had always been quick on his feet, and he tried to defend me. I pushed Jarek back, only to have Samuel throw the first punch. Before I knew it, things escalated out of control. . .and Samuel was dead."

Her eyes squeezed shut for a moment. "I'm sorry, Adam. I really am."

"Don't you see?" Adam's jaw tensed. "Samuel's death was just as much my fault as it was your brother's. If I hadn't been filled with such bitterness for those coming into the area and spoken out of turn—"

"It's over, Adam."

He heard her words but didn't miss the pain in her voice. He knew what she was thinking. Would two lives have been spared if he'd had the sense to keep his bitter words to himself?

Lidia shook her head. "It's time you truly forgive yourself for what happened that day and go on with your life. You can't take back what you said any more than Jarek can erase what he did. It's time we all go on with our lives."

Adam took her hands in his. "If what happened is really in the past, and if you can totally forgive me, then let me court you properly. I can't let you go."

Lidia shook her head, and her eyes welled up with moisture. "I said I forgive you, and I meant it, but it's too late for us, Adam. There are simply too many obstacles standing between us. I saw how uncomfortable you were tonight. My people accept me for who I am. I'm finished pretending to be someone else."

For an instant, he saw the love he felt for her reflected in her eyes. He hadn't been wrong about her. She did care for him. If only he could get her to trust her heart.

He squeezed her hands. "Don't you see? I don't want you to be anyone else but Lidia Kowalski. Polish, American. . . Chinese. . .it doesn't matter to me. It's you I care about."

"I'm sorry, Adam." Lidia blinked back the tears and turned to run off into the night.

Chapter 15

Wait, Lidia."

Adam took half a dozen broad steps before he caught up with her. Reaching out his hand to grasp her shoulder, he turned her gently toward him. Tears streamed down her face as she looked into his eyes. "Adam, please. . ."

"Just tell me why. Give me one good reason why there's not a chance for us; then I promise I'll let you go and never bother you again."

She wiped away the tears from her eyes and shook her head. "You say that you care about me the way I am—"

"And you're not convinced?"

"Why should I be? You obviously despise my Polish culture. Besides, there are dozens of other girls who would jump at the chance to let you court them." She waved her hands in the air. "Dozens of girls who know how to serve a five-course meal or do fancy needlework like a proper lady."

"I'm not interested in any of that." He let his arms fall to his sides. "What is it? The differences between us can't be that great."

"Then you don't know me at all. Don't you see? I'll never be anything more than a common laborer, Adam. I have to work in order to provide for me and my brother, something no respectable Yankee girl would ever do."

She placed her hands firmly on her hips as she continued. "My mother tongue is Polish. I'm the daughter of a poor itinerate farmer who came to this country for a better life. I've had to work my entire life just to have enough to put food on the table. But I'm so much more than a poor immigrant from another country. I love dancing to traditional Polish songs and eating bigos, noodles, and cucumber beet soup. I love stories my babcia used to tell me. Tales of dragons, *Zlota Kaczka*, and other legends my people have passed on for generations."

Adam stifled a grin as she paused to take a deep breath. "Are you finished?"

She flashed him a look of impatience. "For now."

"I see a woman who loves books and poetry. Someone who can see beauty in a starry night and in the taste of maple syrup. I see a woman who can work almost as hard as any man when she has to and who would give up everything to help a stranger. I see a woman who puts God first in her life and has finally discovered that He loves her exactly the way she is." Adam shook his head as he continued. "Just like you can't change who you are, I also can't change the fact that I was born in this country and only speak English. I can't help the fact that I feel more comfortable working my land than mixing at a social. But just because I can't dance and don't particularly like cucumber beet soup doesn't mean that you and I shouldn't take a chance together."

The corner of her mouth quivered upward. He took a step toward her and tilted her chin up with his forefinger. She was so close he could feel her warm breath against his skin, and it was all he could do to stop himself from leaning over and kissing her.

"You once told me that your people were no different from mine." He ran his finger across her jawline. "You said that while some immigrants make mistakes, all they wanted was what was best for their families—political and religious freedom and a place to call home. That's all I want, Lidia. Freedom, home, and a family. I see the way you look at me. Don't deny what your heart is telling you."

⚶

Lidia drew in a quick breath. Adam's words shook her to the core. She was afraid to hear what her heart was saying. Afraid that if she gave her heart away completely, he'd only end up breaking it. She'd spent her life dreaming that one day her own romantic champion would enter her life and sweep her away in one magical moment. Instead, she'd met a man whose past collided with hers. . .and still they had fallen in love.

She swallowed hard. When had love come into the picture? Looking up at him, she felt her chest tighten. The wind ruffled his hair, and she longed to run her fingers through the dark strands. His eyes pleaded with her. If she truly had fallen in love with Adam, then wasn't this a chance she needed to take? Her grandmother's tales of brave heroes and beautiful handmaidens all had happy endings. Perhaps God was offering her a happy ending, too.

Adam interrupted her thoughts as he took a step backward and bowed. "I was wondering, mademoiselle, if I might have this next dance?"

She caught his mesmerizing gaze, and her legs began to quiver. "You want to dance?"

"It's called a mazurra, I believe." Adam looked down at her and winked. "A traditional dance from Poland."

She tried not to laugh, but she couldn't help it. "It's called a mazurka."

"Well, you've got to give a fine gentleman like myself credit for trying at least."

"I. . .I suppose you're right."

Lidia's heart pounded as she stepped into his arms. "You don't give up, do you?"

"On you? No."

A sense of unexpected joy washed over her. Like the night he first kissed her, it was as if this was where she'd always belonged.

She laughed as Adam tried to follow her lead. With her head held high, she let her hands move gracefully through the air. The fast tempo and syncopated rhythm left Adam struggling to keep up, but for the moment nothing seemed to matter except the fact that she was dancing with him beneath a moonlit sky.

He stepped on her foot, and she leaned forward to try to gain her balance. Grabbing her arm, he steadied her, then drew her toward him. His face hovered inches from hers.

She stopped dancing. "I. . ." Her mouth went dry and she couldn't speak.

Adam drew her hands toward his chest. "There's something I've been wanting to ask you all evening."

"Yes?" This time she was ready for his question. This time she knew what she wanted more than anything else.

"Lidia Kowalski, may I have permission to court you?"

ॐ

"I think today's the day." Sarah sat Indian-style on the picnic blanket and dangled a blade of grass between her fingers.

"The day for what?" Lidia rested against one of Adam's sugar maple trees and let the warm sun begin to lull her into dreamland.

"The day that Adam asks you to marry him."

Lidia's eyelids popped open. "Are you sure this time?"

"Well, not 100 percent, of course, but pretty sure."

"Did he say something to you?"

"Not specifically."

Lidia closed her eyes again. "If you don't know for sure, then don't tell me."

"Why not?"

"Because you're making me nervous. On Easter you told me you were certain he was going to ask me, then again at his birthday celebration—"

"Just be patient. He'll ask."

Lidia frowned. She needed more than unsubstantiated feelings from Sarah. During her courtship with Adam, he'd been the perfect gentleman, escorting her to church, accompanying her to socials, and even taking her out to dinner in town twice. But little had been said about their future. Silvia had dared to imply at one point that Adam had no intention of tying himself down to someone like her. While Lidia knew that the woman's words were meant to hurt, it was hard to ignore them all the same.

Sarah helped herself to a second slice of lemon cake out of the tin. "You have to admit that the very thought of Adam proposing is completely romantic."

Lidia didn't answer.

What *would* be romantic would be an actual ring on her finger and a wedding day set, though she'd never be so presumptuous as to say so to Adam. She'd dreamed about his asking her to marry him for weeks, and what their wedding would be like. While she didn't expect Adam to agree that the wedding be strictly Polish, she did want certain aspects of a traditional wedding to be incorporated into the day.

She envisioned the engagement when they would invite friends and family to witness the celebration of their commitment. Then on their wedding day, his parents would give the traditional Bread and Salt Blessing at their house, and later there would be the Unveiling and Capping Ceremony that represented passage from being a young woman to a married woman. Drawing in a deep breath, Lidia could almost smell the tables of rich food that would be set out for everyone. Hunter's stew, dumplings, roasted meats with vegetables—

Lidia started as Adam's puppy jumped onto her lap and began licking her face. "Star!"

"I'll get him." Sarah stood and shooed the dog away before he caused any damage to their picnic lunch.

Lidia yawned as she shoved her half-empty plate to the edge of the blanket, surprised Star hadn't take off with her uneaten chicken leg. "If Adam doesn't come back soon, I'm going to end up sleeping through his proposal."

Sarah laughed. "If Ruby and Anna have their say, he won't even have time to propose to you today. He'll be too busy carrying them around the farm on his shoulders."

Five minutes later, Adam showed up with both girls. One on his shoulders and one holding on to his leg.

He's going to make such a good father. . . .

Ruby climbed down from Adam's shoulders as they approached the picnic blanket and plopped beside Lidia. "Are there any more of those sugary treats you made, Lidia?"

"I think so. Look in the basket."

When Sarah had convinced her stepmother to fix a picnic for the five of them, Lidia had volunteered to make the dessert. These special treats were one of her grandmother's favorites. Lidia's mother had taught her to make them soon after they'd arrived in America.

"They're called *chrusciki*," Adam said, as he handed his sister a handful.

Ruby attempted to pronounce the name of the fried cookie but ended up scrunching her lips together in frustration.

"My grandmother used to call them 'angel wings,' sweetie." Lidia reached out to smooth the back of Ruby's dark hair. "That should be a bit easier to say."

Ruby smiled. "That I can say."

Lidia nodded to Adam. "I'm impressed. Your Polish pronunciation is coming along quite nicely."

Adam let out a deep chuckle. "Considering I know about three words of the language."

Lidia laughed with him. All the doubts she had ever had about Adam accepting her for who she was had vanished in the past few months. So much of the pain she'd experienced over her parents' and Jarek's deaths was beginning to heal. She still thought of them every day and made sure Koby remembered them, but the deep ache she'd carried inside her for so long was finally lessening.

Adam leaned close and gazed deep into her eyes. It always caused her stomach to do flips when he did that. "Don't you want to eat the rest of your lunch, Lidia? You've hardly eaten a thing."

"I'm fine, really." She smiled at him. Even if he didn't ask her to marry him today, the outing still would be perfect. She knew his sisters were important to him, and when they'd asked to spend the afternoon with him, he hadn't even hesitated. Lidia's presence, he'd told her, was icing on the cake.

"If you're finished, then, shall we go for a walk?"

"I'd love to." Lidia felt her pulse quicken.

"Don't worry about us," Sarah said. "We'll finish packing the picnic basket and load it into the wagon so Star can't get into it."

Adam reached down to help Lidia to her feet. His hand enclosed her fingers, sending tiny shivers up her arms. She tried to steady her nerves. Since the night Adam asked if he could court her, she'd known she wanted to marry him. But as ready as she was to get married, she knew they both needed time to get to know each other after all that had transpired between them.

The girls giggled and avoided Lidia's questioning gaze. Maybe Sarah really knew something and just hadn't been able to keep quiet. From the scheming looks on the three girls' faces, something was definitely afoot.

Briefly, Lidia touched the smooth texture of Adam's shirt fabric before pulling her hand away. "What's going on?"

"Nothing." Adam shrugged a shoulder, then winked. "I've been doing a lot of thinking about the farm lately and need your opinion on something."

Lidia frowned. Talking about farmwork wasn't exactly what she had in mind. She took his arm and let him lead her across the path toward the other side of the house. Summer had arrived, and the flowers that dotted the landscape were still in full bloom. The meadows and woodlands spread out before them in varying shades of green. A robin chirped, its cheerful sound mingling with the soft rustle of leaves from the afternoon breeze. With his arm around hers, Lidia smiled, wishing she could capture this perfect moment forever.

Adam pointed toward the south of his land. "I want to take some of the earnings I made from the syrup harvest to increase my herds of both cattle and horses by the end of the year. I know I'll have to start slow, but I want to make use of as much of the land as possible."

Lidia nodded. "I think that's a fine idea."

"One of my neighbors is moving and has promised me a fair deal on some of his livestock. I'm even thinking about dairy cows to produce my own cheese to sell."

"Cheese." Lidia tightened her lips, wishing she could be a bit more interested. It wasn't at all that she thought Adam's dreams were too big, or that he couldn't do it, but thanks to Sarah, she had marriage on her mind.

While she enjoyed listening to his dreams for the future, she didn't want to just hear about it, she wanted to be a part of it. They skirted the edge of the sugar bush, and Lidia couldn't help but feel the swell of pride within her. She had been a part of this year's harvest, working beside Adam once he'd recovered to ensure that the sap was collected and properly processed. It was what she wanted. To spend the rest of her life at his side.

Adam reached out and plucked a green leaf from one of the maples. "Next year I plan to harvest at least twice as much. . . ."

Adam's voice faded into the background as Lidia stared at a bird's-eye marking on the bark of one of the trees. Maybe she should say something to him or at least attempt to draw him into a conversation regarding their future. She knew Silvia and her ugly words weren't true, but if Adam really loved her, wouldn't he be thinking about *their* future instead of the future of his farm?

"I also want to—" Adam stopped and turned to face her. "Have you heard anything I said the past five minutes?"

"No—yes." What could she say? That she was ready for him to ask for her hand in marriage?

"What is it?" A slight grin framed his expression as if he'd caught her with her hand in a penny jar.

"You've spoken about your plans for the house before. . . ." Lidia swallowed hard. "I was wondering about the house."

"The house?"

"Yes." Lidia felt her confidence rise. She'd find a way to discover his intentions if it was the last thing she did. "I remember you saying at one time that you had plans for the house."

He turned to look at the wooden structure. "The flooring needs to be replaced in at least one area, and I'd like to fix the front door. It creaks when you open it."

"Oh." She tried to hide the disappointment that flooded over her. He obviously didn't see the need of a new stove, or kitchen, or any other things a woman found essential.

"What's wrong?" he asked.

"Nothing."

Adam wrinkled his brow as if deep in thought. "There is one thing, though, that I could use your opinion on inside the house. Come."

The girls were nowhere to be seen as they made their way toward the house. Even Star's usual barks as he snapped at birds and butterflies had quieted.

"Where are the girls?" Lidia asked, trying to keep up with him as they took the stairs to the porch.

"Maybe they're in the house."

Adam opened the door, letting Lidia enter first. She stepped inside the living area, then stopped abruptly. The room was full of people.

"Good afternoon, everyone. I didn't know. . ." Confused, Lidia turned to Adam.

There surrounding her was all of Adam's family. Mrs. Johnson with little Daria. Mr. Johnson with his arm around Koby. Matt and the three girls. . .even Star sat quietly on the hearth. Mrs. Gorski from church, who'd always been good enough to lend Lidia copies of her books, stood smiling beside her husband and two small children, as well as several other acquaintances from church.

Adam drew his arm around her. "Lidia, I wanted our engagement period. . . our *zareczyny*. . .to be what you've always dreamed it would be. I know it can't be the same without your parents and brother here, but I still wanted you to have a traditional Polish engagement."

Lidia's eyes filled with tears. "Our *engagement period*?"

Mrs. Gorski joined Adam's stepmother with a loaf of bread in her hands. "Your Adam here has been coming to see me to learn more about our Polish traditions and language. Today, if you say yes, Lidia"—laughter filled the room—"we want to ask God's blessing upon you. That you will always have bread beneath your hands and that your home will be filled with children and love."

Koby took a cautious step toward the center of the room with a white cloth in his hands. "This is so that the two of you will always be bound together."

Lidia's eyes filled with tears. She couldn't believe Adam would do this for her. But he had, and this gift to her was one she'd never forget as long as she lived.

Adam turned toward her and took her hands. "Lidia Kowalski, there's nothing I want more than to spend the rest of my life with you. With these friends and family brought together as a witness of my love for you, I pledge to love and honor you always. Will you be my wife?"

She couldn't speak. She glanced around the room, tears streaming down her cheeks. Her gaze rested on each person, each smile filling her heart with emotion and an abundance of thankfulness.

Sarah caught her gaze and gave her a wry grin. "I promise this was a surprise to me, Lidia. Adam found out I'd been trying to discover when he was going to ask you to marry him, so he never told me."

Everyone laughed as Lidia turned back toward Adam.

"I'm sorry about the lecture on farming," he confessed. "It gave everyone a chance to sneak into the house—"

"And me a chance to squirm a bit?"

"I never said that, but you did deserve it, trying to find out." Adam smiled and squeezed her hands. "Will you marry me, Lidia?"

"Oh yes, Adam. Without a doubt, yes."

Epilogue

Ten months later

The day had finally arrived. Her wedding day.

Lidia fingered the ends of her braid and tried to calm the flutter of butterflies in her stomach. The night before, her customary single braid had been redone into two, symbolizing the step she was about to take in leaving behind her life alone to be joined with Adam in marriage.

She stood before the beveled mirror in Sarah's bedroom, making sure everything was perfect before going downstairs to meet Adam. The dark burgundy dress was by no means fancy, but in making it, she'd added a few extra touches so it would be special for today. Three pearl buttons at the collar and lace around the edge of the sleeves and skirt for trim.

"Are you ready?" Rebecca held little Peter, her and Luke's nine-month-old boy, in one arm while adjusting the edge of Lidia's veil with the other. "You look beautiful."

Lidia offered her a weak smile. "And you're sure Adam will love the dress?"

She worked to steady her breathing at the wave of panic that hit her. Surely this was nothing more than a dream. The thought that Adam was right now waiting downstairs to take her as his bride was too wonderful to be true.

"The dress is perfect." Michaela stepped forward and drew her arm around Lidia's shoulder. "Besides, I have no doubt that he'll be looking at you and not your dress."

Lidia couldn't help but laugh out loud. She was surrounded by people who loved her, and she was about to become Mrs. Lidia Johnson.

See, I have turned your mourning into laughter. Your sorrow into joy.

Her heart swelled with praise at the reminder. While she desperately wished that her mother and father could be here to celebrate this day with her, God had taken away her sorrow and brought happiness back into her life.

"Come now." Rebecca opened the door to the room. "Everyone's waiting outside for the procession to the church. And your bridegroom is waiting downstairs."

Thanking God for His blessings, Lidia glanced up and nodded at Rebecca, who had become like a sister to her already. She was ready.

"I hope I'm next." Sarah's voice was full of longing as she followed Lidia into the narrow hallway.

"You're only fifteen." Rebecca nudged her sister gently. "It will happen one day. Then I'm sure you'll have an amazing and romantic story to recount to your grandchildren."

Sarah blushed as they hurried toward the stairs of the Johnson family home to where everyone was waiting for them.

Lidia saw Adam the moment she began her descent of the staircase.

She drew in her breath as her gaze swept his face. His eyes reflected the smile on his lips. There was no doubt of his love for her. And no doubt in her own heart of her love for him.

Adam tugged on the bottom of his black suit jacket, then stepped forward and took her hands as she reached the bottom. "You look. . .absolutely beautiful."

"Thank you. And you. . ." Lidia felt her cheeks flush.

She'd always thought him handsome, but today his touch left her breathless. He led her toward the front door of the house and out into the bright spring morning. "My father has prepared the traditional Polish blessing for us before we go to the church."

They moved to the front porch for the blessings, a part that was almost as important as the actual wedding ceremony. Everyone was dressed in their Sunday best. Many of the ladies had flowers pinned to their hats.

Mr. Johnson took their hands and pressed them together. "You look beautiful today, Lidia."

He turned to the group of people who stood waiting, and everyone hushed as he began his prayer. "O Lord, we come before You today to ask Your blessing on this couple. May their home enjoy an abundance of love, good health, and happiness. We know that life may be difficult at times, but may they learn to cope. To rely on each other, and most importantly, may they always remember to rely on You. Amen."

Lidia's eyes rimmed with tears.

Mr. Johnson turned and addressed the crowd with a wide grin on his face. "To the church, everyone. We've got a wedding to celebrate!"

Boisterous shouts burst from the crowd, and music began to play from the fiddler and double bass players, who stood in the back.

As everyone got into the wagons, Adam helped Lidia onto his buckboard. Sitting down, she breathed in the fresh spring air that was laced with the scent of fresh flowers. This ride to the church would be the last time she sat beside him as Lidia Kowalski.

The buggy bumped beneath them, but she was only aware of the joy in her heart. So much had happened since the day he'd rescued her from the rabid dog. She was amazed that God had brought them this far. And now they had the rest of their lives to enjoy together.

Adam wrapped his arm around her and pulled her close as they followed the dirt path. "There's something I forgot to ask Mrs. Gorski," Adam said.

"What's that?"

"Am I allowed to kiss the bride on the way to the church?"

"I don't know. I suppose if you wanted to badly enough."

"I do."

Lidia's heart raced in anticipation. "Then so be it."

Adam leaned forward and brushed her lips with promises of what was yet to come. Floods of joy bubbled inside her. She pulled away briefly and looked into his eyes, knowing that she truly had found love in this New World.

A Letter to Our Readers

Dear Readers:

In order that we might better contribute to your reading enjoyment, we would appreciate your taking a few minutes to respond to the following questions. When completed, please return to the following: Fiction Editor, Barbour Publishing, Inc., P.O. Box 719, Uhrichsville, OH 44683.

1. Did you enjoy reading *Massachusetts Brides* by Lisa Harris?
   ❑ Very much—I would like to see more books like this.
   ❑ Moderately—I would have enjoyed it more if _____
   _____
   _____

2. What influenced your decision to purchase this book?
   (Check those that apply.)
   ❑ Cover   ❑ Back cover copy   ❑ Title   ❑ Price
   ❑ Friends   ❑ Publicity   ❑ Other

3. Which story was your favorite?
   ❑ *Michaela's Choice*   ❑ *Adam's Bride*
   ❑ *Rebecca's Heart*

4. Please check your age range:
   ❑ Under 18   ❑ 18–24   ❑ 25–34
   ❑ 35–45   ❑ 46–55   ❑ Over 55

5. How many hours per week do you read? _____

Name _____

Occupation _____

Address _____

City_____ State _____ Zip_____

E-mail_____